CRUSADE

THE SKY JEWEL LEGACY

GREGORY HEAL

ACKNOWLEDGMENTS

To everyone who has helped me reach this point, most notably, my wife, Alison; my extended family and in-laws; my editor; my book designer; my beta readers; and my community, which has grown in size since my debut novel, HERITAGE, came out in 2019.

CRUSADE

Book Two of The Sky Jewel Legacy

by
Gregory Heal

CHAPTER ONE

The farther away Skarmor flew from Watercress Castle, the emptier Jennifer Lancaster felt. As she hugged Treeow close to her chest, thoughts swirled in her head, much like the howling winds that were threatening to buffet her perch on the back of Skarmor, the griffin that had quickly become family over the past several weeks.

As her eyes stung with tears, Jen looked toward the moon of Azumar, which was full and low in the night sky and much bigger than the moon belonging to Earth. It drenched the nocturnal landscape with crisp moonlight, casting deep shadows along the rolling hills. Shadows that seemed to claw at Jen, as if trying to engulf her in darkness.

But she was already in a dark place.

If there was a rock bottom, Jen had hit it—and hard. Everything was falling apart, and she felt as helpless as a newborn child. In the span of one hour, she'd gone from finding out that Victor Huxley was actually her uncle and that her birth father, Charles, had been alive all along, to watching Watercress Castle, the home of the Sorcery Guild, collapse with both of them still inside, dueling Lord Draconex, the ruthless commander of the Dark Watcher tribe.

Jen couldn't believe they were gone.

No!

She shook her head, trying to banish such a horrible thought. She couldn't afford to think that way.

They can't be gone . . . I won't let it.

The only thing that kept her from turning Skarmor back toward Watercress was the promise Victor had made to her—a promise she knew he wouldn't break: he was going to meet her back on Camelore.

Not caring that her hair whipped in her eyes, Jen stole a glance back at her friends, Mira and Gavin. They were both silent and somber, yet each looked determined. She gave them a wan smile and turned back around to face the front. She sighed, ashamed to even be tempted to go back. Her selfishness had almost cost her not only her own life, but those of her friends; if that had happened, all the sorcerers at the Sesquimillennial Jubilee would have died in vain.

Unconsciously, Jen rested a hand on her shoulder bag, confirming for what felt like the millionth time that it still held the fabled lost journal of Merlin and, perhaps most important, the ChronoCrystal, the only MystiCrystal to have been discovered. Whether she liked it or not—or more to the point, whether she was prepared or not—Grand Mystra Cindergray had entrusted those relics to her. She knew what that meant, what she had to do: find the Halostone before Lord Draconex and Malcolm, so that she may prevent them from releasing the trapped soul of Lord Ferox. The best chance of finding the Halostone was with Gavin, the only known sorcerer who could read the lost journal.

Gavin . . . the Light Bringer.

"*Jen . . . JEN!*" Gavin yelled over the screaming winds.

Jen's introspection was broken at the sound of her name, but she was still so racked with fatigue and regret that she didn't budge to even acknowledge that she had heard Gavin. A few beats passed before she heard him speak again.

"We need to put some distance between us and Lord Draconex!" Gavin said. "Let's go through a different portal, not the Eternal Flame Gate, so we don't tip off any Dark Watchers that we're heading to Camelore!"

Jen felt slender fingers grip her shoulder.

Mira . . .

She clenched her eyes shut, feeling another warm surge of tears begin to form.

"You're probably right." She sniffled, then raised her voice. "Are we close to another portal that takes us to Earth?"

"The Rubra Canna Gate!"

Jen took her hand off her bag, shrugged off Mira, and gently patted Skarmor on the side of his neck. She leaned forward and said, "Skar, take us to the Rubra Canna Gate."

Skarmor cawed in acknowledgment and shifted course as a solemn silence descended over the group once again.

A wave of fatigue rolled over Jen, and before she knew it, ahead loomed two large, ruddy pillars that looked to be holding up the night sky. Skarmor picked up speed, and right as they passed between the two pillars, Jen felt a jolt of energy course through her body—a sensation similar to when she'd traveled to Earth through the Gate of Eternal Flame—as her surroundings started to bend and twist as though she were looking through a kaleidoscope. No, as if she were *inside* a kaleidoscope. In a flash, the images normalized, and Jen and her friends shot out of the Cathedral Rock Vortex in Sedona, Arizona, just as an arid dawn broke over the horizon.

The air was calm and had a different smell than Azumar's; it was a smell that made Jen feel like she was home again. As Skarmor flapped his mighty wings and gained altitude, the temperature began to drop, but Jen didn't catch a chill; maybe it was because she was holding the still but warm form of Treeow . . . or maybe it was because she just didn't care anymore.

Glancing down at Treeow, Jen grimaced when she saw how labored the cat's breathing was, his face slightly contorted in a mask of throbbing pain. Just then, Jen thought about having Skarmor heal Treeow once again, but she bit her lip in frustration —she had no idea what Treeow's injuries even were.

Malcolm had me cornered. If it wasn't for Treeow, I wouldn't be here. None of us would.

Jen stroked the top of the cat's head. She wouldn't be able to forgive herself if Treeow didn't survive.

Please . . .

There had already been far too much destruction and death; Jen didn't want to witness any more—couldn't. Looking forward, she blinked away more tears as she made out the curvature of Earth's surface. As Skarmor continued to climb, she caught herself already starting to ponder where the remaining four MystiCrystals were hidden and the long journey that lay ahead.

As they burst through a thick layer of cumulus clouds, Jen caught sight of the beautiful floating fortress of Camelore, casting away her thoughts with its beauty. Her breath caught at its majesty; it reminded her of how she felt when Victor had first given her a tour of that sacred place. Not even a month had passed since then, but to Jen, it felt like a lifetime ago.

As Skarmor came in for a landing in front of the griffin stables, Jen noticed how quiet it seemed; there wasn't a soul in sight.

We must be the first Light Seekers to return, Jen thought with mounting dread.

By the time Skarmor's large lion paws and sharp eagle talons touched the swaying grass of Camelore, Jen's spirits had dropped and in their place her exhaustion had returned. She leaned forward, gently placing her forehead on the griffin's neck, and said while Gavin and Mira slid onto solid ground, "You did it, Skar. Thank you."

Skarmor chirped quietly, sounding just as fatigued as she felt, and stretched his wings, which must have been sore from the long flight. Still holding Treeow, Jen slid off the griffin and to the ground. She felt her knees begin to buckle, and would have collapsed if it weren't for Gavin, who caught her in his arms.

"Whoa, Jen. You all right?" He searched her face for an answer.

"Tired," she said as he helped her back up. His grip was firm yet gentle, and Jen would have wanted to stay longer in his arms, if only it were under different circumstances. "And confused. And worried." She started to shake, her voice cracking. "And angry. And—"

"Hey," Gavin said, consoling her, "so are we." He looked at Mira, gesturing for extra support.

Taking a step closer, Mira said, "You're not alone, Jen. We'll get through this." She was pulling at her braid, fighting the urge to cry, and the conviction in her voice was palpable.

"How?" Jen turned rigid and pulled away from Gavin, her eyes darting between her friends. "We have no idea who even survived that—that—*massacre*."

"There has to be others . . . right?" But even Mira sounded unsure.

Gavin pursed his lips but said nothing.

"That's what we have to believe . . . that's what I *need* to believe." Jen turned around, still clutching Treeow, and stumbled toward the stables. "Come on, Skar. You deserve some rest."

"So do you, Jen," Mira reminded her. She caught up to Jen and touched her arm. "I'll get Skarmor settled."

"I'm fine—"

"Please." Mira locked eyes with her.

Jen wasn't about to concede, but then she looked past Mira, into Skarmor's eyes. They were telling her to listen to Mira and that he would understand. She sighed and closed her eyes, and all she could say was, "Okay."

A heartfelt smile crossed Mira's lips—the first smile any of them had had in what felt like an eternity—and she hugged Jen, making sure she wouldn't squish Treeow between them.

"Thank you." Jen smiled back, though it felt forced, then looked in the direction of her hut, which seemed miles away.

"I'll take you to your hut," Gavin offered, as if reading her mind.

Jen shook her head slowly. "I can make it there on my own, thanks." As she cradled Treeow, he started to move, which was a good sign; relief washed over her as she saw the little cat stretch his limbs, his tail starting to sway.

"Just let us know if you need anything, okay?" Gavin said, and behind him Mira nodded, absent-mindedly stroking the beleaguered Skarmor.

"I just need to rest . . . and wait for Vic to return." Jen was so tired that her lips barely moved, causing her to mumble. Leaving Mira and Gavin to feed and tuck in Skarmor, she started toward her hut.

Camelore was indeed her safe haven, but it felt empty without Victor. Her eyes lazily scanned her surroundings, causing a surreal sense to wash over her. From the gentle swaying of the verdant hills and dogwood trees to the peaceful demeanor of the lazy circle of huts in the area designated as Camelore's living quarters, it felt to Jen as though the horrible events she had fled had never occurred. Like it was just a nightmare, and she was actually dreaming it all as she started another typical day on Camelore.

But no, she fought to remind herself, it wasn't a dream. Lord Draconex, along with his horde of Dark Watcher warriors, had ambushed the entire Sorcery Guild—on a day of celebration, in fact—and had nearly wiped them all out. Jen and her friends were the only confirmed survivors.

Her legs felt heavier with every step, but she forced herself closer to her hut as she balled her fists so hard she thought the skin over her knuckles would split. Just before she could turn her hut's doorknob with one shaky hand, Jen heard a familiar voice call out, "Jenny Jasmine!"

Jen rolled her head toward the voice, still too exhausted to comprehend, but almost immediately her fatigue was cut in half at the sight of her father rushing toward her. As he got closer, he first slowed down as a look of concern swept across his face before quickening his pace again.

"Oh my, are you okay, honey?" Richard asked as he got to her, enveloping her in a big hug.

"Dad," Jen exclaimed, unable to say more.

After letting her go, he hovered his hands over her shoulders. "What caused these scars?"

Jen smiled tightly, crossing her arms. She brought her hands up to touch the opaque scar tissue on the tips of both shoulders. The tips of her fingers played over the raised skin where the scars were, but she couldn't feel it since her wounds were still relatively fresh and the nerve endings hadn't properly healed from the sharp claws of Draconex's dragon, Volcanor, when it had captured her at Draconex's command.

A quick tremor coursed through Jen's body as she remembered being helplessly carried off by that hellish wyvern dragon. She didn't want to think about what would have happened to her if her instincts hadn't cast the moltic spell over herself, encasing her in a protective shell, which had allowed her to slip from Volcanor's vise grip and plummet to the forest below.

"It's a long story. They're just here for decoration now," Jen said, trying to play it off lightly, but still she knew there was residual trauma.

Treeow softly purred in her arms, and her father looked down at him. "Who have you got here? Hopefully I didn't squish him."

Jen sniffled. "He looks all right. This is Treeow. He saved our lives last night."

Richard's eyebrows shot up. " *Our* lives'? Are Victor and Charles with you?"

Uncharacteristically silent, Jen nuzzled her face deeper into his shoulder as she let her guard down. Tears yet again threatened to spill as she thought about what to say—and how to say it.

"This dark sorcerer—Lord Draconex—launched an assault on Watercress Castle last night during our ceremony. I had no choice but to leave Vic and Charles . . ."

At this point, she didn't have the strength to hold the tears at bay. Her shoulders involuntarily bounced up and down with her sobs before she collected herself enough to finish.

"Even after I promised to come back for them."

"Don't blame yourself." Richard looked her straight in the eyes. "I'm sure they're all right."

"So many people died . . ." She shook her head in disbelief, reliving parts of the ambush.

Richard hugged her again. "Victor and Charles will turn up." He rubbed her back gently. "I can't tell you how glad I am that you came back to me, though."

"I thought I'd never see you again, Dad," she said, her eyes suddenly widening in alarm. "Is Mom okay?"

Richard jabbed a thumb behind him at the helioarch, Camelore's ceremonial chamber. The design was reminiscent of an observatory, except there was only a curved track in place of a fully enclosed dome where spherical representations of the sun, moon, and planets would mimic their celestial counterparts. "Your mother's still sleeping in the helioarch. She's been through a lot."

Jen smiled weakly. "Thank goodness. I can't bear to lose anyone else." She sighed again, then immediately tensed up. "Ty," she breathed, then louder to her father, "Tyler!" This realization kicked her adrenaline into motion, causing her heart rate to spike.

Richard's face turned ashen. "I'm a horrible father . . ."

After seeing his tortured expression, she took a breath. "No, you're not. You look like you've been through hell and back." Still holding Treeow in one hand, she reached out the other and touched her father's arm.

"You have no idea." He wiped a tear from his eye and stole a glance at the chamber doors through which her mother rested. "I have to get Tyler."

Jen shook her head. "No. You stay with Mom. I'll get Tyler, and you'll fill me in on what happened once I get him up here, okay?"

She'd never been this forceful with her father, had never bossed him around like this, so she had no clue how he would react. His face tightened at first, but then relaxed after surveying her face.

"Okay, sweetie. I trust you."

"I'm not sure if Draconex or Malcolm know about Tyler," she said, "but I can't take that chance. I know I just got here, but I have to leave. Now."

Richard stroked Jen's cheek, which was dirty with dried sweat and soot. "You've proven to me that you've grown into a very strong and capable young woman. Don't worry about me, Jenny. Go get your brother."

"I'll be back soon." She kissed him on the cheek and, deciding not to disturb her mother's rest, gently placed Treeow on a folded blanket next to her armoire in her hut, then raced back toward the griffin stables with a second wind.

Gavin, who was still tending to Skarmor, did a double-take and held his arms out in front of him. "Whoa, whoa . . . where's the fire?" he asked, gently joking. Mira came in from the other side of the stable holding a drinking bowl that was filled nearly to the brim. Her look shared Gavin's surprise as well.

Out of breath, Jen was able to make a sentence in between breaks to inhale. "I have . . . to get . . . my brother."

"Okay, where is he? I'll go and get him."

She swallowed, catching her breath. She watched Mira put the bowl down in front of Skarmor and wished for a long swig of water too, but she quickly reconsidered. "No, I have to do this. He needs to see a familiar face." She looked back in the direction of where her father had last been, feeling certain he was back in the helioarch with her mother. She turned back to Gavin. "Can you look after my parents, though? Until I get back? They're in the helioarch."

Gavin, seeming to pause, looked over her shoulder, then focused his gaze on her. "I will. Just be safe, all right? If you're half as tired as me, you're not gonna make it down to Earth."

"I'll be fine. As long as Skarmor is ready for the job." She walked over and stroked the back of his neck. "Are you up for helping me get my brother?"

The griffin raised his head to the sky and cawed his approval.

Jen nodded, smiling. "We'll be back as soon as possible. I know exactly where he is." She jumped back atop Skarmor and watched Mira and Gavin get increasingly smaller as Skarmor gained altitude.

The cool, crisp breeze at this height made her more alert.

It felt as if the flight down to her aunt's home in Erie, Pennsylvania, took forever, though Skarmor flew at terminal velocity and only twenty minutes had elapsed. It felt even longer waiting as Tyler packed up to leave with her.

Now, he stared with wide-eyed amazement as Skarmor soared through the air, taking them back to Camelore. Jen smiled as her brother insistently tapped her shoulder and pointed all around them, making her look at all the clouds, birds, and new views as they whizzed by. Knowing that he had been safe with Karen through all the chaos and death warmed her heart and made her thankful that their aunt had taken care of him for as long as she did.

"That's what family does, Jenny," Karen had said, winking.

Family also trusts each other, which was why, thankfully, Jen didn't have to go into great detail about her ragged appearance. Tyler thought it was cool, especially when Jen covered it up by saying that it was the aftermath of a small explosion in her NYU chemistry class.

NYU . . .

Jen remembered her past life mournfully. Just a few short months ago, she'd thought she was on a path toward med school, one step closer to being a doctor. Now, she doubted she'd ever be allowed to go back to her degree in medicine, let alone any semblance of a "normal" life. Her current path was far too important.

But it was also filled with danger and risk. In order to give herself the best chance of success, she needed to make sure the ones she cared about were safe. And there was no safer place than Camelore.

CEEEAWWW!

Skarmor's call carried through the sky as he flapped his wings, gaining altitude. Camelore was just a few minutes away, and Jen finally allowed herself to relax a bit. Tyler's head fell onto her chest, and she peered over to see that his eyes were now closed.

Jen laughed; clearly all this excitement had taken a lot out of him.

As Skarmor settled onto the grassy knoll by the stables, Tyler was still fast asleep. Mira was the only one there, and she helped Jen gently take her brother off Skarmor's back.

"I got him," Mira said as she squeezed the handle of her bull-whip, making the striations of metal pulse white. She then let go and rubbed her hands together before picking up Tyler with ease. He was quickly creeping up to Jen's height and she guessed he weighed more than her already. "Phew, thank goodness for animancy giving me the strength of a gorilla." Mira repositioned Tyler so she had a better hold on him. "Otherwise I would have been left to dragging him to our hut."

Jen laughed with Mira just as a yawn overtook her smile.

"How'd his pickup go?" Mira asked, not even straining as Tyler's head nestled in the crook over her shoulder.

Jen shrugged. "Pretty easy. We've always been able to count on my aunt, though I could tell it was hard for her to see us go so quickly." A yawn appeared out of nowhere, and she tried to hide it with her hand.

Mira just smiled. "Now it's *your* turn to rest, Jen. Come on." She led her toward their hut, still carrying little Tyler.

Jen felt like she was on autopilot as she walked next to Mira toward their shared hut—so many things had happened in the past few hours, and she had no idea how she was supposed to pick up all the pieces. She managed to look up briefly and caught Mira's gaze, and realized her friend was waiting for her to respond.

"Oh, sorry," she laughed weakly. "Yeah, good thing." Her eyelids felt so heavy.

Come on, just a few more steps. Your hut is right over there.

Mira managed to open the door to their hut, and Jen felt a wave of comfort as she looked around the dimly lit room. She hadn't been able to pay it much attention when she quickly dropped Treeow off earlier, but now she noticed how clean and orderly it was—even everything she'd dropped off. Her clothes were folded and put away in her armoire, her diary neatly placed on her nightstand next to her hammock.

Mira deposited Tyler in her hammock, then came back to Jen and, taking her hand, brought her to her own hammock.

"But what about you? Aren't you tired?" Jen asked her friend.

"I took a little catnap while you were picking up Tyler." Mira brushed a clump of sweaty hair from Jen's face. "I'm good for now. Tyler can use my hammock for as long as he wants. I'll see you in a bit."

Sniffling, Jen nodded as she let herself fall into her hammock. It had never felt more comfortable, and she was asleep the second her head hit the pillow.

She was so tired she didn't dream at all—at first.

CHAPTER TWO

The only thing that kept Lord Draconex from fainting from his throbbing wounds was his burning, roiling, stinging anger. It burned because his invasion had failed its intended purpose of acquiring the lost journal of Merlin; it roiled because of how he had let Charles get the best of him yet again; and it stung because Malcolm was still alive despite failing to stop Jennifer Lancaster once again.

As Volcanor carried him away from the smoking wreckage of Watercress Castle, Draconex shot a livid look behind him at the boy: out cold, still bleeding from a deep gash that traveled the length of his face.

Draconex should have ended Malcolm's life when he found him writhing in delirious pain on the shores of Lac Cravath; he would have, in fact, if he didn't so happen to be the only other known surviving Dark Watcher. As much as Draconex fomented, he needed Malcolm now more than ever. Still, the boy was like a bad penny—he couldn't get rid of him.

The only sparse gratification to be had in all this mess was from the huge blow he had dealt to the ranks of both the League of Light and the Sorcery Guild. True that his own forces were just as decimated, but at least he was still alive. Draconex couldn't guarantee the same for Victor Huxley or Grand Mystra Cindergray . . . and especially Charles Lancaster.

Charles, seethed Draconex, still unwilling to believe that his former classmate had managed to intercept the killing spells he'd meant for Victor and Cindergray.

He remembered the acute feeling of shock as he watched Charles block his spells, detonating a devastating explosion between them. He would have been annihilated if it weren't for the quick thinking of Volcanor, partially blocking him from the blast with one wing and then carrying him away as the ballroom collapsed around them.

Well, Charles paid the ultimate price . . .

Draconex felt the slight pull of the wind on his ponytail, which was whipping straight behind him. In his hasty escape, his hollowed-out dragon tooth—a souvenir he'd taken after capturing Silvress, Charles's precious dragon—had been knocked off. For so long, he had become accustomed to the reassuring weight of the tooth resting on his back. Now, with it gone, he felt as if a part of him had broken off, been cast away.

He licked his lips in anticipation; he could not wait to return to Feralot and feel the limitless, intoxicating energy of the Shadow-Crystal as it coursed through his veins and quickened his recovery.

* * *

It was nearly midday before the herculean Volcanor soared through the Wasteland Gate, delivering them to the realm of Nyzanth. Following the deep tracks in the dry, cracked ground made by the roaming citadel of Feralot, the dragon issued a coarse bellow that vibrated through Draconex's entire body, rattling what was left of his shattered soul.

We're almost there.

Draconex looked out in the distance and watched as Feralot quickly grew in size, waiting to feel the familiar pull of the ShadowCrystal . . . but it never came. As they soared closer, Draconex felt a spike of unease; he realized that Feralot was stationary. Furrowing his brow, he surveyed the entire citadel, from its thick legs—which were immobile—to its spired, obsidian towers.

Why has it stopped roaming?

Draconex felt his stomach lift as Volcanor made its descent in front of the central tower's entrance. His wyvern dragon's large, venous wings created such a powerful downdraft as to churn up a cloud of dirt into which they disappeared. Even before it could settle, Draconex appeared through the other side, quickly striding toward the tower's main door, ignoring his still-fresh injuries in his haste.

"Stay."

Draconex didn't bother looking back, knowing full well that Volcanor would obey. He heard a massive snort as its wings made a final forceful flap, sending a wave of fine dirt particles rolling past his boots and dispersing into the dry air.

The large metal door opened before Draconex to reveal a golem, standing solemnly on the other side, hands clasped in front and chin dipped in indefinite servitude.

"Take that unconscious, bleeding cretin to the infirmary now," he commanded, pointing a bony, sharp finger back at Malcolm, who still lay bleeding on the back of Volcanor.

The golem nodded without a word, then ducked out into the harsh light of Nyzanth's trinary suns and trudged toward Malcolm with ground-shaking steps.

Leaving the golem to tend to his apprentice, Draconex used his mastery over animancy to channel the jumping capabilities of a kangaroo, taking the steps six at a time until he reached the enclosed skywalk corridor that led to his den. His head throbbed with intense pain, but he fed on it, fanning his anger into rage.

"Diaema!" he yelled as he kicked in the door. "There'd better be a damn good reason why we've stopped!"

Fuming, Draconex marched over to the Throne of Dragons and impatiently waited for his mistress to come fluttering out and hang on the dead branch next to him.

Silence.

"Di!" he yelled again, balling his hands into fists.

More screaming silence.

Draconex could feel the beginnings of a migraine tug at the back of his skull as he tore through his entire den in search of Madame Diaema, all the while fearing what he knew to be true.

What have you done, Di?!

Draconex wheeled around and sprinted out of his den, across the corridor, and to the open stairwell shaft. Without hesitation, he vaulted over the railing and dropped down the fifteen flights of stairs in mere seconds, somersaulting on the ground as he redirected his downward momentum into another mad dash, this time toward the chamber that held the ShadowCrystal, his gateway to eternal dark magic and the only item to power the juggernaut citadel of Feralot.

Nothing else was on Draconex's mind—nothing could be—until he confirmed why he couldn't feel the pulsing energy of the ShadowCrystal and why Feralot had lost power.

Draconex again felt the dull ache from his injuries as he took a sharp right, nearly clipping his shoulder armor on a corner wall. He panted heavily, and his boots echoed down the long, empty corridors, until it sounded as though there were hundreds of him marching in step.

Draconex picked up the pace once he saw the familiar corroded door not twenty meters away. He channeled the speed of a starving cheetah and the strength of a fully matured white rhinoceros and then rammed into the door, denting it so badly that its metal hinges ripped off as if made of straw.

SLAM!

After the door wisely succumbed to his brute strength, Draconex found himself in an empty chamber—save for the rotting corpse of Madro, the late guardian of the ShadowCrystal.

The item of his desire was nowhere to be found.

"Diaema!" Draconex cursed his vampire mistress before he spun around, spewing a searing wall of flames that engulfed the entire chamber as he uncorked the full extent of his rage, suffering, and betrayal.

CHAPTER THREE

As she slept, Jen's subconscious replayed the events at Watercress Castle's Sesquimillennial Jubilee from the night before, except in the safety of her dream she tried to alter their outcome...

"Jen, go! Take Skarmor to Camelore!" Victor said as he huddled close to her in the castle's main ballroom. He looked scared: sweat rolled down his face and made his salt-and-pepper hair clump together, his breath labored as he kept his staff pointed at Lord Draconex and the traitorous Mystra Simone Chen.

"No, I'm not leaving you!" Jen said with all her heart. She looked at Draconex and shot an ice spell at him.

With ease, he dodged the spell and impressed his will upon it, bringing it back toward Jen. She tried to move out of the way but was too late; before the spell could collide with her, however, Victor slid in front of her, shielding her. The spell hit him squarely in the chest, freezing him solid.

"No!" Jen yelled.

By that time, Draconex was upon her. "You lost," he declared, unleashing a fountain of flames that engulfed her.

Like restarting a level in a video game, Jen's vision returned to Victor, unfrozen and kneeling in front of her, his staff once again pointed at Draconex and Simone.

"Jen, go! Have Skarmor take you to Camelore!"

"No, I'm not leaving you!" Jen said again, holding off on attacking Draconex this time.

Victor looked torn, like he wanted to argue, but instead turned to look at the two Dark Watchers walking toward them. Standing, he began spinning his staff so fast that it soon appeared as a solid, circular shield. Draconex and Simone sent a wave of spells their way, but each either dissipated upon impact with the spinning staff or ricocheted off.

Off to her right, her biological father, Charles, picked himself up and delivered a spell that hit Simone in her leg, causing her to stop attacking and fall to the ground.

They're working together to hold them off! Jen thought as she stood behind Victor, proud. Then, suddenly, her adrenaline spiked at the forceful touch of a hand on her shoulder, spinning her around.

It was Malcolm.

"Miss me?" he asked with a wicked grin and a crack of his knuckles.

"Jen!" Victor looked over his shoulder, distracted.

Draconex, seeing an opening, slammed Victor with an energy blast that snapped his staff in half, causing the two sections to fly off in separate directions.

"No," Jen breathed, and she watched her world crumble all over again as Draconex skewered Victor with a rapier sword and Malcolm, leering at her with his dark, haunting eyes, plunged a blade into her stomach.

Again.

"Jen, go! Have Skarmor take you to Camelore!" Victor yelled once again, once again with pleading eyes.

Jen didn't fight Victor this time and said, "I'll come back for you, no matter what." She touched his shoulder before springing off the ground toward the main gate, expecting Malcolm at any moment.

Malcolm dropped from the skywalk and said while cracking his knuckles, "Miss me?"

Jen slid to a halt and looked back into the ballroom. Victor was holding Charles, but now Draconex and Simone had surrounded them.

Quickly, Jen tugged her veil from her shoulders and blew it toward Malcolm with a strong gust spell, wrapping it around his face and neck. As he struggled to free himself, she ran down the East Wing toward the window through which she knew Grand Mystra Cindergray would come.

"That wasn't very nice," Malcolm said after tearing the veil away, and sprinted after her. He stopped in his tracks when Cindergray burst through the window, showering Malcolm with spells from his radiant sword.

She knew what Grand Mystra Cindergray would tell her to do. It was like her brain was fast-forwarding her to all of the pivotal moments leading up to her decisions she hadn't fully accepted just yet.

"Jen, protect the lost journal and ChronoCrystal!" he said as he sent Malcolm crashing through a door and into a side chamber. Cindergray tossed her his signet ring.

She caught it and was on the move, slipping it onto her finger as she made her way back toward the front gate. Before flagging down Mira and Gavin, Jen risked a glance back into the ballroom and saw both Victor and Charles leap two stories into the air, Draconex and Simone thrown to the ground as their spells collided.

She smiled as Victor landed safely back on the ground. A sense of relief washed over her, sweeping away any doubt or guilt she'd felt about listening to him.

As sorcerers ran past her to help reinforce their allies in the ballroom, she turned toward the front gate to see Mira and Gavin.

"Hey, guys! I need your help—"

But before she could explain further, it all blew away like dust, and she opened her eyes to see blue sky through her hut's skylight.

Her hammock creaked as she shifted her weight to look at Tyler, who was still asleep in Mira's hammock. Feeling slightly more rejuvenated, Jen took a deep breath and let her feet dangle over the hammock's side.

She waited, half expecting Victor to knock on the door and ask for permission to enter, but she knew that wouldn't happen. Not now, nor ever again. Finding the strength within, she stood and walked over to her small armoire, side-stepping the sleeping form of Treeow. She made sure Tyler was still fast asleep before quickly changing into more casual attire.

She wondered who she would see first when she stepped out of her hut—or, more accurately, who was the person she wanted to see the most. Rubbing her hands together to allay her nerves, she walked out into a perfect summer day.

Off to the side of her hut, sitting on a swatch of grass, were Mira, Gavin, and her parents.

At the sound of her exit, they all looked in her direction and stood. Mira and Gavin, looking like they were on the verge of collapse, still wore their scuffed and ripped jubilee attire. Jen's heart leapt for joy at the sight of her parents, but she also ached at seeing just how emaciated and bruised they were. They still wore similar Dark Watcher uniforms to the one Charles showed up in at Watercress. She could only imagine what they had gone through on Feralot.

Her mother was the first to make her way over. "Oh, honey," Beth said, embracing her warmly. "I'm so glad you're safe."

Her mom felt so frail and small in her embrace that she bit her tongue to stop from crying. "It's so great to see you," Jen finally managed. "Tyler's in my hut too."

Beth nodded. "Your father and I checked on both of you once we heard you'd brought him here. Thank you." She squeezed Jen's shoulders but stopped, noticing her scars. "Jenny . . . what happened to your shoulders?"

Jen looked at her bare left shoulder and gave her father a quick look. "I'll tell you about it later. They're completely fine now."

She didn't want to alarm her mother with the true story just yet; she could still see that Beth was overcome with emotion after not knowing if her daughter was alive for the past month.

"You're never leaving my side again, young lady," Beth declared before catching notice of Jen's bracelet. "Oh, my—this is lovely!" She took Jen's arm to get a closer look.

"Thank you. It's a charm bracelet that helps me channel my inner power . . . my nexus."

"Does every sorcerer have a bracelet like that?" Richard asked. "I thought they carry wands."

Jen smiled at her father's comment. "Strictly a wizard thing," she started, fondly thinking back to when Victor had explained the difference to her. "A sorcerer has a specific kind of item, called a *totem*, that helps channel his or her nexus. Everyone's totem is different and completely unique to them."

"Well, then." Richard put his hands up in mock surrender. "That's what I get for asking a sorceress stupid questions."

Jen cocked her head to the side playfully and chuckled. "I have a bracelet"—she jangled it—"and my family ring." She pulled the Ring of Lancaster out from underneath her shirt collar. "Mira has a whip. Gavin has a necklace—"

"An *orb* that happens to be *held* on a chain around my neck," Gavin clarified, holding up his totem and making sure everyone knew it definitely wasn't a necklace.

Jen chuckled, rolling her eyes. "Fine, an *orb*. And Vic had—" She stopped, aghast that she'd used the past tense. ". . . *has*—a staff." With her mood suddenly deflated, she looked down and picked at her fingernails.

"If there's anyone I know who can survive an explosion, it's Vic," Gavin said, walking up to her, Mira at his side. "He's still out there."

Mira nodded and rested her head on Gavin's broad shoulder, intertwining her fingers in his.

Richard put a hand on Jen's shoulder reassuringly.

Jen looked into her father's eyes, placing her hand over his. "That's why we have to stay here until he comes," Jen said with conviction.

Gavin pursed his lips and asked, "Can we talk in private, Jen?"

She looked at her parents.

"Don't worry, we're not going anywhere," Richard said, putting an arm around Beth.

"You better not," Jen said playfully, wagging one finger at them, then followed Gavin to his hut. Mira stayed behind with her parents, already halfway through a new conversation by the time Gavin gestured for Jen to enter his hut first.

He lived alone, so already the interior looked bigger than Jen's shared hut with Mira even though they were the same exact size. Instead of a hammock, he had an ordinary full bed on one side and a bean bag chair on the other, a rustic vanity sink, and a desk, which was placed underneath a shelf full of items.

"You weren't kidding about your doll collection," Jen commented, stifling a laugh as she looked at the shelf.

"Hey, they're *action figures*." He beamed at his memorabilia, which were neatly displayed with the care of a collector.

"Right, sorry," she said, raising her hands in mock-surrender.

He walked to his desk, hands on hips, still looking at his collection. "Mystra Mangstrom rarely found it useful to travel down to Earth, but every so often, when he did, he would bring me back a souvenir." He walked over to his shelf and righted a figure that had fallen down.

"You mean you've never set foot on Earth?" she asked, surprised.

He shook his head. "Mystra Mangstrom thought it would only distract me from my training." There was regret in his eyes as he spoke, but also the maturity of realizing the past could never be altered. Clearing his throat, he changed subjects: "Jen, we need to start looking for the other MystiCrystals."

She blinked, confused. "I agree . . . but you're the one who can read the lost journal. And once Vic and some other sorcerers show up, we can—"

"That's what I wanted to talk to you about," he said, then, seeing Jen's annoyance, added, "Sorry to interrupt."

She crossed her arms. "Why do we need to talk about that?"

He drew in a breath and looked away for a second. "We don't have the luxury of waiting. We need to start the search now, while the Dark Watcher army is at its weakest."

Jen shook her head. "I'm not ready. I've only mastered terramancy so far, and we don't even know if my instructors have survived the attack."

Gavin took a step forward. "You're very strong, Jen—I saw that when we escaped last night." He paused, thinking. "I can teach you astromancy, and I'm sure Mira will jump at the chance to teach you animancy . . . while we search for the remaining MystiCrystals, that is."

Jen stood up a little straighter and slightly cocked her head to one side. "Thanks for offering, but I'm not abandoning Vic and the rest of the League of Light," she said sternly.

He grimaced. "You won't be, Jen, don't you see? You'd be helping out the cause and capitalizing on this window of opportunity."

Jen couldn't believe what she was hearing. "Sometimes the cause can wait until you know that the people you care about are *safe*," she said firmly, raising her voice.

Gavin turned around and braced himself on the edge of his desk. Drawing out a sigh, he finally said, "This is war. A war that has already taken so much from us. Wouldn't you want to end it as quickly as possible if you had the chance? So no other lives are lost?"

"But at what cost, Gavin? If finding the Halostone is all that matters, we're no better than Draconex and his Dark Watchers."

Gavin inhaled, looking like he was measuring his words. Gazing into her eyes, he said, "Vic wouldn't wait if he were in your position."

Jen backed up, shocked at what Gavin had just said. Her bottom lip quivered uncontrollably, and Jen didn't want Gavin to see that so she turned around and walked out of the hut, slamming the door behind her. She was not expecting for their conversation to turn that sour. She stopped after a few paces, hoping he would follow her out and apologize, but the longer she waited, the more she realized she was hanging on to a false hope.

Wiping tears from her eyes, she kicked herself, thinking, *How did I ever catch feelings for him?*

Letting the sun kiss her bare shoulders and legs, Jen stared off into the distance. Her parents and Mira were still conversing on the grass. She wanted to join them, but first she needed some time to gather her thoughts, so she walked in the opposite direction, toward the Pentarena, Camelore's designated training area that housed sections for each Mancy plane.

A few minutes later, she walked through its arched entrance-way, the Arbor Sacré still flowing with vibrant magic, letting every color of the rainbow dance across its trunk, branches, and leaves as it continued its devoted task of keeping Camelore afloat and hidden from prying eyes.

Vic should be here with me, Jen thought in despair.

She opened the barrier to the terramancy section and stepped inside, waiting for the soundproof barrier to reseal before she let out a scream that carried with it all of her emotional strife. Her eyes were clenched so tightly that she started to see spots, and she reluctantly opened them back up. As she listened to her echo fade away, a whistle quickly took its place, growing louder. Jen glanced down and saw that her totem bracelet was spinning around her wrist and realized that she was inadvertently using her terra-mancy to funnel air through the clear chimney vent at the other end of the terramancy arena, but she also noticed that the other three elemental portions of this arena were also being affected: the basin in the fire section was ablaze, sending a wave of warmth at her; the once-placid pond in the water section was churning and starting to form a whipping whirlpool, spraying foam every-where; and the earth section showed boulders of different sizes levitating off the ground, slowly rotating in place and awaiting Jen's next command.

Calming down, Jen collapsed to her knees as the elements crashed around her: the fire disappeared, extinguishing as it turned into smoke that rose into the air in wisps; the whirlpool dissipated like someone plugged up a massive drain, the water's surface becoming quickly pristine; and the boulders shook the ground as they fell.

As the whistling stopped, she was left to ruminate in her thoughts.

CHAPTER FOUR

As the noonday sun shone on the smoking rubble of Watercress Castle, there was a stillness to the air akin to that of a graveyard. Nothing moved—not even the wind—until a carrion bird landed on a heap of twisted metal and shards of glass. A rusted, metallic groan permeated from deep within, startling the bird. As it flapped away, shrieking, the rubble parted to reveal a battered hand, slowly followed by the arm, shoulder, and head of Victor Huxley.

Having used the last of his strength to pull himself out of the pile, he collapsed to his knees. Eventually, he lifted his head to take in his surroundings. The once-magnificent ballroom of Watercress Castle was nothing more than a junkyard of ancient architecture. A destroyed relic of the Sorcery Guild.

"Ch-Charles?" Victor rasped, swaying. Though it felt as though his vocal cords had torn, he called again, looking around. "Charles? Grand Mystra? Heph?"

After only hearing more deafening silence, he stood on wobbly legs to get a better view of the destruction around him. Something reflective caught his eye, and with immense effort he limped over to find his staff, which lay broken in two. Silently grieving, he winced as a gash in his hand revealed itself when he moved it a certain way. It wasn't too deep and blood had already clotted over the cut, but it was still sore. He gingerly picked up the pieces of his staff—the staff that had once belonged to his fallen friend Orin, who now went by the name Lord Draconex.

What happened to you, Orin? Victor pleaded, wishing Draconex could hear his thoughts. He let his broken staff slip from his fingers.

TAP. TAP. TAP.

Noise from falling bricks caused Victor's alertness to return, quickly followed by the rush of adrenaline through his veins. When he saw the face of Grand Mystra Cindergray, contorted in pain, he dropped his defenses and shambled over to help push the wreckage off his mentor and friend.

"You're alive!" Victor exclaimed.

"Just barely, old chap," said Cindergray. "Though I can't say the same for Soter." He tried to lift a cracked slab off the body of his pegasus, but it barely budged.

Victor bowed his head in mourning.

Cindergray brushed a hand softly over Soter's wing. "He battled with honor and died a noble hero." He scanned the ruined ballroom. "Like many of our brethren."

It sickened Victor to think of all the many good sorcerers both the Guild and the League of Light had lost, though he shuddered to imagine what their losses would have been had Charles not arrived when he did.

Jen! Victor stiffened in abject horror, wondering if she had made it out with Skarmor in time.

As if he could read his mind, Cindergray gently touched Victor's hand in reassurance. "She's safe. I can feel it," he said. He closed his eyes and took a deep breath. "I had her take the lost journal and the ChronoCrystal before they could fall into Draconex's hands."

Victor forced a breath out with his worry. "Thank goodness. I bet—" He stopped, hearing footsteps coming from the direction of the front gate. Mindlessly grabbing his staff that wasn't there, he slowly stood, working out the stiffness in his injured wrist as he craned his neck to get a better viewpoint.

"Oi! Anybody in here?" a gruff voice called.

Victor's heart leapt when he realized it was Mystra Sterling Hephalon. Speechless, he looked at Cindergray.

"Go to him. I'll be fine," Cindergray softly told him.

With renewed energy, he attempted to run toward his old friend, momentarily forgetting about his many injuries, though he still had a noticeable limp.

"Heph!" Victor managed as he stumbled over a twisted windowpane, but stopped in his tracks when he saw the person next to him.

"Vic! I'm so glad you survived," Hephalon said as he nudged Simone Chen into the ballroom. She tripped over some debris and fell to the ground, skinning her wrists and elbows as she braced for her unexpected fall. "Look who I found trying to escape."

As Victor tried to contain his anger, he saw that Hephalon had fitted restraints over Simone's hands and wrists so that she could not cast any spells.

"Where's Jennifer?" Hephalon asked Victor, not making a move to help Simone back up.

The anger melted into relief when Victor looked at his friend. "She escaped with Skarmor."

"Thank the billowy heavens," Hephalon sighed, momentarily relieved. His shoulders perked up before slumping as though a different weight was put on him. "I hope Pernissa was able to evade capture as well."

Victor's eyebrows shot up. "Do you know where she is?"

Hephalon shook his head. "I ordered her to take my son to Camelore and watch over him. By now, they should be on their way to safety . . . but if I only knew that for a fact."

Victor placed a hand on his shoulder and gave it a squeeze, saying more than any words could convey, all the while keeping Simone in his peripherals.

She remained quiet, her eyes flitting left and right, until she picked herself up and bolted for the main hallway. But since her hands were bound, her balance was thrown off. As a result, she stumbled and slammed into remnants of the ballroom archway.

The clatter didn't even make Hephalon budge; he merely rolled his eyes and said calmly, "My Pernissa is a survivor, and Resolved is an adept sorcerer like his parents." Clearing his throat, he then decided to turn around and retrieve his prisoner. "I bet you're wondering how I figured out Simone was a Dark Watcher?" He stepped over to Simone and lifted her up by her restraints, causing her to elicit a tight squeal. "I had just pulled up the front gate's drawbridge when lovely Simone here comes along and begs me to lower it." Hephalon scoffed, then continued, "After I refused—considering what was waiting on the other side —she attacked me." He looked at her with contempt.

Victor now focused on Hephalon's bloodied brass knuckles totem, assuming it was stained with Simone's blood. He stepped over a few pieces of crumbled stone and shards of stained glass to get closer to Simone. "When—*how*—did Draconex turn you?" he asked in pure confusion.

Simone glared at him long and hard, but said nothing. When he continued to wait for an answer, all she gave him was a malicious smile.

Victor felt his blood boil as he took hold of her shoulders. "Do you realize the atrocity that you let happen here?!" He shook her, hoping an answer would rattle loose.

"Vic," Hephalon warned, still holding Simone's hands.

Victor stopped, remembering that the Grand Mystra was still behind him. Cindergray wouldn't want anger to dictate his actions. With a clenched jaw, he released Simone.

"It was a needed cleansing," Simone finally said between swollen lips.

Victor's heart nearly stopped when he heard her voice; it sounded more like a cheap imitation than the real thing, almost as though the Simone he had loved for so long had died in the mayhem the night before. With his heart already shattered in several pieces, he held no pity for Simone. Not anymore.

"And now that the Guild and League of Light are nearly wiped out," she went on, "there's no one to protect Jennifer Lancaster or the lost journal of Merlin."

"All right, that's enough out of you," Hephalon said, pulling at her arms and taking her toward Cindergray.

Victor's feet remained planted where they were as he watched Simone scuffle past him. "You underestimate her," he whispered when she was within earshot.

Simone only raised her chin in defiance, not acknowledging his comment.

Clamping his eyes shut, he let his sorrow and anger flow out of his body and mind before he turned around to join the other survivors. By this time, the Grand Mystra was standing strong as Hephalon brought Simone before him.

Fleetingly, Victor noticed that Cindergray's attire still looked regal and bright. Even in the worst of circumstances, Cindergray looked as though he had everything under control—and that included the presence to calm everyone around him. A true gift, and Victor was thankful for that.

"You would have been luckier if you had died in the explosion," Cindergray said to the traitor, his voice filled with scorn.

"Of course—you lack the strength to kill me," Simone said smugly. "That's why Draconex will ultimately prevail."

"True strength is when the urge to kill is abolished, even when it is most deserved," Cindergray said, respectfully nodding at Victor, who returned the gesture.

"Spare me your aphorisms," Simone shot back, shaking her head dismissively.

"You are getting too comfortable," Hephalon said. "Would you care for another quick tap on the cheek? You've heard that we will not kill you, but that doesn't mean I have to make your continued existence painless." He raised his hand that held the brass knuckles, which muted her instantly. He directed his next question at Cindergray: "What would you like me to do with her, Grand Mystra?"

"She cannot alert any other Dark Watcher of our survival, so she must remain with us for the time being," Cindergray said.

Just then, his eyes caught something in the distance. His

demeanor changed to one of uncertainty and dread as he stepped closer to the ballroom's center.

Victor turned to follow Cindergray, getting an ominous feeling in the pit of his stomach. He left Simone with Hephalon, wishing again that he had his staff for balance as he stepped over the wreckage. But that thought and everything else seemed inconsequential when he saw what the Grand Mystra was drawn to.

A bloodied, burnt arm sticking from a pile of bent metal and broken glass.

"No . . ." whispered Victor, praying the arm did not belong to Charles, his brother-in-law. *"No,"* he repeated, this time more fervently. He immediately started digging, not caring that his hands were being sliced and torn by the scraps and shards of metal, stone, and glass.

"Victor," Cindergray said empathetically, watching as Victor blinked away tears and proceeded to throw slabs of stone behind him.

Charles can't be gone . . . not after I'd only just found out he was alive all this time.

Victor clenched his teeth and felt his strength leave as he slid a steel girder away to reveal a horribly burnt body, curled up in the fetal position. The only thing that seemed to not have been singed off was the torn front of the Dark Watcher uniform that Charles had been wearing when he escaped Feralot. Stifling a sob, Victor stared loathingly at the Dark Watcher patch on the uniform before taking it in his hands and ripping the dried fabric in two.

Cindergray put a hand on Victor's sore shoulder. "There's only one thing we can do for him now . . . him, and every other fallen sorcerer."

Victor barely heard his words. His thoughts were consumed with how he would break the news to Jen when he saw her. Carefully, he pulled the withered body from the deep pile of rubble, and only then did he realize just how malnourished Charles had to have been.

No one moved—not even Simone—as Victor took off his cloak and draped it over the body. He then knelt and, with deep sadness, placed two fingers on the part of the cloak that covered the head.

Victor recited the Sorcerer's Oath, forcing himself to watch as the body of Charles Lancaster slowly disintegrated, releasing the remaining nexus energy. Tiny orbs of white light floated up from where the body had rested, carried by an unseen, mystical force. Victor watched the orbs for as long as he possibly could until they disappeared into the bright, noonday sky.

"We have a lot of brothers and sisters to honor," Victor said, his face grim as he eased himself up and replaced the cloak on his back, starting toward the next fallen sorcerer.

After Cindergray placed Simone under a spell, freezing her in time and space, he, along with Victor and Hephalon, spent the next hour solemnly giving ritual passovers to all the sorcerers who had fallen. The silence was broken only by recitations of the Sorcerer's Oath; the bright sky twinkled as one nexus after another returned to its respective Mancy plane, completing the mortal cycle.

"We've lost more than I care to admit, Grand Mystra," Hephalon muttered as they stood over a graveyard that was once a ballroom.

Cindergray pursed his lips, surveying his once-tall kingdom. "This is the worst massacre since the Great Battle fifteen hundred years ago," he admitted. "But Draconex's Dark Watchers have sustained equal or greater loss to ours."

"And they still don't have the lost journal, thanks to Jen," Victor added. He wished for the dozenth time that he were holding his staff; he felt naked without it.

The Grand Mystra raised a long finger. "Yes, we mustn't forget that."

Hephalon stirred, surprised. "Jen escaped with the lost journal as well?"

"And the ChronoCrystal," Victor added with a smirk.

Hephalon wiggled a pudgy finger at his old friend. "That lassie is a special one, I tell ye."

Victor looked down at his dusty boots and nodded. "Very." He only hoped she had made it back to Camelore safely.

Victor fell into stride with Hephalon behind Cindergray as they made their way back to Simone. "Camelore is the rendezvous point for any surviving League of Light sorcerers. We should make it our mission to get there before more precious time passes," he said.

"Seconded," Hephalon heartily agreed as he picked up the spellbound Simone and flung her over his shoulder as if she were a bag of griffin feed.

"Without our guardian animals, we'll have to go by foot." Victor squinted up into the afternoon sky, gauging the time, as he made his way to the front gate. "And it'll be nearly impossible to reach Camelore without them . . ."

"What are you proposing, Vic?" Hephalon asked, switching Simone to his other shoulder so he could better follow his friend.

Before Victor could respond, he caught a glimpse of a pointed object off to the side of his path. He bent and plucked it from a pile of rubble: it was a hollowed-out dragon tooth—the dragon tooth that had been worn by Lord Draconex. Victor dusted debris from the glazed enamel, running his thumb over the brushed silver cap at its tip. He had always thought he would be able to save his old friend, but after this most recent battle, he knew Orin was too far gone.

He truly was Lord Draconex now.

"We need to find the Cstesian Crossing." Victor looked at Hephalon, then Cindergray, as he put the tooth into the folds of his cloak. A tense silence surrounded them until Victor motioned for them to follow. "But first, we need to make a stop at my cottage."

CHAPTER FIVE

Malcolm was jerked awake by the sensation of falling as he lay motionless on a smooth, ice-cold, stone slab. The left side of his face felt prickly, so he opened his eyes—and froze.

Terror seized Malcolm's body and senses as he saw arachnid-like creatures skittering across his field of vision in the dim light. With his voice suddenly trapped in his throat, like in a nightmare, he swiped at the creatures, causing them to fall to the ground, chittering in *clicks* and *pops* as they fell from his face.

Once he thought he'd taken care of them all, Malcolm sat up and looked around. He was in Feralot's infirmary. The harsh, decrepit state of this area of the citadel reminded him of just how little the Dark Watchers cared about the health and safety of their inmates and fellow tribesmen.

Shaking from frayed nerves, he tried to calm his breathing. He could still hear the chittering of those hideous creatures on the hard ground below him; he dared not look.

What the hell happened?

Malcolm tried to remember how he got back to Feralot after . . . after . . .

Jen.

With the full force of his terramancy powers, he slammed his fist on the slab where he sat, cracking it like balsa wood. This time he did scream, his voice finally free, and felt veins protrude from his neck as the chittering below stopped.

"I *had* you!" he yelled aloud. "You were *mine*, Jen!"

He grabbed at his short-cropped hair in exasperation, then ran his hands down his face until he felt a raised mark on his left side. With dread mounting, he traced the curved mark from his forehead down to his earlobe.

Momentarily forgetting about his anger, he slid from the slab and made his way to the closest mirror, which happened to be at the infirmary's wash station. Wiping away the mirror's filth and grime with his sleeve, he at first didn't recognize the person who stared back at him.

His hair was matted with sweat and caked in dried blood, and the left side of his face was swollen with a deep red scar slicing over his brow and eye socket, curving around his cheekbone all the way to the tip of his earlobe.

Without warning, his mind rewound to the fleeting seconds of Jen's escape. He had been about to shoot Jen and her friends out of the sky when—*SLICE*—Skarmor's talons came out of nowhere and ripped through his face like a hot knife through butter. It was so quick and sharp that Malcolm had thought it was nothing to worry about, nothing but a light graze; now he knew it was a much deeper gash.

Carefully touching the scar again, he saw that it had been recently stitched together, but with what, he didn't know—until he noticed one of those arachnid-like creatures still latched onto the bottom tip of his scar.

With an expression mixed with both disgust and fascination, Malcolm pulled it off and examined the creature. It had the body of a small centipede with the spindly legs of those Earth spiders called daddy longlegs. Letting it drop to the ground, he squished it with the heel of his boot and looked back in the smudged mirror.

As he stared head-on at his reflection, Malcolm's heart skipped a beat when, for a split second, he thought he saw the blood-thirsty visage of Lord Draconex leering back at him. He realized that his scar was nearly in the same place at his master's.

Rage boiled in his nexus and he punched the mirror, shattering it into tiny, sharp pieces.

CRASH!

As the shards scattered to the floor, Malcolm gripped the edges of the sink to steady himself.

"Am I being punished?!" he yelled.

No matter how hard he tried, Malcolm could not escape Draconex. And now, thanks to Jen, whenever he would look in a mirror he would be reminded of his twisted, maniacal master.

And he couldn't stand it.

CHAPTER SIX

"Hey, Gav, where's Jen?" Mira asked her boyfriend as she caught him coming out of his hut. She went on her tiptoes to give him a light kiss on the cheek.

With hands still in his pockets, Gavin looked distracted and didn't meet her gaze. She turned around to see the Smiths walking up toward them.

"I'm not sure . . ." He grimaced. "Probably the Pentarena. That's where I go when I need to blow off some steam."

"What happened?"

He crossed his arms and continued to look off into the distance. "We disagree on what to do next."

Mira grimaced, too, and ran a hand through Gavin's dirty-blond hair. "Hey, there's no right or wrong answer here, babe. We're all faced with a tough situation." She paused, lightly scowling after he still didn't give her attention. She moved into Gavin's line of sight so he would be forced to make eye contact with her. Mira relaxed a bit when she saw the strained look in his eyes. "You look exhausted. Why don't you get some rest? I'll go talk with her."

"I think that's a good idea," Gavin agreed, letting his eyes droop closed as he nodded. Looking at Jen's parents, he then said,

"It was nice meeting you both." He waved as he headed back toward his hut.

"Likewise," Richard said as Beth nodded in agreement.

Once Gavin had returned to his hut, Mira turned toward her best friend's parents and before she could say anything, Richard said, "I think we'll check on Tyler again if you don't mind."

Mira clasped her hands behind her back and said, "Sounds great. Would you like me to walk you to his hut?"

Beth smiled warmly but shook her head. "We'll be fine. I think Jen needs a friend right about now, so we'll let you two talk."

Mira nodded, concerned about Jen's mental state. If it was anything like hers or Gavin's, it was more than slightly frayed. She focused her attention back on the Smiths. "Well, let me know if you need anything in the meantime." She touched an ear and said, "I have the hearing of an African elephant, so just call my name and I'll rush on over!" She smiled her usual smile: big and genuine.

Richard chuckled. "Thank you, Mira."

He led his wife in the direction of the huts while Mira took a few steps back, watching them recede into the distance before turning toward the Pentarena, and launched forward with the speed of a cheetah. As she got closer, there was activity in the terramancy section, confirming that Jen was indeed there, and once she walked through the open atrium, she stopped right in front of the terramancy section and tried to get Jen's attention. She waved and shouted out her friend's name, but Jen seemed to be too focused on whipping around fireballs to notice.

Sighing, Mira gave up, put her hand on the scanner, and walked in. The closer she got to Jen, the more conflicted she could tell her friend was. The ferocity with which she threw the flames in a white-hot arc above her head was jaw-dropping, but every so often her footing would get tangled up and she would stumble, breaking the smooth display of her fire-wielding.

Jen, having tripped and fallen back on her butt, proceeded to punch the charred, ashy ground with a grunt of frustration.

"Hey, stranger," Mira said, now only a few steps away. She

held out her hands instinctively just in case she caught Jen off guard.

"Everything okay?"

Jen wiped her forehead with one wrist and shrugged. "I just wasn't expecting this to happen," she said, then, finally, seemed to relax with the presence of her friend.

"None of us were," Mira agreed sadly. When she realized that Jen wasn't going to say anything, she added, "What did Gavin want to talk about?"

Jen pursed her lips as Mira sat beside her. She waited, not wanting to push her friend into any conversation she didn't feel comfortable with.

"Oh, well . . ." Jen finally said. "How he disagrees with my plan to stay here on Camelore until more Light Seekers return." She looked at Mira, hurt in her eyes. "And he brought up Vic."

"He's still out there, Jen. I know it." Mira put a hand on Jen's forearm.

"Gavin said that if Vic were in my position, he wouldn't wait around."

Mira's eyes widened in surprise. Shaking her head and aimlessly looking around the arena as she collected her thoughts, she squeezed Jen's arm. "He shouldn't have said that."

"It was out of line," Jen said forcefully, getting up and walking toward the pond that was as still as glass in the water section.

Mira's shoulders slumped in mild defeat.

Jen stopped and looked up toward the sky. "But not untrue," she added, her voice more vulnerable than before.

Mira bit her lip, unsure how to respond to that. She couldn't help but agree, but she was glad that Jen came to that realization on her own. Getting up and closing the distance between them, she wrapped Jen in a hug from behind.

"Vic is family," Jen said as a lone tear streaked down her cheek, "and I know he would want to make sure I was okay, but with how fast things are progressing, we need to act now." She turned around and embraced Mira head-on.

"In times like this, every decision we need to make is a

hundred times more difficult. But if we can all agree then we can overcome anything that comes our way. I hope Mystra Wingelius survived, too, and is on her way here, but we have to stay strong together and push forward."

Jen nodded, clearly trying to curtail more tears. "Sorry, I'm more of a private crier." She laughed, then fanned herself, drying her tears.

"Sometimes you need to share a good cry, girl." Mira squeezed a little tighter, then pulled away and winked, wiping another tear from her friend's cheek.

Jen nodded. "Now more than ever. Thanks." She smiled, then said, "I guess I'm also scared to start the search because I don't think I'm ready, even though I've got a handle on terramancy."

Mira scoffed and pointed at herself with both hands. "Hey, you're looking at an almost-Paladin! I can teach you animancy in my sleep."

Jen played with her totem bracelet. "Thanks. Gavin said you'd be willing."

"He's not wrong." Mira's eyebrows shot up when she thought of an idea. "And he can teach you astromancy!"

"He offered," Jen said as she wiped another tear streak off her cheek. "I can't express how grateful I am to have you both by my side for this."

"So are we, babe. We're family, too, and don't you forget it." They both laughed, and Mira could feel the weight of the world lift from Jen's shoulders. "I just wanted to make sure you're okay, and I think you're much better than that. I'll get outta your hair now. We'll be waiting for you whenever you're ready."

Jen smiled—and for the first time in what felt like a long time, Mira felt it was genuine.

"Thanks, Mira. I'll see you soon."

Waving, Mira hopped out of the terramancy section and headed back toward her hut.

* * *

Jen watched her friend go, then turned back toward the pond and, with renewed spirits, closed her eyes and began to calm her mind. She quickly fell into a deep meditative state so she could safely face her fears and perceived shortcomings and then work through them separately, finding ways to overcome them. She needed to understand and trust in her abilities and those around her.

As if her body were telling her she had reached the end of her meditation, her eyelids sprang open. Jen didn't know how long she was under, but she felt revitalized and self-assured in what needed to be done next.

Stopping in front of the Arbor Sacré, she gazed at the magnificent tree before her. Even in the daytime, its energy was as vibrant as ever; its trunk, branches, and leaves swayed with a rainbow of colors made by the magic spell that kept Camelore aloft and hidden to the human eye.

Jen stepped closer and placed a palm on its trunk, right over one of its veins of energy, and she suddenly felt as if some of the magic was beginning to travel into her. Closing her eyes, she prayed for continued strength in the coming days and for the well-being of all the sorcerers who were lucky enough to have survived Draconex's ambush at Watercress Castle.

With a peaceful smile, Jen walked out of the Pentarena, ready for a much-needed shower. She followed the path back to her hut, which took her around the lake she had fallen into with Gavin after he broke the news that he was dating Mira. She shook her head at the memory; it was still too tender to even think about how she felt about Gavin in that way . . .

As she walked under her favorite dogwood tree, she lifted her hand to feel its soft white leaves brush across her fingertips. Continuing on her way, she looked down at her shadow in front of her, which was starting to elongate with the setting sun, but quickly noticed another shadow—one a great deal larger—sneak up behind her.

Jen smirked, turning around. "Gavin, if you're here to apologize—"

Surprise and a twinge of fear cut off the rest of her sentence as she realized it wasn't Gavin, but an enormous creature. It had skin as coarse and cracked as tree bark, and a bed of green leaves—except for one clump of leaves that had the same coloring as a ripe, yellow pear—as hair and a beard. Easily standing ten feet tall, it towered over Jen as it stomped closer.

Jen inadvertently let out a sharp scream and backpedaled, losing her balance. She fell to the ground, just as the creature's gnarled hand swiped through the air in which she'd stood just a second before. Jen's heart raced as she tried her best to get her feet beneath her again so she could run—but she stopped in confusion when she saw the being meekly recoil.

"I'm sorry—I'm so sorry—I didn't mean to scare you. I'm so very sorry," it repeated in a thick Russian accent. Jen was not expecting it to speak, much less apologize. "I knew I should have stayed in my feline form, but I say 'No, Dimitri, you need to change back to heal faster, and Jen would understand'—"

"Treeow?!" Jen blinked, not believing her eyes. Frantically, she tried to remember what Mira called Treeow after he'd saved them from Malcolm's killing spell. "You're a—a—"

"A *leshij*," Treeow—Dimitri—finished for her. "Or 'leshy' in your native tongue." Seeing that she was still just as confused, he continued, "We are protectors and guardians of the forest and worthy travelers. I'm sorry I didn't show you my true form until now, but I was afraid of how you'd react."

"Probably the same way," Jen said, finally breathing easier as she slowly stood back up. "You look to be in better shape now. You said you heal faster in your leshy form?"

"*Da.*" Dimitri nodded. "It takes lot of energy to remain in my feline form, much less heal from injuries."

Jen lightly nodded. That made sense. "I can't thank you enough for saving me and my friends. I'm indebted to you." She covered her heart, which was beginning to beat slower, with both of her hands.

"It is my sworn duty, Jennifer Lancaster." Dimitri dipped into a low bow, the leaves in his hair and beard rustling.

She cocked her head slightly. "To protect me?"

He stood from his bow and gestured to the shady trunk of the dogwood tree. "Let's sit."

Forgetting that she needed to shower, Jen quickly walked over to the base of the tree, sat, and crossed her legs, eagerly awaiting Dimitri's answer. She watched as the leshy practically pressed himself to the ground, barely getting enough clearance from the overhanging branches. His impish grin made her feel even more at ease.

"I was given orders from one who cares for you very, very much."

Jen thought for a moment. It couldn't be Victor, because he'd thought Dimitri was just a feral cat from the Amaranthine Forest. The only other person she could think of was . . .

"My father, Charles?"

It still felt so weird for her to say those words aloud. *My father.*

But Dimitri slowly shook his head and said, "Merlin."

Jen opened her mouth, but nothing came out; she was speechless. Hope blossomed in her chest.

If Merlin is still alive, he can help us find the other MystiCrystals!

But that thought immediately brought yet another question.

How could the most renowned sorcerer—one who was thought to have vanished over a millennia ago—still be alive?

Finally, she managed an attempt at speaking: "M-Merlin? How could that be? Vic told me he disappeared shortly after the Great Battle."

Dimitri playfully waggled a finger. "He is not wrong, but 'disappeared' does not necessarily mean that he *died*. In his search to find the remaining MystiCrystals, Merlin came across a *ved'ma*—a witch—deep in a Russian forest and she turned him into a tree, helpless, bound to be eternally trapped as the world continued to change around him." He shook his head in sorrow.

CEEAAAAWWWWWW!

Before Jen could ask any other questions, she heard Skarmor's cry; it wasn't a warning cry, but one denoting surprise and elation. Turning, she spied another griffin slowly descending near the direction of the stables.

"Vic?" she whispered as hope flooded into her heart.

Pushing up from the ground, she sprinted toward the stables, not caring how stiff her legs had become from sitting so quickly after her training. Tears of relief blurred her vision as she broke over the top of the hill, refusing to slow down. Blinking them from her eyes, Jen realized that the griffin was Pernissa, Hephalon's griffin.

"Heph . . ." Jen breathed, willing herself to run faster.

Pernissa looked beyond tired as Skarmor met her in midair, flying up beneath her to place his body carefully under one of her wings and stabilize her descent.

When Jen saw the rider on Pernissa's back, she faltered slightly, coming to a standstill. It wasn't Victor—not even Hephalon—but a lanky boy with curly, fiery-red hair who couldn't have been much older than herself. He was resting on the strong neck of Pernissa, seemingly unconscious.

Jen's legs refused to budge from the shock she was experiencing; they were glued to the ground as thoughts swirled in her mind:

If that's not Heph or Vic, then who could it be?

Does this mean that Heph couldn't escape the massacre? Or Vic?

Where are they now?

She watched, frozen, as Pernissa's hind legs nearly gave out once she landed, saved only by Skarmor.

Rushed footfalls behind her signaled the arrival of Mira and Gavin. Mira was the first to get to Jen, saying, "What's going on?" She put a hand on Jen's shaking shoulder, concerned.

With her mouth as dry as cotton, Jen couldn't bring herself to speak; all she could do was point toward Pernissa and the boy slumped on her back.

"*Rez?*" Gavin said as he made his way up the hill, squinting as though his eyes might be deceiving him. "Rez!" He rushed past Jen and Mira to help the boy off Pernissa's back while Skarmor gently stroked Pernissa's head with his own.

After a few hard swallows, Jen finally attempted to speak.

"Gavin . . . knows him?" She gestured at the boy who was now beginning to regain consciousness.

"We both do," Mira said. "He's a fourth-year tenderfoot, one year behind me. His name is Resolved, but he goes by Rez." She slid her hand from Jen's shoulder and took her hand. "He's Mystra Hephalon's son. Come on!"

As another wave of surprise attempted to paralyze Jen, Mira took her arm and gently tugged her along toward their unexpected visitors.

"Heph has a son?" was all Jen could say, which came out as barely a whisper.

As they got closer, she noticed a few slight resemblances—the curly, red-orange hair; the height; the rounded dimples—but that was as far as it went. Rez was stick-thin, and his outfit opposed that of his father; he wore skinny jeans, a white V-neck, and a black, silk, low-cut buttoned vest, all of which were disheveled most likely from the ambush at Watercress, leading Jen to believe that he must have been at Watercress during the time of the ambush.

By the time they closed the distance, Rez was finally coming to. His eyes fluttered open. One glance and Jen found another resemblance to Heph that made her wish he'd arrived on the back of Pernissa as well.

"Rez, oh my gosh," Mira breathed. "I'm so glad you're here!" She wrapped him in a gentle hug before pulling back.

"Hey, Mira," Rez said weakly as he hugged her back. "All thanks to m'lassie, Pernissa, here." There was a subtle Irish tenor in his voice. He stroked the feathers on Pernissa's neck as she softly chirped. "She found me just in time before the explosion. Otherwise I woulda been a goner . . ." His eyes seemed to be replaying the atrocities he had witnessed.

Jen wanted to introduce herself, but she was still processing that the person in front of her was actually Hephalon's son.

Rez broke out of his reverie and asked, "Hey, is m'da here?" As the shoulders of every person around him sagged, he swallowed, saying, "Is he . . . ?"

"No." Jen was quick to reply, which surprised her. She cleared her throat and brushed back a few strands of curly hair. "He's too resourceful of a terramancer." She rocked on the soles of her feet, hoping she could keep her emotions in check.

Rez grimaced. "I wish I knew him as well as you."

There was an awkward pause.

"Uh, Rez," Gavin said, breaking the silence as he walked over to Jen. "Let me introduce you to Jen."

"Pleasure." Rez straightened, revealing more hidden height, and gave her a slight bow.

Jen was expecting a handshake, but instead she improvised and curtsied awkwardly.

"A thousand pardons, but I cannae recognize you . . . are you one of the traveling Paladins?"

She smiled slightly. "No, I just recently became a tenderfoot."

"Oh . . ." He looked confused. "You seem to be a little old for a beginner tenderfoot." Shrugging, he then asked, "Which Mancy Plane are you studying?"

She looked around and smiled again, raising her arms innocently. "All of them?"

Rez laughed at this. "I like you." He playfully wagged a finger in her direction. "Don't we all wish to be an omnimancer, eh?" His chuckling faded when no one else seemed to think that Jen's response was a quippy joke. Uncomfortably clearing his throat, he shifted his weight and offered, "You're *truly* an omnimancer?"

Jen nodded. "Yes—well—not yet. I've only just grasped terramancy."

Nodding in return, Rez looked over Camelore, scratching his chin in thought. "So . . . then you must be related to one of the First Five clans."

Gavin leaned toward Jen, whispering, "Rez is a little rusty on his sorcery history. He prefers conspiracy theories from Earth and learning magic tricks instead of hitting the books."

"Oi, they're not *magic tricks*," Rez countered, putting a slight defensive edge in his voice. "They're pure sorcery. Far more than just simple illusions or sleight of hand." He posed as if performing onstage. Putting one hand behind his back, he lifted the other skyward. An instant later, he brought it back down to eye level, and he was suddenly holding a miniature version of a griffin that looked just like Skarmor.

Jen involuntarily smiled as she saw Skarmor reel back in shock. The miniature copied his every move, as if a small mirror-image. Sniffing, Skarmor cautiously stepped toward Rez's hand, trying to make sense of what he was seeing.

"Look, Skar, that's you!" Jen said, only making Skarmor cock his head to the side in mounting confusion.

Rez waited a few more seconds, then blew on the miniature Skarmor, turning it into a bouquet of blooming peonies, which gave off the freshest flower smell. Jen smirked as Skarmor blinked in amazement and leaned in to sniff the flowers. Smiling coyly, Rez brought the flowers to Jen as Gavin and Mira clapped, ever the raptured audience.

"For you, m'lady."

Taking the flowers, Jen remembered that Hephalon would call her that as well. "You are your father's son."

Rez seemed to stiffen slightly, but then relaxed when he saw Jen's totem bracelet. "The dragon . . ." he murmured, entranced by her charms. "The mark of the Lancaster Clan. You're a Lancaster!"

"You don't seem as rusty as Gavin lets on," Jen said, smelling the brightly fuchsia peonies.

"There we go," Gavin teased, clapping. "It only took him a few minutes."

Rez shot him a playfully annoyed look, but quickly focused back on Jen.

Softly chuckling in amazement, Jen commented, "Peonies are my favorite flower."

"I know." Rez winked, tapping his head. "Just as you are an omnimancer, I'm a telemancer."

Suddenly, it made sense. "Telemancy channels the power of the mind and illusion . . . and you're a magician?"

"I prefer the term 'telemagician.' " Rez bowed again.

"Resolved Hephalon: always the showman," Mira said, nudging Jen playfully.

Turning around, Rez petted Pernissa. "Yeah, well, when you're surrounded by sorcerers, your elegant illusions don't garner the same amazement that comes from the humans on Earth. But one day! I plan to follow in the footsteps of the most famous tele-mancers, like David Copperfield."

Jen's jaw dropped. "David Copperfield is one of us?"

"To name one of many. Did you know that my mother helped him make New York's Statue of Liberty disappear?"

Jen looked to Mira and Gavin, then back at Rez.

"I jest not. For a split second, it was a part of Azumar's skyline."

Jen laughed out of pure amazement. "That's nuts!"

Rez smiled, then craned his neck to see over his friends and down the hill. "Um, guys? Did I hit my head harder than I thought, or has that tree been getting closer and closer to us? I know I haven't been to Camelore in a while, but . . ."

They all looked back, and Jen smiled as she saw Dimitri realize that he had been made and freeze in place, not bothering to cover up his noticeable face.

"Guys, that's Treeow," she started as her friends took a cautionary step or two back. "The leshy who saved us during the massacre." She looked back down toward Dimitri, who was starting to lose his balance. "I was talking with him before I came up here."

"That's *Treeow*?" Gavin blinked, surprised.

"His real name is actually Dimitri, and you'll never guess who sent him to look after us."

After no one made a motion to float a guess out, Jen said, "Merlin."

CHAPTER SEVEN

CREEEEAAAAK!

The old, double-latched door to Victor's cottage swung open, causing light to tear through the dimness inside. At first, the torches didn't light right away; instead they remained dormant, making Victor's place of solitude seem like an empty husk . . . not entirely unlike how he was feeling at the current moment. Light streamed in through the windows, but not enough to win over the shadows.

"*Rallumé,*" Victor said, his voice barely a whisper. On command the torches softly glowed, like embers fighting to stay alive in a fireplace, before growing into a warming light.

"This wench is getting heavy." Hephalon grunted as he put Simone down near the door. Stretching out his burly arms, he said, "I could really go for some Azumarian ale right about now. Do you have some stashed away in here?" He patted his stomach, looking around.

If Victor wasn't so burdened, he would have laughed. "You're more than welcome to search."

"That sounds like a *no.*" Hephalon winked, then walked over to the kitchen table and plopped down on one of the chairs; it creaked under his weight but did not break. His demeanor changed from one of kidding to complete seriousness. "So are you serious about journeying to the Ctesian Crossing? You do realize that the location changes every yearly cycle?"

"If we need transport to Camelore, Azumar doesn't exactly have the greatest selection of creatures that can fly," Victor countered, "and equivols have been said to be the easiest to tame."

"If you can manage to capture one, that is," Cindergray added from across the room. He walked to an empty chair next to Hephalon and slowly sat down, placing his hands on the table for balance. "There's a reason why the humans on Earth can never manage to see one and have since turned them into creatures of myth. Their elusiveness is legendary."

"I've never understood the moniker that humans bestowed upon the equivols: *unicorns*." Hephalon shook his head. "If anything, they should be called uni*horns*." He put the back of his hand on his forehead and pointed outward with his index finger, making it look as though a horn protruded from his forehead.

Victor knew Hephalon was only trying to lighten the mood, but he brushed off the invitation, saying instead, "Regardless, we have to try. We don't have time to journey to the Vallei Mortic realm to track down and train a dragon."

Hephalon dropped his hand and rested it on the table. He made a fist, clenching and unclenching it over and over, looking to be in deep thought. Finally, he said, "Wherever you go, I will follow."

Victor nodded with the faintest of smiles.

Cindergray added, "I would normally offer my support, but given the current circumstance"—he gestured at their unconscious prisoner—"I shall stay here and see if I can glean anything from Simone."

Victor clenched his jaw and nodded. "If we can figure out why —and how—she was turned, that might give us insight into Draconex's methods."

"And potentially give us the upper hand," Cindergray agreed.

Victor nodded again, then slowly walked across the room toward the door that led to his chambers. "And now, the reason why we came here . . ."

Not quite sure why he was feeling so anxious, Victor turned the doorknob and stepped into an immaculately clean room. Inside, he knelt before a mahogany chest that lay at the foot of his bed and unlatched its leather straps. It opened to reveal all his mementos accumulated from what seemed like several lifetimes. Victor glanced back toward the door to see both Cindergray and Hephalon waiting in the wings.

"How long has it been?" Cindergray asked.

Victor audibly exhaled as he gripped the chest's edges. "Longer than I'd care to admit," he confessed.

Slowly, as though not to startle anything inside, he took out a belt that was coiled and held together by a strap of worn-out leather. The belt buckle's brushed silver gleamed a warm yellow from the torchlight as he ran a thumb over its surface.

"I almost forgot what my first totem looked like . . ."

Victor angled the buckle so that the light could highlight more of its design, which was of a masculine *H*—the initial of his surname, Huxley—inlaid with Celtic knots. Bordering it on both sides were small outlines of circles that glinted with different metals. He lightly tapped the center of one of them, and a copper ring rose up from the surface.

Picking it up between index finger and thumb, he slid it onto his right ring finger; it fit almost effortlessly.

"Still fits—surprisingly," Victor remarked, looking at Cindergray, then Hephalon. "Albeit a little snugly."

Hephalon let out a single chuckle. "Leave it to the great Victor Huxley to barely change over the course of two decades." He patted his belly. "I remember when *I* had a six-pack."

"Of what? Azumarian ale?" Victor said as he slid the copper ring off and placed it back into the belt buckle.

Hephalon inhaled but then stopped, seeming to begin a rebuke but reconsidering, and smiled instead. "It's good to have you back, my friend," he said kindly as he walked over and patted Victor on the back.

"You practically handed me that one." Victor closed the chest and stood, the belt still in one hand. Looking at both of them, he said, "Now if you'll excuse me, I'm going to change into something more practical for our journey."

"Don't have to tell me twice," Hephalon said, and he walked out of the room.

Cindergray, leaning on the doorframe, didn't yet move. "This situation is becoming more dire with every passing second."

"Yes, Grand Mystra," Victor agreed.

Cindergray pushed himself off the doorframe and stepped closer to Victor. "For the first time since the Great Battle, our way of life is on the brink of extinction."

A lump formed in Victor's throat and he looked at the floor. "I know."

"There cannot be any hesitation in protecting what we've spent millennia cultivating."

Cindergray's tone was firm, but there was a hint of something in the Grand Mystra's voice that made Victor look back up and into his eyes. He didn't have to read between the lines to know exactly what Cindergray was alluding to.

Cindergray went on, "The survival of our species demands strength . . . and conviction." A long pause. "You are part of our last line of defense."

Victor shut his eyes and swallowed.

"Let nothing through."

"Yes, Grand Mystra." Victor opened his eyes and stood straighter.

"There is a reason why you're among the few left." Cindergray put a hand on Victor's shoulder. "It is part of your destiny, my son."

With that, the Grand Mystra left, closing the door behind him.

Alone now, Victor looked down and, deep in thought, instinctively squeezed his coiled belt.

* * *

Several minutes later, Victor stepped from his room clad in trekking clothes, his terramancy cloak squarely on his shoulders.

He felt recharged for the journey ahead. His hands naturally grasped his buckle totem like it was a part of his daily wardrobe, not stored away for a couple decades. Smiling inwardly, Victor felt the buckle's familiar, comfortable weight, making him partially feel like his younger self.

He caught the gaze of Cindergray, who said with a telltale smirk, "Now go and find your niece."

Victor nodded, deciding to smirk back. Clearing his throat, he managed to Hephalon, "We have work to do."

Back in the main room, Victor noticed that Simone was still unconscious, exactly where Hephalon had placed her upon entering the cottage. With her eyes closed, she seemed almost at peace. How, Victor hadn't a clue; after all, she'd betrayed the Guild and everything for which it stood.

The Grand Mystra exhaled, pulled out his pocket-watch totem, and wound up its central knob. Looking stoically at Victor, he reached out his hand in the Guild's parting gesture and said, "May your nexus protect you."

Victor grabbed Cindergray's forearm and the Grand Mystra did the same. "And yours as well."

As Cindergray bid Hephalon the same parting gesture, Victor stole one last glance at Simone before opening the front door. Before he followed Hephalon out, he said, "Don't go easy on her."

Victor didn't wait for a reply from the Grand Mystra; he didn't need one. He knew that Cindergray wouldn't have an issue in extracting the answers they needed, but even so, he feared what exactly Cindergray would learn.

Victor closed the door to his hut and stopped next to Hephalon, sliding his thumbs behind his belt buckle as he surveyed the rolling hills. "There's only one person I can think of who can help us find the Ctesian Crossing on such short notice."

"*Teska,*" Hephalon grumbled. "The one woman I cannot stand."

"Sorry, Heph," Victor said, putting a hand on his friend's shoulder.

"Well, if I cannot sway your mind, I need more weapons in my arsenal than just my totem." He slid his brass knuckles onto his fingers and shook his fist at Victor. "Events have never transpired accordingly whenever *Teska* is involved."

Victor let out a chuckle, starting east and motioning Hephalon to follow. "That, I can agree with. Last I heard, after she left the Guild, she went on a meditative retreat into the Amaranthine Forest . . . which just happens to be in the same direction as your metallurgy."

"Of course she did," Hephalon groaned, begrudgingly follow- ing. "It'll be a bloody miracle if we can track her down . . . *alive.*"

Victor waited until Hephalon caught up to him before saying, "I've heard whisperings that she made it to the forest's central lake."

"Lake Myctoph? Well, if she's decided to go there, then she must not want to be found—especially by the Guild."

"I'll convince her otherwise," Victor said confidently.

"What on Azumar are you going to do to convince *her* to help *us*?"

Victor looked at Hephalon out of the corner of his eye as he picked up the pace, smiling mischievously. "I have a plan."

* * *

By the time the duo had reached Sterling Hephalon's place, the Azumarian sun was about to dip below the horizon behind them. Its far-reaching rays illuminated the nearby cumulus clouds in radiant hues of pinks, purples, and oranges while, farther east toward the edge of the Amaranthine Forest, the sky smoothly transitioned into a vast black with dots of white to signify the realm's constellations.

After taking some time so that Hephalon could change out of his jubilee attire (as well as down nearly a full cask of Azumarian ale), Victor was itching to start off on finding Teska. As they stepped out of the cottage with full stomachs, he could already hear the droning sounds of the forest's nocturnal creatures; it was oddly calming, but at the same time equally foreboding. It had been seven years since he last set foot in that forest; he was a part of the search-and-rescue team for Erik Flanagran, Gavin's friend who had become lost in its disorienting paths and was never seen again.

And here he was, about to willingly head into that treacherous maw yet again.

May our nexi protect us.

"So what is this idea of yours? It'd better be genius, since you made me wait with boundless anticipation until we reached my place."

Hephalon's question broke Victor out of his thoughts. "Oh, it is . . . but you might not fully appreciate it," he predicted as they walked to the metallurgy, past the cottage and griffin stables.

"I'm sensing a pattern here, Vic," Hephalon said, half joking, as he walked up the steps and made his way to the main door. "I just came to grips with us enlisting Teska's aid . . ."

Victor caught up to Hephalon and put a hand on the door, leaning on it to prevent it from being opened. "It's dangerous," he started, "and most likely involves battle."

His friend let go of the door handle and folded his burly arms, interested. "I'm listening."

Victor smirked. In that moment, he felt like a paladin again, trying to convince his old friend to help him out with his newly hatched scheme.

"What is the most reviled and deadliest creature in the Amaranthine Forest?" he asked.

Hephalon smirked back and jutted a thumb behind him at the thick trees that lined the edge of his property. "Serknids." Then it dawned on him; his eyes grew wide, and he leaned forward as if sharing a secret only he and Victor could know. "We're going serknid hunting?"

Victor took his weight off the door and said, "If they happen to be in our path, yes . . . but what we're after are their eggs."

"Vic, you're wrong," Hephalon said flatly.

Victor scrunched his eyebrows and stood straighter, confused at this reaction and unsure of what to say.

His old friend grabbed the handle and slowly pulled the door open. "I reckon I'm beginning to piece together your genius plan . . . and I love it." Hephalon gestured into the metallurgy with his free hand. "After you, old chum."

Letting out a sigh of relief, Victor accepted the invitation and was the first to enter. "I'm glad you're on board, because I know how much you despise those enormous scorpion-spider beasts."

"I'd despise them a whole lot less if there weren't as many of them skittering about, terrorizing the forest," Hephalon countered, shutting the door to his factory. "They make this bloody awful screeching that wakes me from my slumber at least twice a fortnight," he lamented as they walked toward his armory in the back, lighting the wall torches along the way.

"And we can't have that, now, can we?" Victor winked. Getting back on topic, he continued, "So, the plan is to get their eggs."

"Which just happen to be the hardest and most dangerous items to collect in the entire forest."

"Well, for good reason," Victor agreed. "The fluid inside of those eggs masks any and all scents, so if applied, you are practically invisible to them."

"Aye, and quite ironic, really," Hephalon agreed, but then stopped in his tracks as he looked to be piecing more of Victor's plan together. "Does Teska rely on those eggs' fluid to survive?"

"It only makes sense. And I doubt she will turn down a few of those eggs in exchange for helping us."

Hephalon threw back his head and guffawed. "Merlin's beard, you *are* a genius!" he said as he unlocked the latch on the armory door, entering. As the torches sprung to life, Hephalon rubbed his hands together and said with anticipation as he surveyed his marvelous collection, "Hello, my children."

Victor waited as Hephalon walked over to his work bench and slid on a leather harness, which held a thin, magnetized, metal disc that nestled between his shoulder blades when he put it on. Like a kid in a candy store, he then made his way to the wall of glistening weapons and plucked from it two identical battleaxes.

SHING-SHING-SHING!

The sharp, crescent blades sliced through the air as Hephalon swung them with masterful ease before letting them magnetize to that metal disc on his back.

"Say by the Magic of Merlin we find these eggs and manage to escape with them . . . How do we ensure that we don't lose our bearings and end up like every other poor soul, doomed to be forever lost in the Amaranthine Forest?"

As Hephalon spoke, he picked up a long-shafted mace club with a steel head dotted with sharp spikes. He tested its weight and, thinking better of it, set it back down.

"We won't lose our bearings," Victor started, expecting that question, "because those who get lost are focused on escaping, not trying to find a location already in the forest." He shifted, excited to share how innovative his plan was. "The Amaranthine Forest only alters the direction of those wanting to get out, not stay in."

"How did you reach such a daring conclusion?" Hephalon asked, momentarily distracted from his weapon foraging.

"I figured that's how Teska found the lake. By focusing on her marker so that the forest wouldn't play tricks on her," Victor concluded.

"Ever since we were wee lads, you were always the brains, Vic, while I was—and still am—the brawn." Hephalon shook his head in amazement, then let out a quick shout of surprise as he noticed something behind Victor. "Come to Hephy," he said under his breath, as if about to devour a thick, juicy slab of a seasoned wild boar thigh.

Hephalon reached the other side of the armory in four massive strides and took a quiver from the far wall. Putting it on, he let the quiver hang snugly behind his right shoulder as he side-stepped to the right to retrieve some arrows.

"It's said that Loch Myctoph is the natural center of the Amaranthine Forest, where its creatures gather to water, which is due east from here. As long as we keep that heading, we shouldn't have issue finding it," Victor surmised.

Helphalon let out a quick chuckle. " 'Should'? It's bold, I'll admit." He brought each of the twelve arrows to his eye and sighted them, making sure they'd fly true before sliding them into the quiver on his back. "But what other option do we have?"

"Desperate times," Victor said. "Are you all set?"

Hephalon slid the last of his dozen arrows into the quiver, then raised a finger and said, "One last thing to complete my ensemble." He shuffled over to the adjacent wall, picked up a heater shield, and slid it onto his left forearm. "Ready," he said. Adorning the shield was his family's coat of arms: a crane holding a stone in its beak with a lightning bolt splintering off diagonally behind the stoic avian.

Victor placed a hand on Hephalon's shoulder armor. "You sure you want to come? I honestly don't know what will happen," he said, unable to take the seriousness out of his voice.

"You are my oldest and dearest friend," Hephalon said. "I would follow you into any battle . . . even if it were surely suicide." He smiled, gesturing at all the weapons that now hung from his person. "Hence my protection!"

Victor smiled back and patted Hephalon's brushed silver shoulder plate a few times before admitting, "I don't deserve a friend like you."

"No, you don't," Hephalon agreed, winking. "But you have me anyway."

Hephalon pushed ahead out of the armory. Turning to follow, Victor noticed one last thing they would need for their mission: a compass. He picked it up and slid it into one of his many pockets before exiting.

Hephalon locked the door and then slid the keys into one of the pouches on his belt. "I figure the sooner we embark, the better. Are you sure you do not need anything from my armory?"

Victor chuckled, rubbing his belt affectionately. "No thanks. I think I can manage with my trusty, old totem. And I think we might need this." He produced the compass from his pocket.

Hephalon rumbled with a quick burst of laughter. "Aye, that would come in handy!"

"Anything else would just slow me down." Victor kept the

compass in his hand as he made sure it was reading Azumar's magnetic field correctly.

"You might have a point . . . these weapons are getting a little cumbersome." Hephalon shrugged, letting the weapons lightly clang against each other as he moved. "But I cannot bring myself to leave any of them behind. I might need each and every one before our journey is through."

"Better to be safe than sorry," Victor said as he walked past Hephalon, toward the main door of the metallurgy. "Come on."

Hephalon followed and again, once they were outside, he locked the main door. By then, the midnight moon was the only thing illuminating their surroundings, bringing both a calmness and an eeriness to the night. The line of trees that marked the entrance to the Amaranthine Forest, as silent as the statues adorning Watercress Castle's hallways, looked even more fore-boding as both Victor and Hephalon quietly stepped closer.

Raising the compass, Victor pointed at the tree line. "East." He lightly tapped the glass casing of the compass, augmenting the magnetized needle and setting it firmly eastward. "Ready?"

Hephalon stirred, repositioning his quiver and bow more toward the center of his back. "Are we ever?"

"Let's find those eggs," Victor said, then stepped into the Amaranthine Forest.

The crisp sound of leaves crunching beneath his boot elicited a response from some unseen creature shrouded deep within the cover of the trees. Hephalon tensed and reached for one of the battleaxes lodged to his metal back plate, just waiting for a reason to draw it.

This, Victor thought, *is going to be interesting . . .*

Lord Draconex hadn't moved in he didn't know how long; it could have been minutes or hours, but it felt like days. He remained kneeling on the cold, cracked cement ground of the chamber that had once housed his ShadowCrystal shard, deep within the bowels of Feralot. Now it resembled nothing more than a mausoleum, containing only stifling reminders of his withering powers and the plague of failures that had seemed only to compound since his ambush at Watercress Castle the night before.

With his body slumped and mouth agape, his hands rested weakly at his sides, palms open. Draconex seemed catatonic, but in his mind he was frantically concocting what his next move should be.

Should I track Diaema down and retrieve the ShadowCrystal and then kill her for her betrayal?

Should I instead focus on capturing the Lancaster girl while she's weakened and all alone, without anyone protecting her?

Or should I go to the one place where I swore never to return . . . a place where my strength and powers will be restored, but at a high price . . . ?

Trailing echoes reached him from the darkened corridor outside, startling him from his thoughts and halting the formation of his plans. At first, he foolishly thought that it might be Madame

Diaema, returning with her spoils and a remorseful conscience; but then he distinguished the exasperated grumblings of his leech of an apprentice. Trying to regain some semblance of his former ruthless self, Draconex stood just as Malcolm entered the room.

With his most seething leer, he said in his hardest tone, "The prodigal son returns."

Malcolm stopped and stared at Madro's corpse in the corner of the chamber then turned his gaze to Draconex, not giving a reply.

The torchlight revealed a bruised and battered face with an inflamed, sutured scar traveling down its left side. Draconex hadn't realized the true extent of Malcolm's injuries—probably due to his lack of concern, as he had carelessly thrown his apprentice onto the back of Volcanor during his escape from Watercress Castle. But now that he was face to face with the boy, Draconex was equally startled and surprised that it resembled his own scar —the one Charles Lancaster had given him all those years ago.

Looking at those swollen eyes, he saw in his apprentice contained rage—could there also be a hint of budding defiance?—roiling beneath the unwavering gaze. Tense silence continued, which filled Draconex with a slight . . . unease?

My, that's a new feeling . . . he thought, *and I don't like it.*

He fought to keep his composure. He could not let Malcolm sense his newly weakened state, for he knew that his apprentice would surely capitalize on it.

"Don't shoot me with that stare, *boy*." Draconex slowly circled Malcolm, hoping that he could still command respect—and fear. "You're the only one to blame for letting that Lancaster girl out of your feeble grasp."

Malcolm didn't budge; he just continued to stare at the place where Draconex had once knelt, which was near the empty containment field that once held the ShadowCrystal so that it may spread its unlimited energy throughout all of Feralot.

His eyes narrowed. "Where's the ShadowCrystal?" he said, emotionless.

"It was taken during the unexpected escape of Charles and the girl's foster parents."

By this time, Draconex had completed his sweep and now brought his hand to where the ShadowCrystal had once levitated. There were no words to explain the emptiness he felt now that the lifeblood of his dark powers was gone without a trace.

"Well, who took it?"

Malcolm now sounded almost as exasperated as Draconex felt, but he was too wrought with fatigue to smite the boy for his disrespectful tone; instead he stayed as still as stone, only allowing his eyes to pierce Malcolm's before giving him an answer that still felt too surreal to be true.

"Diaema."

* * *

Malcolm tensed, inhaling in surprise. He saw Lord Draconex pick up on his slight change in demeanor, but for some reason he did not expose it, as was his usual wont, and dismantle him on the spot with a condescending remark about his lack of vision or limited intelligence.

What has gotten into Draconex? He seems . . . different.

Shaking off that question, he focused again on the thief that absconded with the ShadowCrystal.

Madame Diaema . . .

"Why—why would she take it?" he chose to say aloud. Malcolm waited for Draconex to respond. He searched his master's torchlit face for some indication until he saw a slight twitch from the edge of his mouth nearest his scar.

"She remembers," Draconex breathed, barely audible.

"Remembers what?"

Malcolm furrowed his brow in confusion. He couldn't help but think back to his time alone with Diaema in Draconex's den, when she convinced him to sit atop the Throne of Dragons while she divulged to him its secret power, her deeply guarded resentment toward their mutual master, and the façade that Draconex wore that allowed him to rise to the rank of Dark Watcher Commander.

"She's starting to remember what I did for her—what I made

her into . . . but how could she *possibly* remember?" Draconex touched the scar on his left cheek, visibly shaking. "It's impossible." He then made a fist and thrust it back to his side. "In death, how can *he* still be ruining my life?"

Malcolm saw that familiar rage emanate from his master but not nearly with the same magnitude as before. Without warning, Draconex spun and started toward the door, only blocked by Malcolm. In any other circumstance, Malcolm would have cowered and let Draconex pass, but for some reason he remained still and stolid, waiting for this long-awaited confrontation.

"Move, *boy* . . . or *be* moved."

The words spilled out of Malcolm's mouth before he could stop them: "Why don't you try . . . *master*."

Malcolm expressed no intention of stepping aside. He felt a sudden jolt of adrenalized pleasure surge through his system at the sight of his master's stride faltering ever so slightly. Draconex continued walking toward him—slower than before—and stopped inches away, the top of his breastplate almost touching his nose.

Malcolm looked down and saw that Draconex's ring had begun to glow a sickly blood-red. He focused on his ring to do the same, then slowly craned his neck to look at his master; he was more than primed for a duel.

Instead, Draconex snickered derisively, and Malcolm saw his ring power down. "Nothing would please me more . . . but where we're going, I need you to be at your best. Or"—he ran a bony finger across his own scar—"as close to your best as possible."

Malcolm felt his face get warm and fought the urge to touch his new scar. He stared into the ghoulish eyes of his master. Determined to focus on their similarity no longer, he instead demanded as sarcastically as possible, "To where must I follow you, O Lord?"

Draconex exhaled, and Malcolm could smell hot, acidy brimstone on his breath. A sparkle briefly played across the deep abyss of Draconex's pupils. Malcolm thought he sensed hesitation and fear from him, but Draconex said, "You'll soon find out, my apprentice."

He stepped to the side and continued his exit, deliberately striking Malcolm on the shoulder with his jagged, armored vambrace.

Malcolm closed his eyes and waited for the urge to retaliate to finally subside. Just before he turned around to follow, he heard Draconex say, "Oh, and the new look suits you."

CHAPTER NINE

FLAP FLAP FLAP.

Madame Diaema's wings erratically cut through the air as she fought to both keep the ShadowCrystal from falling from her meager grip and increase the distance between herself and Feralot. Ever since the prison escape of Charles Lancaster, she'd been in a panic; she had no idea where she may go—or what she may even do—but knew that, whatever she decided, it must be as far away from Lord Draconex as possible.

How could he?! she wanted to scream.

Every so often she would glance back, paranoid that he might be hot on her trail, even though Diaema knew that her echolocation ability would alert her to his presence well before her eyes ever could. She'd been flying for hours, searching frantically for shelter under the scorching red giant sun of Nyzanth, but the barren landscape offered little succor. The only thing that kept her going was the suffocating memory of Lord Draconex's stifling manipulation that was all too clear now.

What have I done?

Between bouts of near heat exhaustion, her failing vision seemed to pick up a stone quarry sled in the distance. She cared not if it led to a gateway portal at that particular moment—just as long as it could give her shade and a chance to rest, for every flap of her wings was harder than the last.

As she slowly drew closer, she saw that the sled was in fact composed of several covered cars filled with blasted stone, and was in motion, pulled by four massive beasts known as felsen. These creatures, forged under the harsh sun of Nyzanth, dragged the tonnage as if possessed; their steps were gradual but powerful as their rocky, muscular legs drove dense hooves methodically into the cracked ground, providing sturdy anchor points to keep them moving forward.

She was now close enough for her eyes to begin stinging from the dust that the felsen and sled were kicking up, but that didn't stop her from reaching the last attached car in the line. Her rough landing caused her to lose grip of the ShadowCrystal, and her adrenaline spiked as she used up the last of her energy reserves to stop its roll with one of her wings just in time to prevent it falling off the side of the car.

Before she succumbed to her growing fatigue, she found a small tear in the corner of the car's tarp and, with increasing effort, crawled her way toward it and slid under, out of the unforgiving rays of the sun. As she tried to find a comfortable position between two jagged stones, her mind, now temporarily free of her main task of survival, quickly shifted to the events that had led up to her sudden escape.

She remembered being jostled awake from a nap in Draconex's den by a less-than-subtle tremor; this was quickly followed by a deep-throated growl that made the hairs on her neck stand up. Quickly, she changed into her albino bat form, fluttering through every chamber in an effort to find Draconex; once she realized he was not there, she burst out into the corridor and flew down the open stairwell. More bone-chilling noises rose up, coming from the throats of both dragons and humans alike.

It was mass hysteria by the time she made it to the immense main chamber that provided a central view of the four main wings of Feralot: the entrance to the prison bay, the exit to the outer grounds, the admittance wing of the infirmary, and the descending staircase that led to the dungeon.

She managed to catch the vanishing forms of Draconex and Malcolm as they jumped out of sight into the smoking hole that used to be the dungeon's entranceway. She tried calling out both of their names, but over the cacophony of screams and the shuddering, moaning frame of Feralot itself, they didn't hear her. Getting increasingly worried, she decided to follow them down, when she was suddenly struck by a stray piece of falling rubble. Feeling the beginnings of a concussion, she pushed it aside to get close enough to still see her master and Malcolm.

What was waiting for her was something that she never could have possibly imagined: Draconex, staring furiously at an empty cage, spitting out a name that she'd never realized she knew.

"Charles."

CHAPTER TEN

In the hours that succeeded the arrival of Resolved Hephalon and Pernissa, Jen asked Mira, Gavin, and Rez into Camelore's helioarch ceremonial chamber so they could be debriefed on Tree-ow's true identity—a leshy named Dimitri—and the revelation of who it was that sent him to protect her. Tyler was out in the stables with their parents, playing with his newfound best friend Skarmor.

Gavin was the last one in after quickly stopping by his hut to pick up the lost journal of Merlin. Everyone was slack-jawed as Jen continued explaining her newest revelation.

"Merlin is actually *alive*?" Mira breathed.

"Well, 'alive' is . . . generous," Dimitri said, chuckling. He was standing by the door after discovering that he was too big and heavy to sit in one of the chairs. "He was cursed millennia ago and turned into big *derevo*—" He gestured to himself while seemingly trying to find the right words to explain further. "Um, *tree* . . . so is he *living*? Yes. Alive? Remains to be seen."

Jen softly chewed on her lip, thinking. "Well, can't we find him and see if he can help us?"

Dimitri crossed his arms, which were covered by thick bark. "That will prove more difficult than you might think. The curse also made Merlin mute. The only reason I can sense him is because I am *leshij*. We are connected by the forest."

"If we find him, can you translate for us, then?" Gavin asked, staring down at the lost journal in his hands.

The leaves on Dimitri's head rustled as he sadly shook his head. "*Nyet*. He doesn't really speak to me. It's more like a feeling. It's . . . hard to explain." He looked down and shrugged.

Jen sat up a little straighter and looked around the chamber. "I think we need to at least try. Right now we need to follow every possible lead, even if the odds aren't in our favor."

Silence spread over the small group until Gavin said, "Jen's right. We need to know for sure." He looked her in the eye and flashed a tight smile. Jen returned the smile and watched as his face turned more serious. He cleared his throat and said, "I'm . . . also having trouble reading parts of the journal, so . . . maybe he can help me understand that too."

That caused both Mira and Jen to lean forward in surprise.

"Wait," Jen said, "what?"

Gavin cleared his throat as he placed his open palms on the table, the journal laid out between them. "After our . . . talk," he said to Jen, "I decided to look through the journal and see if I could decipher anything about the locations of the other Mysti-Crystals. After flipping through the pages, I found that I could only read the foreword passages of every chapter, but nothing after that."

Jen and Mira made their way over to Gavin as he opened the journal and trawled through the pages.

"I assumed I could read it all after I opened the journal in the Sacrarium, but I only had time to read the first page before we had to escape."

Jen couldn't believe it. She looked over his shoulder at the pages, but of course she couldn't make out any of the symbols herself. "Does this mean that you're *not* the Light Bringer?"

Gavin looked up at her and shrugged. "I don't know what it means . . . but what I do know is that there might be more clues in here that I won't be able to figure out, so that might make finding the other MystiCrystals a bit harder."

"Well, maybe the foreword passages will give us something to go off of?" Mira offered. Jen could tell that Mira was trying to be positive, but she couldn't help but feel disheartened by this news. "We definitely have to find Merlin now."

"Agreed," Gavin said.

Jen looked at Mira, then Rez, still sitting in his chair. "How about you two? Are you also in?"

Mira nodded with no hesitation. "Now's the time when we desperately need to stick together."

"I'd feel wrong if I stayed here," Rez confessed. "We've all sworn an oath to the Guild and the League of Light."

Jen took a deep breath and nodded once, making her way back to the chair she had been sitting in. "Okay, then. It's settled."

She was reluctant to say her next thought, because that meant she would leave earlier than expected. But she knew she had to.

I'm sorry, Vic . . .

"We are going to find Merlin."

"When would you like to leave?" Gavin asked.

Jen looked up at the helioarch and noticed that the sun was getting farther west, signaling late afternoon. "First thing tomorrow morning. Is that okay with everyone?"

They all nodded in agreement.

"Ah, if I may," Dimitri politely interjected. "Your idea is good, but it cannot be so."

"Didn't Merlin send you here to bring me to him?"

"*Nyet*, Sky Jewel. I have been tasked with protecting you. As part of that task, he also warned me not to take you to him, for he had predicted that if you choose that path, the MystiCrystals would be lost." He reached out, gently pressing his forefinger to her forehead. "It is *your* destiny to find the crystals, not his."

Tears welled in Jen's eyes, but her emotions were so raw that she didn't even bother to blink them away. "This is impossible . . . I don't even know where to start!" She put her head in her hands, feeling as though the weight of the world might suffocate her.

A few seconds later, she felt a warm hand on her shoulder. Looking up, she saw Mira by her side. Nothing was said between them—nothing needed to be. Jen put her head back in her hands and prayed for an answer. Every so often, the silence was broken by the turning of the lost journal's rough pages as Gavin went over the passages again and again.

Pinching her eyes closed, Jen tried to imagine Victor by her side. What would he say at this moment? More importantly, what would he *do*? Jen knew that no matter what, he would choose to do something; he would make a decision and he would act upon it, because the worst path one could take was the path of indecision.

He would choose a way, and he would stick to it.

"Okay," Gavin said, still looking intently at the journal, "I'm picking up a pattern across all of the passages that I can read."

Feeling a surge of hope, Jen lifted her gaze to Gavin who was across the table. He looked up with a smirk on his face, and she unexpectedly found herself blushing; that smirk was one thing she would never tire of.

"Well?" Mira prompted.

"They're all based in riddles," he said. "For instance, here's the passage for the first chapter:

"For this crystal I have traveled far and wide,
   Leading me to places where people can hide.
   In one night and one day, their civilization was washed away,
   Under the deep blue, foamy ocean spray.
   With rings of cut and polished stone,
   It shelters a race once purer than our own.
   They can see the world from their shrouded Eye,
   But the outside world will not know them, for three millenia
have passed them by."

"I love riddles," Rez said, clearly delighted. Rubbing his hands together, he stared off into the sky, muttering, " 'One day and one night' . . . 'ocean spray' . . ."

"Yeahhh," Gavin said, drawing out the word, "I got nothing. I've never been down to Earth, so I have no idea what Merlin's referring to."

"You can read the lost journal, but you have no idea what to make of it," Mira jabbed playfully. "Ironic."

Jen was more distracted by Rez than actually thinking about the riddle herself. He looked like he was having an internal dialogue with himself, favoring one idea then dismissing it for another. After a few more seconds, Rez boasted, "I may not know a lot about the Guild's history, but I can't get enough of Earth's conspiracies and legends."

When he didn't follow this up with anything else, Gavin asked, "So, then, do you have anything you'd care to share with the class?"

"Indeed, I do." Rez stood and settled into the pose of a stage magician. With arms outstretched, a glorious cityscape surrounded by water appeared before their eyes with the help of Rez's telemancy.

" 'With rings of cut and polished stone, it shelters a race once purer than our own.' "

His voice was much deeper than his usual tone. It was his showman voice, Jen realized with a smirk.

" 'In one night and one day, their civilization was washed away under a deep, blue, ocean spray.' "

Rez wiggled his fingers, and the gleaming city was swallowed by a huge tidal wave, leaving nothing but churning, white foam, and water that steadily turned darker and darker.

"He's stalling." Gavin rolled his eyes. "You're just repeating the riddle!"

Rez gave him a look. "Patience, patience."

He continued quoting the riddle as the illusion disappeared.

" 'They can see the world from their shrouded eye . . . for three millennia have passed them by.' "

He snapped his fingers twice and leaned on the table. "Which city of legend did Plato say had technology far beyond its time and sunk into the sea?"

Jen knew the answer. "Atlantis!"

Rez bowed flamboyantly before sitting back down. "My work here is done."

Dimitri clapped in astonishment. "Well done, Magic Boy. Very impressive."

Jen's amazement quickly turned to concern. "So now that we have a heading, how do we find it?" She looked at Gavin. "Does it say anywhere in that chapter?"

He flipped through a few pages before stopping and shaking his head. "The rest of the chapter is still coded. I'm sorry."

"There are many different accounts of where Atlantis might be," Rez pointed out. "Some say that Atlantis had even spread to control several regions, all ruled from their main kingdom."

"And how would we even know if we found it?" Gavin asked. "Based on this riddle, it seems like they want to stay hidden."

Gavin had said what everyone was thinking: How could they find a lost civilization that had eluded explorers for centuries? The brief flicker of excitement at cracking the riddle soon vanished, and Jen felt like they were nowhere closer to finding any Mysti-Crystal.

Gavin, re-reading the riddle, paused. "Huh."

Everyone seemed to straighten in their chairs, eager to hear any possible revelation. "What is it?" Jen asked, hopeful, even though she was hanging by a thread.

"Every word that starts a new line of this riddle is capitalized, but so is the word 'Eye.' "

A few seconds passed as they all let this revelation sink in, and then Rez exclaimed, "Merlin's Beard! That's it! Merlin must be referring to one of the debated locations of Atlantis in Mauritania. That one *must* be their main kingdom."

Jen shook her head in amazement. *He definitely is Heph's son.*

"And where's that?" she asked.

"It's on the western coast of Africa. In Mauritania, there's a very interesting landmark. Many people call it the 'Eye of the Sahara.' It's quite fascinating, really. From a bird's-eye view, you can see large concentric circles and eroded channels that lead out to the ocean."

The second surge of excitement hadn't yet faded from Jen's chest. "It makes sense." Looking around at everyone, she offered, "I think we should first check out Mauritania. This lead is too good to pass up and continue to debate."

Dimitri smiled and nodded in agreement while Gavin closed the journal and Mira let out a sigh of relief that Jen could understand.

"Rez, thank you," Jen said, making sure to acknowledge her new friend's massive contribution.

"Anytime, m'lady." There was that flourishing bow again.

Jen still thought that tomorrow morning was a good time to embark, and with the sun sinking even lower in the sky, she felt the fatigue that she had been fighting for the entire day finally begin to overtake her body. "Okay, at first light tomorrow we'll pack up and head to the Eye of the Sahara."

"We're actually going to find *Atlantis*," Mira breathed in awe. She beamed at Jen before getting up and stretching her legs. "I don't know about you all, but my next stop is the mess hall. Would anyone want to grab some dinner before we call it a day?"

Putting a hand over her stomach, Jen debated internally if she wanted to sleep more than eat, but with the way her stomach was rumbling, she quickly decided. "Count me in."

"Yeah, let's whip something up," Gavin agreed.

"Twist my arm, why don'cha?" Rez licked his lips in anticipation.

"Dimitri," Jen said, "would you care to join us?" She slid her chair back toward the table before making her way to the chamber's doorway.

"Leshies don't need to eat nearly as often as you humans," he replied, "but there's something about the cat food that you have given me that really—as you say—hits the spot."

Everyone laughed. "I think we can find some on this floating island," Jen said with a smile.

They all walked to the mess hall where Jen found her parents and Tyler, who joined them for a quick meal before a much-needed rest.

CHAPTER ELEVEN

Hephalon cursed . . . again. After being in the Amaranthine Forest for half an hour, he'd managed to stumble over several fallen branches, prick himself on thorns that he believed were not poisonous, annoy a small family of furry rodents in a hollowed-out tree trunk, and tangle his long, red locks with bits of twigs and leaves.

"I sure hope you'll fight those serknids better than how you're hiking in this forest," Victor said, half amused, half serious.

"Oi, you'd be in the same boat if you had this much battle armor and weapons on you," Hephalon huffed.

"Which is exactly why I don't." Victor looked back at his old friend and tapped his belt buckle totem.

"Serknids are wily creatures. They may be born blind, but they'll match you at every turn."

"We have little room for error," Victor agreed. "Just remember that these guys paralyze their prey with their noxious breath. If we're ever unlucky to get into close quarters with them, take a deep breath first." He ducked under a low-hanging branch that proceeded to smack Hephalon straight on the forehead.

"*Oof,*" the metallurgist grunted, snapping the branch off the tree and rubbing his forehead. "How could I forget *that* important detail? But that begs the question: remind me, why did I decide to follow you into this horrid place?"

Ahead, Victor saw that the trees looked different than the others he had passed. Forgetting his friend's question, he slowed his pace and signaled that Hephalon do the same. As he got closer to these new trees, he noticed that they had tendrils hanging from every one of their branches. It wasn't until he got closer that he realized that those tendrils were thick webbing, dripping with some sort of viscous fluid. He scanned the canopy left and right.

"We've found them," Victor said, barely a whisper.

He looked back at Hephalon, who, without stating the obvious, became as quiet as a cunning warrior, blending in with his surroundings and waiting for Victor to make a call.

Scanning the trees again, Victor tried to get a glimpse at what was in store for them. In order to do that, he had to part two thick branches. He could feel the wet, sappy fluid on his fingertips, sticking to them.

Perfect . . .

From whatever moonlight that was able to be filtered through the dense canopy, Victor could make out several webs haphazardly spun between tree trunks like hammocks, which held a dozen or more sleeping serknids. Their weight seemed to push the limits of the webs' tensile strength, but they did not break; some of the serknids' spindly, knotty legs were dangling through the webs like fearsome stalactites in a nightmarish cave.

In the middle of the perimeter of webs lay the serknids' bulbous eggs. Some of the shells were so thin that Victor could make out the larvae moving underneath, pressing every part of their devilish bodies up against the shells in an attempt to break free; others did not move. Victor homed in on the latter because they were the fresher eggs—and the more perfect targets.

Detaching the rings from his belt buckle, Victor slid them onto his fingers. Turning around to Hephalon, he gave him a look that said, *Hold your charge, but be ready.*

Hephalon nodded once, and then didn't move a muscle, waiting.

For as long as Victor had known Hephalon, they both had been able to work so easily together. It was like they shared the same mind, thought the same way. Their strategy was unmatched when they were Paladins in school, and it felt like nary a day had passed since then. He wouldn't have wanted anyone else to be with him during this moment, because there was no one else he trusted more . . . and failure meant that he would never see Jen again.

Blinking away the tears before they could form, he slowly extended his hands and reached out toward the eggs with his nexus. He let his senses run along the vine-covered, mossy ground until he could feel the warm weight of the eggs. A tight smile played across his lips as he tipped his fingers inward toward his palms ever so slightly and saw the closest egg start to sway under the movement of the mossy ground. Realizing he had been holding his breath, Victor allowed himself a moment to inhale the humid, stagnant air before regaining focus. Blinking twice to square himself again, he curled his fingers a few more times as the egg slid one more meter—and then stopped at the lip of the nest, stuck.

Scowling in annoyance, Victor bit his lip and brought his hands together like he was already holding the egg. He lifted his hands a few inches, and so followed the egg—until he heard a faint rustling sound in front of him and off to his right.

He remained still and, only with his eyes, looked in that direction. As if his mind had been read, he saw Hephalon slowly move in that direction, beginning a search of that area.

Knowing that his friend had things under control over there, Victor refocused on the task at hand. All around the nest, he could still see the sleeping forms of several adult serknids. He squinted, focusing on one webbed hammock in particular. In the dead of night, their shiny, black exoskeletons gave them near-perfect camouflage, so it was hard to get a decent head count, but it seemed as though there weren't as many of them as before . . .

Another rustle of leaves.

A few quick footfalls not too far away.

Victor tensed just long enough to forget about the eggs and

turn to his right. Out of the Stygian darkness emerged Hephalon, wiping blood from his battleaxes.

"Thought they could pull a fast one over ol' Hephy. They were sorely mistaken," he whispered.

Almost immediately his arrogance drained away the second he looked up at his friend.

"Behind you!"

Twisting both axe handles in his hands to get a better grip, he flung them straight at Victor. If he hadn't ducked just in time, Victor would've been the one impaled instead of the drooling beast crouching right behind him, seconds away from striking.

As Victor lay there, he first heard the large body of the serknid thump to the ground, then looked up to see its head on a trajectory to land inches away from his own. He quickly took a deep breath and rolled away from the corpse just as it elicited its death rattle. Victor didn't have to be next to it to know that it had released its airborne toxins—if he had inhaled its breath, Victor would have been incapacitated and no help to Hephalon.

"Thanks," Victor said, grateful.

"You can thank me once we have the eggs and are out of this death trap."

Hephalon wasn't wrong. Now wasn't the time to stop and let your guard down. Victor looked back toward the nest and grimaced when he saw more serknids start to stir from their slumber.

Feeling an even more dreadful sense of urgency, he quickly reached out and felt his nexus use the undergrowth to grab ahold of the first egg and push it over the nest's lip. It started to roll, crunching dead leaves and breaking small twigs along the way. Victor no longer cared about stealth—all he wanted was to keep this egg intact; without it, he would have no bargaining chip with Teska.

The egg wobbled haphazardly, picking up speed as it rolled closer. Darting his eyes from his prize to the awakening monsters and back again, Victor hoped he could at least get one of the eggs before the swarm of serknids overtook both of them.

"Vic, we no longer have the element of surprise!"

Hephalon cut through the thorax of a large serknid and moved to block the charge of another that seemed intent on taking Victor's head from his body.

"What gave you that idea?"

Victor didn't expect a sly response—both of them had their hands full. He spotted a female serknid crawling toward his egg, and with a swift flick of his right hand, the ravenous monster was flung back toward one of the webbed hammocks by a thick, knotted branch now under his control.

Almost there, Victor told himself, extending his senses into the ground directly below him and outward, covering a radius of fifteen meters. He could feel Hephalon off to his right, darting quickly across the mossy forest floor as he sliced through one serknid after another.

Just as the egg was within his reach, Victor sensed a heavy weight on the ground off to his left side. He dared to shoot a quick look in that direction, and he was glad he did. His instincts kicked in, causing him to lean back so that he just missed a deadly blow from a sharp pincer. Victor fell into a backward somersault, temporarily out of harm's way, but his life-saving maneuver added more space between him and the egg. He clenched his teeth, angry at being forced to deal with this overly aggressive obstacle.

Well, to be fair, I am stealing their eggs.

The beast snapped its claws together, getting ready for another onslaught. Victor backed up a few paces, still using his nexus to feel the ground for any more unseen surprises around him. Hephalon seemed to be maintaining great control of the perimeter, hopping from one serknid to the next, but he could sense his friend slowing down from fatigue.

Needing to make this bout quick, Victor used his size and speed to his advantage, rushing the unsuspecting serknid and sliding through the gap between its long, spindly legs. Like pendulums, the claws swung down to grab him, but his slide was too quick for his opponent's reflexes. Before it knew it, he was out the other side, and he brought his hands together and toward his chest. Vines sprouted from the forest bed and took hold of the monster's shiny, armored claws and legs before it could turn around to face its prey.

With all the force Victor could muster, he funneled all his power into the vines and pushed his conjoined hands downward. Immediately, the vines retracted into the ground, bringing with them a surprised serknid. It tried to fight the vines, but the forest was too strong, and its blind face bit at the air as it was swallowed up by the roiling vines as if they were the tentacles of a kraken.

Victor could still hear its muffled wailing as he ran over its grave toward the egg, which was miraculously in the same place he'd left it.

"You don't even have *one* yet?" Hephalon bellowed.

Victor looked over to see him staring as he stood atop a fallen serknid, a javelin stuck deep into its thorax.

"Working on it!" Victor bellowed back as he tucked and rolled under a swinging claw from another serknid.

Hephalon jumped to the ground and sprinted toward the new assailant, making quick work of it as Victor finally made it to the egg.

He picked it up; it felt lighter than he'd expected.

Hephalon came to his side. "Now that we have our spoils," he started, out of breath, "how on Azumar are we going to get out of this?"

Victor looked all around him, seeing the remaining serknids fully surrounding them, and they were tightening their circle. Cycling through all of their limited options in his mind, Victor extended the egg to Hephalon.

"Break it."

At first Hephalon was about to retort, but seeing how much closer the serknids were getting, he resigned himself to the new plan and used his brass knuckles totem to crack their only serknid egg.

"Revolting. Simply revolting," Hephalon muttered as he pulled out his arm, now fully covered in viscous albumen.

Without hesitation, Victor lifted the broken egg over his friend's head and let a fair bit of the albumen coat him before doing the same to himself. The fluid was warm as it coursed over his head and down his chest and back.

"I see an opening at nine o'clock," Hephalon advised once he'd wiped clean his eyes.

"I see it too."

Victor could see the serknids slowing down their approach, arching their heads upward as they began to lose the scent of their trapped prey.

"Go!"

They both rushed toward the narrow opening between two serknids, barely making it out of the death circle.

The serknids seemed to not even register that their prey had escaped, for they were still closing their circle and sniffing more ferociously.

Aggravated shrieks echoed through the forest as Victor and Hephalon rushed toward the unprotected nest of remaining eggs. Victor pulled his pouch out from underneath the folds of his travel cloak and placed three eggs snugly inside, cinching it shut. Hephalon tried to grab one with his hands, but the slimy fluid made his grip poor and it kept sliding through his fingers.

"Butterfingers," Victor joked, quieter this time so as to not alert the serknids, who were still scrambling around the battleground, bumping into each other as they tried to find their prey.

Hephalon repeated Victor's jest mockingly, wiping his palms on his trousers before finally succeeding in holding one. He took another in his other hand. "Are we good to go? For the first time in my life I am looking forward to seeing Teska."

Victor snickered. "I'm gonna tell her you said that." He looked once more back at the serknids, then turned the other way. "Time to leave."

And with that they were off—toward the center of the Amaranthine Forest that held the mythical Loch Myctoph and their old classmate.

CHAPTER TWELVE

THUMP! THUMP! THUMP!

A particularly aggressive jostle of the boxcar jerked Diaema awake.

She was still in her bat form, huddled under a tarp that covered dusty stones collected from the cracked wasteland of Nyzanth. Somewhat rested, she suddenly remembered why she was here: she'd stolen the ShadowCrystal after hearing Lord Draconex say a long-forgotten name.

Charles.

That common name stirred something deep inside her, but she could not pinpoint it.

Why is that name so familiar? And what did hearing it do to me?

Her usual self-assuredness and strategic mindset had all but evaporated when she'd decided to haphazardly flee Feralot with the dark MystiCrystal. Diaema knew that she had surprise on her side, but that advantage wouldn't last much longer; Draconex would inevitably return to his fortress and realize that she had absconded with his main source of power. She surveyed the cramped area, checking to see if the ShadowCrystal was still with her. Luckily it was safely nestled in between two massive stones. It wasn't going anywhere.

Thankful for the rest—however brief it had been—she started

to plan out her next move. She crawled on her winged arms to peer out of the crack in the tarp to see where the felsen were taking this stone quarry sled. It was hard to gauge her location, since Nyzanth had very few unique landmarks; everywhere looked the same with its cracked ground splintering in all directions like withered veins, hemmed in by the seemingly endless jagged mountaintops on every horizon. Peering away from the mountains, she caught sight of the silver lining she needed.

Amazingly, there in the distance, almost like a rippling mirage, lay the Everworld portal, perfectly flush with the cracked ground. If she weren't so alert, hadn't been able to rest, she would have completely missed the portal. She stared at it in relief. The Everworld portal was widely known to be the hub to the eleven known realms. Like a lost soul finding a new purpose, Diaema knew where she needed to go, and, more importantly, who to find when she got there.

She waited a bit longer, trying to save as much energy as possible until the quarry sled was close enough to the portal. Feeling a bit more like her old self, she clamped onto the ShadowCrystal and shot out of the ripped tarp, setting the straightest course for the portal. Her heart urged her to fly as fast as she could so that she could get off-world and farther away from Draconex.

Immediately she felt the harsh sun start to sear into her fragile white skin, but that only pushed her to reach her destination even faster. Almost on top of the portal now, she wrapped her wings around her body and the ShadowCrystal and dove straight down, feeling the energy of the portal pass through and around her until she emerged into a new realm. Overcast skies took away any chance of heatstroke and the ground changed from sun-dried mud to slate-gray volcanic rock.

Diaema was now one of many floating volcanic mountains high above a thousand-year-old storm that endlessly ravaged Everworld, an immense gas giant that had been burning for several billion years. Far in the distance, she saw multiple portals, each leading to a different realm. As luck would have it, the last portal she saw—seemingly cut into the side of the main volcano on this mountain range—was the one leading to Vespre, home to her people.

The beings of Earth would call her species vampires, but she knew them as Vesperites. And the one particular Vesperite she needed to see was her old nest leader, Ephram La Proutagne. If anyone was able to give her insight into how she knew Charles Lancaster, it would surely be him.

Swirling winds buffeted her tiny form as she fought to keep a straight path toward the Vespre portal; some puffs of air seemed to be actively trying to rip the ShadowCrystal from her tiny grasp. Miraculously, she crossed the cooled lava pool without draining herself too much and fluttered into the opening, feeling that familiar energy exchange as she crossed realms once more.

The humid, mossy air hit Diaema immediately, causing her to feel as though she were flying through molasses. She fell toward the ground, fighting to stay airborne as she adapted to the new climate. As she noticed condensation forming on the Shadow-Crystal, something hit her from the side, wrapping around her and causing her wings to constrict around her body.

Fear shot adrenaline through her veins as she careened to the ground, sliding through patches of thick grass and over mossy roots. Clamping her eyes shut, Diaema waited to come to a complete stop, praying that she wouldn't ram into anything. She lay there a few seconds, catching her breath, and opened her eyes.

I'm in a net?!

The net seemed to be made of small fibers sturdy enough to hold a bat or other small animals, so she risked morphing into her human form. Luckily the gamble paid off, tearing her encumbrance apart as she gained size and mass.

Waiting a few more seconds and not hearing any noises, she then found a large leaf to put the ShadowCrystal in so none of the toxic energy would infect her human form.

She stood and continued her way toward Ephram's nest. Not two steps later, she was hit to the ground again, this time by a blunt object. She rolled onto her back and stared at the dreary canopy of trees as her vision blurred.

A figure, clad in dark green, approached her as darkness enveloped her sight.

* * *

DRIP. DRIP. DRIP.

Diaema awoke with a nausea-inducing headache, not knowing where she was. The steady rhythm of water droplets echoing through a large room helped her focus and gather her senses, though her head felt like it was going to burst.

Slowly, she raised herself from a sofa covered in velvet and cautiously opened her eyes, though her lids had become slightly puffy. Looking around the dim room, she could make out several candelabras placed randomly around her and a large chandelier which took up the majority of her sight when she looked upward. Diaema did not recognize this place, and she wasn't particularly keen on meeting whoever took her here.

Faintly, she heard whispers emanate from one of the deep shadows where even the light from the candelabras seemed too scared to reach. Her acute echolocation told her that there were two beings in the room with her, hidden amongst the shadows.

"Who's there?" Diaema asked, fearful.

No one responded, but footsteps echoed all around her, shooting up her heart rate as she spun around, not knowing where they were coming from. Instinctively she reached for the ShadowCrystal to protect it, but it was nowhere to be found.

"No need to fret," a very calm, familiar voice said. "Your token is safe with us."

Almost immediately, Diaema relaxed. "Ephram," she breathed. She fell back to the ground, finally letting her fatigue set in. "Thank you for saving me."

She closed her eyes and fought to focus through her throbbing headache to find where her old leader's voice was coming from.

Opening her eyes, she looked in the direction that her senses pointed toward.

"It was nothing but a simple misunderstanding," Ephram La Proutagne said just as the candelabras burned a little brighter, casting their light to cover most of the room.

He was a tall man, and if a stranger met him in the street, they would assume he was in his late thirties, but he was actually somewhere around four hundred years old. His features were still chiseled and those sharp gray eyes almost blended in with his skin tone, reminding Diaema of a marble sculpture. In true fashion, he wore vestments of a bygone era, but still looked good in them: a flowing linen long-sleeved shirt tucked into a pair of black velvet trousers; a tight vest, buttoned halfway up his chest and splayed outward to reveal sharp, staunched collars reminiscent of a bat's elegant wingspan. His long, immaculately maintained fingernails danced across his shoulders as he unclipped the gold chain of his cape, letting it fall in swelling folds along the opposite end of the sofa.

"One of our warriors mistook you for a Grey scout and captured you." He smiled warmly. "It's so great to see you, Diaema." Ephram sat down next to her, putting a hand on her thigh.

Diaema didn't know where to start, but she led with a hug. "I never thought I'd see you again."

Ephram chuckled warmly. "Come now, my child. I knew we'd meet again." He returned the hug and looked into her eyes.

Diaema wanted to ask how he was, but she decided to first ask, "Why are you trying to capture the Greys? They've been our allies for centuries."

Ephram took a deep breath. "Now they are our enemy. Shortly after you left, their leader was slain during a coup orchestrated by his half-brother, Mil, and under his reign, they have been trying to take our land and enslave our people ever since. The Greys of the old order that are still alive have been forced into service of his bloodthirsty army. It is a dark time for us all." He put a hand on her shoulder. "I'm glad we found you before any of the Greys did."

Diaema touched his hand and squeezed. "You have no idea how great it is to see you, Eph. I have never felt so lost." She could feel tears starting to form.

"You are here now, my child," Ephram consoled. "What is wrong?"

She pulled away and put her head in her hands, saying, "Everything. I don't know where to start. I feel like I don't know who I really am anymore." She looked up at Ephram, whose posture was now extremely rigid.

"Have you spoken of this to Lord Draconex?"

"No . . . mostly because he said something that made me question everything." She looked at her hands, which were slightly shaking. "I panicked and rashly took his piece of the Shadow-Crystal."

"What did he say?" Ephram seemed to ask too quickly, almost as if he was afraid of her answer.

"He said the name 'Charles,' " Diaema said, remembering how contemptuously Draconex spat out that name in Feralot's dungeon.

There was a long moment of silence, as though Ephram was choosing his words carefully. Then he stood and walked toward the nearest candelabra. Running a hand over the flickering flames, he said solemnly, "You know I have always protected you, yes? That I would never do anything to hurt you?"

Diaema looked over at him, unsure of what was to come next. "Of course."

He bowed his head. "I thought I was doing the right thing . . . I am sorry."

"Sorry for what?" If Diaema had a beating heart, it would have been racing. "You're scaring me, Eph."

Ephram inhaled and turned toward her. "Back before you knew me, I was more . . . impetuous. I got in over my head and Lord Draconex saved my life. Of course, at that time, he was called Orin."

Orin . . . ?

Diaema grabbed the arm of the sofa, feeling lightheaded.

How do I know this name too?

Ephram continued. "Years later he came to me, looking to collect the debt I owed him. He brought with him a severely wounded sorceress, asking me to turn her so she could get a second chance at life. I'm a man of my word, so I obliged."

Ephram looked Diaema square in the eyes.

"Her—*your*—name was Jocelyn. Jocelyn Lancaster."

Her lightheadedness quickly turned into something akin to vertigo as a rush of memories from another life—both images and sounds—unloaded upon her like a tidal wave.

Ephram was by her side in seconds. "You were so badly injured that the transition made you lose your memory completely—which is exactly what Lord Draconex had wanted."

Speechless, Diaema was having a hard time even hearing her old nest leader. She was suddenly feeling emotions she had never known she could feel. "What is happening to me?" she groaned, falling into Ephram's lap.

"Whatever trauma you recently endured has made your old life's memories resurface," he surmised. "Fascinating . . ."

Happiness, joy, love—all of these emotions and everything in between were bubbling to the surface for Diaema, too quickly for her to fully appreciate each one. She squeezed her eyes shut to stop tears from flowing, but then the face of an adorable baby girl entered her mind's eye, and that was when she stopped fighting the inevitable.

She broke into sobs as she looked up at Ephram. "I-I have a daughter . . ."

"Yes," he said, his voice filled with melancholy.

Diaema sat up straight and said, as realization dawned on her, "Draconex has been hunting down my only daughter." She sniffed, wiping tear streaks from her cheeks. "And I stood there —*by his side*—letting him!"

"You had no memory of her or your past life, Diaema. It wasn't your fault. You were led to believe what Draconex told you."

Diaema shot daggers at him with her eyes. "And you let him do that to me."

Ephram looked down at his hands, crestfallen. "I realize my mistake now, but at that time I felt like I had no choice but to obey him." He looked at Diaema, and she'd never seen such anguish in his eyes before. "I apologize, my child."

Diaema didn't say anything as she stood, looking for an exit. Picking one direction, she started walking.

"Where are you going?" Ephram said. He was still sitting, but concern was in his voice.

Diaema didn't stop to look back at him as she continued to walk farther out of the candlelight. "To find that bastard and put an end to him." She couldn't find a door, so she picked a new direction.

"Diaema, I would advise against that," Ephram warned. "By now he probably has figured out that you are gone, along with the ShadowCrystal, and he might even be on your trail already."

"Angrier than ever," Diaema added.

She wanted nothing more than to tear out Draconex's throat, but Ephram was right. Nothing meant as much to him as that broken shard of the ShadowCrystal . . . not even her. And if she were to confront him—tired, unsteady from all these memories, all this emotion, and without a plan—he would surely kill her without breaking a sweat. She needed to first figure out who she really was before facing the person she had blindly followed for two decades.

Calming down, she stopped trying to leave and faced Ephram.

"You need to keep running," he said, grimacing. "It won't be long before he comes here looking for you."

Diaema didn't know what to do. The only person she felt safe around was Ephram, but she knew that if she stayed, she would be a sitting duck. "But where would I go?" she asked.

Ephram stood and walked over to her. "Let your heart guide you. Use your newfound memories to your advantage."

Diaema focused even more on slowing her breathing. Then,

looking her old friend in the eyes, she said, "I'll only leave if I can take the ShadowCrystal with me."

"No. It is too dangerous."

"We both know that Draconex will show up here because of me, and there will be unnecessary bloodshed if you try to keep it from him." She grabbed Ephram's cold hands. "You know me—I'm a survivor. Once he finds out that I still have his most prized possession, he will leave."

Ephram seemed to weigh both options in his mind until he finally conceded. "Fine . . . but I need you to promise me one thing."

"Anything."

She searched his face and saw something she didn't expect.

Is he holding back tears?

"No matter what happens to me . . ." He unlatched a small pouch that was attached to his belt and pulled out two dodecagonal earrings that were the size of dimes. "Do not come back here. We are too deep into a civil war, and now that your memory is restored, you need to find your true family."

"Ephram, I—" she started.

"My child," Ephram cut her off, "you are a Lancaster. I know that your daughter needs you now more than ever." He handed her the jewelry. "These earrings were once yours. I managed to convince Lord Draconex that it was too dangerous to keep your totems on his person. He agreed to never run the risk of you finding anything from your old life."

"I have a totem?" Shocked, she gazed at the earrings glistening in her white palm. Smooth, amber jewels gave off a warm reflection in the candlelight, held in place by a swirling dodecagonal border, making it look like an optical illusion of an endless knot.

Putting the earrings on, she felt a familiar comfort. "I was a telemancer, wasn't I?" She couldn't explain the feeling, but it was telling her that this was true.

"A very powerful one, based on my reckoning." Ephram smiled. "Your totems never left my side."

She walked to the only mirror in the room and admired her

new jewelry. Her face turned sullen, and tears once again rolled down her pristine skin. "I remember now . . . Charles gave me the amber gemstones as an engagement gift. I loved them so much that I asked Sterling Hephalon to add them into my new totem."

"Lord Draconex took your old life from you—and I foolishly helped." Ephram looked toward the ground. "For that, I am eternally sorry . . . but now you have a new purpose." He straightened, reminding Diaema of the Ephram La Proutagne of old. "Come, now. I will take you to the ShadowCrystal."

CHAPTER THIRTEEN

Daybreak came on Camelore once more and Jen awoke to a sliver of light hitting her face from the slight part in her curtains. She stared at the hut's thatched ceiling for a few minutes as she slowly woke up.

She let her head roll to the left and saw Mira still sound asleep in her own hammock. Smiling to herself, Jen realized how lucky she was to have Mira as a friend.

And Gavin too, she thought. *Gavin . . .*

She'd never properly cleared the air with him since their disagreement, so as quietly as possible, Jen rolled out of her hammock and crept across the room toward the door. Praying that it wouldn't creak and disturb Mira, she opened the door only enough to squeeze through, and was met by a pleasant warmth on her face and arms. The sun's rays were already pretty strong this early in the morning, the lack of cloud cover certainly helping.

After closing the door as softly as possible, she started straight toward Gavin's hut, reciting in her mind what she wanted to say. She made it to his door quicker than she would have liked, but after taking a deep breath and unconsciously running her hands through her hair, she was ready to knock—when the door swung open.

Surprised, Jen completely lost what she was about to say. Instead, she started with, "Hiya." She raised her hand in a stiff wave.

"Oh! Hey, Jen." Gavin squeezed the towel that was draped across his shoulders, hiding his bare chest. The only thing he was wearing was a pair of athletic shorts and flip-flops. "I was just on my way to a quick shower before we headed out," he said, breaking the awkward silence.

Jen caught herself starting to blush and tried to look anywhere but at him. "I'm sorry, if—if this is a bad time, I can—"

"No, not at all," Gavin said, cutting her off. He pulled the towel off his shoulders and held the door open while he stepped aside. "Come on in. What's up?"

Brushing a stray curl behind an ear, Jen walked in. "Thank you." She walked to the center of the hut, then turned around and continued as he shut the door, "I just wanted to get a chance to privately clear the air between us. I didn't feel like last night was the best time with everyone around, and I didn't want to kill the vibe at dinner." She tried her best to maintain eye contact, but it was tough.

He nodded, absent-mindedly folding his towel a few times as he said, "I've been thinking about that too. There really wasn't a perfect time last night." He looked up at her and grimaced. "It wasn't my intention to hurt your feelings and make it seem like your idea of waiting for Vic was wrong."

"I know."

This was the first time that Gavin had actually opened up to her like this, so she let him continue. He was twisting the towel like he was wringing out his true feelings. "I just felt like we had a limited window to get a jump on Draconex and whoever is still alive in his Dark Watcher tribe."

"I know," she said again.

"Now that I've thought about it, I'm glad that we took a beat to first come up with a game plan. I know Vic means a lot to you —as he does to me—so it was wrong of me to insinuate that he wouldn't approve of what you were wanting to do. I'm sorry, I—"

Now it was Jen's turn to cut him off. "Hey." She stepped closer to him. "It's okay. I came here to also apologize. I'm sorry that I had an attitude . . . you didn't deserve that. Everyone had high emotions—not to mention being hungry and sleep-deprived." She looked at his eyes, his lips, then back up to his eyes. "Tempers were bound to flare up." She took the towel from his hands and folded it again. "I just wanted to check in with you to make sure that we're okay before we, you know, try to save the world." She looked up at him again and grinned.

He smirked and nodded. "Yeah, we're cool. I know we were both just focused on making the best decision."

"Exactly." She gave back his folded towel, saying, "Now go shower. Make sure it's a quick one so we don't fall behind schedule."

He kept the towel folded and gingerly held it out in one hand like a waiter would a tray of drinks. He mock-saluted with the other. "Yes, ma'am!"

Jen had the impulse to go in for a hug, but repressed it, thinking better. She took the lead and made for the door. "Thanks for making time to talk. I feel a whole lot better."

"So do I." He deftly moved in front of her to open the door. "We're a team, Jen, and now we have a really good lead to go off of. I'll see you in a bit."

"I couldn't agree more." Jen said, feeling like a weight had been lifted from her shoulders.

Gavin followed her out and shut his door.

Smiling at each other, they parted, Gavin to the shower stalls and Jen back to her hut. She glanced back after several paces to see him disappear behind a hut on the opposite side of the housing compound. She was beginning to sense her initial feelings toward him creeping back into her heart.

Easy, Jen, she tried to remind herself, *that's your best friend's boyfriend.*

By the time she got back, Mira was already up and in the middle of her yoga routine. "Hey, girl!" Mira called out as she went into Downward-facing Dog. "Wanna get in on this with me?"

Jen smiled. "I'd only distract you from your stretches. Yoga's more your thing, but thanks for asking." She went over to her armoire closet to put on something more travel friendly. "How was your sleep?"

Mira got up and switched to the first of the Warrior poses. "Surprisingly good. I had such a deep sleep, I don't even remember dreaming."

"I had something similar," Jen commented. "I guess we just had to reset since the Jubilee." Involuntarily, her mind brought her back to that night, one filled with immense destruction and bright spells whizzing around left and right. Shaking her head to clear the horrible memories, she said, "And a good night's sleep really helped me put things in perspective." She took off her pajamas and slid on a plain white top and some slim jeans, making sure her family ring was still on her necklace.

"I feel more self-assured too," Mira admitted, sitting down on her yoga mat and dabbing her forehead with a towel, workout over. "Even though we don't know what we'll encounter once we start finding the MystiCrystals, I'm glad I'm doing it with you."

Jen's heart filled with gratitude at that. "Mira, you know how much I value you and our friendship, right?"

"I know, Jen." Mira smiled at her.

"I'm so lucky that you're doing this with me. It's a lot to ask someone—we don't have any guarantees that this will even work, or that we'll be safe the entire time . . ." Jen trailed off.

"Hey." Mira stood up and placed her hands reassuringly on Jen's arms. "This is exactly what we swore to do when we took our oaths as sorcerers. It's even better that we're such close friends."

Jen hugged her and didn't respond—she didn't have to. The admiration and loyalty were shared equally between them.

After a few seconds of embrace, Jen said, "I'm going to say goodbye to my family before I pack up. I'll let you cool down."

Mira gave that sweet, understanding smile again. "Sure. I'll see you soon."

"'Kay." Jen walked back out of her hut, gaining more confidence with every passing second. She wouldn't let Victor, Hephalon, or Cindergray down.

* * *

Tyler and her parents were sitting at the shore of the lake next to her favorite dogwood tree, and after a few tears made their appearance, Jen spent some time convincing Tyler that he needed to stay back to protect their parents. Shortly thereafter Jen rushed to meet up with her friends at the griffin stables. As she got closure, she was able to hear the happy cawing of Skarmor. Gavin handed her the lost journal as she came to a stop and, smiling tightly, she put it in her shoulder bag next to the ChronoCrystal.

"Sorry I'm late," Jen apologized as she petted Skarmor.

"No need," Gavin said. He shifted his weight to his other foot while holding Mira's hand. "How're you doing?"

"A little raw, emotionally speaking, but glad my family's staying here on Camelore. It's the safest place for them." Jen walked over to Skarmor's stable to let him out. "Hey, boy," she said, ruffling the griffin's feathers as he vibrated his vocal cords in happiness and stomped his two front lion paws. "I missed you too," she giggled lightly.

Skarmor seemed alert and ready to fly as she guided him out of the stables, quickly followed by Pernissa with the help of Rez. There was a slight wind that made the long grass sway lazily atop the hill. Jen looked down toward the lake and spotted her favorite dogwood tree shed some of its snow-white leaves.

"Thank you all again for coming," she said as she turned back to her group of friends.

"Think nothing of it," Rez said as Jen climbed on Skarmor's back. "I'd feel horrible shame if I were to sit back and do nothing while my friends and teachers gave their lives to protect our way

97

of life." He hopped on Pernissa, who backed up slightly to rebalance under his weight and stretched her wings.

"I wouldn't be anywhere else," Mira said, letting go of Gavin's hand and reaching up to Jen, who smiled and helped her up.

"You can always count on me," Gavin said with a single head nod. He deftly straddled Pernissa right behind Rez.

The only one left on the ground was Dimitri, back in his cat form.

"Come on, Dimitri," Jen said, making sure her bag was positioned comfortably on her hip. "We won't leave without you."

Meowing, the leshy pounced and landed in Jen's lap. She waited a few seconds to make sure he was settled, then she uttered a phrase that made her believe she was dreaming.

"To Atlantis!"

CHAPTER FOURTEEN

As Skarmor and Pernissa dove out of the stratosphere above northwestern Africa, Rez pointed in glee down toward the continent, no doubt excited to see the Richat Structure in person. Jen wasn't expecting to feel this overwhelmed, so she whispered in Skarmor's ear to slow down so she had enough time to gather her thoughts and plan next steps. Pernissa matched his speed as they glided through the air, which was slowly getting warmer the lower in altitude they dropped.

She hadn't heard of this place until twelve hours before, and even though this was their first lead, Jen hoped that they were on the right track to Atlantis—or at least on track to find a new clue that would get them one step closer to the TeleCrystal.

Jen also had a creeping thought laced with paranoia about Lord Draconex and if he was already on his way to intercept her. She couldn't afford the luxury of believing that he had been defeated during the ambush; he seemed too skilled to be caught in the collapse and buried in the debris.

Then there was Malcolm. He had been the last person to stand in her way that night, trying to stop her from fleeing, but instead he'd gotten one of Skarmor's claws to the face and plummeted to the ground. His screams of surprise and pain still echoed in her head. For a reason unclear to her, she felt an unexpected ping of sorrow and . . . worry, maybe?

Why are you feeling this? she asked herself. *Malcolm lied to you about who he is, kidnapped your parents, and tried to capture you multiple times. He doesn't care about you! Why are you worried if he is okay or not?*

Those were the kinds of questions that Jen didn't have time to dissect—especially since she could now see the coast of Mauritania between intermittent flaps of Skarmor's great wings. She knew that for her to stay focused, she would have to believe that both Malcolm and Draconex had survived and were already hot on her trail.

A squeeze from Mira's hand brought Jen back to the present, and she realized that she had tensed up. Her muscles thanked her as she made herself relax. She acknowledged her friend with a smile over her shoulder.

Mira pointed downward. "We're getting there faster than I thought!" The wind was near deafening, but thankfully Jen was decent at lip-reading.

She nodded and patted Skarmor on the neck before leaning down toward his ear. "You're doing a great job, Skar." She pointed down at a large set of concentric circles that seemed to be etched into the landmass: the Richat Structure. "Head toward the center of those rings!"

Skarmor let out a single caw to show his understanding and pitched slightly to the left, turning them closer to their destination.

Now that Jen could see this ancient marvel with her own eyes, her heart began to race. They could be on the verge of finding a new MystiCrystal for the first time since the ChronoCrystal was rediscovered all those centuries ago.

And a lost civilization that was only believed to be a myth.

Jen's peripherals caught Pernissa flying closer to them; both griffins flew parallel to each other now, and they masterfully navigated shifty winds as the ground quickly came up to meet them. The twenty-eight-mile-long formation fast overtook Jen's vision, and now she could distinguish with more clarity several concentric circles emanating from its center along with fault lines near its vast circumference.

"Keep steady and aim for the center, boy," Jen reminded Skarmor, and he obeyed, touching down in the dead center of the vast Richat Structure after a few more minutes of careful approach.

Not a single cloud dotted the sky as Jen and the rest of her friends dismounted both griffins and looked around. It didn't seem special at all—just sediment and volcanic rock for as far as the eye could see, blending into the Saharan sands. Near the edge of her vision, Jen could see slight wavering mirages, reminding her that she was in a desert.

"Well, if there was a major city here, it's long gone now," Gavin mentioned as he cupped his hands around his eyes, blocking the harsh rays of the noonday sun.

"Just imagine what Atlantis would have looked like all those years ago . . ." Rez placed his hands on his hips and spun around in a slow circle.

Mira was holding the hilt of her whip, looking alert and a little wary. "What should we do now? Split up and expand our perimeter to see if anything catches our eye?" Her gaze fell on Jen.

Nodding, Jen said, "That's a good idea, Mira." She was about to follow it up with another suggestion, but just then she felt a low, steady vibration. She couldn't quite determine from where it was emanating, so she knelt down and placed her hand on the warm, hard ground.

"What's wrong, Jen?" Mira asked, kneeling beside her.

"Do you guys feel that?" Jen couldn't tell if the ground was vibrating or not, so she awakened her nexus to channel terramancy so she could feel the particles in the sediment. They were as solid and still as a glacier. She pursed her lips, unsure.

"What vibration?" Gavin asked, looking concerned. He widened his stance.

"I reckon it just might be you," Rez chimed in, shrugging.

Dimitri, still in his cat form, walked across Jen's field of vision and stopped in front of her bag, purring.

Furrowing her brow, Jen lifted her hand off the ground and opened her shoulder bag's flap to see the ChronoCrystal emitting a soft, white light. Her eyes widened in surprise as she reached in and grabbed it.

"Guys, the ChronoCrystal is the thing that's vibrating," Jen said as she pulled it out to show everyone. "And look—it's glowing a little!"

Almost immediately after taking the crystal out, Jen saw a mirage form around it. Wherever she moved the crystal, the mirage followed, bending light and air around it.

Mira instinctively jumped back. "Is it just me or is the crystal doing something funny?"

"I'm seeing it too." Jen could not believe what was happening. This was the first time the ChronoCrystal had done anything. "This must mean another crystal is nearby!"

"Amazing," Gavin breathed, stepping closer.

He was about to touch the ChronoCrystal when Skarmor and Pernissa both let out a cry of surprise. Jen looked behind her to see Skarmor and Pernissa on their hind legs, flapping their wings vigorously. They were blocking whatever was in front of them, but Jen didn't have enough time to act as her muscles seized up, causing her to crumple to the ground.

The ChronoCrystal rolled out of her stiff hand, barely a foot away from her, but she could not move at all to retrieve it.

Her friends and Dimitri were also frozen on the ground, their faces contorted in shocked surprise. Tunnel vision quickly crept in, overtaking her peripherals, but just before she blacked out, Jen saw chrome-plated boots stop right in front of her and a muscular hand reaching down to pick up the ChronoCrystal.

CHAPTER FIFTEEN

It's like they were expecting us! Malcolm thought as he fought off the third vampire in as many minutes.

He hadn't quite known where Lord Draconex was taking him when they left the desolate Feralot, but he knew it was somehow connected to Madame Diaema's disappearance. For as long as he'd known Draconex, Malcolm always regarded Diaema as that mysterious woman in the shadows, always tending to her master's infinite whims. Malcolm saw her more than he heard her speak, which only increased his desire to know who exactly she was and from where she came.

When he realized that it was Diaema who had absconded with the ShadowCrystal, he wasn't entirely surprised—after all, there was his little confrontation with her in Draconex's lair not too long ago. She had convinced him to sit on the Throne of Dragons while giving him reason to doubt Draconex's legitimacy and question why he should be taking orders from him in the first place.

She can definitely be convincing, Malcolm thought, chewing on that memory as he decapitated yet another vampire reckless enough to charge at him. *Say what you will about Lord Draconex, but he does know how to train you, and well.*

Malcolm couldn't forget one of his last training exercises,

where Draconex left him for dead, paralyzed, in a locked room with his venomous pet anaconda, Quickfang. He still couldn't believe he'd escaped with his life.

Malcolm's ring pulsated like glowing embers as he deftly moved his hands in conjunction with an incantation, causing the ground to eat a fresh vampire soldier. He quickly glanced over his shoulder to see Draconex mutilate another opponent just before a few more of the ravenous undead ambushed him.

Malcolm squinted, trying to make sense of what he was seeing. Lord Draconex, Commander of the Dark Watchers, had allowed himself to be double-teamed? And it looked like he was about to be overtaken—until, at the last second, he let out an earsplitting roar, which preceded a burst of white-hot flame from his mouth.

Even from more than ten meters away, Malcolm could feel the intense heatwave as it melted vampire flesh and blackened the surrounding trees, which were as enormous as redwoods. As if on cue, the gloomy, overcast sky of Vespre turned a searing orange as Volcanor strafed the battlefield, charring up any opponent that still moved. His large, demonic wings carried his brimstone-scaled body farther ahead, stirring up fallen ash with each flap.

Malcolm wasted no more time marveling at the wyvern dragon, picking up the pace to Chateau Noir: the command post of Ephram La Proutagne. Draconex was not far behind, cutting down the few remaining stragglers still determined to stop their charge.

Malcolm never understood that steadfast loyalty to a leader. He always thought of it as a game of chess: find the King, learn from the King, then *become* the new King. He served no one unconditionally, and up until a few days ago, Malcolm believed that he was on phase two of his plan, "learn from the best"—but now, after seeing how different Draconex was without the strength of his piece of ShadowCrystal, the time to strike was near.

Soon, I will become the best.

Malcolm relished the thought. It would help him succeed and eventually become Lord Ferox's best chance of resurrection.

Malcolm intentionally slowed down as he reached the front gates of the vampire stronghold, for if he beat Draconex there he would not hear the end of it and would most likely be punished for upstaging his master.

How strange . . . the tables have begun to turn, Malcolm thought as Draconex lumbered past him. *He looks weaker than ever. The husk of the man I once idolized—and feared.*

The ground shook as Volcanor, letting out a fearsome roar, dive-bombed the front ramparts, ripping and clawing through scores of guards.

"Ephram is in here . . . I know it," Draconex spat. Malcolm could tell that he was trying to hide how out of breath he was. "When we find him, do not engage . . . He's all mine."

"As you wish," Malcolm said, knowing that he might have to get involved regardless of his master's wishes should Draconex prove to be too tired or slow for the vampire leader.

Then again, why would he *have* to?

Outside of Diaema, Malcolm hadn't encountered another vampire until today, when they'd started to decimate the ranks to get to their commander. Malcolm knew that they'd made quick work of Ephram's pawns only with the help of Volcanor; surely, if La Proutagne was a commander in every sense of the word, then he must be a very resourceful fighter and tactician. That kind of worthiness in an opponent made Malcolm think that Draconex was outmatched.

But only time would tell.

✳ ✳ ✳

Channeling the ramming speed of an African rhinoceros, Lord Draconex rushed the front gate of Chateau Noir, buckling the steel girders and tearing it from its holdings.

BOOOOOMMMMM!

The sound of the enormous gate crashing on the polished

marble floors echoed through the cavernous stronghold, revealing a black abyss. Draconex walked over the mangled frame, followed closely by his apprentice. No words were exchanged between the two Dark Watchers, for they were using their nexi so they could acclimate to the Stygian darkness and the eerie quiet. Draconex channeled the echolocation of horseshoe bats of the European tropics, latching on to to the faint ringing emitted by his steel-toed boots as he walked through the corridor, to alert him of any potential danger.

TACK-TACK-TACK.

With the loss of his ShadowCrystal shard, he could no longer channel all the Mancy planes, so he had to rely solely on animancy, his birth-given plane. He knew Malcolm's natural plane was terramancy—just like Victor's—and he would be looking for other clues in a similar fashion.

Volcanor's roars became fainter and fainter as Draconex stepped deeper into the chateau, knowing that his loyal dragon was making quick work of any remaining vampires.

TACK-TACK—

His ears picked up a faint squeaking sound, which quickly multiplied and increased in decibels. Immediately, he knelt to the ground and draped his flowing, obsidian cape over his body, ducking his head just in time before a wall of bats flew at him. He could feel that they were larger than normal bats—and more aggressive. Their teeth and feet tore at his cape and pierced his armor along his forearms, back, and neck. Not knowing how long this annoying barrage would last, he drew in a breath and channeled the ability of a giant armadillo, making his skin sprout overlapping, hard plates that covered his hunched body, which better protected him from the bats' onslaught.

Inexplicably, the screeching changed pitch, almost making Draconex think that the bats were scared or surprised. He could feel the amount of bats slamming into him diminish until they left him alone entirely, but their screeching remained. Blinding light broke through the tears in his cape, and it didn't take him long to realize that Malcolm was the reason why the bats were evading him.

Shading his eyes, he glanced behind to see his apprentice not a few steps behind him, emitting a harsh light from his ring totem. The bats avoided the light as if it were a protective shield around them. As long as Malcolm continued to give off that light, they were safe.

Nodding approval to his apprentice, Draconex resumed his march deeper into the castle, first stepping slowly before picking up his pace as the bats continued to part in front of him. He slowed as he noticed himself getting closer to the edge of the light, knowing that was the only thing repelling the bats. Eventually they came to an enclave that offered three separate doorways, and without hesitating Draconex chose the left pathway. Even after all these years, he still remembered exactly where Ephram's chambers lay, and it wouldn't be long until he reached them.

After a few more minutes of determined walking, hearing nothing but the leathery flaps of the bats' wings and their random screeching and the *tack-tack-tack* of his steel-toed boots, Draconex made it to a wide staircase in one of the several towers. Almost as if giving up, the bats left just as suddenly as they had arrived.

Ephram knows that I won't be stopped, Draconex reasoned.

Standing at the base of the staircase, he craned his neck upward, following the staircase as it disappeared into more darkness. Malcolm dimmed the light he was emitting, now using it more as a tool to see instead of a bat repellent.

Taking a few more steps toward the center of the tower's base, Draconex looked around, letting his memory take hold. He slowly pointed his finger at the area to his left and stepped toward the wall. Its cold stone was slightly damp to the touch, but he paid it no heed. He could tell that Malcolm had followed him, for the light became more concentrated on his hand. Draconex grazed his fingertips along the surface until his nails caught a seam between two stones. Following it down, he faced the wall just as his heart began to beat faster.

"Almost there," he whispered through sharp teeth.

And then he felt it: the faint outline of a lever. A smile cracked Draconex's lips as he dug his nails farther into the wall, allowing his fingers to wrap around—just as he thought—a small lever.

He pulled.

Muffled reverberations came from inside the wall and below his feet as the center of the tower began to move. Malcolm lost his balance, but quickly recovered after jumping out of the way so a winding staircase could be revealed, leading into the bowels of Chateau Noir.

Exactly where a vampire would prefer to spend time.

Slight hubris overcame Draconex, making him feel more like his old self.

"Remember what I said, *boy*," he reminded Malcolm as he walked toward the descending flight of stairs. "La Proutagne is mine. Do *not* get in the way."

"I didn't forget," Malcolm said flatly, casting the light where the staircase began.

"Good."

Draconex started down the stairs, knowing he was mere seconds away from his final destination. Licking his cracked lips, he could practically taste the battle that would ensue—as well as the blood that would be spilt.

Draconex dispensed with his stealth, figuring that Ephram already knew how close he was from the rumbling cacophony of the secret staircase opening up. As he made his way around the last turn, he could see the faint glow of centuries-old torches framing the chamber's door.

I have you now, mused Draconex as he slowed down, descending the last remaining steps deliberately and drawing his fists up into a guard position.

SHING!

Draconex didn't feel pain, but he heard the swing of a sharp blade cut through the air and a dull *thud* on the ground in front of him. Before he could look down, he instinctively ducked as the same blade passed over his head, nearly decapitating him. Forward-rolling out of his duck and into a low fighting stance, he finally saw what was on the floor.

His left hand.

In disbelief, Draconex looked at the stump of his arm, which was just below his elbow joint where his forearm armor stopped. His heart rate spiked as he immediately wrapped his arm with his cape to slow down the hemorrhaging and cursed himself for his reckless stupidity.

He then looked at the base of the stairwell but couldn't find Malcolm anywhere. Had he been quickly defeated by Ephram, or was he hiding like the miserable rodent he was?

Draconex didn't have time to investigate the whereabouts of his apprentice, for Ephram was already on the counterattack. In the dim light, the faint hissing of the vampire shot tingles up his spine.

"You should have retreated when you had the chance."

The voice seemed to come from every angle simultaneously.

Still in shock from the loss of his hand, Draconex spun around, trying to ascertain where his enemy truly was. He was slow in channeling the night vision of a horned owl so he could better see in the dark passageway, but as luck would have it, he was able to catch the reflection of one of the torches in Ephram's sword just fast enough to successfully side-step to the left, causing the sword to miss dissecting his skull and instead strike his right shoulder armor, where the blade caught between two of its decorated dragon claws.

Sensing his good fortune, he quickly capitalized on it and spun backward, yanking the sword from Ephram's hand and dislodging it from his armor. The massive sword slid into the darkness, far away from its former wielder, sending up sparks as the sharp blade skittered on the stone floor.

But that did not seem to slow down Ephram La Proutagne. He came at Draconex more aggressively now, unsheathing a small knife from his side and covering the distance between them in a heartbeat.

Draconex backpedaled and fell to his back, bringing up his right arm in barely enough time to block a forceful knife thrust.

He felt as though in a dream, one in which he couldn't move his body as fast as he wanted. He watched helplessly as Ephram masterfully countered with a precise redirected strike into Draconex's obliques in the space between his chest and back armor.

A plume of heat erupted in his side as he felt the cold knife slide into his muscle and fracture a rib. He let out a stifled grunt as Ephram pushed the knife in deeper for good measure. The pain arrested Draconex just long enough to give his opponent the extra second to grab his sword and return to hover over the defeated Dark Watcher commander.

"This is for Jocelyn," he said as he raised the sword over his head.

Giving in to his fate, Draconex spat at Ephram but did not move.

KRAKAACK!

In the millisecond before Ephram brought the sword down, he became a dark silhouette as a fierce light exploded from behind him, followed quickly by a deafening crackle. Ephram let out a surprised wail as his body convulsed and his hands dropped the sword yet again. It landed blade-first just inches away from Draconex's head as the vampire crumpled to the ground, spasming as if he had been electrocuted.

Draconex glanced back in the direction from which the light had come and saw Malcolm running toward him. Without saying a word, the boy used terramancy to break apart the ground and push the rubble toward Ephram; the stones swept up the dazed vampire and pinned him to the side wall.

Shivering, Draconex used his good arm to push himself to his feet, then pulled the sword from the ground. He hugged his injured arm to his chest as he stepped over pieces of rubble toward Ephram, waiting for the pain to set in as the adrenaline wore off.

Ephram's face was contorted in a mask of pain and shock, but he didn't let out any cry; he was a noble warrior, after all. But that would only help him so much.

Paying no attention to Malcolm, Draconex climbed up a few larger pieces of shattered stone so he could reach the same eye level as his enemy.

"Where is she?" Draconex hissed in Ephram's ear.

Ephram winced in pain and Draconex caught a glimpse of his sharp, pronounced, right canine tooth before he closed his mouth and turned to look him in the eye. The vampire said nothing.

"She was here, I know it." Draconex brought the blade to touch Ephram's pale skin. "I can still smell her."

Finally, Ephram spoke. "You're going to have to be more specific." He tried to move his body, but the rubble was so tightly held by Malcolm's spell that it didn't allow him to budge.

"Don't get cute with me," Draconex said through gritted teeth. "I'm in no mood." He pressed harder with the sword, puncturing Ephram's throat—though only slightly.

Ephram clenched his jaw as he bounced his gaze from Draconex to Malcolm then back again. His breathing was labored, but his eyes gave no hint of the pain he had to have been feeling.

"She's aware . . . of everything," he said with effort.

Draconex's cheeks began to boil as he felt rage resurface, and he allowed it in. He let out an ear-splitting yell as he spun away from Ephram, stumbling over the uneven surface of debris.

Draconex could feel all the years melt away in vain. All the years he'd spent keeping Diaema away from Charles as he lay prisoner, weak and forgetful, in Feralot. All the years he made a life for her in his new kingdom, his new . . .

Draconex's eyes bulged as a sudden realization hit him like a stampede of angry elephants.

He had let his initial desire of having Jocelyn all to himself be eclipsed by his lust for power. And that lust had overtaken his life as he rose through the Dark Watcher ranks, finally murdering the tribe's former leader and becoming the seated heir to the Throne of Dragons. Draconex had inadvertently cast Jocelyn to the side, making her his mistress who did petty tasks for him.

Now, all his accomplishments faded away, leaving cold regret for what could have been, how he could have focused on the only person he desired.

He brought his only hand, still clenching the vampire's sword, up to his head as he doubled over, succumbing to white-hot rage and flesh-tearing regret. He couldn't tell if he was angry because Jocelyn now remembered her old life or because he had been so obsessed with gaining more and more power that he had forgotten her, leaving her to be sucked up by his ego.

Breathing heavily through clenched teeth, he slowly looked in the direction of Ephram, and with more composure, he strode back up to within inches of the vampire's face and said, "I'm going to ask you one last time . . ."

CHAPTER SIXTEEN

Victor was beginning to make out more of the surrounding forest now, which meant that dawn was fast approaching. He and Hephalon had spent the last few hours putting as much distance as possible between them and the serknid nest they had just ravaged, all the while focusing on reaching Loch Myctoph, the mythical lake in the center of the Amaranthine Forest that was the rumored home of their former schoolmate, Teska.

The egg's runny yolk that they had poured over themselves for protection had begun to dry and flake off, leaving both sorcerers stiff and smelling not particularly appealing, but it still seemed to be warding off the menacing predators lurking behind the fallen trees, overgrown bushes, and thick grass.

"We've got to be getting close," Victor mustered as he trudged through a dense cluster of mushrooms. He could feel the effects of lactic acid in his arms and legs, which had been slowly building up since their rushed escape from the serknid nest.

He glanced down at the compass he held, still pointing true East. *What I would give for this compass to also tell me how much farther we need to go,* he thought, beleaguered.

"I reckon you said that . . . over an hour . . . ago . . ." Hephalon wheezed. It sounded like his friend wasn't faring any better.

Just as he was about to offer a chance to briefly rest, Victor saw that the ground sloped downward up ahead. Setting his teeth, he put the compass back in his pocket and pushed forward.

"And I was just about to see . . . if you wanted to break . . ." Hephalon grunted behind him.

"I think we've made it, Heph." Victor looked back and flashed a fatigued smile.

He picked up his stride as a second wind hit him. The trees in this area were denser—usually a sign that a body of water was nearby.

"It has to be the loch," he said, more to himself than to Hephalon.

He could make out yellow speckles of sunlight dotting the line of trees ahead, meaning a clearing of some sort was only meters away. Fully panting now, he cleared several feet with every stride. Stray branches scratched at his face and neck, but he didn't care— his sights were locked in, and after maneuvering around a few large tree trunks, he could hear the soft lapping of water.

Victor glanced behind his shoulder to make sure Hephalon was nearby. His friend was several meters behind him, barreling down the sloped terrain, his many weapons clanging together in a chaotic orchestra of sound. Content enough, Victor turned back around and could now see glimpses of glistening water between the trunks ahead. Ducking under a rather large branch and holding on to it for support, he found himself at the shoreline of what could only be Loch Myctoph. He stood there for a few heartbeats, realizing that the only people who had seen this lake either never lived to tell outsiders about it or—hopefully in Teska's case —never left.

Victor took off the pouch holding the eggs to give his shoulders a break, then pulled out his water flask for a few large gulps as he waited for Hephalon. He surveyed the calm, dark-green waters of the lake, which must have spanned nearly a thousand acres. After quickly finishing off his water reserves, he noticed something break the lake's surface near its center. Squinting, he started to focus on the unidentified figure when he was knocked into the water.

The water was surprisingly deep this close to shore. Victor pulled himself back to the surface, finding his friend to his right and just as wet as he.

"I tripped," was all Hephalon said, trying to tread water despite the enormous weight of his weapons.

Victor didn't respond—he just glared at his clumsy friend.

"Oh, come now, we needed to wash up anyway," Hephalon said as justification, wringing his braided beard of excess water.

Victor was going to retort, but movement in his peripherals caused him to forget what he was about to say, and his senses sharpened. He felt sluggish in his thick cloak and trekking boots, but he twirled around just in time to see a large dorsal fin submerge twenty-five meters away, followed by what looked like a group of tentacles.

"Did you see that?" Victor said as he tried to track where the creature might have gone. He didn't wait for a response, lowering his head into the murky water. He couldn't make anything out aside from dancing streaks of light straight below him, beckoning him deeper into the lake. He dared to close his eyes quickly enough to touch his eyelids, using his nexus to form air bubbles around his eyes. When he opened them up again, his vision was as clear and crisp as if he were wearing swimming goggles.

Victor's timing was exceedingly lucky because he just barely caught sight of a pair of reflective eyes piercing the dark green water straight below him—followed by glints of countless sharp teeth that were headed straight for him and Hephalon. Without thinking, Victor risked a glance back at his friend. Hephalon was sucking in water, having a hard time keeping his head above the surface. Instead of making a coy remark about his friend's choice of wearing his entire weapons arsenal, Victor channeled his terramancy at the water surrounding Hephalon. His mastery over his nexus created a geyser that launched the burly metallurgist safely to shore just as massive jaws cut through the surface of the water, missing Victor by only inches but clamping onto his cloak.

He was effortlessly lifted out of the water by jaws belonging to a horrific creature that resembled a great white shark but with thick, writhing tentacles in place of a lower torso and back fin. It looked like it came straight from the depths of hell. As it breached the surface and shot into the air, an enormous, gelatinous eye focused on him while the monster opened its jaw, no doubt trying to readjust its grip and tear into the flesh of its prey, but that was enough to afford Victor the opportunity to kick off the side of its jaw, breaking free and sending him into a free fall. Rotating his hands in a circular motion, he made the lake water meters below start to foam. He straightened his body out and entered the water in a pencil dive, feeling the cold water softly envelop him. Fully submersed again, Victor discarded his cloak and boots so he could move with more ease now that he had a second chance at life.

He would not be caught off guard a second time.

A muffled *SLAM* sent reverberations through his body as the hulking sea creature dropped back into the lake. Victor, ready to defend himself, searched all around him, trying to notice where his opponent went through the floating bubbles. For a beast as large as this one, Victor was impressed at how quickly it camouflaged itself seconds after it reentered the water. His rings were already on his fingers as he began to summon a spell that would freeze the predator the instant it attacked again, but it never came. Instead, a soft rainbow glow floated closer to him, causing Victor to drop his guard and deactivate his rings.

Teska . . .

* * *

"You're lucky I got to you before Sinear had a second chance," Teska said as she handed Victor and then Hephalon each a cup of warm tea.

Victor took a sip of the herbal tea, feeling its warmth flow down his chest. All his and Hephalon's clothes were hung up by the fire, drying out. Currently, they were both draped in large towels.

"I still can't believe how you were able to tame that thing. It looked like something straight from a nightmare."

Teska shrugged. "I am an animancer after all. You just have to understand it." She took a sip of her tea. "And 'that thing' is a lusca."

Victor raised his cup, acknowledging her reasoning. He then furrowed his brow, asking, "Wait . . . I think I've heard stories about that creature during my time on Earth. A sea monster from Caribbean folklore?"

"That's the one. Half great white shark, half octopus." She shrugged again. "Or at least that's what it most closely resembles."

"Well, I just hope Sinear knows Heph and I are friends," Victor commented, making a mental note to never go for a swim in Loch Myctoph without Teska by his side.

Teska chuckled as she swiveled on her stool to pour more tea into her cup.

She hadn't changed much since she left the Guild. She was still very trim and spry, but Victor could tell that years of living in the Amaranthine Forest had aged her. What hadn't changed the least bit was her beautifully flowing, multicolored hair, which seemed to defy gravity, making it seem as though she was perpetually underwater even when she was on dry land.

"It's good to see you, Vic," Teska said, "and you, too, Sterling . . . I guess." She offered just a glance over at the metallurgist.

Victor turned to look at his old friend, hoping his gaze would remind him to play nice. Hephalon hadn't taken a single sip of his tea, but he was still holding the mug in both hands, no doubt keeping it close for warmth. Their little foray into Loch Myctoph's waters sucked the heat right out of them.

"Do you have any ale around here?" Hephalon grumbled, shooting a tired look back at Victor.

"You haven't changed a bit," Teska said, getting up and tending to the fire she had started for her visitors.

Be nice, Victor mouthed to Hephalon. If they had any chance of convincing Teska to help them find the Ctesian Crossing, both of them had to be on their best behavior, especially Hephalon.

"Er, but tea suffices . . . I suppose," Hephalon reluctantly put out, trying a sip and wincing as if he had just drunk spoiled milk.

Teska didn't turn around; she just hummed while poking and prodding the dry wood through the flames, launching hot embers into the air.

After Victor and Hephalon's raucous arrival to the lake, Teska was the one who called off Sinear and brought them down to her home, which was at the deepest part of the lake in a subterranean cavern dug out by gigantic burrowing creatures now gone extinct. Here, away from the dangers of the murky waters and the surrounding forest, they were able to drop their guards and enjoy not being on constant high alert.

"Thank you again for coming to our rescue," Victor said. "We weren't sure how long it would take to find you, but I'm sure glad you found us when you did."

Teska smiled at Victor. "To tell you the truth, you two were the last people I'd expect to see here. Especially you, Sterling."

Hephalon slightly choked on his sip of tea. Clearing his throat, he mustered, "Well, I want to inform you that we have exhausted all our options and you are our last resort."

Victor eyed Hephalon, none too pleased with his tone. Before he could speak, Teska said, "This must be pretty important."

Victor set his cup on the table. "It's a long story, but one you should definitely hear . . ."

He proceeded to fill Teska in on the last several months, from confronting his former tenderfoot, Malcolm, to taking in Jen, who had been believed to be the last living Omnimancer until her father, Charles, turned out to be alive. He also explained that the Dark Watchers ambushed Watercress Castle during the Sesquimil-lennial Jubilee, laying waste to the Guild's ranks and their own, not to mention destroying the castle itself.

As Teska stood silently listening, Victor mentioned that the last known place Jen and her friends had gone to was Camelore, ChronoCrystal in hand, and he ended with asking the favor he'd come all this way for.

Teska was stone-still, only her eyes moving from Victor to

Hephalon and back again. He could only imagine what she was thinking. She hadn't seen them in years, her relationship was rocky at best with Hephalon, and Victor was asking her to leave her safe home to find a migration pattern that was constantly changing.

The muscles around her eyes and mouth softened. "So there is hope," she breathed. She sat back down on her stool and looked at her hands for a while, her hair ebbing and flowing like a soft tide full of effulgent colors. She chuckled. "Charles is alive. And so is his child." She looked up with tears in her eyes. "That was one of the main reasons why I left the Guild, you know. Once they were presumed dead and their child missing, I felt as though the realms had become imbalanced, and there was no light to fight Orin's mad descent as he grew the Dark Watcher tribe."

Victor said nothing and knew that Hephalon would do the same.

Teska straightened and looked Victor square in the eye. "I'll lead you to the Ctesian Crossing," she said resolutely.

Victor let out a breath and relaxed his shoulders. "Teska, you have no idea how grateful we'd be."

He looked back at Hephalon, and he saw his friend wearing a look of sincere appreciation. Without saying a word, the metallurgist placed his now-empty mug on the table, stood, and walked over to Teska. He stopped right in front of her and, before she could react, he enveloped her in a great bear hug. At first Teska's arms tensed, but after a few seconds she wrapped them around Hephalon's waist.

"You big softy," Teska teased once the hug was over.

Hephalon didn't say anything, just sat back down, but his blushing cheeks said enough for him.

Victor suppressed a grin, swallowed his last sip of tea, and mentioned, pointing at their pouches by the hut's hatchway, "We thought you would be a tougher sell, so we brought some extra serknid eggs to sweeten the deal."

Teska let out a quick laugh as she got up and went to stoke the fire. "Abodiala."

"Abo-who, now?" Hephalon stumbled over the new word.

"Abodiala," Teska repeated, this time a little slower. "It's that mushroom you see growing in clusters all around the forest. It's completely safe, and if you put just one of its spores on you, it will give you as much protection as the serknid eggs, with less of a mess and stench." She turned back to look at them.

Victor massaged the bridge of his nose with his thumb and middle finger, realizing his oversight.

"Don't beat yourself up, boys," Teska said, going over to pick up the pouches. "It's not all a waste. They still make a mean omelet."

For the first time in what felt like ages, Victor shared a genuine laugh with his friends.

CHAPTER SEVENTEEN

Wh-where am I?

Jen tried to lift her eyelids, but they were heavy as sandbags. Unfamiliar voices echoed in waves as she fought her nausea. Her neck muscles stung with pain as she tried to lift her head, thinking better of it and slowly rolling her neck instead, working out the tight knots that had formed while she was unconscious.

She finally managed to open her eyes, and as they adjusted to the dimly lit room she tried to figure out where she was. She could make out that she was several feet above the ground, pitched slightly forward while uncomfortably strapped to a plank of some kind by her wrists and ankles.

What she saw when she lifted her head made her want to scream, but she could only issue a silent whisper between cracked lips. It felt like she was in a nightmare where she couldn't alert anyone for help or move to escape.

Staring directly back at her with a glowing set of sunken eyes was a gaunt, lifeless, floating head.

Her tongue didn't want to work, making it hard to swallow. Jen tried controlling her breathing first instead. As she calmed herself, she realized that the massive head in front of her was only a bust. A statue, somehow levitating high above the ground and emanating a xanthic glow from both its eye sockets and its lazily opened mouth.

Eerily, the longer Jen stared at the bust, the calmer she became—calm enough to take her gaze from the floating head and notice that her friends were in the same chamber, still unconscious but hanging in the same fashion as her. They were all equally spaced out, in a circle, each of them with a floating head in front of them.

Testing the strength of her bindings, Jen tried to break free, but she was fastened quite securely to her plank. Next, she closed her eyes and reached deep into her nexus, hoping to break her bindings with terramancy, but the material that held her captive was one she had never felt before. She didn't think it was even of this earth.

A soft rumble made her open her eyes to see the lights from the floating head turn from yellow to deep magenta. Hers was the only one to change—all of her friends' stayed the same color.

Three guards entered the room. Jen froze, now knowing that she had triggered some kind of an alarm. The guards stopped right below her and looked straight up at her. At first Jen thought about pretending to be unconscious, but she realized that it would probably be in vain—since the only bust that had changed colors was the one in front of her, her movements were most likely detected by some kind of magic—so instead she locked eyes with one of them, waiting to see what they would do next.

"Bring her down," said the one Jen stared at.

He was a tall, muscular man who, along with his other cohorts, wore an armored tunic; streaks of red light created intricate designs across their armored plates, but the guard who spoke was the only one who had a forehead band of the same color. The band came to a point in the middle of his forehead which made him look more menacing.

He must be the superior officer, Jen presumed. The other male guard tapped his gauntlet and the plank she was fastened to began to descend.

"Looks like you win, Sc'ran," said the only female guard to the other man as Jen came to a stop at eye-level. "I had my coin on the blond to arouse first." She nodded at Gavin, who was still out cold.

"Sorry to disappoint," Jen said sardonically, and was surprised to see them stiffen, the woman taking a step backward.

Looking at the taller man, the woman asked, "She can understand us?"

Before he could respond, Jen interjected. "English is my native language." She stared at them for a few seconds, confused at their reaction.

The commander didn't break his stare at her. "You're not speaking English . . ." he said slowly. "You're speaking *Atlantean*."

Jen blinked, even more confused. "I— How can that be?" she said, more to herself than anyone in particular.

The commander set his teeth. "Take her to *Roi'ta*," he said firmly.

Roi'ta?

The female guard walked up to Jen with her arms outstretched and gently pressed her fingers to Jen's temples. Immediately, her vision left her and she felt claustrophobia begin to set in.

"Hey, I can't see! Where are you taking me?"

No one answered, but she felt the plank that she was attached to move so that she was now laying prone on her back. Jen could hear the footsteps of the guards and feel a slight breeze float over her, causing her to believe that she was being transported somewhere else.

Jen started to hyperventilate, and as she felt the pull of unconsciousness, she tried everything in her power to follow a breathing technique that Victor had taught her. This thankfully helped a little, though she was still scared about what was about to come next. After another five minutes of unspeaking movement in which she persisted with her breathing exercises, she felt a thin veil of serenity drape over her. She didn't know why this feeling came to her, but she did know that if these people were hostile, they wouldn't have spared Jen and her friends.

"You have something important to show me, Tactos Kl'to?"

A new voice filtered its way into Jen's ears. She must have

been so focused on her exercises that she hadn't realized they'd arrived at the guards' intended destination.

"Yes, *mah Roi'ta*," the head guard, Kl'to, said. "She awoke before the others."

Jen was still blind, but she felt the plank raise her so that she was again upright.

"Surely you did not interrupt me to only show me that she is now awake?" This new voice, which dripped with haute pretention, was feminine and laced with judgment.

She must be in charge here.

"Yes, *mah Roi'ta*," he said quickly. "This girl . . . she speaks our tongue."

Jen counted the seconds as they slowly added up before the woman replied. "That is impossible," she said briskly. "Nobody outside of our walls has ever come across an Atlantean to learn our language."

Jen flinched as slight pressure was put on her temples once more, causing her vision to be restored. Blurs coalesced into shapes and different shades of gray bloomed into colors. She was now in a large room that reminded her of a Roman cathedral, with its central dome being made of what Jen could only guess was glass. Its style was a perfect mix of natural, organic design and immaculate, noble architecture to honor the person sitting before her.

Raised high on a dais, the older woman wore a robe that shimmered with striations of purple light. She held a staff that looked like a thin, frozen waterfall, and atop her long, braided hair rested an ornate tiara that glowed with the same purple light as her robe. Her skin was a deep ebony with subtle flecks of copper, and it looked weathered with age and perhaps the stress of wearing the crown of an ancient, clandestine civilization. Behind, flanking her on both sides, two younger men sat silently on thrones set into the gleaming, marbled wall.

Out of her peripherals, Jen saw that the guards stood in a loose triangle, from the head of which Kl'to took a step forward. They all shared the skin tone of their queen, but they looked younger—especially now, since Jen was out of the dimly lit prison.

"I would never fool you, *mah Roi'ta*," was all Kl'to said before crossing his arms and extending them out in front of him, now with his hands clasped together—probably the Atlantean version of a salute.

Jen looked at the queen again to find that she was staring daggers back at her, tapping a long fingernail on the armrest of her throne while her other hand slowly rotated her staff.

"Can you understand me, foreigner?" the queen asked.

Jen found her mouth suddenly dry, so she swallowed. "Yes, I can understand you."

The queen gasped and straightened, and Jen caught the young man on the queen's right slightly smirking, seemingly in good humor. "How can this be? Where did you find this girl?"

Kl'to spoke again: "We found her along the third ring with a small party of other humans and three creatures."

"I am P'tara, only daughter of King Qan'to the Wise, queen-warrior and sovereign ruler of the last surviving kingdom of Atlantis," the woman declared loudly and proudly, dismissing her commander's answer. "And to my sides are my twin sons, Prince Mb'alo and Sh'tam."

Both nodded in unison.

After a few seconds of silence, the queen asked, "Who are you, and what are you doing here, girl?" Her eyes were harsh and narrowed in suspicion.

"My name is Jennifer Lancaster, the last surviving omnimancer of the Sorcery Guild," Jen started. "My friends and I mean you no harm. We've come here to ask for your help."

The queen eyed her warily. "How did you find us?" Clearly Jen's identity wasn't her prime concern.

Jen took a deep breath, remaining calm. "I will show you, but you must release my friends. We mean you no harm. We are here to ask for your help," she repeated.

"Out of the question," the queen snapped. "You claim that you are an omnimancer—a sorcerer that is said to have been extinct for some time. You are very bold. Why in Atlantis should I trust someone who was caught snooping around our land uninvited?"

Jen felt her cheeks get warm and her blood pressure increase.

"Mah Roi'ta," she started, hoping to diplomatically show deference, but then she stopped.

She'd noticed that the Ring of Lancaster, still on its necklace around her neck, was suddenly glowing a soft purple. Reminded of what happened the first time it accidentally glowed, on the night of her birthday—an accidental spell shot out and struck Malcolm when he was attempting to kidnap her—Jen looked back up at the queen and continued.

"We are friends of Atlantis. We come as messengers to tell you of a great evil on the brink of falling over this world—including your kingdom."

Out of the corner of her eye, Jen saw the sky take on a violet hue and in turn cast a purple coloring over everyone in the chamber.

"We humbly ask for your help, and I will gladly tell you everything you want to know, but first, please, release my friends."

The queen's lips were taut and her eyes wide as she looked at Jen's glowing necklace, then up at the sky. The guards exchanged glances and awaited their queen's response, as did Jen. She didn't know what was happening or why the sky had turned purple, but their reactions made it difficult to ascertain if it was good or bad. She prayed for "good" as her heart thumped in her chest.

The queen inhaled deeply and brought her chin up. Her eyes narrowed as she stared down at Jen. "Release them and bring them to me this instant," she ordered her guards, but still did not break her eye contact with Jen. "But if I see the slightest move toward violence, I will have you all disposed of immediately, do I make myself clear?"

Jen nodded. "Yes, *mah Roi'ta.*"

The two other guards left, presumably to get her friends, while Kl'to remained. She knew that the only way to have a chance at obtaining the TeleCrystal was to win over the queen, and Jen was determined to try everything to appeal to her.

"I greatly appreciate you granting us counsel."

The queen said nothing, but instead nodded to her commander, and Kl'to pressed down on a part of his left chrome forearm bracer. Jen instantly felt relief as the bindings seemed to evaporate, freeing both her wrists and ankles. She dropped a few inches to the ground, silently thanking her legs for not buckling beneath her.

Before she could thank him for releasing her, there was a dull *CLANG!* and the ground below her moved and suddenly she was rising. She looked down and saw the ground that Kl'to and her stood on had now become a circular platform, slowly twisting around in a full three-hundred-sixty-degree circle until it nearly reached the level of the queen's dais.

To her right, she could now see Atlantis's expansive skyline more clearly through the dome at this elevated angle. The structures were clearly inspired by ancient Rome and Greece. One building particularly stood out to her which looked to be in the perfect center of the city. It had a similar design of melding the natural with the man-made, and its crystalline structure made it rival even the most architecturally stunning buildings across the globe. There was a flowing elegance to the crystalline exterior as it twisted toward the sky and atop its peak rested a large, perfectly spherical orb which emanated that now-familiar purple glow.

"That is our Akt'aron," the queen said, pointing to the same structure at which Jen was looking. "It is our spiritual palace, named for the crystal that came from the heavens. It is what bathes our kingdom in a protective light every night and supplies my kingdom with the power to keep secluded from the uncivilized world outside."

Jen remained looking at the Akt'aron for a few seconds more before turning her gaze upon the queen again. "But how does—" Jen started, but caught herself, just now realizing the answer to her question. "The TeleCrystal," she breathed.

"The what?" the queen asked haughtily, scrunching her nose while she waited for a response.

A rumble from below caused Jen to instinctively steady

herself, but her platform stayed stable. A few seconds later, two more platforms rose up to meet hers, and carried on them were familiar faces that sent warm joy through her heart. There was Mira, Gavin, and Rez, all free of their bindings as well, but looking uneasy.

"Guys!" She turned to give them a hug, but the two guards swiftly blocked her way.

"I have released your friends, Jennifer," the queen announced from behind her. "Now it's your turn to deliver on your promise: tell me why you are here."

Jen gave one last look at her friends from between the guards' shoulders before she turned back around, standing to her fullest height. "I have good reason to believe that the crystal that powers your hallowed Akt'aron is what we call the TeleCrystal." She waited a beat and looked at all the Atlanteans. When no one made a motion to speak, Jen continued. "It is one of the MystiCrystals that were lost during the Great Battle a little over fifteen hundred years ago."

The queen's eyes turned to slivers. "Lies," she spat. "The gods sent down a celestial crystal to shield us from the degradation of the rest of the races inhabiting this planet. They answered our prayers and allowed us to remain pure and untarnished."

Jen's lips were sticking to her teeth. She needed water. Swallowing hard again, she asked, "When did the gods gift you the Akt'aron?"

"During the rule of D'gar, my ancestor who reigned seventy generations ago," she responded, but then added quickly, "But that being when you claim this great battle ensued is nothing but coincidence."

"If I may speak freely, I have a strong sense that we are talking about the same crystal," Jen said, trying to sound respectful. "Not only was it lost during the Great Battle, but it was also a part of a set of five crystals that, once collected, will show the way to the Halostone, a lost relic that holds a very dark evil."

One of the queen's sons—Mb'alo—straightened in his throne.

Queen Pt'ara's defensive anger quickly turned into denial.

"No, I shall not hear any more of this." She looked straight at Jen. "You dare waste my time with your lies, girl? Why would you want to collect these crystals if it will lead you to a known evil?"

Jen's cheeks warmed. Taken aback, she said, "We have no choice but to find it! So we can protect it from falling into the wrong hands, hands that would release the evil it holds inside. There are dark forces also after this relic, and they know the only way to the Halostone is by gathering all five MystiCrystals, including the one that you have." Jen pointed straight at the Akt'aron in the distance. "As an omnimancer of the League of Light, I have vowed to find the Halostone first."

"You do realize that by giving you the Akt'aron crystal, my kingdom will not be protected any longer, and the outside world will know of our existence?" The queen shook her head vigorously. "That would surely cause our downfall."

"I believe that Atlantis will greatly help the rest of this world," Jen said. "The stories of your advanced medicine, your technology . . . that is something we desperately need taught to us from a leader like you."

The queen grasped the arms of her throne and leaned forward, eyes like daggers. "You presume to counsel me like you are my advisor?" She scoffed, then made a quick motion with her head, and Kl'to and the other guards seized Jen and her friends. "I have heard enough of this. You—Jennifer Lancaster—only want to use the crystal and its powers for your own gain, just like every other corrupt human."

"But—"

"Take them to the edge of our gates, Tactos," the queen said, cutting Jen off, then returned her glare to her. "Do not mistake my mercy for kindness here, young lady. I am allowing you and your party to leave unharmed. But if you ever try to enter Atlantis again, that will be the last decision you will ever make."

She made that head motion again and the guards pushed Jen and her friends onto one of the platforms, which almost immediately began to lower.

As they descended, Jen turned to her friends, but the guards touched their temples and their eyes turned a misty white. Before she could react, Kl'to touched the side of her head and her vision was lost again.

* * *

"Wait!" Jen yelled as her vision returned.

Kl'to and his guards were repairing to the gate portal that led back into the city of Atlantis. One by one they disappeared, and Jen was too far away to reach them before the portal closed and she was left standing in the arid, blistering temperature of the Sahara with the wind whipping her curls across her face. She didn't care enough to brush them aside, and they were left to dance over her eyes and cheeks.

A beak gently nuzzled its way under her right arm, and she felt warm feathers.

"Hey, Skar," Jen quietly said with chagrin. She turned and hugged the griffin. "I'm so glad you're okay." Pernissa was next to him, cawing slightly in a sympathetic way.

"Okay, what just happened?" Mira said from behind. "And how the heck could you understand them *and*"—she raised a finger in emphasis—"speak their language?" She was standing a few feet away, next to Gavin, Rez, and Dimitri.

"I'm not sure, exactly, but I don't think it ended well, considering where we are at the current moment," Rez quipped, shading his eyes with his hands.

Jen exhaled, letting it draw out as she scratched the side of Skarmor's neck. She turned to them and said, "Basically the queen of Atlantis doesn't trust us and thinks we are after her crystal to topple their secret kingdom and use it for our own personal gain."

"So that's what Atlantean sounds like," Gavin mused, walking over to check on Pernissa.

Jen rubbed her forehead. "I guess my omnimancy involuntarily kicked in and helped me understand them, just like how I could understand the Elder Synod when they were speaking in

130

their Mancy tongues right before they tested me and put me through the Chimera Course." She looked up and saw her friends stiffen, all their faces showing a look of unease, which made her spasmodically turn around.

"Jennifer Lancaster," said one of the queen's sons, extending his arms in a gesture of peace. "Please do not be alarmed. I am Mb'alo, Prince of Atlantis." He went into a deep bow before continuing. "My mother does not know I am here, but I wanted to say that I believe you." The bright sun above made his azure eyes and light-blond hair contrast with his ebony skin even more so than when she first saw him in the throne room.

Jen was so surprised that she forgot to return the gesture and just stood there, gawking.

"My mother has an antiquated view of civilization outside of our kingdom. I don't blame her, but she has never tried to really understand who it is that lives outside of our walls. Atlantis has so much to offer to the world to help make it a better place, and in turn there is much we can learn from your society."

Jen studied Mb'alo's face before responding. "Why do you believe me?"

"Your eyes," he said, smiling. "They're kind. And your heart energy." He extended his hand, which held something wrapped in what looked to be linen. "Here."

"What is it?" Jen took the offering and held it in her hands.

"You may unwrap it," Mb'alo said, gesturing to his gift. "It is one of my ceremonial daggers."

Jen unfurled the long strand of linen to see a gleaming dagger about a foot long. Its blade was slightly curved, coming to a trailing point at its tip. The hilt was a perfect mix of the same chromelike metal on Mb'alo's armor and translucent glass that swirled with pinks and purples when light hit it.

"I can't accept this," Jen said, rewrapping the dagger to return it to Mb'alo.

"No, please," he urged, placing a hand on hers. "This is me telling you that I am on your side and will work with my mother to help you on your quest."

Jen paused and nodded. "Thank you, Mb'alo."

"I hope to see you again, Omnimancer Jennifer," he said, bowing low once more before turning to disappear back into Atlantis's invisible dome.

Jen looked at her friends.

"Is everything okay?" Mira asked, walking closer.

Jen smiled slightly, looking at her new dagger. "Yes. One of the queen's sons believes us."

"*He's* a prince of Atlantis?" Gavin asked incredulously, pointing at where Mb'alo had disappeared.

"One of them." Jen hefted the dagger in her hand, feeling a new sense of determination fill her. "We seem to have an ally who will help us get the TeleCrystal, and I don't want to force ourselves back in so soon." She looked at Gavin. "You up for reading the next passage, Gav?"

He threw a roguish grin her way as he pulled the lost journal out of the shoulder bag. "With pleasure."

CHAPTER EIGHTEEN

DRIP . . . DRIP . . . DRIP . . .

Water droplets splashed on the jagged surface of the cave, echoing their lonely existence, as stalagmites silently stood sentinel for the hopeless and lost Madame Diaema.

Jocelyn.

Wife of Charles Lancaster.

Mother of Jennifer Lancaster.

After forcing herself to leave Vespre and the comforting reunion with her old mentor, Ephram LaProutagne, Diaema couldn't think of anywhere else better to hide except for in this cave. Nestled deep within a marsh a few hours south of Watercress Castle on Azumar, it had once acted as a secret meeting place for her and Charles Lancaster, back when they were paladins, young and newly in love.

As far as either of them could tell, this cave was unknown to the headmasters and their classmates, which gave them much-needed privacy, considering that Charles was the last omnimancer at the time and all eyes were constantly on him throughout his schooling.

Hanging upside-down as a bat, trying to catch some sleep, Diaema could now remember again the beautiful moments they shared in this cave, from feeling Charles's warmth as they just held each other in silence to gossiping about other paladins and tenderfeet. Tears formed as she wished those days could be shared again, and they flowed freely when she realized that she would never feel his warmth again. Those memories should just as well have been those of a different person in a different life.

With contempt, she craned her neck to look at the Shadow-Crystal, tightly wrapped in fabric and tucked in a small fissure in the cave's wall. That small crystal shard now held a completely different meaning for her. At first, she'd seen it as a tool to augment Draconex's powers so that he could channel every Mancy plane and unify his misguided acolytes. Now, it stood as a reminder of everything she had lost and would never regain.

Too emotional to sleep, she just hung there, trying to find some serenity before deciding what to do next and where to go from here. She was just starting to feel the pull of slumber when her acute bat ears picked up the distant crackling of firewood in between the cave's waterdrops.

CRACKLE—POP—CRACKK!

She unlatched from the cave's ceiling and let gravity take her, effortlessly changing into her human form and landing with the grace of a cat on the uneven ground. The cave slowly curved to the right as it opened toward the exit. Where she crouched, Diaema could barely make out the dancing firelight being thrown onto the craggy, slate walls.

Her heart raced as she cycled through what—or who—could be just outside of eyeshot. She quietly slinked her way forward, hoping to get a better vantage point. The cave straightened out, allowing Diaema to see the silhouetted form of a large, sleeping dragon.

Volcanor?!

Diaema almost lost her footing as she backpedaled around the turn. How had Draconex found her so quickly? Could he sense the pull of the ShadowCrystal? Or even worse, had he somehow wrung her whereabouts from Ephram? However it happened, there was nothing she could do about it now, which caused her to stop retreating. If Draconex was here, she needed to act, because deep down she knew full well that this would not end until either she or him fell dead.

Diaema would never agree to follow him again now that her memory had been restored.

Glancing back toward where the ShadowCrystal rested, Diaema set her teeth and targeted the sleeping dragon, using her vampiric speed to hopefully catch Volcanor and Draconex unaware. Her blinding agility allowed her to cover the distance quickly, but as she was halfway there, the dragon stirred, looking up. It roared in abject surprise and quickly covered something with one wing. Its open mouth glowed a fiery orange as it prepared to spew hot flames at her.

Now even closer to it, Diaema realized that it wasn't Volcanor, but a different dragon, still somewhat familiar, with steel-blue scales.

Diaema's surprise made her falter and clip a stalagmite, causing her to hit the rough ground and roll to the opposite side of the cave. A heartbeat passed before hot flame engulfed a rocky outcropping to her left, sending her leaping for cover behind a thick stalagmite to her right.

Panting heavily, she felt unbearable heat from all sides as the dragon belched intense fire at her natural shield. She now had to find a way out of this mess. After what seemed like an eternity, the barrage stopped, leaving her drenched with sweat. She hugged herself, trying to become the smallest target possible. She was so scared that the thought of turning back into a bat didn't even cross her mind.

She used to be one of Ephram's most elite warriors in his Vamp Legion, and now she couldn't even execute a surprise attack on a sleeping dragon. What had she become?

The stalagmite she was using for cover rumbled and chips flew all around her as the rock formation broke free from the ground and was thrown into the depths of the cave, eaten by the shadows that once protected her. Completely vulnerable, Diaema clamped her eyes shut and waited for the next fire blast to engulf her.

But it never came.

She slowly turned around to see a man—who was not Draconex—kneeling with an arm outstretched and half-protected by a wing of the blue-scaled dragon.

"Who are you and why are you attacking us?!" the man demanded, his voice familiar but distraught.

Diaema started to bawl even before she realized that she recognized the voice.

"It can't be . . ." she croaked softly between sobs.

* * *

Charles Lancaster looked at his attacker, priming his nexus to collapse the side of the cave that held her. But when she turned around, he managed to catch a glimpse of her earrings in the firelight before she cowered away and his breath caught in his chest, a cold shiver running down his spine.

There was only one person who ever wore those earrings—but she was dead.

"Who are you?!" he yelled again after regaining his voice, his bottom lip quivering. He didn't care that the yelling caused his injuries to flare up and send pain through his midsection.

As he waited for the stranger to respond, he wanted equally for her to be Jocelyn and for her not to be; because even though she would then be alive, the thought of knowing that they had spent twenty years apart would devastate him.

"Who are you?" Charles repeated, this time a little less intense.

The only response he received was quiet sobbing.

He started to stand, but Silvress snorted her disapproval.

"It's okay, Sil." Charles put a hand on his dragon's snout. "I'll be fine. Thank you for protecting me."

Silvress snorted again, but then closed her eyes and raised the wing that blocked him from leaving. He held on to Silvress's neck to stand and slowly walked toward the other person, whom he and Silvress had deemed to be no longer a threat.

"How did you get those earrings?" he asked, this time even

softer, but his senses were still on high alert. He cursed his lips for starting to quiver again, his eyes blurring with fresh tears.

The woman still had her back to him, her bleached-blond hair in sweaty strands, shoulders shaking from her heavy sobs.

Charles took one step closer, his heart pounding in his chest, silently confirming what his brain already knew.

"Jocelyn?"

After hearing that name, the woman froze, her sobs momentarily forgotten. Her head lifted and she turned to look at him.

When their eyes met, Charles knew that it was her, though she looked as though she hadn't aged a day since the explosion in Draconex's compound all those years ago. He fell to his knees and wrapped her in his arms, and they both cried tears of everything: joy, sadness, shock.

"I can't believe it's you," Jocelyn whispered, caressing Charles's face.

He let out a chuckling sob before leaning in to kiss her.

"You're so cold," he mentioned after he'd soaked in the first kiss they'd shared in twenty years. "Here, let's get you closer to the fire."

He picked her up, pushing through his injuries as he set her by Silvress. Even his dragon seemed to have a flicker of recognition toward his wife.

"Thank you," she said with a faint smile. She let out a long exhale to calm herself. "Oh, my . . . you're hurt." She gently touched his right side.

"It's nothing, my love." He picked up her hand and kissed it. Her hand felt even colder despite being inches from the fire. "How are you not shivering?"

Jocelyn grimaced and said, "A lot has happened since we were separated."

* * *

Under the moonlight, with Diaema wrapped in Charles's arms as the fire bathed them in warm light, she explained how she'd survived the explosion all those years ago. How, in order to save her, Draconex had her turned into a vampire, and in the process caused her to forget everything up until that point. She explained how she was then trained by Ephram LaProutagne to become an elite vampire warrior before Draconex convinced her to join his cause of restoring order to the ways of sorcery. Diaema started to choke up when she told Charles how memories of her old life came to her once he broke out of Feralot's prison and destroyed the dragon's dungeon. Finally, she ended by recounting how she had taken the ShadowCrystal shard and gone back to Ephram, only to fully remember after his confession that he was complicit in helping Draconex turn her.

Diaema turned on her side and studied her long-lost love's face, awaiting a reaction. All Charles did was stare unblinkingly at the fire, slowly caressing her arm.

Finally, he said, "You are Jocelyn." He tore his gaze from the fire and looked at her with steely eyes. "No matter what you were told. No matter what they made you into."

Diaema closed her eyes, feeling tears pool below her eyelids. Her throat swelled and she didn't dare try to speak. She could feel her husband's heartbeat as he breathed, so steady and strong. She placed her hand on his chest as the fire slowly turned to embers.

They stayed in silence for a while before Diaema finally spoke. "I feel like I'm *not* Jocelyn, though, even though I can remember my life before becoming Diaema. I've done things I'm not proud of."

"But the *true* you fought back," Charles countered. "The Jocelyn I know and love broke through and you're here to stay." He reached across and brushed a few strands of her long hair behind her ear.

She quivered and broke down, the tears streaming down her face anew and soaking into Charles's shirt. Diaema—the person who she'd thought she was—was beginning to evaporate: the cold, conniving mistress who loved to seduce and sow dissension among the Dark Watchers. Jocelyn—the person who she thought she may never be again—was beginning to bloom once more: the loving, considerate, kind-hearted telemancer who only cared about two things in the eleven known realms . . . her husband, Charles, and the daughter she'd had with him, Jennifer.

And of all the prayers that were recited across the realms, hers was answered that night. Jocelyn was at peace, held by her husband in their secret cave as the fire continued to burn, much like their enduring love.

CHAPTER NINETEEN

Aldred Cindergray poured himself a cup of tea to usher in the morning, wondering if today would be the day that Simone Chen would awaken.

Once a loyal sorceress and a trusted confidante, Chen had fallen far, had betrayed the entire Sorcery Guild to work alongside Lord Draconex as a Dark Watcher. Cindergray still couldn't believe that she had pulled the wool over his eyes, but it did make him realize that he was too obsessed with finding the Halostone, too focused on his fight with the Dark Watchers; in his obsession, he hadn't made the time to check in on his allies, his warriors—his *friends*.

And now, he was staring at what he had created from his lack of proper leadership.

Mother would be so disappointed in me, Cindergray admonished himself.

As he blew on the steaming tea to cool it down, he sat there and watched Chen sleep, just as he had for the past two days. He took a sip and felt the liquid slide down his throat, warming his insides. Out of all the things he had experienced in these realms, there was nothing quite as comforting as the first sip of piping hot tea in the morning.

He crossed his legs and was prepared to sit in silence as he finished his tea when Chen stirred. Cindergray silently set his cup on the table and withdrew his pocket-watch totem, ready for whatever might come.

With a wince, Chen turned toward Cindergray and opened her eyes, squinting. She seemed to remember her situation quickly, and pushed herself off of the sofa, poised to issue a spell directly at Cindergray.

But he was faster.

He held out his hand and motioned like he was turning a doorknob, and Chen froze in place, a gasp caught in her throat.

"I've been waiting for you to wake up, young lady," Cindergray said matter-of-factly. He looked at his pocket watch, which was softly glowing an icy blue, its minute and hour hands frozen from the spell he was using. He searched her eyes for any glimpse of emotion and he saw . . . fright.

"There's no need to be frightened, my dear," he said, leaving the table and kneeling on one leg so he was eye to eye with Chen. "If you answer my questions truthfully, no further harm will befall you." He popped open the glass face of his pocket watch and turned back the minute hand and Chen seemed to rewind in time, falling back into the position she'd held while sleeping, but still awake—wide awake, in fact.

"Now," the Grand Mystra started, "were there any other Dark Watcher agents inside the Guild?"

Chen didn't say anything, and the fear in her eyes turned to hatred.

"You do realize that you forsook all your training and devotion to not only your bloodline but also the entire history of what we sorcerers stand for?"

That got a reaction from Chen. "My devotion to your corrupt cause died a long time ago," she spat. "You are the blind one if you haven't seen the writing on the wall."

"And Draconex's vision is a path toward righteousness?" Cindergray asked. It hurt hearing Chen say those things about the institution he'd fought for and took over to lead, but his years of experience had brought him clarity of mind, so he suppressed any rise in emotion. "He promised you a better world, didn't he?"

"I know who you really are," Chen said with a sickening smile, evading his question.

For the first time in ages, Cindergray's heart skipped a beat. He could feel a bead of sweat forming on his brow.

How could she possibly know?

"You hide behind a mask and let your followers do your work," she continued. "They give everything for you while you sit back on a throne of lies." Chen raised her voice. "At least Lord Draconex is clear with his intentions!"

Acting on instinct, Cindergray fluttered his left index and middle finger, causing Chen to hyperventilate. Her eyes bulged and her mouth opened wide, almost like she was trying to get as much oxygen as possible.

"W-what are you doing to me?" she gasped.

He needed to know if Chen really knew. "I am Aldred Cindergray, Grand Mystra of the Sorcery Guild."

"You can say that all you w-want, but it d-doesn't make it t-true." Chen's chest heaved up and down like she was sprinting a marathon. "Ph-Phillip."

Cindergray couldn't believe it. He began to see red and, without realizing it, he clenched his hand. Chen let out a shriek so loud it jolted him out of his current manic state.

She slumped deeper into the sofa, dead.

TICK, TICK, TICK.

The sound of Cindergray's watch started up again, leaving him catatonic and letting him know that time paid no heed to his rash actions. After he took a second to regain his composure, he fumbled with his watch, popping the face open again in an effort to rewind time to just before he stopped her heart—but he caught himself before he put the spell into motion.

"Wait," he said aloud.

He slowly lowered the watch's face and put it back into the folds of his robes, then stared at Chen's body, his eyes now slivers.

The more he thought about it, the more Cindergray realized

that Chen would only complicate things if she were alive. She knew his real identity, and that could not get leaked to anyone else. And if she knew his true identity, she clearly knew what he was planning to do when the Halostone was found.

Aldred Cindergray, the Grand Mystra of the Sorcery Guild and headmaster of Watercress Castle, could not allow anyone to know that he was actually Phillip Lancaster II, son of Genevieve and Phillip I, the latter henceforth known in infamy as . . . Lord Ferox.

CHAPTER TWENTY

Loch Myctoph was not only the center of the Amaranthine Forest, but also the sole life-source for its vegetation and wildlife. It was so expansive that it even had networks of long underwater tunnels and caverns that fed directly into the bogs and marshes of its lowlands, which was exactly where Teska first led Victor and Hephalon as they began their journey to the Ctesian Crossing.

"I never want to do *that* again." Hephalon rang the water out of his braided beard. "Merlin's Beard!" he exclaimed.

Victor, just as soaked as his friend, smirked and patted Hephalon on the back. He looked behind him and saw three luscas slide back into the deeper part of the bog with the help of their massive tentacles, their shark snouts submerging below the water's surface to leave only bubbles in their wake. He couldn't believe that he and Hephalon were able to hang on during the luscas' swim to this part of the forest; they had to have reached a top speed of eighty miles per hour.

Victor pressed his hands together and a stream of air bellowed his clothes out, drying them almost instantaneously. He then proceeded to do the same for Hephalon.

"Thank you, my friend," he said as he picked up an axe that had fallen off his backplate when the blast of air first hit him.

Victor motioned toward Teska, but all she did was wave him

off. "I'm good, terramancer." Her hair was as vibrant as ever, flowing in suspended gravity; it was still a bit damp, though, which gave it more of an effervescent sheen. "We're at the northernmost edge of the forest." She motioned ahead of them. "Even though equivols have unpredictable migration patterns, they're creatures of habit when it comes to a nice place to graze. I should hopefully be able to pick up their scent."

Victor nodded and, along with Hephalon, followed Teska for a few hundred more meters until they broke the tree line and entered into a wide clearing. The sun shone down with such brilliance that Victor had to cover his eyes. He patiently waited for his sight to acclimate to the extreme change, from the dark, shadowy forest to the bright, open field he now found himself in.

Wind gently brushed the long, grassy knolls in every direction, and he could make out abandoned remains of a castle several hundred meters off. That sight reminded him of the destruction that had taken place at Watercress. He looked skyward and prayed that his fallen brethren were watching over him—him, Hephalon, and every other sorcerer who'd survived after Draconex's ambush. It seemed a lifetime ago, but it was only a few days fresh.

Victor realized he was lagging behind Teska and Hephalon, so he made a point to catch up. As he got closer to his group atop one of the hills, Teska froze briefly and glanced back at him and Hephalon before sprinting down the hill, quickly falling out of sight.

He furrowed his brow in mild confusion and quickened his strides, reaching the lip of the hill alongside Hephalon to see Teska, several hundred meters away, crouched next to a black form, trying to protect it from a serknid.

Instant shock spiked his adrenaline levels. "I thought serknids couldn't leave the cover of the forest?" Victor asked. He was in a dead sprint with Hephalon.

"Things are getting weirder with every passing day," was all Hephalon said, clearly just as confused.

They were just under one hundred meters away when the

serknid reared, showing signs of spearing Teska with its sharp, scorpion-like tail.

"Eyes open!" yelled Hephalon. He drew an axe from his back-plate and tomahawked it with such force that Victor heard the blade slicing the very air as it twirled toward its target.

SCHLUNK!

With precision, the axe struck the serknid's thorax, piercing its organic armor and lodging itself deep into its underbelly. The beast didn't seem fazed by the attack, but it was jarring enough to momentarily distract it from skewering Teska. As green fluid oozed from the fresh wound, the serknid eerily looked at Victor and Hephalon, repositioning itself to meet their charge.

"Something's off with this one," Victor said as he opened his right hand and turned it over.

Obeying his command, the patch of grass underneath their target shifted and broke from the surrounding ground, cata-pulting the serknid into the air. Its legs and tail squirmed uselessly as it slammed into the ground twenty meters away.

By the time it came to a stop, Victor and Hephalon were by Teska's side.

"Are you all right?" Victor asked as they made a barrier between the serknid and Teska.

"Yes, I'm fine." Teska was clearly focused on the wound of the other creature.

Breathing heavily, Victor waited for movement from the spider-scorpion beast, but it was still. Throwing a quick side glance at Hephalon, his friend returned the same look of caution and hesitancy.

"You reckon it's dead?"

Victor's peripherals caught movement before he could respond. He turned in time to see the serknid spasm, inverting its joints to pick itself up and glare back at him, fluid still dripping from the puncture made by Hephalon's axe. Its head wobbled slightly before it launched off the ground, showing terrifying speed as it closed the distance between them.

"Enough of this," Hephalon grunted, unsheathing his dual

swords and meeting the serknid halfway.

Despite his size, he deftly slid between its long legs and wind-milled his swords, slicing the beast clean in two.

Now bisected up to its skull, the gargantuan serknid fell to the ground, its spindly legs still moving, mindlessly clawing at the air. Hephalon, dripping in the green fluid, slowly walked toward the head and cleanly decapitated it, which caused the legs to twitch violently before becoming forever still.

Victor rushed to his friend's side to look at the fallen serknid. Hephalon took his slimy swords and wiped them on the long grass before resheathing them. Upon closer inspection of the carcass, Victor noticed bulbous tumors clumped all across the serknid's head and upper torso. He knelt to get a better look.

Almost as if Teska read his mind, she yelled, "Don't touch it! Those spores on its body came from contact with a parasitic fungus found in remote parts of the forest." She was still kneeling by the other creature.

"Did you get any of it on you, Heph?" Victor asked, looking up with concern.

His friend surveyed both arms and legs. "Not that I know of. Just its innards, which makes me realize I need another deep clean."

"Sooner rather than later," Victor commented, scrunching his nose at the smell. He got up and walked back to Teska, keeping fair distance from Hephalon. "Were you able to get to it in time?"

Teska didn't break her gaze from the wounded animal, still struggling to breathe where it lay. "I think so. Its breathing is labored, but it looks like we got here right as the attack started." She was gently stroking its head with one hand and holding the wounded side with her other.

The creature looked like a gigantic leopard, but instead of sporting rippling fur, it had hard, leathery skin much like a rhinoceros. Its tail branched off into two ends near the tip, one a lot sharper than the other. Its muzzle, like a hippopotamus's, was wide, but it had sharp canines curving from both upper and lower jaws like a saber-toothed tiger.

"I don't think I've ever seen an animal like this before," Victor mentioned.

"I have," Hephalon said, "but only once before, when I was exploring the pyrite hotbeds along the equator looking for ore to smelt."

"This guy belongs to the species relicontus," Teska added. "They are a solitary species that usually never strays from their birthplace. Guardians of the hotbeds that Sterling mentioned. I wonder why this one ventured so far away from his home . . ." She trailed off as she opened her carrying sack, rummaging through it.

"Wait," Victor said. He reached into his robes and pulled out a small bottle. "If I may." He popped the cork and let one drop of the liquid fall into the wound. "Griffin tears, courtesy of Skarmor." He smiled at Teska as she watched the wound bubble and repair itself, closing the gash and leaving only a scar behind on the animal's leathery skin.

"Thank you," Teska said gratefully.

The relicontus stirred, inhaling sharply. This caused Teska to stand, and all three of them took a cautious step backward. Its eyes fluttered open and regained focus as it propped itself up on its legs, looking at Victor. He was amazed at how large the creature was now that it stood to its fullest height, easily dwarfing him and Hephalon, who were seventy-two and eighty inches tall, respectively.

This guy has to be over seven feet tall, Victor thought as he craned his head to look the creature in its eyes.

It exhaled powerfully as it shook its head, almost like sloughing the remnants of its injury off. Victor could hear its tail thumping the ground methodically like a metronome. No one moved as it stared at each of them in turn. Victor didn't sense any aggression in the creature, and the last thing he wanted to do was spook it. Its muscular tail stopped hitting the ground and the relicontus dipped its head toward Victor as it let out a low rumble.

"He-he is thanking you for healing him," Teska breathed, shooting Victor a look of astonishment.

Victor smiled and slightly inclined his head in return, holding eye contact. "You're welcome." He didn't move as he let the relicontus sniff his head.

Seeming to approve, it moved to greet Hephalon but quickly thought better of it, and finished by Teska, sniffing her too. She put her palm on its forehead while it was still bowing and closed her eyes.

"There was a horrible sandstorm," Teska recounted. One of her special gifts was being able to communicate with all living creatures when she touched them, much like reading their minds, Victor remembered. "He was separated from his pack during a particularly deadly heat storm. He spent days searching for them, but found all dead." A tear streaked down Teska's face as she spoke, as if she was experiencing the creature's pain. "He couldn't bear staying in the place where his pack died, even if it was the only home he knew. So he left and searched for a new place to live. He quickly made it to more fertile land, but grew weak after spending days without feeding . . . and that brings us to the present and the serknid attack." She wrapped her arms around its neck, hugging it in true sympathy.

After letting go, Teska rummaged in her pack and pulled out something rectangular. "Here, eat up."

She put it in front of the creature's mouth. It sniffed it before engulfing it, chewing with such force that it snapped the bar like it was a toothpick.

Teska smiled, then looked at Victor and Hephalon. "This guy needs a ration pack more than we do now. We still have four more for our journey, which should be more than enough."

Victor nodded as he watched the relicontus finish its first meal in who knew how long. "Our timing couldn't have been better."

Teska exhaled, clearly releasing her pent-up worry and stress. "Yes." She rubbed behind the animal's ears. "I was able to pick up the scent of a few equivols too. Faint, but enough for me to glean the direction in which they're headed." She pointed off to her right. "I figure that's a good start."

"Aye," Hephalon agreed. "Let's mush on." He repositioned a

few of his weapons, patted the relicontus on the side, and waved his friends to follow. "We have a ways to go."

"After you, my dear," Victor said to Teska, letting her lead.

"Careful, terramancer," she said, flicking him a side-eye and a lopsided grin, "or I'll fall in love with ya." She gave the creature one last rub before starting toward Hephalon.

With Teska now in the lead, all three started in the direction she'd pointed.

"Now, I don't know how far ahead they are, but we'll know when we're close because the sky will be filled with colorful, dancing lights. The energy that equivols give off bends the electromagnetic field in their area."

Victor was now abreast with Teska. "Dancing lights in the sky . . . kind of like the aurora borealis on Earth?"

Teska gave him another side look and nodded appreciatively. "Exactly like the aurora borealis." She raised a finger. "In fact, every time humans see that phenomenon, they don't realize that they are near a herd of equivols."

"Merlin's Beard," Hephalon exclaimed. "Truly astounding."

Victor looked behind him and flashed an expression of similar amazement, but also caught movement farther behind his friend. "Well, it looks like we made a friend." He tapped Teska on the shoulder to turn around.

The relicontus was following them, and gently nudged Victor's shoulder once it caught up to them.

"He wants to join us," Teska said, scratching the underside of its neck.

"Well, having a ride to the Crossing will certainly help get us there faster," Victor thought aloud. "Would you ask him if he could carry us to our destination?" He looked at Hephalon, and his friend shrugged before nodding in agreement.

"He would be honored," Teska relayed to the men. "I feel such gratitude and loyalty from this relicontus," she commented, then smiled. "I think it's gonna be hard getting rid of him."

The creature knelt low enough so everyone could get on its back.

With Victor between Teska and Hephalon, he was reminded of being on Skarmor, riding with Jen. With his desire to get to Camelore stronger than ever before, he said, "Whenever you're ready, Teska."

She nodded and looked ahead, placing a hand on the relicontus's neck. It crouched slightly, then launched forward, causing Victor to grab onto its sides a little harder to stabilize himself.

As the Azumarian sun made its journey across the blue-violet sky, they continued their journey, taking them farther north and closer to the deducted location of this cycle's Ctesian Crossing.

* * *

Victor was astounded at the relicontus's speed and stamina as it carried him and his friends several hundred miles across Azumar's surface in very little time. The sun had barely moved two finger-lengths in the sky before Teska pointed out the faint glow of auroras ahead.

"We're getting close!"

Victor could tell they were getting closer to Azumar's northern pole: the air had turned more frigid, and he'd noticed snow replacing open fields of grass. He channeled more power from his nexus to stir the air molecules enough to increase the temperature around him, Teska, and Hephalon.

"Remember," Victor started, peering over his shoulder at Hephalon, "we must get to Camelore as quickly as possible, so there's only enough time to tame one equivol."

"Aye," was all Hephalon said, clearly distracted by trying to keep all his weapons attached to his armor. Victor was thankful that they had come across a creature large enough to hold all of them and fast enough to make up time they didn't have, but it certainly wasn't the smoothest ride.

He looked back ahead and noticed that Teska was leaning forward, saying something to the relicontus that was just out of earshot. He'd just discerned the smallest hint of movement ahead —probably a few hundred meters away—when he felt the creature slow down and break to the left, bringing them down into a sloped basin between two small, snow-swept knolls.

The relicontus snorted loudly, expelling clouds of warm air as it knelt—a sign for them to get off. Teska was the first to slide off the massive creature, followed by Victor, then Hephalon.

"Thank you, friend," Teska said gratefully as she scratched behind one of the relicontus's ears. "We are about a hundred meters from the herd." She swiveled her neck to look at Victor while continuing to give scratches. "Equivols are a true specimen to behold. They not only can fly, but also have hearing and eyesight to rival the best apex predators—even though they are relatively docile. Thankfully, this wind"—she swirled her free hand in the air—"is masking our scents and almost all of our noise." She peered judgmentally at Hephalon, who was counting his blades to make sure he didn't lose any during the trek.

"I'll have you know that neither of you minded my arsenal during the several times we've been attacked," Hephalon whispered, straining not to be too loud. He pointed at Victor and Teska in turn. "So what if it is a little loud?"

"For the exact purpose of not frightening the equivols!" Teska bit out. Hues of red rippled through her hair to show her irritation before reverting back to waves of all the colors. She rubbed her forehead before clearing her throat, trying to find the strength within to keep calm. "Now, these guys are fast." She pointed back in the direction of the herd of equivols. "We only have one shot to catch one by surprise."

Victor bit his lip absent-mindedly as he thought. "Is there anything that can capture their attention," he said, "like bright lights or certain noises?"

"Well, they do prefer colder climates—hence their current location—but warmer temperatures make them sluggish and more agreeable to approach."

Victor flashed a smile as he rubbed his fingers together, causing the air around the group to heat up and leave a perfect circle of green-brown grass underneath them.

"I think we can work with that."

CHAPTER TWENTY-ONE

"Okay, so . . . even though we *are* human, we have the ability to connect with every other living animal on a higher level due to us all being a part of the same domain," Mira said.

She was leaning up next to Jen, who sat with her back against the wall of the cave in which they were currently taking shelter, waiting out a horrible storm that had rolled in during their flight from western Africa.

Gavin had just read the next chapter of the lost journal, and Jen and her friends had deciphered fairly easily that the Terra-Crystal was somewhere in Antarctica. The riddle that Merlin wrote for this one was:

Very few survive in sunless days,
When the moon rules the heavens while the sun hibernates.
Out of the elements it's like a new world,
Sealed and preserved under a constant white swirl.

Wishing that the TerraCrystal had found a warmer place to hide, they all reluctantly agreed to start flying south, but in an attempt to avoid several weather systems, they'd flown farther east than they had initially wanted. Eventually a squall came out of nowhere, ushering in torrential rain, shifting gale-force winds, and an intense lightning storm, the last of which finally forced them to seek shelter in a cave nestled in Cathedral Cove, New Zealand.

"Once you unlock that connection, you are able to borrow literally any ability of any precious animal found on this amazing planet." Mira balled her fists and brought them to her chest, breathing in as she closed her eyes and smiled.

Jen stared at Mira. She had never before seen such a genuine care for Earth and its animals than she did from her friend. "You truly care about every living thing, don't you?"

Mira opened her eyes and stared at the cave's ceiling. "Yes . . . more than anything. What's crazy is that once Mystra Wingelius taught me how to elevate my state of being, I felt even more deeply in tune with life in all its forms." She looked down to meet Jen's gaze. "Even the animals I had never seen with my eyes before. I now know they are out there and as much a part of me as my own heart."

Jen nodded, astounded at how spiritual animancy truly was. Her ears slightly twitched, picking up quiet chittering and cawing from Skarmor and Pernissa, both of whom were resting deeper in the cave. Looking that way, she wondered what they were talking about.

Off to the side were Gavin and Rez, playing some type of card game, next to Dimitri, who'd remained a cat, curled up next to a small fire Jen had created when they first took shelter. Jen was glad to see Gavin and Rez having some fun, especially after how caught up Gavin had become in reading the lost journal since they'd set down in this cave. She felt a little more relaxed herself as well, making her ponder if this was Mother Nature's way of telling them to take a small break.

"All right, Mystra Mira," Jen said as she stood up, dusting her hands of sand and bits of broken shells. "Teach me your ways."

Mira blushed a little. "I never thought I'd be called a mystra, like, ever." She laughed with a quick snort. "Okay . . . you have to start by clearing your mind." She brought Jen closer to the mouth of the cave and, just before the curtain of rain hit them, let go and stared out at the beach and its lapping waves. "Let the ambient noise of rain wash away any past, present, and future thoughts. And every time you hear a thunderclap, inhale and go deeper within yourself."

Jen looked out at the gray landscape, seeing the mist-covered sea stacks and saturated sand that reflected the constant lightning strikes like soaked blacktop. Even though an intense storm raged all around them, there was an eerie calmness that came over her as she continued to look out from the cave.

Her eyelids closed unintentionally, and as the crisp thunderclaps echoed off the cave walls, Jen found herself involuntarily breathing in, and every subsequent thunderclap seemed quieter and quieter until they were nothing but a distant afterthought. She now felt as if she were floating; her eyes caught flares of light softly dancing across the undersides of her eyelids, each flash a different, dazzling color which morphed into images of different animals.

A bear! Jaguar! Now a shark!

They moved across her field of vision quickly, but Jen was able to discern almost all the animals presented. She felt the brute strength of a black rhino as it flashed white; the athletic stealth of a puma in yellow; the agile dexterity of a lemur in purple; the exhilarating speed of a sailfish in blue.

Then the images dissipated and a rush of consciousness came flooding into her body. Jen inhaled sharply, but quickly choked and coughed out water. She flicked her eyes open and found herself wading in the churning waters near the largest sea stack, partially protected from the deluge of rain.

How did I get out here?! Jen thought, rolling with the waves around the sea stack.

Mira appeared from out of the cave opening, kicking up clumps of wet sand as she sped toward the shoreline with blinding speed. "Jen!"

Jen kicked off of the rock wall and swam to the shore. The

waves certainly didn't make it easy for her to reach Mira, so she tried channeling the powerful strokes of a sea lion with her newfound animancy, but Jen found it difficult to retain that ability, whether because she was tired or new to this or what. Her muscles were aching and her lungs fighting to take in as much air as they could, and by the time she crawled up to the shore she was gasping for air.

"Holy cow!" Mira exclaimed as she grabbed Jen's arm to help her out of the shallow water. "You took off like a bat outta hell! Weren't you gonna warn me?"

Jen bent over to catch her breath. "I didn't . . . mean . . . to." She swallowed hard, then continued, "I thought I . . . was still in the cave until I . . . was splashed in the face with a wave."

Mira was covering her eyes from the slanting rain, shaking her head. "Well, it looks like the animancer in you wants out now that you awakened her. Come on, let's get you by the fire before you catch a cold."

* * *

Mira seemed more excited to share Jen's breakthrough than she did with everyone else as they sat by the fire and tore at some packed ration bars for dinner. She couldn't stop repeating how amazed she was at Jen's inherent speed and connection she had with her nexus.

Inversely, Jen was more terrified than excited. She had never before been in less control of her body. Apparently, she'd sprinted over a hundred meters in less than four seconds, jumped onto the side of the closest sea stack and then dove like a needle into the ocean, staying underwater for a few minutes before resurfacing and wading behind the protected part of the same sea stack.

At least with terramancy, Jen knew exactly what she was doing every time.

"I don't know if I could do that again if I tried." She shrugged. "I wasn't even aware of doing those things." She bit off a piece of the crumbly ration bar.

"The first time an animancer unlocks that channel, it is always the strongest. So many connections overload your synapses and some come out before you can rein it in consciously," Mira explained, rubbing Jen's back. "Over time, and with practice, that pathway slides more toward our conscious self, allowing you to turn it on and off at will." She smiled. "That will be what you need to work on next!"

"Okay," Jen said, accepting that answer and feeling a little better about herself. She needed a break from her animancy lessons; her energy was sapped. She looked at Gavin and Rez, who were intensely focused on the deck of cards before them. "So what game were you two playing over there?" she asked them.

Both looked at each other and stifled a laugh. "Egyptian Rat Race," said Rez, showing the back of his hand, all red.

"No way, I love that game!" Jen said. The last time she'd played it was in high school. "You both up for another round, or are your hands too sore?"

The boys laughed. "Oh, ho ho," Gavin said playfully. "Already talking some smack, huh?" He reached over and began to shuffle the deck of cards.

"I'm just getting started." Jen looked at Mira. "Let's wipe the floor with these boys."

Mira raised her eyebrows in surprise. "Oh, I don't know . . . I've never played that game before." She crossed her arms and rocked slightly in place.

"Oh, come on, babe, it'll be fun," Gavin egged Mira on as he dealt out the cards.

"It's super easy to learn, and I guarantee you'll love how fast-paced it is." Jen winked and playfully bumped shoulders with her.

Mira held in a smile as she looked at everyone. "All right, all right," she relented, sliding closer to Gavin as Jen helped form a rough circle with her friends.

* * *

They played until the rain let up, when Rez asked, "So how are we supposed to find the TerraCrystal in one of the largest continents on Earth?"

Jen looked at the shoulder bag that held the ChronoCrystal. "I'm not sure, but do you remember how the ChronoCrystal glowed and turned invisible when we were near the TeleCrystal?"

Everyone nodded.

"No one knew that the MystiCrystals would activate like that around each other," Gavin mentioned. "This could really help us locate the others."

"Exactly," Jen said, smiling. Now they had another trick up their sleeve. "I don't know how close the crystals need to be before they are able to communicate. I'm just thankful that we have one to help us speed up our search."

"Let's hope that the TerraCrystal isn't guarded by a group of beings who would rather wage war against us than work with us." That was Mira, sounding uncharacteristically pessimistic.

"Or eat us," Rez put in, half joking.

"Hey." Jen rested a hand on her friend's shoulder after giving Rez a look. "Even if we do find another hidden civilization and they don't allow us to have it, remember: that means it will be just as hard for Draconex to obtain it for himself . . . if he can even find them. Remember, he doesn't have the lost journal—something he can't even read—or another MystiCrystal to act as a beacon for the others."

Mira smiled tightly and nodded. "When did you become such a great leader?"

Jen felt her cheeks blush. She looked at the dying fire, watching the embers shoot out from the crackling wood. She sighed and looked back at her friend, replying, "When I decided to trust in my friends and believe that what we are doing is the right thing."

Skarmor softly cawed, lifting up his beak in what she took as agreement. Dimitri, who was curled up on the opposite side of the fire, raised his head and nodded, purring.

Jen took a quick moment to survey all her friends and

companions. Seeing the way they looked back at her with their genuine eyes was further testament that there wasn't a better group she could have chosen to go on this journey with.

But there was one person who was missing.

Her thoughts briefly flashed to her uncle Victor. Jen wished he was here with her, but she knew full well in her heart that he would have echoed her sentiments. Jen had come a long way since she learned that she was a Lancaster, mostly due to Victor's mentorship and true compassion, and she felt even more connected to him now that she knew that they were related.

She blinked away the onset of tears that were a mix of happiness and sadness. She had to believe that they would reunite—some way, somewhere. Her journey was certainly not over, and Victor would still play a large role in it, but at the current moment, Jen also realized that she would have to face more tough decisions —with or without Victor—as she and her friends edged closer to collecting all of the MystiCrystals.

"You guys ready to see what Antarctica has in store for us?"

CHAPTER TWENTY-TWO

A few hours later they caught sight of the white terrain of Antarctica. Winds howled around the griffins as they glided a few hundred feet above the frozen landscape, venturing farther inland; the swirling wind did not affect them, nor did the continent's intense cold, due to Jen's protective sphere of warm air that she had created from her nexus.

She silently thanked Victor for teaching her a few life-saving tricks. Terramancy was definitely coming in handy. She gripped the ChronoCrystal harder, noticing that it had begun to glow brighter; this could only mean that they were headed in the right direction.

Her sphere of charged, warm air dampened the sound of howling winds outside, allowing everyone to be heard. Most recently, Rez was in the middle of passionately sharing all his favorite conspiracy theories about Antarctica, from secret bases to a lost civilization to subterranean alien strongholds.

"I've even heard that explorers found preserved pyramids and sphinx here," Rez said with more than a hint of excitement as Pernissa kept up with Skarmor. "Do you think we'll find any of them?"

Sitting behind Rez, Gavin chuckled briefly. "Remember, our main priority is the TerraCrystal, Rez." He peered down at the snow-swept, icy terrain below. "I don't want to stay here any longer than we need to."

"Agreed," Jen said as she used the ChronoCrystal as a compass to the next MystiCrystal, adjusting their course slightly when she pointed the crystal more to the right. Seeing Rez's mood change at this, she added on a more positive note, "Maybe the TerraCrystal is near one of those structures?"

He gave a wan smile as he petted Dimitri, who was curled up in between him and Gavin. "I really hope so."

From the corner of her eye, Jen saw Mira shoot Gavin a look and mouth his name. At the sight of Rez, Gavin quickly added, "Once we save the world, I'll take you back here and you can lead an expedition."

Eyes lighting up, Rez said, "Really?"

"I promise." Gavin looked behind him and patted his friend's leg.

"Bang on!" Rez flashed his straight teeth in a big smile and held Dimitri up, wiggling the cat slightly before plopping him back down on Pernissa's back, his excitable mood returning.

"Hey, is the ChronoCrystal glowing a bit brighter, or is it just me?" Mira asked from behind Jen.

"I think you're right," Jen responded, looking over her shoulder at her friend, who was peering intently at the crystal. "It's starting to vibrate too."

"I'll take that as a good sign!" Gavin said from across the way.

Visibility was spotty once they reached land, and had since become even worse. It seemed to Jen almost as though they weren't gaining any ground: any direction yielded the same white haze. Essentially flying blind, both griffins slowed their pace in hopes that visibility would soon return.

"I wonder how much longer—"

Jen cut off her question when Skarmor suddenly clipped something jagged and hard, sending the ChronoCrystal spinning from her grip, quickly swallowed up by the thick snowfall. She didn't have time to react; Skarmor had been knocked off course and was now plummeting to the ground, spiraling. Her concentration broke, her nexus's protective shield stuttered and fell, allowing the elements to assault them. Bitter cold bit into her skin and made her eyes ache. Jen and Mira clung to Skarmor, and the boys, Dimitri, and Pernissa quickly disappeared as well.

"Hold on!" Jen yelled as she tightened her legs' grip on Skarmor and extended her hands to both sides. Mira grabbed Jen's midsection tightly as she flexed her diaphragm, feeling the warm power of her nexus activate again. With the buffeting winds, she couldn't properly discern in which direction they were falling, but, though briefly, the white haze broke long enough for Jen to catch something gray as it flicked across her field of vision. Using that as a reference point, she pushed outward in that direction and prayed.

Air swirled from her palms as the gray image grew larger in her vision and quickly passed beneath them—right before they crashed into rough and crunchy snow and ice. Jen's best efforts prevented a fatal landing, but it still hurt like hell. She went limp and waited for their momentum to stop. Thankfully, her years of playing rugby had taught her how to fall properly.

The shoulder on which she'd come to rest ached quite a bit, and she noticed that Mira was still holding tightly to her even though they had come to a stop and were now lying still, probably because of the intense cold. Bringing back the sphere of warmth and protection from the wind, Jen stayed lying on the ground alongside Mira as Skarmor picked himself up to stand.

Jen rolled onto her back, staring above her and trying to catch her breath. "Is everyone all right?" she finally asked, giving Skarmor then Mira a quick look.

Skarmor cawed softly, shaking his head to dispel clumps of snow from his feathers.

"Yeah . . . I guess." Mira sat up, patting herself to make sure there weren't any hidden injuries.

Jen, where are you?! a voice echoed in Jen's mind.

"Rez?" Jen asked aloud, blinking in surprise. "Are you okay?"

We're fine. We're coming to ya, Rez communicated.

Within a minute, Jen saw a white-blue light cut through the

haze—most likely Gavin's totem—and then one large silhouette of Pernissa and her other friends as they glided closer.

"That was a wicked tumble you took," was the first thing Rez said after entering Jen's protective sphere. He slid off Pernissa at the same time as Gavin and they both rushed to the girls.

"Are you both all right?" Gavin said, deactivating his totem and kneeling to touch both Jen and Mira on their legs before he caught Mira's hug. His hair was tousled every which way from the unforgiving winds, but he pulled the look off.

"What'd ya hit?" Rez said from behind Gavin.

Dimitri ran through Rez's legs and came up to Jen, cocking his head slightly, and touched a paw to her arm. Jen smiled down at Dimitri, giving him a quick brush on his head before responding to the telemancer.

"No clue, but it came out of nowhere." Holding her injured shoulder, she went over to Skarmor and checked on his talons and paws. He seemed uninjured, which was great, so Jen stood back up and rested her head on the side of his while she caught her breath. "I'm glad you're not hurt, Skar." She softly caressed his feathers. "How'd you find us so quickly?" she asked Rez.

Hephalon's son clamped onto his blazer's lapels, beaming with pride. "Well, I wouldn't've been able to focus had Gavin not used his astromancy to right us and heat our molecules up so we wouldn't freeze." He winked at his friend before continuing. "Once I opened up a channel to communicate with ya, it was like I could see ya—even though I couldn't, y'know, *see* ya." His eyes went wide in emphasis.

"That's something you'll have to teach me, Rez." Jen flashed an awe-struck smirk. "Otherwise we would have been separated for who knows how long."

His cheeks, which were already pink from the brief encounter with Antarctica's cold winds, turned a deeper hue. "Gee, thanks, Jen," he said, scratching his full head of amber-red curls.

She walked over and gave him a strong high-five with her good arm and hugged him, favoring her injured shoulder. She finished her hug with Rez and turned to see Gavin rushing closer to her.

"Jen, there's something up with your left shoulder?" the astromancer asked.

"I think it was how I landed." She stretched her shoulder but winced and realized she couldn't rotate it past forty-five degrees.

Gavin's eyes showed concern as he reached out. "I can already see it starting to swell." He gingerly ran his fingers over her bare skin.

Jen couldn't help but softly hiss from the pain that pin-pricked her shoulder. She quickly followed it with a sheepish giggle. "If this is what I walk away with from a crash landing, I'll consider myself lucky."

He chuckled softly back at her, still focused on her injury. Jen was looking straight into his eyes when she saw them turn a bright white-blue. Both of his irises disappeared and every bit of his eyes were softly glowing. She glanced down at his necklace and noticed his pendant giving off that same colored light.

Almost as if on cue, her shoulder got even warmer where he was touching as tingles spread across her skin where the rash was, and just as quickly as the sensation came, it left, and she looked down at a perfectly healed shoulder. Pressing gingerly at first, she squeezed her shoulder a little more firmly after not feeling any tender spots.

"That is . . . *wow*," was all Jen could formulate, still processing what she'd witnessed, let alone felt. She rotated her arm a few times, pleased that it felt completely normal.

Gavin smiled, satisfied with his work. He cracked his knuckles before crossing his arms, which showed his muscles' definition underneath his thin long-sleeved shirt. "Astromancy, at its purest, harnesses the building blocks of life down to the atomic level." He walked back toward Pernissa to check on her. "Astromancers are able to isolate every atom and rebuild them if needed. It also helps that all living things are just reconstituted particles of stardust."

"Yeah," Mira breathed as she stroked her braided hair. She looked to be completely enraptured by Gavin, which made Jen aware that she was also feeling that way toward him . . . the same guy. Mira's boyfriend.

Clearing her throat and quickly shaking her head in an effort to snap out of the infatuated trance Gavin seemed to hold over her, Jen quickly said, "Um . . . thank you, Gavin."

"Can't have the last omnimancer not up to her fullest out here," he volleyed back without missing a beat. "You're welcome. You'd do the same for me."

"I didn't even know any of the Mancy planes had command over healing properties," Jen said. "Heck, Victor gave me some Advil for my headache the night he rescued me." Jen touched her forehead, remembering that time fondly.

The start of my new life.

"I'm very thankful that astromancy allows me to heal others," Gavin commented, finishing his check on Pernissa, who seemed eager to go over to Skarmor. "And it's my honor that I get to teach you that power, Jen, along with some other cool ones." He smiled at her.

She smiled back, careful not to make it seem like she was flirting with her best friend's boyfriend. Jen had thought she was over Gavin after their heated discussion back on Camelore, but it seemed that had been only a brief emotional tear that had already healed. Reminding herself she valued Mira's friendship more, Jen picked at her nails—and just then realized that she was not holding the ChronoCrystal; those prior thoughts quickly evaporated as anxiety hit her.

Mira furrowed her brow. "What is it, Jen?"

"The ChronoCrystal!" Jen blurted out. "Did any of you see where it landed?" She surveyed the stormy landscape around them, wishing for the conditions to clear up. As her anxiety edged toward a panic attack, an idea came to her.

With a hint of desperation in her heart, Jen took a quick breath in and held it as she dropped deeper into her nexus until she felt more of her reserves activate. She blinked and looked down at her totem bracelet, seeing that familiar glow from her terramancy pendant. Smiling, Jen spun her hands counterclockwise, as if spinning a basketball, and her protective sphere expanded, pushing the maelstrom out an extra fifty meters.

As she looked around the barren landscape along with everyone else, Jen fought hard to prevent her anxiety from getting the better of her. Everywhere she looked yielded no clues as to where the ChronoCrystal might have landed, and with the subzero storm raging around them, who was to say that the crystal didn't get taken by the shifty winds in the complete opposite direction and was still rolling along the hard-packed surface of Jen's least favorite continent, never to be found again?

Almost as if he could feel Jen's sense of building worry, Skarmor would nudge her playfully with his head every so often as she continued to look around, allowing her to pet him. It certainly kept her from spiraling. Dimitri was on her other side and Jen was thankful she had decided to pick him up as she continued her search; his warm, soft fur and purring gave Jen a much-needed spike of serotonin. She had wandered away from her group when she heard Rez's excited tone.

"Hey, I think I found it!"

Jen turned around and closed the distance between her and Rez with several quick strides. She let Dimitri jump from her arms before she withdrew more power from her nexus and the radius expanded another twenty meters to uncover the ChronoCrystal, firmly stuck in the frozen ground, pulsating.

"Glorious!" exclaimed Rez, and he jumped into a run to get closer to their only MystiCrystal. Everyone quickly followed and he waited for Jen to come pick it up. "Well, I'd be daft," he said, pointing at the crystal. "Looks like it's givin' us a pathway to somethin'."

There was a glowing line in the snow that emanated from the ChronoCrystal like a jagged bolt of lightning laid flat across the landscape.

"Like the TerraCrystal?" Jen hazarded a guess, trying not to get too excited.

She waited for her whole party to surround her before

deciding to follow this new marker in hopes that it would further their expedition.

"Hey, I think the storm's abating!" Mira said.

Jen looked skyward and noticed the sun for the first time since that tropical storm had forced them to harbor in Cathedral Cove.

"About time," Jen said, shooting everyone a quick look before turning back to the marker. It was easier to follow with the nicer conditions, and before long, she noticed a sight that made her heart skip a beat.

"Merlin's Beard!" Rez exclaimed, echoing something similar to what Jen was feeling.

In front of them—not even a full twenty meters—was the base of a massive, snow-swept pyramid. It was so enormous that Jen had to crane her neck to see the top of this megalithic structure.

"Rez, I take back everything I said about your crazy conspiracy theories," Gavin commented, gazing up in awe.

This arctic structure reminded Jen of the great pyramids of Egypt, but it looked slightly different: the portion of the pyramid that wasn't covered in snow was as smooth as weather-worn slate; it didn't look to have been created from piled stone slabs at all.

"Is this what Skarmor flew into?" Mira asked, coming up on Jen's side.

"It's gotta be." Jen looked behind her at Skarmor, who let out a derisive snort and shook his head, clearly not pleased that the pyramid had been inconsiderate enough to be in his flight path. "Well, it looks like this is where the ChronoCrystal marker points."

The bright green light on the ground jutted its way to the closest corner of the pyramid, which was partially obstructed by wind-swept snow. By the time Jen and her friends had reached the corner, she was overcome with a very familiar feeling. Without knowing why, she reached out and placed a hand on the cold, smooth base, and she immediately understood why it was so familiar.

"I don't think the TerraCrystal is here," she said, removing her hand from the pyramid.

"Wait—what?" Mira asked. "Then what could the Chrono-Crystal be sensing?"

"This pyramid is made out of pure carbon," Jen breathed, remembering back to the test she'd taken when she was in front of Cindergray and the rest of the Elder Synod back at Watercress Castle. "Just like the wall that Mystra Étoilier created in the Chimera Course."

"Mystra Étoilier is an astromancer," Gavin said, catching on. "Are we near the—"

"The AstroCrystal," Jen finished, smiling at him. "I think so."

"Psych!" Rez said from behind. "But then, why did the lost journal say this is where to find the TerraCrystal?"

"Merlin heavily implied this is where the TerraCrystal *might* be," Gavin put in. "His journal entries were based on his research and deduction. He never actually *found* the other crystals—other-wise, we wouldn't be searching for them now."

"Where could the TerraCrystal be, then?" Rez responded.

Jen took in a deep breath and placed her hand back on the pyramid, not caring that it was uncomfortably cold. The atoms were aligned in such rigid columns, and as her nexus channeled her consciousness farther into the structure, she made a startling revelation.

"This pyramid is actually much bigger than I thought. I can feel it miles below the surface."

Jen's eyes were closed as she focused on finding the exact dimensions of the pyramid. She felt Gavin come up next to her and make contact with the fused carbon wall as well. This was the first time she'd felt someone else's nexus as it passed through and worked with hers. It was very comforting.

"She's right," he agreed. "This thing is even more massive than it lets on. I also feel some spots that are less dense."

"Kind of like . . ." Jen trailed off, trying to think of the word.

"Passageways," she and Gavin said simultaneously.

Jen opened her eyes and smiled when she locked eyes with him.

* * *

With Gavin's help, Jen discovered that there were four weaker spots along the base, almost like doors, all in the midpoints of each of the pyramid's sides. After Jen retrieved the ChronoCrystal and stuffed it in her shoulder bag next to the dagger M'balo gave her, she focused on the midpoint closest to them and carefully created an opening with the help of Gavin.

It wasn't long before they were inside the pyramid, standing in an antechamber of sorts, out of the wind and freezing temperatures. Dropping the spell that protected them from Antarctica's climate, Jen felt a surprising rush of warm, humid air.

"Whoa."

Everyone else seemed to feel it too.

"Well, this is much welcomed," Mira chuckled, fanning herself.

Jen smiled, quickly doing a once-over of the antechamber: the floor, ceiling, and walls had square indentations and protrusions that stuck out, but only for a few centimeters, which helped reflect any light that was still coming from the outside. The shimmering obsidian of the carbon left Jen with a feeling that they were on an alien world.

"Okay," she said, breaking the silence and regaining focus. "So it seems like all of these passageways converge in the center, then branch downward in some sort of shaft."

Even though they were making headway, she couldn't help but start to feel the slight constrictive pull of claustrophobia as it continued to get darker. She made sure that Skarmor and Pernissa, who were just able to fit inside the passageway, were doing okay before continuing on.

"I sense that too," Gavin said, then pursed his lips, shaking his head. "I think that's where this warm air is coming from, but that's as much as I can gather. The shaft seems to stop a few hundred meters down . . . then I go blind."

"That's because it connects to another subdermal layer in the Earth's crust," Jen explained, letting her nexus take her mind deeper into this undiscovered part of the Earth. "I can feel rock, wood, even soil, all effortlessly merged with the pyramid's carbon."

Now that they were a substantial distance away from where they'd entered and natural light no longer helped them, Jen conjured a few balls of flame while Gavin turned his totem orb into a makeshift lantern, allowing them to go farther inside. The temperature remained the same, but she could tell the humidity was rising. Looking back and seeing their opening a mere pinprick in the distance, Jen turned back around and met the shaft's opening a few steps later. She ran the flame along its perimeter; it looked to be the size of a professional hockey rink. Jen cautiously peered over the drop-off and noticed a dot of light shining from far below. It was so far down, it looked like a pinprick.

She pulled back and faced her friends. "I think I can see the end of the shaft."

Gavin, Mira, and Rez all threw a glance over the edge and came back with expressions just as confused as her own.

Rez was the first of her friends to speak: "It defies all logic, but if you're sayin' that there's another layer of Earth down there, that leads me to one conclusion."

After a few seconds of silence, Jen slowly said, "Which is . . . ?"

Leave it to Rez to always be the showman.

"A lost civilization!" he said, letting his voice echo through the tunnel.

"Well, he did bring up pyramids on our way down, and look at what we're standing in," Gavin tried to reason.

Jen rubbed her forehead. She'd hoped she wouldn't need to convince yet another race of people to let her take something they'd had for centuries.

"Well, we've come this far. If there are people down there,

we'll do our best to plead our case, just like we did with the Atlanteans." She shrugged, smiling tightly. Putting her hand out in front of her, palm down, she said, "Who's with me?"

One by one, each of her friends placed their hands on top of hers, making Jen feel even more confident. Even Skarmor and Pernissa cawed and smacked the rough ground with their lion tails, and Dimitri softly purred at her feet.

"I wouldn't be able to do this without any of you, you know that?" Jen said, tears suddenly threatening to spill over her bottom eyelids.

"We're here for you, girl," Mira said, her voice just as emotional as Jen's.

Gavin gave Jen a thumbs-up with his other hand, and Rez bowed his head slightly and tipped an imaginary hat.

She steadied herself and tried her best to keep from breaking down. How could she have ever ended up so lucky? The odds were surely stacked against her in finding a group of sorcerers who were just as purehearted and dedicated to the cause as she was. To say that the last month had been challenging would be a tremendous understatement; it had been filled with tragedy, yes, but also with hope. And Jen was holding on to that hope as steadfastly as she could.

"Three?" Jen said, choking back a sob.

"Two," Gavin followed.

"One," they all said in unison, right before they threw their hands up into the air.

Setting her teeth and using that internal momentum to propel her onward, Jen walked toward Skarmor. "Mira, you're with me. Gav and Rez, you got Pernissa."

"Aye, aye," Rez said as he hopped on to the female griffin, Gavin right behind him.

Skarmor lifted Jen and Mira up once they were settled on his back. His powerful legs and talons balanced perfectly on the ground, remaining slightly bent as he prepared to leap over the edge of the shaft at Jen's command.

Jen paused to feel the warm breeze run through her wavy hair, letting her eyes close to help her focus on finding the strength to meet any challenge she and her friends would face as they emerged from the shaft.

A soft cooing noise caused her eyes to flutter open, and Jen noticed that Pernissa had walked over to Skarmor. She looked scared, and Skarmor seemed to be consoling her by rubbing his head on her neck and chittering softly in her ear. Jen hazarded a glance behind her and saw that their tails were intertwined. Her heart nearly burst when she saw that, and she petted her griffin's neck as he finished calming Pernissa.

"Just head toward the light, okay, Skar?" Jen leaned back and looked at the boys on Pernissa. "Follow Skarmor's line as tightly as possible, okay?"

"Copy that," Gavin said.

"It's time. *Allez!*"

Without hesitation Skarmor leapt into the air and, just as Jen extinguished her balls of flame, completing the arc of his jump, nosedived straight for the center of the shaft.

The light from below was bright enough to cast reflections and shadows along the coarse walls of the shaft. Instinctively, Jen clenched her legs tighter around Skarmor's body as they picked up speed, quickly reaching terminal velocity. She could feel Mira get a firmer hold on her as well. She reached down and found her friend's hand and gave it a quick squeeze before regaining her grip around Skarmor's neck. Trusting that Pernissa had followed Skarmor's lead, Jen locked her gaze on the light source below, which still looked like a distant star in the night sky. The rush of wind hitting her face caused her eyes to water. Since the end of the shaft was so far away, it looked as though they weren't moving, but Jen knew they were clipping along at a speed that borderlined on terrifying. Not letting any other thoughts invade her mind, Jen didn't deviate from the goal of getting to the bottom of the shaft and whatever awaited them below. She blinked away an endless amount of tears and eventually held her eyes shut for a few seconds at a time in an effort to keep them from drying out. After resting her eyes for a third time, she noticed that the dot of light was expanding, first slowly, then speeding up at an alarming rate until she saw something even brighter in the dead center of the hole.

"Skarmor!" was all Jen got out before the griffin splayed his mighty wings out wide, halting their velocity to such an extent that she felt her stomach drop. He instinctively rolled to one side, narrowly missing the glowing point of a massive stalagmite that was positioned exactly in the center of the shaft's opening.

She didn't have long to breathe a sigh of relief. Almost instantly after Skarmor brought her and Mira out of harm's way, he began to struggle staying aloft. He screeched in surprise, beating his wings almost futilely as gravity pushed them toward the ground, which was about one hundred meters below.

Some invisible pressure was making it hard for her to stay upright, and Jen knew that Skarmor could only fight it for so long. "Hold on!" she said loud enough for both Mira and Skarmor to hear. By that time, they were losing altitude by the second, the ground an inevitable obstacle they wouldn't be able to avoid. With all her might, Jen reached into her nexus and felt the familiar grip of terramancy latch onto her. Straightening her arms toward the ground, she opened her palms—

And *pushed*.

Two focused tunnels of air blasted the approaching ground, rippling the dense dirt outward like solid waves. Jen didn't feel their speed slow much, so she did all she could do: she pushed harder. Her arms felt like they were going to hyperextend and snap. She winced and clenched her teeth together, feeling her molars dig deeper into her skull. With only a few meters separating them from the ground, Jen gave one last, desperate push and felt a jolt as they met the ground forcefully.

Jen barely managed to jump off Skarmor so she wouldn't crush him on impact, and so did Mira, who'd had the same idea. Like magnets, they stuck to the ground, with Mira on her belly and Jen on her back, her shoulder bag slipping from her shoulder during the rough landing.

With wide eyes and no way to warn them, Jen saw the small

form of Pernissa corkscrew away from the deadly, glowing tip of the stalagmite just as they had seconds before.

Jen felt something akin to *déjà vu* as she watched Pernissa and her riders fight against the gravitational pressure. She tried to point her hands toward them to help soften their descent, but she felt chained to the ground, the gravitational pressure too great to overcome. Her anxiety was through the roof, but Pernissa regained control somehow and swooped down, landing easily and without exertion.

What . . . ?

Jen's head fell back to the ground, her muscles aching from tilting her head as she watched her friends get off Pernissa. Gavin's eyes and pendant were glowing that icy blue again. Just inside her peripherals, she saw Gavin lead Rez and Pernissa away until they were out of sight. With effort, she turned her head to the right to see Gavin releasing Mira and Skarmor from their invisible prisons. He brought them to a small grassy knoll twenty meters away, where Rez and Pernissa waited, the strong gravitation effects seeming to not reach there.

Even though Jen couldn't move, the pressure wasn't causing her pain. She watched, amazed, as Gavin marched toward her, a lopsided smirk pulling at his lips before it vanished and he slowed down, pointing behind her. With effort, Jen turned her head all the way to the left to notice her shoulder bag bulging upward. The gravity kept the bag from floating up, but something inside was seemingly being drawn upward—perhaps to the glowing peak at the mouth of the shaft.

"Okay, what's happening over there?" Gavin said as he reached Jen's side.

Jen was still looking at the bag. "I don't know." She turned back to look at him, awaiting his help.

Gavin didn't reach for her. Instead, he knelt and rested his forearms on a bent knee. "I can't explain it, but there's an astromancy spell here. Now's as good a time as any to start teaching you some astromancy."

Jen all but scoffed. "You can't be serious."

"Very," he replied, bringing back that roguish grin. "First, you have to stop fighting the pressure and instead use it to reach a depth in our nexus that you've never gone to before. Your center."

Blinking away her disapproval, Jen said nothing and closed her eyes. She counted out four long breaths and relaxed her muscles, which she hadn't realized were tensed to the max.

"What am I looking for, exactly?" she asked.

"You'll know when you find it. You'll be in perfect stasis when you reach your nexus's center, and you won't feel like you're in freefall any longer."

Gavin's voice started to become muffled as Jen let the outside gravitational pressure suck her into her nexus. As she rocketed downward, she felt the familiar sensations of terramancy and animancy pass her by, almost too quickly to register as things became darker and denser.

Her mind marveled at the expansiveness of her nexus, not knowing where it truly began or ended, almost like a whole universe. She was lost in herself, but she felt a calmness envelop her when she stopped falling. Floating now, she noticed a pinprick of light ahead. Not knowing how close she was to it, Jen reached out and was surprised to touch it with the tip of her finger. The light exploded, engulfing her in warmth and energy, reflecting outward in every direction. Her aura tingled with dazzling light as she felt her awareness and connection heighten, expanding further, beyond her physical body. What she could best describe as nebulae and galaxies rushed past and around her, making Jen feel like a passing comet.

She caught the familiar pull of that initial ball of light, so she reached out for it and held it in her hands. The tighter she gripped it, the faster the swirling galaxies rushed past her until they became streams of light. Jen's heart began to race, but she dared not let go of the glowing ball, feeling the onset of vertigo. She clutched the ball with both hands now, and that's when she opened her eyes. Her vision was mottled with spots of light, so she vigorously tried to blink her sight into focus.

Gasping for air, she propped herself up on her elbows, panting. "What just happened?"

Gavin hadn't moved from the last time she saw him. He clapped slowly. "Looks like you've activated your astromancy!"

Jen looked at him, her mouth slack with disbelief. She glanced at her bracelet and saw it floating around her wrist. She slowly stood, no longer feeling the gravitational pressure though still a little weird, like she was walking on the bottom of a pool, fully submerged.

"I don't even know how I'm doing this."

Gavin stood to his full height. "Don't overthink it. Just focus on maintaining that grip."

Jen nodded, clenching and unclenching her fists as she turned to look down at her bag, which was still bulging out at the center. Slowly, she approached it and released the latches.

The ChronoCrystal, glowing a similar hue to the light above, slipped out of the leather-worn folds and floated up to the tip of the enormous stalagmite before Jen could grab it. It finally came to a stop, levitating about one meter away from the light source. A crooked finger of lightning shot out from the light source and struck the ChronoCrystal, dimming the light enough to reveal a startling revelation.

"I think that thing we almost hit is a MystiCrystal." She pointed up at it, and Gavin followed her line of sight.

"I think you're right. Definitely not the TerraCrystal though, considering the spell it's casting," he said, bringing his hand up to act as a visor from the still-bright light above. "We should update the others. Come on."

Jen picked up her bag and followed him to the others.

She surmised that this new crystal was the AstroCrystal as it slowly rotated in sync with the ChronoCrystal. She was amazed that she and her friends were quite possibly the first sorcerers to lay eyes on another MystiCrystal in fifteen hundred years since the Great Battle.

Her reflexes kicked in when the tip of her boot hit an uneven surface, forcing her to look down, her arms shooting out to brace her fall. Thankfully, she kept her balance and only stumbled, windmilling her arms a few times before her feet planted firmly on the ground again. Her grip on astromancy slipped and she collapsed to the ground, feeling the immense gravitational pressure returning. She clamped her eyes shut, trying to regain her grip on her new powers before she started to panic. Thankfully she did not have to search far to reel in her focus and tap into astromancy, but Jen could feel that her grip on that plane wasn't as strong as the first time she tried. She opened her eyes slowly and exhaled in relief.

Gavin was a few steps away, coming back toward her. "Everything okay, Jen?" He extended a hand to help her up.

"Yeah, but I feel like my grip is starting to weaken."

Gavin helped her up and said, "Astromancy is like working out a muscle. The more you practice with it, the stronger it gets." He cocked an eyebrow. "We're almost there."

Jen let Gavin slip a strong arm under her shoulders and help her to the edge of the gravitational barrier. She let her head naturally fall on the edge of his chest, nestling between his bicep and his pectoral muscles. She felt comfortable, but quickly pulled her head away as she realized how it looked. She fought to keep her cheeks from reddening even more by focusing on anything other than Gavin's strength and solid frame, which led her to take in this new world they had dropped into. Ever since coming out of the shaft, her sole focus had been on survival, and now that things seemed to be more under control, she took a few seconds to get her bearings.

For a place where the sun never reached, its foliage and vegetation were surprisingly verdant and thick. Towering trees rivaling Californian redwoods lined the clearing they were in. No doubt the AstroCrystal discouraged any proper tree growth within a fifty-meter radius. The only light source seemed to be from this place's MystiCrystal, which was still shedding a good amount of light even though it was glowing at a fraction of what it had been before connecting with the ChronoCrystal. With its light, Jen could make out the perimeter of the carbon pyramid, flushed almost imperceptibly with the underside of the Earth's crust.

Stepping up on the grassy knoll, Jen could feel the release of the AstroCrystal's power; it felt like the lifting of a humid fog. As Mira came up to hug her, Jen let go of her astromancy, falling into her friend's embrace. After exchanging a few words with her and Rez and making sure no one was hurt, Jen convinced her friends to let her check out the situation with the two MystiCrystals.

"Come on, Skar, that's it," she said as the griffin took her skyward.

Making sure they stayed out of the AstroCrystal's powerful effects, Skarmor arced his way over the invisible gravitational dome, closer to the side that had the ChronoCrystal. Jen swallowed a gasp as her higher altitude brought a new perspective to this subterranean world.

Just like the ocean, the dense canopy of trees seemed to bend with the curvature of the Earth in every direction. Maybe when everything was over and she had more free time, Jen thought, she would come back and study this fascinating new world.

Maybe—

But that thought quickly evaporated when Skarmor slowed into a holding pattern about half a meter away from the Chrono-Crystal, which floated in tandem with the AstroCrystal. Up close, the AstroCrystal was even more breathtaking. Its deep, rich, purple body glistened with thousands of small silver specs, like the infinite blanket of the cosmos. Those same silver specs winked in and out as the crystal slowly rotated, giving off a palpable energy.

With her nexus fully open to the power of astromancy, Jen couldn't help but feel a kinship toward the AstroCrystal. She patted Skarmor on the neck, letting him know that it was okay to take her closer. She reached for the ChronoCrystal and held on to it for a few seconds before gingerly tugging. It gave way after a few loose sparks shot off its surface and were absorbed by the AstroCrystal as it regained its initial, brighter glow. Hefting the seafoam-green crystal in her hands, she smiled and put it in her shoulder bag. It lightly clinked against the Atlantean dagger, reminding Jen of the work that still needed to be done to get the TeleCrystal.

Jen was now also half a meter away from the AstroCrystal, and she looked straight at it, not needing to shield her eyes for some reason. A faint buzzing emanated from the crystal that lulled her into a trance and before she knew it, her hand was already grasping the AstroCrystal.

Then the world shook.

* * *

"Jen, stop!" Gavin screamed at the top of his lungs, waving his arms frantically in hopes of catching her attention, but she was too high up to notice.

Dimitri, now back in his leshy form, watched as Jen slowly reached for the AstroCrystal. How her eyes were not blinded by its light, Dimitri did not know. Out of the corner of his eye, he saw Gavin leap onto Pernissa, taking off toward her as fast as the griffin's wings could carry him.

"What's Jen doing?" Mira asked in disbelief.

"I thought we agreed to keep the AstroCrystal where it's at until Jen got back from scouting it out." Rez was just as confused.

Both kept their eyes trained on Jen and what her next move would be.

Dimitri stepped up behind them and hoped Gavin could get to her before she did anything rash. Pernissa was getting closer with every flap of her wings, but Dimitri's ears picked up something from behind that made him turn around. A faint rumble, starting deep within the forest. Before long he could hear the violent shaking of its trees as an earthquake rolled from the tree line to where he stood with Mira and Rez.

Intense vibrations coursed up his trunklike legs and into his head, completely destroying his balance. Immediately he bored into the ground with his strong toes and grabbed the two young sorcerers in a protective embrace. Pieces of the pyramid's underside cracked and chipped away, sending massive carbonite shards careening down all around them. Dimitri wished they were closer to the edge of the forest so they could make a mad dash to relative safety, but before he could act, the shaking subsided just as quickly as it had come, leaving him hunched over Mira and Rez and waiting for the earthquake to return for a second round.

He slowly stood to his full height, sparing a quick glance around him as he reluctantly released the humans. Sharp tiles of obsidian carbon jutted out from the ground all around them, one piece not more than a meter away. The leaves atop his head rustled as a shudder ran through his body, releasing his tension with relief. He looked up and could see both griffins coming in for a landing, first Pernissa then Skarmor.

"Gavin!" Mira shouted, running over to her boyfriend.

Rez stayed put, seemingly lost in thought as he stared at the same carbonite shard that Dimitri had seen, its sharp side impaling deep into the ground. Dimitri made a move toward the group, but was pulled to look back in the direction of the forest. His eyes became slits, unsure of what he felt, but there was definitely something out there that had been awakened by the earthquake.

And it was calling to him.

* * *

Jen was stricken. What had she been *thinking*? She could have killed herself and all her friends. She looked at the clearing, now littered with pieces of the crustlike ceiling. Still on Skarmor, she put a palm on her forehead, unsure what had come over her. If it wasn't for Gavin bringing her out of that trancelike state . . . She didn't want to continue the thought. She slowly brushed Skarmor's feathers, hoping her hands would stop shaking.

She was still lost in thought when Mira came up.

"Jen, are you okay?" She rested her hands on Skarmor's side, looking up with those large eyes now full of concern.

All Jen could say was, "Physically, yeah." She bit her lip,

fighting back tears. Their journey had almost come to a screeching halt a few minutes before—all by her hand.

"Well, we're okay, too, thankfully." Mira shot a look back at where she had stood. Rez hadn't moved, but Dimitri was already halfway to the edge of the clearing.

Jen caught sight of his receding form, too, and slid off Skarmor. "I'm sorry. I was reckless. The AstroCrystal did something to me . . ."

Mira hugged her unexpectedly, taking a little bit of wind out of her.

"I—" she continued, "I didn't know what I was doing until I had already touched it."

"Hey, we made it through." Mira pulled away. "Now we know we can't just take the AstroCrystal from its spot up there."

"But there's got to be a way." That was Gavin, a few paces behind Mira. He was just as pensive as everyone else seemed to be. In no way was this challenge going to stop them, but they had to be smart about their next steps.

Rez scratched his head. "We could try replacing it with something of similar weight? Like in those old adventure films?" He brought his hands in front of him, one palm facing up and the other down, then rotated both wrists so his palms switched directions. "But it never seemed to help, actually. The place would always come crashing down." He scratched his head, trying to find another idea.

Dimitri had now stopped at the tree line, seemingly to stare at something through the dense rows of trees. He looked so small next to the dense canopy beyond. The vegetation was lush and full, making Jen grimace. In no way did she want to destroy this untouched, purely balanced ecosystem . . . this, this Shangri-La. But Gavin was right: there had to be a way.

Jen made her way over to where Dimitri stood, her friends following. The leshy didn't stir; he remained looking longingly out into the unexplored forest.

"Hey," Jen said. She put a hand on his rough arm. "Why're you over here?"

Dimitri didn't turn to look down at her. "There's something out there. Something familiar, Sky Jewel. The earthquake stirred it awake." A soft breeze rustled his leafy hair, accentuating the yellow leaves that Jen had decided were a birthmark.

"Is it hostile?" she asked, feeling a lump start to form in her throat.

"*Nyet*," he said, making Jen instantly relieved. "But it didn't like the AstroCrystal getting taken. Can't you feel it?"

Jen thought for a moment, hands resting on her hips. She glanced back at her friends, who seemed to be trying to make sense of this new development, too, before she closed her eyes and let her nexus take over. She concentrated, scrunching her face as she opened her astromancy plane, assuming that was what she needed to search for. She cocked her head in mild surprise when her terramancy plane seemed to be beckoning to her.

Of course! Terramancy. That's why Dimitri can feel it too!

Jen's epiphany came with a small squeal of excitement. Eyes flicking open, she felt her heart beat faster as her adrenaline spiked. Were they this lucky?

Mira was instantly by her side. "What is it, Jen?"

Jen exhaled, then almost laughed. "There's another Mysti-Crystal here."

CHAPTER TWENTY-THREE

Jen stepped up to the shore of a large oval lake, gazing out over its serene waters, which tricked her eyes into thinking its surface was made of glass.

Once Dimitri had echoed her initial feeling that the Terra-Crystal was somewhere deep in this underground forest and was the reason for the earthquake, they both had led the rest of the group along the winding river that passed through the clearing, and soon they had been wrapped up in the dense foliage and vegetation of this untouched land. Treating her nexus like a compass, Jen had walked with a purposeful gait alongside Dimitri, not stopping to look at or get worried about the curious sets of eyes that followed her every step, protected by the forest's shadows.

Her nexus had led her to this lake, beckoning her to explore deep in its waters. Now, she knelt and let her fingers make figure-eights on the placid surface while using it as an access point to stretch her reach deeper into the lake. The resulting ripples silently traveled toward the center and edges of the lake, giving it a different sense of awe. Jen wondered when the last time any waves had lapped across these still waters.

The lakewater felt charged with a certain energy that paired well with her terramancy plane, which became more concentrated as she extended her senses deeper into the depths—almost like she was getting pulled to the deepest part in the center. Jen asked Mira to accompany her into the lake to explore further, because she didn't want to go alone and be the cause of another earthquake . . . or something worse.

The water was soothingly warm as she waded farther away from shore. The drop-off was gradual, but shortly thereafter she was forced to tread water to keep her head above the surface. Her knee and ankle joints thanked her for this brief reprieve, especially after experiencing that intense gravitational pressure from the AstroCrystal earlier.

"Come on, slowpoke!" Mira egged Jen on as she swam effortlessly to the center of the lake. "Okay, now close your eyes." She grabbed Jen's hands and held them tightly.

Jen obeyed and let her nexus take control.

The familiar portal to animancy opened in front of her and as Jen stepped through, she felt Mira's presence. Jen followed Mira into a swirling neon cloud. As Jen entered the cloud, she found it to be filled with outlines of animals passing by so fast she could barely distinguish them all, but she stayed on Mira's heels and jumped out of an opening that almost instantly gave her the abilities of one of the *Oncorhynchus*, the world's fastest freshwater fish: the rainbow trout.

Jen opened her eyes, finding herself a few meters below the surface of the water with Mira. She could see her friend as clearly as if she were still above the water's surface. Jen breathed in and out effortlessly as gills alongside both sides of her throat opened and closed, letting water rush through them and extracting the oxygen.

"Let's go!"

Jen could hear Mira crystal clear. Awestruck, she followed her friend deeper into the ever-darkening depths of this secret lake. Immediately reminded of how her first foray into animancy had gone, Jen forced herself not to overthink her control as she glided through the water.

Light fought to keep up with them as they swam deeper, but

as they left its grip a distant glow blinked into sight farther down. Not sparing a second, Jen caught up to Mira and was at her side by the time they made it to the bottom, where they saw dense rock and sediment formations, reminding Jen of the freshwater reefs found in Lake Erie. What was nestled in a section of the reef caught her full attention, though . . .

What could only be the TerraCrystal.

The rock reef had grown around it and even accepted it as part of its ecosystem. Tiny veins of the crystal's power pulsated out into the lakebed, creating a certain calming harmony.

Jen let her body sink closer to the TerraCrystal, but before she could reach out, Mira's hand gently grabbed her shoulder. Jen looked back and her friend slowly shook her head. Nodding, Jen turned back toward the lakebed and placed a hand just next to the TerraCrystal. Its energy stretched miles below the lakebed and to either side, revealing its deep-seeded connection with the ecosystem of this hidden world. Jen also sensed a strong symbiotic bond between it and the AstroCrystal. The perfect harmony that resulted was so pure that she was overcome with a meditative peace she had never experienced before. It took every ounce of her willpower to pull away and report back to the others.

Forgetting that she could speak with the help of animancy, Jen turned back toward Mira and pointed toward the surface. They spanned the distance in mere seconds, breaking the water's surface.

"That was amazing!" Jen let out an incredulous chuckle, but just as soon as it had left, a different feeling overcame her. One that made her realize how difficult it would be to add the Terra-Crystal to their collection.

They swam to the shore where the rest of their party waited and Jen filled them in on what she and Mira had found.

"So you think there's no way to extract the TerraCrystal?" That was Gavin, wiping droplets of water off his forehead after Jen used her terramancy to dry off both her and Mira with blasts of air.

"Without doing untold damage to this place? No." Jen sighed.

"It seems like it's more responsible for this ecosystem than the AstroCrystal, which now I understand is more a fulcrum for the TerraCrystal than anything, a sort of backup generator in case more power is needed."

Silence pervaded the group, the only noise a soft humming from the AstroCrystal as it floated above, vigilant over its domain.

"It's impossible to take these MystiCrystals with us," Jen finished.

"*Nyet*, not impossible." Dimitri spoke for the first time since they'd left the clearing. "There is a way, Sky Jewel."

Jen furrowed her brow and looked at the leshy. He seemed very calm and resigned. He walked over and put a large hand on her shoulder, and Jen was confused when she felt warm tears pool on her lower eyelids.

"It's time I fulfilled my promise to Merlin."

CHAPTER TWENTY-FOUR

Daybreak came too quickly for the reunited couple, and Charles was already yearning to be back in the cave holding Jocelyn. He was in the forest below the cave in which they spent their first night together in twenty years.

Still in a surreal sense of disbelief as he dropped his last handful of berries into his makeshift basket, Charles prayed that this wasn't some elaborate dream. He looked up at the mouth of the cave where Jocelyn still slept next to his dragon, Silvress. Popping a berry in his mouth, he smiled and let a happy tear streak down his cheek and fall into his basket. Now he just had to find Jen and their family would be whole again.

He took a deep breath—and froze.

Brimstone.

The basket slipped from his hands and the berries seemed to tumble out in slow motion as he craned his neck skyward. To his everlasting horror, a massive wyvern dragon with two cloaked riders swooped down, its sickening gaze locked in on the cave.

"How did Orin find us?" he whispered.

Directing his thoughts to his wife, he sent a warning to her. Forgetting about the berries, he bounded up the natural rocky steps with the leg power of a kangaroo.

He was a few seconds late, which proved to be lucky, because even though Volcanor had already landed at the mouth of the cave, its body was too large to enter. Charles changed his course away from the center of the cave as he channeled terramancy, causing the lip of the cave to crumble and wash away the dragon and the two Dark Watchers in a current of fragmented rock and loose soil.

He didn't bother to look at the stunned faces of Draconex and Malcolm as they were caught up in the forceful rockslide. Volcanor belched out a bone-shuddering roar as his venous wings were pinned between rolling boulders and slabs of cracked rock. Charles mustered all his strength to continue pushing them as far away as possible as he reached the cave, careful not to fall into the fresh opening he had just created.

"Joss," he breathed as he rushed to her side.

Silvress had a wing around her, protecting his wife. He could see the faint glow of a fireball ready to shoot out of the dragon's mouth the second their intruders might come closer. Charles expected Draconex and Malcolm to be back, and soon; all he wanted was to slow them down.

He wrapped Jocelyn in a tight embrace. "Are you okay?"

Jocelyn was shaking. All she said was, "How did he find us so quickly?" She closed her eyes and burrowed her head into Charles's shoulder. A laugh made Charles look over his shoulder, forgetting how that made his injured side feel.

Instead of Draconex, what Charles initially thought was a ball came arcing toward them. It hit the rough cave floor with a hollow *THUD*, not bothering to bounce. It rolled a few more meters before settling at his and Jocelyn's feet. Jocelyn let out a shriek as Charles realized that it wasn't a ball at all.

It was a decapitated head.

Motion in his peripherals made Charles look back at the cave's mouth in time to see the form of Orin—Draconex—step into the cave. Malcolm was right behind him, his silent right hand.

"Of *course* you're alive, Charles!" Draconex spat. "Why wouldn't you be?"

Charles didn't respond. He hugged Jocelyn tighter.

"Ephram sends his regards," Draconex said, his tone changed to smug satisfaction. "And his head."

His throaty laugh returned as Charles looked back down at the crystal-blue eyes of the head at his feet, more resembling lifeless marbles than the windows to a soul. He caught the gleam of a long, sharp canine tooth of the vampire Jocelyn had recently told him about.

He felt Jocelyn start to move, sensed her desire to get to something that was deeper in the cave, but he held tight to her, shaking his head. Instead he got his feet under him and helped his wife stand. Silvress was growling; he could feel the heat coming from her open maw. Charles used telemancy to touch his dragon's mind and give her patience, telling her to wait.

"You have something that belongs to me, Di."

Draconex had stopped a few meters away from them, clearly favoring his right arm, which he hugged to his chest. It didn't have any armor on it and looked . . . weak?

"Where's my ShadowCrystal?!"

* * *

Victor hadn't realized just how much he missed being airborne until the equivol soared through the stratosphere. They were making good time, just recently exiting the nearest portal to Earth. The majestic beast that was called a unicorn by humans was much larger and heavier than Skarmor, allowing for a smoother flight, but Victor realized with chagrin that the truth was he preferred being buffeted by the occasional shifty air currents as he rode on his trusty griffin.

Granted, Victor was in no place to complain. It had been rather easy to tame the equivol once he'd warmed up the atmosphere around the herd. Even though they had been lulled into a faint stupor with the rise in temperature, all but one of the equivols had trotted away from Victor and his friends. Teska's innate power to communicate with animals had greatly helped them win over that sole equivol, but he could tell that this one was different from the rest. It was strong and curious. And shortly after Teska had said her goodbyes and rode off on her relicontus, Victor and Hephalon had taken to the skies.

He was surprised he wasn't in rougher shape with how quickly they were flying after their dive with Teska and her luscas. He knew the rule of waiting twenty-four hours between those two activities, but they couldn't risk letting any more time pass. He didn't even know if Jen was still on Camelore, but he had to check. Victor wasn't convinced that Hephalon wasn't affected either, because even though his old friend said that he was fine, whenever Victor would look behind his shoulder at Hephalon, his pale and clammy face said otherwise.

"We're almost to Camelore, Heph. Hang tight."

Victor patted the thick neck of the equivol as it cut through a cloud, feeling its dense humidity as water vapor settled on his bare skin. As they broke out of that cloud and curved around another, Victor was met with the glorious sight of the League of Light's floating fortress, Camelore, the Arbor Sacré glowing with that comforting array of colors in its center.

"Hey!" He reached behind and tapped Hephalon on the leg. He felt the metallurgist stir as Victor pointed toward their destination. "We're finally here—"

Vic . . . Victor!

Vertigo hit the terramancer. That voice. That familiar tone. One that he hadn't felt in decades, hadn't ever expected to feel again, yet here it was.

His sister . . . but how?

He didn't realize he was swaying until Hephalon steadied him with his large hands.

"Whoa, Vic. I got ya."

Victor heard the concern in Hephalon's voice. Even the equivol must have felt something, because it slowed to a stop, flapping its wings as it hung in the air.

Camelore was only a few seconds away, but he knew where he needed to be. "You're not going to believe this, Heph, but we need to go back to Azumar," Victor said. He shook his head, trying to get the vertigo to release its nauseating grip. It seemed to be working.

Hephalon exhaled behind him, not relenting his sturdy grip. "Is Jen there?"

"No. Jocelyn."

"Your *sister*, Jocelyn?" Hephalon said, completely surprised.

"I—I know it sounds impossible, but I think she just reached out to me." Victor glanced back at Hephalon and locked eyes with him. "She's in danger and needs our help."

Hephalon's focus shifted from Victor to Camelore and back. Victor knew what he was thinking. The place they had been fighting to get to for the past two days was finally within sight, but now it felt as unreachable as the sun. Hephalon nodded once, pursing his lips and patting Victor on the shoulder.

"Well? What are we waiting for?"

Victor smiled and faced forward again.

"Hya!"

He turned the equivol around and, without sparing a parting glance at Camelore, directed it to the nearest Azumarian portal.

* * *

Draconex saw red. His façade of uncaring cracked apart the longer he looked at who was in the cave. Not only was Charles alive—*How did he survive my killing spell at Watercress?*—but he was with Diaema!

Between Silvress's hot breaths of white fire, Draconex was throwing everything he had at his life-long rival and former mistress, not caring about his form or proper counterattack strategy. Eventually they would tire, and then he would claim victory. Diaema was as good as dead now; all he desired was his piece of the ShadowCrystal.

The injuries from his duel with Ephram cut his stamina in half. Not only was his reaction time a shadow of its former self, but the power of his spells was also diminished. He would have eviscerated them if he was at full health. Draconex's right forearm and hand had been cut clean off, yes, but after he killed the vampire commander, he had channeled the abilities of a salamander to start the regenerative process. His right arm was useless, the nerves still not fully connected, so all his spells were forced to come from his nondominant hand. There were times when he even used well-timed kicks to give his left hand a break.

Malcolm was off to his left, getting in a few of his own strikes in between his master's attacks. The boy seemed determined and focused. His terramancy launched a broken piece of stone from the landslide and caught Silvress in the shoulder. The steel-blue dragon staggered backward as Draconex and Malcolm dove into the cave with purpose.

Draconex inhaled and felt quills grow out of his back and through his serrated armor. Using the force of a porcupine, he whipped around and launched the quills with deadly accuracy at Charles.

SHING-TING! SHING! SHING!

The quills, blocked by Charles's forearms, which were glistening tetrachromatic colors only found in clear-cut diamonds, scattered on the ground.

Draconex bit the insides of his cheeks in frustration and rushed toward Diaema, dodging flying shards of cave and fireballs with the quickness and grace of a ring-tailed lemur. If he could get his hands on Jocelyn, then Charles would have no choice but to agree to hand over the ShadowCrystal—he knew he would.

Draconex was a mere two strides away from the cowering Diaema when he slammed into an unforgiving stalagmite a few meters deeper into the cave, knocking the wind out of him. His neck twitched as he felt a splintered rib puncture his lung. His legs trembled a bit, but he set his feet for another charge until he felt a familiar pull from behind. The ringing in his ears could not hide the intoxicating whispers that emanated from the part of the cave where no light reached.

Come get ussssss . . .

You need ussssss . . .

"The . . . ShadowCrystal," he strained to say, falling on all fours and forgetting about his battle with Charles—which, if he had taken the time to turn around, he would have noticed that what had knocked him down was not a terramancy spell from the omnimancer, but the hooves of an equivol ridden by none other than Victor Huxley. Draconex no longer cared about this confrontation. He'd only needed Diaema so he could wring the ShadowCrystal's location out of her, and now that he had a read on it, she could go to hell. He would track her down later and end her miserable life; he made himself that promise.

We will give you back your power!

There it was! Stuck in a large crack in the cave's wall, a small cloth sack half covering it. The whispers were getting louder, overlapping each other. Draconex curled his cracked lips into a sneer, his eyes full and wide. He used his good hand to reach out for it as his ears picked up a set of flapping wings receding in the distance. His prey was gone . . . for now. Let them live in fear for another day. He would come back stronger and more ruthless than ever before. They hadn't tasted his full power. They—

The tips of his fingers were inches away from the Shadow-Crystal when he froze, his breath caught in his throat. Then the pain set in.

* * *

Malcolm kept his hand outstretched for several seconds after the impact. Part of him couldn't believe he'd actually acted upon his urge; the other part marveled at his accuracy. There, from across the way, knelt the pathetic shell of his master, Lord Draconex, trapped by a reinforced quartz spear that Malcolm had crystallized from melting down and quickly cooling loose rocks found around him.

Malcolm had planned to sneak up on Charles's left side and attack him while Draconex grabbed Diaema, when he hesitated, seeing Victor ride in on an equivol and collide with Draconex. They were clearly outnumbered, and so he hid in the shadows and watched as Draconex crumpled to the ground and then seemed to focus on something deeper in the cave. It took Malcolm only a few seconds to deduce that the only thing capable of diverting Draconex's attention from Madame Diaema and Charles Lancaster was the ShadowCrystal.

His master looked in rough shape, falling to his knees and crawling with a bad shuffle toward his new target. With a slight twinge of disappointment, Malcolm saw Victor lead everyone out of the cave before he turned back toward Draconex. Without a single breath of hesitation, he formed that quartz spear that was now deeply embedded in the cave wall . . . but not before cleanly impaling his master's neck.

As he stepped closer, Malcolm could see Draconex straining to touch the ShadowCrystal, two agonizing inches from his finger-tips. Keeping his distance, Malcolm knelt down a meter in front of his master. Suddenly, Draconex's hand, moving with lightning speed, reached for Malcolm's throat. The long fingernails barely grazed the young man's Adam's apple.

Malcolm did not so much as flinch, but still Draconex laughed. It was a wet one, sporadically gurgling blood which cascaded down his ashen chin.

"I've been . . . wondering . . . when you would strike . . ."

Malcolm could tell that his spear had struck Draconex's vocal cords, his voice a mere serrated whisper. His hand finally dropped to his side as Draconex began to realize his plight.

Malcolm swallowed, biting his tongue so he wouldn't be able to retort. If there was one thing that agonized the dark lord most, it was a lack of reply after he addressed someone beneath him. Malcolm broke his glare from Draconex and slowly looked toward the ShadowCrystal embedded in the cave wall. Draconex spoke again, but he did not turn back.

"I lost sight," he conceded. "I made . . . that crystal my entire being." He coughed up more blood, painting fine droplets across the nape of Malcolm's neck and shoulder. "Don't make my mistake, boy—"

Malcolm turned and slid forward on his knees, plunging his dagger into Draconex's heart.

"I never told you this, but I *hate* when you call me that."

He twisted the blade deeper, feeling the give as the sharp point popped Draconex's spleen and chipped a vertebra.

Draconex inhaled sharply, his eyes strained, imperceptibly shaking with shock and pain as he grabbed Malcolm's shoulder. He let go and slowly traced the scar on Malcolm's face, from the tip at the forehead, across his eye, and down his cheek, before his hand fell limp to the side again, swaying like the body of an anaconda that had just been skewered and died.

Malcolm pulled the dagger out of his late master and wiped the blade on the corpse's ruffled cloak before resheathing it. He stared at the soulless eyes one final time before he turned and slid the ShadowCrystal out of its cloth sack.

The cold, jagged edges of the ShadowCrystal cut into his skin like a samurai's blade, but he didn't loosen his grip. He absorbed the sharp sensation as he inhaled deeply, reminding himself that this crystal shard was also once held by Lord Ferox all those centuries ago. His eyes fluttered closed as his ears pricked with whispers that blew into his mind like the fleeting wisps of an extinguished candle. They silenced themselves after a few seconds, almost as if they knew Malcolm would speak.

He said, "Tell me what to do now."

CHAPTER TWENTY-FIVE

Everyone was set. Jen and Mira were at the shore of the lake with Skarmor; Gavin by the AstroCrystal atop Pernissa; and Rez and Dimitri in the clearing, counting down. Rez was using telemancy to connect everyone's minds, since timing was everything. They had one shot to do this, and no one was particularly happy about it. But it was the only way.

Jen could hear Rez echoing through her mind.

Ten . . . nine . . .

She knelt at the shore next to Mira, looking down into the water. She gripped the dagger Prince M'balo had given her after she was escorted from Atlantis. She envisioned his face, how genuine and hopeful it had been. She wanted to feel hopeful at the current moment, but her emotions were churning like a stormy sea. She let a single tear roll down her cheek and fall into the lake, causing her reflection to waver like a desert mirage.

Eight . . . seven . . .

When Jen heard Dimitri's plan, she'd become numb. There was no way she'd let him sacrifice himself just so she could have a chance at getting both the AstroCrystal and TerraCrystal without destroying this beautiful subterranean world. But then he had explained that, as a leshy, he was born from the mystical forces of Earth—the ones that were, in turn, born from the Terra-

Crystal. That was why he was so drawn to the TerraCrystal when it awakened. And that was why he knew what he must do.

Six . . . five . . .

Jen still couldn't accept his decision to willingly give his energy back to the earth in the hopes of filling the void that would be created when the TerraCrystal was taken. And his physical form would compensate to replace the AstroCrystal's role. He hadn't explained exactly what that would look like, but Jen could see how confident Dimitri was.

Four . . . three . . .

Jen had cried even harder when Dimitri told her what an honor it was to serve her, and after her protest of his plan, he wrapped her in a big hug. Jen would never forget that hug. Dimitri had saved her life at Watercress when the Dark Watchers attacked, and he had never left her side since.

"I will always be with you, Sky Jewel," he had told her after the hug.

Now, as much as she was dreading the next few moments, she knew she had to commit; otherwise, Dimitri's sacrifice would be in vain.

Two . . .

Jen exhaled, mentally visualizing her next move. She wished she had already learned chronomancy so she could slow down time.

One . . .

She looked at Mira and they both nodded. Jen slipped into her nexus.

GO!

By the time Jen dove into the water, she already felt the exhilarating speed of the sailfish course through her body. In mere seconds, she'd reached the freshwater reef where the TerraCrystal was. She gingerly dug around the perimeter of the TerraCrystal with the tip of her dagger until she felt confident enough that she could get a good grip on it. She then felt Gavin reach for the AstroCrystal through Rez's mind-meld, and as he wrapped his fingers around his crystal, Jen did the same with the pulsing TerraCrystal.

She knew Rez would sense when they both were ready for his signal.

And . . . PULL!

Jen used all her strength to pry the TerraCrystal out from its resting place, and thankfully there was only mild resistance, probably comparable to what Gavin was feeling several hundred meters up. The light green pulse that the reef was exhibiting had stopped, its color slowly fading.

Mira tugged on her arm, keeping her focused. Together they sped through the hazy water to the surface. Several orbs of white light caught Jen's eye, entering the water and spiraling down toward them. Both girls diverted their path to let the light speed past and sink deeper. Aware enough to not let up her speed, Jen flutter-kicked furiously while she looked down, her eyes following the white orbs deeper and watching them drop into the space where the TerraCrystal used to be.

Dimitri, Jen thought, knowing that those orbs were his life energy. With water all around her, no one would have known that Jennifer Lancaster was crying.

Catapulting out of the water with the velocity of a mackerel shark, Jen landed spryly next to Skarmor, TerraCrystal in hand, and quickly got on. Mira was milliseconds behind her, and Skarmor was airborne moments later, setting his sights on picking up Rez in the clearing. A surprising gust rose up and buffeted Skarmor as the familiar rumble of another earthquake rustled the leaves of the dense forest below.

In the distance, something was growing in the clearing. It quickly dwarfed the jagged outcropping on which the Astro-Crystal had once rested. As they flew closer, Jen realized that the growing mass was Dimitri—well, his body. His eyes were closed, his arms extended above him. The underside of the pyramid's base looked to be lowering, almost as if the earthquake had shaken it loose from its housing and it was sinking into the

Earth's mantle. Thankfully, Dimitri's enormous hands rose higher and caught it securely.

Skarmor now descended into the clearing, and Jen could see Rez in a shoulder-length stance, deep in thought, his index fingers touching his temples. Gracefully, Skarmor landed in front of the young telemancer, causing Rez to look up from the ground.

No words were spoken since everyone knew what was happening from their collective mind-meld. He jumped on Skarmor's back behind Mira and handed Jen her shoulder bag.

"Thanks!" Jen decided to say aloud.

She looked up and saw Gavin keeping Pernissa at fifty meters above ground level. She then looked across at Dimitri's peaceful face and ran her eyes down his body until she saw that his feet had rooted securely into the ground. Skarmor turned to the side, preparing to launch in the air again, when Jen saw veins of color spring up from the ground and travel up Dimitri's legs. As Skarmor took off, Jen pointed with incredulity.

"Are you guys seeing this?" Jen was immediately reminded of the brilliant-colored veins of the Arbor Sacré on Camelore.

"Yeah," was all Mira said, sounding stunned.

The place they'd called Shangri-La quickly became illuminated by Dimitri's glowing body, more than replacing the light source from the AstroCrystal.

As they met up with Gavin, Jen could see him also marveling at what was happened below them, but he didn't acknowledge it. Instead, he said, "We gotta get outta here!"

Jen nodded, then looked around after she glimpsed the Astro-Crystal in his hand. The opening in the pyramid they had entered from was now fully blocked by one of Dimitri's large palms.

Great.

She looked left and right, trying to see where this place would lead them if they just picked one direction.

"Here, put this with the other MystiCrystals!" Gavin said, startling Jen. Pernissa and Skarmor were nearly touching as Gavin extended his hand.

With her heart pounding like a jackhammer, Jen took the

AstroCrystal, but it slipped from her hands. She tensed up, shooting her one open hand out and catching it at the same time as Gavin. For an instant, they both held the MystiCrystal, their hands touching. She looked in his eyes and smiled. She was going to say "Thank you," but before she could, Mira screamed.

She looked up along with Gavin and saw that another carbonite shard had chipped away from the pyramid's underside, this one much bigger than any of the previous shards. It appeared larger and larger as it dropped, threatening to slam into them at lethal speed.

Jen didn't let go of Gavin's hand. She squeezed him just as she squeezed the TerraCrystal in her other hand. She knew that they wouldn't be able to clear the shard's edges no matter which way they flew. She closed her eyes and yelled, not willing to accept death after all that they had gone through—all that they had sacrificed.

But she went deeper. Her consciousness was transported to her nexus. She was careening around the limitless space, activating all the Mancy planes she had been taught—and others she didn't know she could tap into yet. It was all too fast for her to even comprehend, but in an instant, everything became muted, and then a cacophony of a million sounds erupted outward.

CHAPTER TWENTY-SIX

Victor couldn't remember flying back to Camelore; it was almost as if he'd blacked out. As if he wasn't already maxed out from everything he'd gone through over the past forty-eight hours, the news that not only his sister was still alive but also Charles gave him every reason to faint. But he stayed strong through the intense rescue at the cave on Azumar and the arrival on Camelore.

Jen and Skarmor were not there when he landed on the floating fortress. Victor surmised that they had most likely started their search for the other MystiCrystals with the help of Jen's friends. So then, did that mean she was the prophesied Light Bringer? Victor couldn't think of anyone else who it might be. He grimaced, knowing that she was doing the right thing, but with him not being by her side, Victor had no clue of Jen's current condition or if she was seeing success in her efforts. It was like half of his heart was lost.

Silvress let out a small roar that brought Victor out of his thoughts. With Charles and Jocelyn atop her, the steel-blue dragon landed a few meters behind Victor's equivol. Victor was the first off his ride, helping Hephalon down. Back on Azumar, the metallurgist had arguably had the harder job of distracting Volcanor, Draconex's dragon, during the rescue. He'd survived with a few burns and scrapes, but had been absolutely down-trodden when Volcanor swallowed his throwing axes.

"I pray the beast gets indigestion," Hephalon grunted once both his feet were on solid ground.

Victor patted his friend on the back. "You can always smith more axes, Heph."

Hephalon grumbled in response.

Victor squeezed Hephalon's shoulder once more, then walked back to the equivol, which had neighed, and held its large face in his hands, placing his forehead between its eyes.

"Thank you," he whispered.

He pulled back and was met by an unblinking stare that made his eyes well up with tears. Just then the realization hit Victor that he was tremendously lucky to have found a creature not only willing to help him reach his goal of getting to Camelore, but also brave enough to fly headlong into an unknown battle against a dragon and dark sorcerers so Victor could rescue people it had never met before. In that moment, he knew he had developed a strong bond with this equivol.

"So what are you gonna call 'er?" Hephalon asked. He stepped closer so he could run his hand along the equivol's silky mane.

Smiling, Victor said without hesitation, "Kuirhan."

"Well, very nice to meet you, Kuirhan." Hephalon patted the equivol on its side.

Victor's smile faded when he saw Charles holding Jocelyn like his life depended on it and struggling to get off Silvress, who had collapsed seconds after landing on the flowing grass of Camelore. There were slashes of dried blood and missing scales all over Silvress's svelte body, her wings showing equal wear and tear from the confined battle in the cave with Draconex and Malcolm.

Victor hastened over and put a hand on the dragon's snout, still warm from the fire it had breathed while protecting her master. He could see her stomach rise and fall, a great sign that she was still hanging on. Victor's eyes then gravitated toward his sister. Jocelyn looked ashen and her hair was a frigid bleached-blond. Tears blurred Victor's vision as he walked over to them, limbs slightly trembling.

"Is she all right?" Victor breathed, not daring to break his gaze from his sister out of fear that she might disappear and reveal that it was just a fever dream. He brought his hand up to touch her face but stopped inches away, unable to go through with it.

Charles smiled grimly. "Yes. I'm afraid her nerves got the best of her. But she does need to rest. She's been through more than you or I could ever imagine."

Knowing that he would soon learn about what Charles meant, he didn't push the issue. What question he felt entitled to press was: "How are *you* alive, though? That spell from Draconex during his ambush of Watercress Castle was one of the most wicked killing spells I've ever seen."

Charles cradled Jocelyn closer to his chest. At first Victor thought he was grinning, but then he saw that the other man was actually biting his lip. "To be honest, I couldn't tell you. One minute, I thought I was too weak from spending those twenty years in prison. The next, I was letting my nexus completely take over . . ." He looked up. ". . . and did what I thought was right. Next thing I knew, I woke up on Silvress's back as the suns were rising. She took me to that cave that you found us in."

Victor had always been amazed by the man standing before him. Even if you took away the fact that Charles Lancaster was an omnimancer and an extremely skilled sorcerer, the man's unreachable character, unerring focus, and blinding altruism made Victor look up to him with such admiration. Victor knew he could never reach his brother-in-law's level in this regard, but he was surely glad he was on his side.

"Here, I'll take her," Victor said. "Tend to your dragon." He motioned to take Jocelyn, which elicited hesitation from Charles.

Finally, he relented and gave her up, then knelt next to Silvress as he gingerly touched her armored body.

"I'll put Jocelyn up in your daughter's hut. She'll be safe there," Victor said.

The omnimancer abruptly looked at Victor, eyes going wide. "Jennifer's here?"

"Not at the moment." He sighed, looking up at the clear azure sky. "I think she's using the lost journal of Merlin to search for the remaining MystiCrystals."

Charles squinted with uncertainty. He rested his hands on his bent knees, saying, "But how? Is Jen the Light Bringer?"

"She has to be, otherwise I think they'd still be here." Victor noticed Charles's expression cloud over at this. "Don't worry, my friend. We'll find her. We won't stop until we do, or until she finds us."

Victor returned the nod that Charles gave him, then started toward the huts.

* * *

Charles watched Victor recede into the distance as he put his hands back on Silvress, already missing being there for the love of his life, but he knew they would soon be reunited once he finished tending to his dragon. With the help of astromancy, his vision altered so that he was able to scan Silvress's anatomy like an X-ray machine. Charles bit his upper lip as he came across a few injuries that were graver than others, but Silvress would live; she just needed time to heal. He reached over and rubbed her strong head and neck as her steady breathing continued.

She was a fighter.

This place was as good as any to keep her, so Charles let her stay resting on the grassy knoll next to the griffin stables. He stood and reminded himself to take a deep breath. Between Silvress, his wife, and Jen, he wanted nothing more than to solve all the problems in which they found themselves, but he had to remind himself that rash actions would only lead to more, sometimes bigger, problems. Like more heads growing from the stump of a hydra's neck.

He took another long breath in, forcing himself to look away from Silvress and at his lush surroundings, drinking in the sights of Camelore. Not much had changed since he last stood upon this floating island, except now there were more huts in the living area. To his left was the captivating Arbor Sacré in the distance, shimmering with the full colors of a rainbow in the bright afternoon sun. He hadn't seen this place in such a long time—not since everything had been ripped from him. He vowed to never let that happen again.

Hephalon walked up to him and extended his hand. "Charles," he said with sympathetic but warm eyes.

Curling his lips into a smile, Charles broke out of his reverie and clasped his hands with Hephalon. "Hey, Heph." He sighed, reminding himself that the past was the past and could not be changed. Not even a chronomancer had enough power to travel years into the past. "Sorry about your axes."

Hephalon snorted. "That sacrifice was deemed more than necessary. I can't fathom the luck the gods must have bestowed upon you to survive that spell, and now to find out that Jocelyn lives?" He pulled away, hovering his open palms over his head in a *mind-blowing* gesture. "We are surely blessed to have you both still among us."

Charles put a hand on Hephalon's shoulder and said, "I've seen better days, that's for sure." His tone turned more serious. "But thank you for rescuing us. Truly. I don't know how we would've escaped if you hadn't been the one distracting Volcanor."

The burly terramancer put his thumbs in his belt holes, clearly pleased with the acknowledgment. "Wyvern dragons, I've learned, are a lot like felines. They like shiny objects and, well . . ." He slowly turned around, letting Charles see the weapons—the ones that hadn't been swallowed—adorning his body. "I'm the shiniest object they'll ever see."

Charles began a slow-clap for his friend when he heard something akin to a static electricity discharge—but loud. He could feel it traveling through his bones. Instinctively, he used terramancy to quickly construct a protective shelter over Silvress before turning his head toward the genesis of the sound. He was able to catch the tail-end of a flashing light go out near Camelore's lake, along with what seemed to be a yell.

"What in the—" Charles started, rushing toward the flash, Hephalon close on his heels.

Adrenaline made Charles suddenly fleet of foot, almost gliding over the flowing grassland. He wanted to make sure that if it was hostile, it wasn't getting anywhere near Jocelyn. An extra boost of speed came when his nexus gave him the acceleration of a Savannah cheetah. He was nearly flying now, his feet spending more time in the air than touching the ground.

As he cleared the hill, Charles saw a downed dogwood tree in the distance, its snowy petals spread around it, and a group of forms in a fresh crater not too far from the lake's shore. He could hardly believe who he was seeing. He was about a hundred meters away when he realized he was yelling his daughter's name.

"JEN!"

Startled, the girl whom he believed was Jen reached toward him and a bright green ball of light crackled out with blinding speed.

Charles somersaulted to the side, and the projectile whizzed past and nearly engulfed Hephalon, who was a score of meters away. The burly man slammed his fists into the ground, causing a slab of dense dirt to rise up to meet the ball of energy. Immediately it exploded, showering Hephalon with clumps of dirt, mud, and pieces of root.

Now only twenty meters away, Charles could see that Jen's eyes had been shut the entire time. Once he saw her violet eyes open—the same ones that had looked up at him twenty years ago while he rocked her to sleep—Charles's heart nearly burst with happiness. He slowly jogged the remaining distance with his arms outstretched.

"Jennifer?"

Jen blinked, momentarily confused, before she got off her griffin and reoriented herself as she looked around. She seemed shocked to be back on Camelore. He could only imagine where she had come from. When Jen's eyes fell on his, she tried to meet her father halfway, but she faltered. Gavin caught her and helped her stand again, but her gaze never left Charles's face.

"Charles . . . ? You're alive?"

He got to her and wrapped her in a hug. Jen relaxed, letting him hold her for a few silent seconds.

Charles pulled away from her and smiled. "That was some spell you casted," he said.

"I—I'm sorry," Jen said, putting her palm on her forehead. "I thought you were someone else."

"It's okay, it really is." He gingerly placed a curly strand of her dark hair behind her ear. Charles couldn't begin to comprehend how Jen got here. The crater behind her was no small one, but it seemed like she wasn't injured.

"Well, I beg to differ!" shouted Hephalon from behind. Charles turned to see his old friend striding closer, trying to pick stuck wads of dirt from his armor and hair. He winked. "I've never seen such an inconsiderate greeting in my life."

"Heph!" Jen squeezed Charles's arm before running to the metallurgist. "I'm so glad to see you too." She pulled quickly away, tensing. "Is Vic here?"

Hephalon nodded. "Yes, m'lady, but I have something for you." He pushed aside a dangling mace and dagger to find a pocket and dug in it for a second before pulling out a velvet pouch cinched tight. He delicately opened it and deposited its contents into his other hand. "I believe you need these now more than ever."

Jen gasped.

Charles walked to Jen's side to see three gorgeously crafted charms of brushed silver and gold. One reminded him of a galaxy, a flowing ellipses of swirling metal with the smallest diamonds sprinkled all around; another was a miniature hourglass filled with fine, glittering sand; and the last charm was a disk, both of its faces covered in specks of color that spiraled outward and became more elongated. Looking at it further, it seemed as though the entire disk was rotating, but it was an optical illusion.

"I'm sorry I was unable to give them to you sooner," Heph said as Jen took the charms and clasped them onto her bracelet next to two others.

"Heph, these are incredible." Jen shook her wrist and a satisfying *cling-clang* of metals in their purest forms resonated outward. She hugged Hephalon again, letting out a happy sigh. When she pulled away, she asked, "Can I see Vic?"

Hephalon smiled again, the crow's feet on the sides of his eyes becoming more pronounced. "Yes, indeed. He's—" He trailed off as he spotted someone else, behind Jen, who was coming out of the crater. At the same time, Victor came over the hill to be in full view.

Charles smiled as Jen, with another quick thanks to Hephalon, raced toward Victor. He watched his daughter run straight into his brother-in-law's arms. He could hear a faint laugh from Victor as he lost his balance when Jen hugged him.

This . . . this feeling; this reunion. Charles needed this.

CHAPTER TWENTY-SEVEN

Dusk arrived all too soon, and Jen found herself in Camelore's banquet hall, which had a similar feel to the interior of the helioarch, except that it was covered by a flowing canvas much akin to a large tent. Sconces adorning the circular walls illuminated the space, growing in brightness as the sun continued to dip below the horizon.

Two solid oak tables were pushed together so the whole group could visit while they dined. Jen was the first to finish cleaning her plate—the first real meal, she realized, that she'd had in several days. She hadn't noticed how hungry she was. She took a moment to look at everyone present: there were her foster parents, Richard and Beth; her brother, Tyler; her uncle, Victor; father, Charles; and friends, Hephalon, Mira, Gavin, and Rez. She also said a silent prayer to Dimitri because she wouldn't be here if it weren't for his sacrifice. Skarmor and Pernissa were enjoying their time in the stables while everyone had a heartfelt reunion. Tears of relief and happiness didn't seem to stop coming from Jen's eyes, and her mouth grew tired of constantly smiling, but she welcomed the soaked cheeks and sore muscles. She looked down at her totem bracelet, now complete with the remaining Mancy charms. It looked beautiful and uniquely hers as she rolled her wrist on the table so she could see the newest three. Her eyes landed on the chronomancy and telemancy ones, reminding her of the work she still needed to put in.

Before she could fill in Victor and his group on what she had been up to since they were separated at the Jubilee, the table went quiet when Victor said, "Charles, the last thing I want to do is trigger anything unpleasant for you, but do you remember why you went missing in the first place?"

Jen's father slowly put down his silverware on his plate as if it were extremely brittle, then tucked his hands underneath the table. "Yes," he said, looking at everyone in turn. "Our claim that Jocelyn and I had discovered the Halostone. But it's not what you think."

"I'm thinking, now that you've evaded death twice, we don't have to worry about collecting the MystiCrystals and instead have you lead us directly to the Halostone," Victor said, his elbows on the table and hands clasped in front of him.

Charles exhaled. It was several seconds before he responded. "Jocelyn and I thought we could turn the tide of the war." A look of regret washed across his face. "Twenty years ago, the League of Light and the Guild had been forced into a corner. We were losing battles that we otherwise should have won, and the Dark Watchers were one step ahead of our battle plans. Their attacks were too precise. There had to have been a mole deep inside the Guild."

Everyone, including Jen, was hanging on his every word. After no one made a move to say anything, Charles continued.

"The day after our crushing defeat on the western edge, Jocelyn and I knew we had to do something, even though we'd just had a baby." He looked at Jen, his eyes shimmering with tears. "We didn't know which part of the Guild had been compromised, so after ensuring Jen was safe"—he motioned to Richard and Beth Smith, lowering his chin in respect—"we spread the news that we'd located the Halostone, which was entirely fabricated."

Those words left Jen hollow inside. For a second, hope that there was another way to reach the Halostone without going back to Queen Pt'ara—that lioness—and her den. That her parents had risked everything to discover the identity of a potential mole was as equally brave as it was foolish. But if it had paid off, then they would have been hailed as heroes and possibly ended the war or found the Halostone in the process. That was the thing with risks —you either have luck on your side and become revered as a genius, or you draw the short end of the stick and accept the consequences, whatever those end up being.

"We immediately left for the Ocuul realm, trying to lead the mole away from the Guild, but we weren't expecting the celerity of Draconex's response. Our plan started to fall apart faster than we could keep it together." He put his hands on the table and examined them. "That . . . explosion"—the crow's feet at the edges of Charles's eyes deepened as he seemed to be reliving the event —"prevented us from ever snuffing out the mole until, I believe, the Sesquimillennial Jubilee."

"Simone . . . yes," Victor concurred. His eyes were boring into the sturdy oak table, lost in a memory? Jen couldn't tell for sure.

Jen felt her father's eyes on her. "I'm sorry, Jennifer. If I could do it again, I wouldn't."

Her bottom lip quivered slightly as she tried to blink away tears. She lifted her right hand and placed it on top of Charles's. "No one blames you, Father. I don't." She saw him relax, almost as if he had been waiting all those years for her to say that, but her next sentence made him tense again. "And you have to stop blaming yourself." She had to take a few breaths to compose herself or she would be lost in this raw, vulnerable emotion. "You can't change the past, and I admire the guts you and my mother had to do something so selfless in order to ensure the Guild's survival and put an end to the war." She rubbed her thumb affectionately over the back of his hand.

Thank you, Charles sent to her through telemancy.

You're welcome, Jen sent back, smiling at her father.

Aloud, she said to everyone, "And that leads me to update you all on what Mira, Gavin, Rez, and I have been up to since the Jubilee . . ."

Jen started with the reveal that Gavin was indeed the Light Bringer, then followed with their journey to Atlantis and then below the Antarctic crust, to a place they'd dubbed Shangri-La. When it came time to talk about how Dimitri, the leshy sent by Merlin to protect Jen, had sacrificed himself so that she and her friends could escape, she described that final earthquake and the impending doom of their escape, leading to their mysterious and confounding appearance here. Charles explained that the Astro-Crystal, in conjunction with her nexus, more than likely saved her and her friends, transporting them back to Camelore.

Jen could see the awe on the faces of Victor, Hephalon, and Charles as she pulled the ChronoCrystal out of her shoulder bag alongside two new MystiCrystals, all three glowing due to their close proximity. And she had to admit: now that she was out of danger, the reality of what she held in her hands was sinking in. Their collection of MystiCrystals had now tripled to three.

"No one has laid eyes on these in fifteen hundred years," Victor breathed as he cradled the TerraCrystal with both hands. It made sense that he'd gravitated toward that one, since he was a terramancy mystra.

"They look even more beautiful than the texts describe," Charles said, holding the AstroCrystal. The silver and gold specks danced in a sea of deep, rich purple as he rotated it around, drinking in its every angle.

Jen beamed proudly at Mira, Gavin, and Rez, making sure to credit their hard work in helping her retrieve the crystals. But then she remembered she had failed to get the TeleCrystal . . . and the AniCrystal was still out there somewhere.

"What's wrong, Jen?" Victor asked, a look of concern furrowing his eyebrows.

Jen realized she had slid slightly down in her chair and was pursing her lips. "Oh, it's just that the TeleCrystal and AniCrystal are still out there, and who knows how we'll manage to get them."

"Don't negate the marvel of what you have accomplished," Hephalon said as he ripped through his fourth wild boar leg, his other hand grabbing his mug of ale as he held eye contact with Jen. "You have managed to do something that thousands of sorcerers have only dreamed of doing." He picked up the mug and swirled its contents around, saying before he took a long swig, "And besides . . . you've got *us* now."

This was all true, but Jen was suddenly distracted from the feeling of more tension from Rez, which had started when his father went up to him as he was getting out of the crater back near the lake. She looked over when she heard Rez exhale in time to see the most over-dramatic eye roll. He crossed his arms and leaned back in his chair. Jen cocked her head slightly, confused at his reaction, but it was something between them and clearly private, so she decided to respect that.

Victor's next comment pulled her attention away from the brooding telemancer. "Hephalon is right. Maybe I can try diplomacy with the Atlanteans while you retrieve the last MystiCrystal." He absentmindedly tapped the tines of his fork on the side of his plate as he thought aloud.

Jen shook her head. "I don't feel like the right move is splitting up, especially since we just found each other again."

Easy, girl . . .

Jen felt her cheeks heat up and her vision started to blur. She reached below the table and pinched her thigh to distract her emotions from opening the floodgates. It was working . . . for now.

She cleared her throat and continued, "I feel like we should decipher where the AniCrystal is, then focus our full effort on getting it. If we then go to the Atlaneans and show them every other MystiCrystal, that might help them trust us."

Victor placed his fork on the table and nodded, looking around the table, seemingly waiting to see if anyone would argue with her plan. Jen found her way to Richard and Beth, who were beaming at her, clearly proud of the woman they had raised. Tyler just seemed awestruck, happy to be included as he piled mashed potatoes into his mouth.

Movement off to her side made Jen notice Gavin slide his plate to the side and place the lost journal on the table in front of him. "Let's see what ol' Merlin has in store for us next."

The centuries-old binding softly cracked as Gavin opened it up, flipping deep into the book. A feeling of anticipation hung in the air as he settled on a certain page, sliding his index finger across it, reading Merlin's coded riddle.

Jen, realizing she had been holding her breath, finally let it out. She looked at Charles, who was sitting as straight as a board, clearly as anxious as her.

Gavin began:

"Follow the path formed by multiple volcanoes' bursts.
Therein lies a winged progeny of heaven and Earth,
Forever guarding a host of hidden treasure.
What you seek is the object of Fuzanglong's pleasure."

A silence fell over the hall as Merlin's riddle lingered like a dispersing fog.

Volcano? Fuzanglong?

Jen was at a loss. Her eyes bounced around the entire table to see if anyone's body language belied the confusion Jen was currently experiencing.

Then a gasp.

Rez shot up from his seat, scrunching his eyes shut and snapping his fingers as if something was on the tip of his tongue and he was trying to coax it out.

"Rez . . . ?" Gavin said uneasily.

Rez started pacing. " 'Winged progeny' . . . 'heaven and Earth' . . ." He shuffled past Jen. "Fuzang . . . *LONG!*" He clapped his hands and did a little jig, causing Mira to giggle.

Jen couldn't help but smirk. If Rez could solve another one of these riddles, she would finally agree to watch his one-man magic show he'd been trying to get her to see. Her heartbeat steadily grew in anticipation.

"*Long* is the Chinese term for dragon." He waited a beat to see if anyone else had had the same epiphany as him. Nothing, so he continued: "And the prefix *Fuzang-* is a *type* of Chinese dragon. The one of hidden treasures."

"So somehow this dragon found the AniCrystal and is guarding it?" Jen hazarded a guess.

Rez flashed a big smile. "Not just the AniCrystal, but also literally mounds upon heaps upon hordes of treasure from 'round the world—and from other realms."

Jen caught a flash of pride from Hephalon. He was sitting back in his chair, hands in his lap, not paying any attention to his fifth steaming boar's leg.

"Okay," Gavin said, "but what's with the mention of volcanoes?"

"The reasoning is so cool," Rez gushed. "Watch and learn."

He channeled telemancy to show a holographic depiction of an erupting volcano in the middle of the banquet hall's table. Red-orange molten lava spurted from the volcano, showering down in all directions. Tyler gasped and covered himself with his napkin to protect himself from the illusion. Jen laughed, then paused, mesmerized by Rez's telemancy. A particularly large eruption was occurring, and what she'd initially thought was another plume of lava was actually the long, writhing body of a dragon, its scales shimmering with the same color as the lava.

Rez continued, "Fuzanglong creates volcanoes whenever he wants to travel back to heaven. In fact, it's said that volcanoes first formed when Fuzanglong an' his brother, Zhulong, fought thousands of years ago.

"Y'see"—he clapped his hands together once, clearly getting more excited by the second—"throughout the ages, dragons battled each other fer supremacy over Earth's land. Even though all dragons have an affinity fer treasure, Fuzanglong and Zhulong, the first of several dragons tha' ended up takin' eminence over present-day Asia, cultivated a desire fer nah' only infinite riches but also a power that would lead to immortality, omniscience, an' control over terrestrial weather . . . to name a wee bit."

He brought his hands together and the hologram vanished, leaving the torches along the walls to carry the burden of lighting the hall once again. "A flamin' pearl is said to hold that power, an' some say that they're still searchin' fer it."

Rez won another round against the riddles of Merlin's journal.

Charles looked pensive. "Does any volcano lead to Fuzanglong's lair, or do we need to search for a specific one? This could take a while." He leaned forward, putting his head in his palm.

"Rez, you said that some volcanoes formed while the two brothers fought in what is now China, right?" Jen asked. Seeing him nod, she then said, "So I suggest we start looking for the oldest ones in that region." She thought that would be the most logical approach, considering that time was clearly not on their side.

"Seems sound to me," Victor said. "I agree with Jen, and we can use terramancy to pinpoint the volcano that has most recently erupted in mainland China."

A murmur of assent spread around the table as Gavin closed the lost journal and Rez sat back down. Jen blinked, her eyelids suddenly as heavy as sandbags. She couldn't help but notice that Hephalon had let his head fall back to rest on the top of his chair's backrest, the half-eaten fifth helping of boar's leg lazily clutched in his right hand.

"All right, time to rest, weary travelers." That was the first time her foster father, Richard, had spoken since they started dinner. He picked up Tyler, who was quickly falling asleep, and started toward the large circular doors.

Jen was hit with fond memories of the many times she had drowsily woken up in those same arms as a child, carried by Richard up to her room back in Erie, PA. She always felt so safe in his arms, hearing his steady heartbeat as she nestled her head close to his chest. Jen knew that he would do anything for her and Tyler, and she now felt a sense of guilt for not making time to talk with them since she'd arrived back on Camelore, but she could tell that her parents understood the weight of the current situation. Hopefully, in the near future, they would all be able to relax and be together again.

Richard reached for the door handles when someone who Jen didn't recognize burst through.

"Jocelyn," Charles said, shooting up from his seat.

Jocelyn . . . ?

The heaviness of Jen's eyelids suddenly went away, like someone had ripped a weighted blanket off of her, and her heart involuntarily sped up. Looking at the pale, blond woman in the doorway, she was speechless.

Jocelyn . . . as in, my mother, *Jocelyn?*

"Did I miss anything?" the woman asked quietly, clearly having just woken up.

The room suddenly felt insanely small, as if it were just her, Charles, and the woman he called Jocelyn inside.

Charles was by her side in an instant, taking her hand and leading her to his seat. "You shouldn't be up."

"I feel fine, Charles," she said reassuringly, though she did accept the seat he offered her.

Jen looked at Richard, who was still holding Tyler by the door. He tightly smiled at her as Beth went to his side. He nodded, almost as if he were a telemancer and could read her mind.

Jen was pulled back to look at Charles and the woman when she heard her biological father say, as if in a dream, "Jen, I'd like to introduce you to Jocelyn, my wife and"—the words got caught in his mouth—"your mother."

Jen's own mouth suddenly went as dry as the Gobi Desert and her tongue wouldn't cooperate to form any of the right words. She tried swallowing, but forcing it only made her want to dry-heave, so she gave up on that and just said, "Mom?"

That word felt odd coming from her mouth, directed at a woman she had never met before. She silently hoped that the woman who helped raise her, Beth, wouldn't be offended.

Jocelyn seemed equally as gobsmacked. She quietly placed her hands on her legs and looked up at Charles for reassurance. He rested a hand on her shoulder, and she seemed to calm down at his touch, looking back at Jen with watery eyes.

"Hi, Jennifer," she finally said.

Jen was lost in her own thoughts, unsure of how exactly to process this new information. Her biological mother—the one who was said to have perished in an explosion twenty years ago *with her father*—was somehow alive, both her and Jen's father sitting not three meters from their grown daughter. She jolted when someone touched her shoulder. Looking up, she saw Victor.

"We'll leave you three alone for a bit, Jenny." He smiled softly and squeezed her shoulder.

She watched him file out of the banquet hall behind everyone else. No one remained except the Lancasters. Jen stood on trembling legs, willing them to walk the short distance to her biological mother for a hug.

* * *

It was coming up on an hour since Victor had left Jen inside with Charles and Jocelyn. He was the only one still waiting outside the banquet hall, sitting on folded knees on a soft patch of grass and meditating deep within his nexus. He had bid everyone a good-night as the rest of the group broke off, trickling back to their respective huts, the last to remain with him Gavin and Mira. They looked completely beat, so he soon convinced them that Jen would understand if they retired for the night. Now it was just himself and the pleasant nighttime breeze. It played across his face, running its invisible hands through his thick, silvery mane.

A lot of sorcerers had asked Victor what he thought about when meditating, and his answer was different every time. It came down to what good fortune had given him at that time, and how to be mindful going forward, no matter how smooth or treacherous the road ahead might be. Tonight, he meditated with the feeling of gratefulness; of how, though lost to him for so long, he was able to find both his younger sister and his niece unharmed and back with him in one piece.

He floated in his nexus, drinking in its power and the harmonious connection he shared with all the elements, when finally he sensed the banquet hall's door opening. Happy with where his meditation session had led him, he brought himself back to the present and saw Jen leading Charles and Jocelyn his way. The calming, oscillating rhythm of crickets returned as well.

"Hey," Jen started with. She brushed a long, curly strand of hair behind her ear.

Victor got up and looked past Jen to see Charles and Jocelyn sharing a smile. He looked back at Jen and said, "How did it go?"

Jen spared a quick look behind her before answering, "Surreal."

He got the sense that she was at ease—maybe even happy—though clearly still processing this news. Victor didn't blame her; he still wasn't fully convinced this wasn't a dream himself. He'd had a heartfelt moment with Jocelyn when he put her in Jen's hammock. The slight disturbance had awoken her, and brother and sister hugged, crying out their pent-up grief that they no longer needed to carry. It was cathartic, and Victor wondered if Jen had done the same during her private conversation with her birth parents.

Victor hugged Jen before either of them could say anything else. He felt her thin but strong arms wrap around his lower back.

"I'm scared," Jen said into his shoulder.

Victor gently squeezed her, not saying anything.

"I have everything I could ever want . . . which means now I have more to lose than ever before."

He pulled away and could see that Jen's lower eyelids were now damp. "I want you to see this as a strength, Jen. These people love you just as much as you do them. And we won't let anything harm that. Together we are stronger, and don't you forget that."

Jen sniffled, letting out a single chuckle, probably to release her recent onset of anxiety. "You're right. It's all about perspective." She dabbed her eyelids with a finger. "I guess I just need to sleep through it."

"I'm in need of a good rest myself." He smiled and rubbed her back.

Jen nodded, clearing her throat. "Then, at first light, we should scout out that volcano."

Victor was amazed at his niece. With all the trials that Jen had experienced in such a short period of time, she was still trying to figure out where her place was in all of this, yet through everything she never lost sight of the end goal. She pushed through fear, exhaustion, and the unknown, no matter what.

Victor stole the line Hephalon had once told him, and he wasn't ashamed of it: "Wherever you go, I'll follow."

Jen smiled broadly, though he could see in her eyes how tired she was. "Thank you," she said as she squeezed his hand, then quickly turned around to hug Charles and Jocelyn again. "I'll see you both in the morning."

As Jen headed to her hut, Victor stepped closer to his younger sister and brother-in-law. "And how are you?"

Charles sighed and Jocelyn inhaled, pausing.

Jocelyn was the first to speak: "I can't believe what an amazing woman my baby has turned into." She placed a hand over her mouth and rested her head on Charles's shoulder.

"What we wouldn't give to get these last twenty years back," Charles said.

Victor stepped closer and rested a hand on Charles's shoulder, then put his other hand on Jocelyn's. There really wasn't anything he could say to that. They had not only been ripped from their daughter, but their memories stolen from them for too long. He guessed the only silver lining—and a truly bright one at that— was that they now remembered and were able to reunite with their only daughter.

He shot a thumb toward the huts and both nodded back in agreement.

They were all walking side by side, still a fair distance from the huts, when a light flared up in the night sky. Victor stopped, unsure what to make of it. The light grew, turning into a ring, and out of its center dropped a dark silhouette, landing below the crest of the hill just beyond the huts. A similar light emerged on the edge of his peripherals, and he turned in time to see another black form drop from the sky, this one much closer than the first. It landed with a heavy *THUD*, causing the ground to rumble and the leaves on a nearby dogwood tree to shake.

Unconsciously, Victor touched his belt buckle and started slipping his totem rings onto his fingers as he stepped forward. "Stay behind me," he said, more to Jocelyn than to Charles.

The silhouette was running full-steam toward them, and as it got closer, the quarter moon's light revealed what Victor was about to go toe to toe with. He felt another rumble, and guessed that a third one dropped in somewhere behind them.

"Golem!" he yelled.

Victor quickly slid into a fighting stance, and before he could start worrying about the rest in their huts, he felt Jocelyn envelop him and everyone else in a mind-meld, alerting them all to the ambush outside.

"I'll take the golem on your six," Charles said to Victor.

Without breaking his concentration on the lumbering stone creature getting exponentially closer, he nodded and let his nexus activate the familiar plane of terramancy.

A faint metallic *SHING* let him know that his rings were snug on his fingers before he funneled his terramancy powers through them. Victor unleashed a cyclone of air toward the golem, which was already airborne, having jumped moments before, intent on delivering a rib-shattering flying low kick squarely at Victor's chest. The cyclone wrapped up the heavy creature, and with the skill of a mystra, Victor used the golem's forward momentum to carry it well over the trio and slam it into the second golem as it squared off against Charles. A lucky direct hit caused both golems to be torn asunder, cascading shards and chunks of stone in a two-meter radius.

"Nicely done," Charles said, surprised.

"Don't mention it," Victor responded. He turned to Charles and his sister. "Everyone all right?"

Then his heart sank when he saw the rubble roll back to where the collision had happened. The pile grew as every broken piece returned, reforming into a single golem twice the size as the initial two. And this juggernaut had four arms.

Victor cursed just as screams emanated from near the huts. He caught a glimpse of the third golem as it plowed through a hut, sending pieces of thatched roofing and clay high in the air.

Charles must have seen Victor hesitate because the next thing he said was, "Jocelyn and I will take care of this guy. Go!" He swung back to face the hulking, four-armed golem. He launched into a butterfly kick, spells from all of the Mancy planes shooting from his feet.

Victor took off in a dead sprint. He lanced spears made of fire at the golem that was one hundred meters or so away. He focused intently on guiding the searing projectiles to their quick-moving target without hitting any of his friends. A few exploded as they hit the golem's shoulders and back, but that wasn't enough to faze it. It kept bulldozing whatever was in its way, but it looked like the sorcerers who were in the thick of the battle, Jen and Hephalon, were holding their own.

Grunting, Victor leaned into his sprint, letting his cumbersome cloak slide off his back. He balled his hands in preparation to sink the golem deep into the ground when a fourth ring of light illuminated the sky, causing him to instead dive into a somersault, a massive fireball decimating the spot he was just in.

He rolled into a run once more, his joints reminding him of his age. Victor looked skyward and saw the unwelcome nightmarish body of Volcanor rumbling over him, strafing the ground as it glided toward the huts, its large, venous wings spread wide to minimize drag and maximize speed.

Victor had known he would have to face off against Draconex again sooner or later, but what he didn't understand was how his former schoolmate found the location of Camelore. This place should have been protected by an ancient spell concealing it from everyone who wasn't admitted into the League of Light.

In the distance—about twenty meters or so—Victor could see colorful spells being exchanged between Jen and the dark sorcerer atop Volcanor as Hephalon focused on the golem. Another hut exploded in flames from an errant fireball from the wyvern dragon as Volcanor was pounded with spells, too big to move quickly enough to evade all of Jen's terramancy. The grace with which Jen moved as she navigated between casting offensive spells and twirling into defensive evasion tactics reminded Victor of Charles's style mixed with his own. He remembered the night Draconex brought Volcanor to ambush them minutes after Jen had received her totem and terramancy charm, and how defenseless Jen had been during that aerial battle.

She was getting better . . . much better.

Victor's nerves screamed with anxiety as he cleared a meter with every stride, just getting within range to pick out the form that slid from the massive, brimstone-encrusted dragon, but—

It wasn't Draconex.

The voices of the ShadowCrystal chattered in Malcolm's mind as he willed the golem to take its fight with the burly metallurgist farther away from Jen. He wanted there to be nothing standing between him and his ex-girlfriend.

Malcolm smirked. He no longer felt that tug from his heart for Jennifer Lancaster. After he'd grabbed the ShadowCrystal, his inhibitions immediately shriveled up like a long-dead carcass. With a clear mind and the power of dark magic, Malcolm was astounded at the clarity of mind he'd been awarded. He didn't thank Draconex for a lot, but his master's final act of usefulness had come in the form of a dragon scale lying in the cave, torn from Silvress by Draconex's final attack before Victor's equivol checked him into the cave's wall. That one small piece had allowed him to track his prey to this clandestine floating island.

Malcolm sneered. It didn't look that impressive.

As Volcanor came in for a landing, its massive wings buffeted Jen with gale-force winds, causing her to throw her hands up to protect her face. The blast of air also extinguished a few ancillary fires ravaging several of the huts in the immediate vicinity. Volcanor let out a ground-trembling roar as Jen flung pieces of a decimated hut at its head, managing to block most of the debris with one large, leathery wing.

On the opposite side of the attack, Malcolm slid from his perch on his late master's dragon, using its massive body as a shield from Jen's onslaught. On his right hand he wore a gauntlet that held the ShadowCrystal in its center. Malcolm had crafted it from scavenged debris from the downed Watercress Castle before he had left for Camelore. He deliberately made it so the underside of the crystal touched his skin at all times, feeding him with the unlimited power of the ShadowCrystal. He clenched his fists and was satisfied to see that his forearm veins bulged a bruised-purple glow as the dark magic radiated through his body.

Volcanor made a move to charge at Jen, but Malcolm, with a strong telemancy prompt, willed his mighty dragon to pause. Frustrated, nonetheless it obeyed.

The familiar voice of Victor Huxley cut through the crackling of the ablaze huts.

"Malcolm, *stop!*"

Malcolm turned to see his old mentor standing not ten yards away. He could sense Victor's surprise to see him instead of Draconex. Malcolm relished that emotion.

"Expecting someone else, *Vic*?" He snickered, feeling the slight pull of the scar tissue on his face. "Well, you'd be waiting forever if that's the case."

He let his gaze bore deeper into Victor while he cracked his knuckles, ready for anything this old man might throw at him. He then slipped his un-gauntleted hand into the folds of his robes, pulled out Draconex's totem ring, and slid it on, winking at Victor.

"You're looking at the new commander of the Dark Watcher tribe."

He turned back around to get a clear view of Jen, not waiting for a response from his once-trusted master. After quickly making sure that his golems were occupying both Hephalon and Charles Lancaster, he sent an icy spell straight at Jen.

A wave of superheated air rippled in front of the girl, negating the spell that would have frozen her to her core. She fell into a side roll and stayed low on one knee, breathing heavily. Between matted strands of hair stuck to her temples, those violet eyes glowed bright in the night. Malcolm stared back as he sorted through all the possible next moves allowed him by the Shadow-Crystal.

A barely imperceptible flicker of violet from Jen's eyes alerted Malcolm to another presence behind him. Without looking, he reached out a gloved hand, extending his limited chronomancy powers behind him, and closed his fist. There was a satisfying muffled grunt, and after seeing the concern on Jen's face, Malcolm decided to look back to see who he'd caught.

To the naked eye it appeared as if there was no one there, but Malcolm squeezed his fingers together even tighter and a tall, lanky boy flickered into sight. He was frozen in stride, clearly trying hard to break away from Malcolm's spell.

Ah . . . a telemancer, Malcolm thought as he cocked his head, probing the boy's mind.

Movement at the edge of his sight revealed two airborne griffins racing toward him. He channeled the eyesight of a bald eagle, picking out the likes of Gavin Kingsland and Mira Amian as their riders. Mira's griffin was slightly ahead of Gavin's, her bullwhip drawn and trailing in the wind. The hilt glowed a bright yellow as she prepared to crack a spell at him. Gavin had his orb totem levitating above an open palm, a soft blue aura surrounding him.

Malcolm timed it out so that right before both sorcerers would have inundated him with their attacks he yelled, vibrating his vocal cords with the intensity of a howler monkey—

"STOP! OR I'LL AGE HIM SO FAST HE'LL TURN TO DUST RIGHT IN FRONT OF YOU!"

—and he wasn't expecting that voice. He gave himself chills when he heard that the ShadowCrystal's tone was now synched up with his voice but an octave lower.

Both Gavin and Mira reined in their griffins, their totems still activated, though neither of them dared to cast any spells.

"I don't think I know you," Malcolm commented to the ginger boy in his grasp. He knew he wouldn't get a response—the poor boy was frozen in time—though he did seem to resemble someone Malcolm knew . . . but he couldn't put a finger on who.

Probing the ginger's mind further, his eyebrows raised in recognition when he found out his name: Resolved "Rez" Hephalon. So the boy caught in his clutches was the son of the great Mystra Sterling Hephalon. The one who had been second fiddle to his father's position as the Guild's totem maker and his blind allegiance to that cult, the likes of which Malcolm was once a part.

Your golem pawns have been neutralized.

The eerie whispers of the ShadowCrystal alerted him as it vibrated on his wrist. He'd known that eventually his golems would get overpowered—they were mindless stone guardians after all—but he'd hoped they would have at least given him enough time to obtain however many MystiCrystals Jen had possessed. Guess not.

Kill the boy.

Malcolm locked eyes again with the frozen telemancer and did a final probe.

Rip him asunder.

A wicked smirk etched itself across his face. He flicked his fingers up and down, increasing the boy's heart rate while shriveling his brain with the manipulation and acceleration of time. He felt searing heat on the nape of his neck and the edges of his ears as Volcanor laid down a wall of white-hot fire to prevent Jen and Victor from stopping him.

Blasting through the intense fire wall, Sterling Hephalon roared with unparalleled rage. Malcolm's heightened instincts saved his face from being bludgeoned by a deadly right hook, but his new armor was severely dented by terramancy-charged brass knuckles, splitting in the deepest part and puncturing his skin. Malcolm had no choice but to relinquish his hold on Rez and spar with the man who had made his first totem ring back when he was a young tenderfoot.

"You have signed your own death warrant, *mac ghalla!*" Hephalon roared, transitioning his jabs into a blindingly fast uppercut. His brass knuckle totem moved so fast it was nothing but a blur of upward motion, narrowly missing Malcolm as he kicked back into a back handspring.

It hurt Malcolm to breathe too deeply, but he couldn't help it as he landed on his feet again. Hephalon moved with him, not allowing Malcolm enough space to position himself effectively. Like lightning striking twice, Hephalon hammered his chest with a one-two punch before twirling into a low leg sweep, briefly cutting Malcolm off from the ground. He grunted as he landed straight on his back, but he was able to roll away from a pile driver that carried the weight of a three-hundred-pound man, armor and all.

Placing his palms on the ground above his head, Malcolm shot up into a kip, regaining his feet before he executed a tornado axe kick, spinning three-hundred-sixty degrees in an instant and using his momentum to send his boot heel crashing down on the metallurgist with the kick power of a red kangaroo. He felt his boot connect with the bottom edge of Hephalon's chest armor. Another few inches and he would've vanquished the old man.

Volcanor was still fending off Jen and Victor, but Malcolm could sense Gavin and Mira moving in from above. His plans were disintegrating before his eyes, and if he didn't try to escape this instant, he knew he would eventually be subdued. Malcolm rammed a boot tip across Hephalon's face, hearing a wet *CRUNCH* before his opponent went unconscious, then proceeded to jump on Volcanor.

Cursing, he commanded the hellish dragon to fly. The griffins were too close now, so Volcanor spat a quick round of fireballs in their direction before gaining more altitude. Malcolm glared at Jen as she turned into a receding speck on the ground.

You retreated.

You don't trust how strong we are.

Malcolm chewed on his lip so hard he tasted blood. "No! Their MystiCrystals are too heavily guarded." He swiveled around to look ahead. "It's smarter to get to the other ones before they can."

And Malcolm knew exactly where to look for the AniCrystal.

Besides, having another dragon on his side would surely turn the tides.

* * *

While Gavin and Mira relentlessly but futilely volleyed spells at the retreating form of Volcanor until the dragon was gone, Jen rushed to huddle alongside Victor and Rez around the beaten and unconscious form of Hephalon. Victor dropped to his knees and gingerly placed his friend's head in his lap and conjured up a water-healing spell as Jen knelt beside him. She rested a hand on his chest armor, feeling the slick, cold temperature of the curved metal as she watched the water course over Hephalon's face, turning his amber beard a shade darker, and down his throat to the rest of his body underneath his armor. Crackles and pops from dying flames were white noise to her ears as Jen smelled singed grass and hay.

Camelore was no longer safe.

Jen leaned over to Victor and whispered, "You think Malcolm really killed Draconex?"

Victor didn't budge. He kept his eyes closed as he continued to focus on healing what he could out here before bringing Hephalon to Camelore's infirmary. Jen didn't know if he had even heard her.

"Is . . . is he okay?" Rez asked, choking back tears.

Jen, torn away from her focus on Victor, looked down at Hephalon. The metallurgist bore the forming bruises and cuts of a man who had been badly beaten, but Victor's healing spell would quickly repair those topical injuries. Through astromancy, Jen was able to feel a strong pulse and normal release of brain synapses. Looks can be deceiving, and for her sake as much as Rez's she wanted to make sure.

"He'll be fine. He's a fighter." She stood and squeezed Rez's hand just as Mira and Gavin landed. She didn't quite know how to console Rez; they still barely knew each other, but she knew he needed comforting.

"Your parents and Tyler are safe in the stables," Mira said as she led Skarmor to the group.

"Thank you," Jen said. She held up a finger to Rez to give him a *one-minute* sign before she hugged Mira, and she felt Gavin wrap them both in his broad arm span seconds later. She was still breathing heavily, not because she was out of breath, but because her adrenaline had finally succumbed to her other emotions and sobs now softly racked her body. Jen exhaled forcefully and wiped her teary eyes when she pulled away from her friends, their faces now etched with worry at their downed mentor.

"He's in rough shape, but internally he's fine, thank goodness."

Jen spared a glance at Rez, who looked as white as a ghost and also catatonic. Her heart ached seeing him standing there all alone, and she knew what she had to do. She walked over to him and gave him a hug. Jen could almost feel the bottled-up animosity Rez still held for his father, which, for her, had yet to be explained, suddenly leave his body. He'd seen that Hephalon was willing to sacrifice his life to save his son's, and whatever squabble he had with his father was now less than trivial.

"I felt Malcolm touch my mind," Rez said in her ear. "He knows where to look for the AniCrystal."

Jen tensed, but didn't let him go. That explained why he'd left and didn't continue to fight. She closed her eyes and took a few breaths. There was no sense in getting worked up about that. God knew Rez had been through enough, and she was sure that it happened so fast he couldn't have put up a wall to protect that information.

"It's okay, Rez . . . it's okay."

Jen finished her hug and smiled sweetly at the telemancer before turning around to see her birth parents run up, and she was surprised when Jocelyn embraced her. Jocelyn was cold to the touch, which made Jen want so badly to warm her up, but she knew that vampires weren't like other living beings and didn't need to have a warm internal body temperature.

Gavin was the first to ask the question that was on everybody's mind.

"How did Malcolm know where to find us?"

His jaw was clenched and his eyes, which were normally softly piercing and caring, were now biting and churned with anger. Jen could envision him reacting intensely if she, without preamble, disclosed what Rez had just told her. She needed to first talk to someone who was more collected at the moment, which was a difficult thing to be, all things considered, but she knew both Victor and Charles were those people. They would take the news the best and help her come up with a plan before she updated the rest of the group. Thankful that no one had chimed in yet, Jen gave Mira a signal to calm Gavin while she focused on what she had felt during her fight with Malcolm. She had been able to sense Rez, even though he was invisible. She looked at him and hoped that feeling was the gateway to telemancy.

Don't say anything yet.

Rez straightened up and looked her in the eye. *Merlin's Beard, you can channel telemancy?*

Jen gave him a smirk but repeated her thought to him before saying, "Excuse me." She touched Victor on the shoulder and Charles's mind to get them to follow her, and in a couple of seconds they were standing in a circle.

"Rez thinks Malcolm used telemancy to read his mind, and I think that's why he left so quickly. He knows we're after Fuzanglong's lair," Jen said softly. She was glad Gavin wasn't a telemancer, and fought the urge to look back at him.

Victor stroked his chin while Charles bit his lip. Jen was astounded to realize that she did the same thing when she was deep in thought.

Like father, like daughter.

Victor was the first to respond. "In that case, we have to assume he also knows you've found the TeleCrystal in Atlantis and have already tried getting it. And after this show of force, I figure he has a pretty inflated ego, especially after killing Draconex and making Volcanor his dragon. My best guess is that he is going for the AniCrystal because another dragon guards it, and he's already made one submit to him, so how tough could another one be?" Victor scoffed at such a delusion. "Let him find it," he said, indifferently and with a vein of anger. "I wasn't all that eager to go up against a dragon to retrieve it, and we all know he needs the MystiCrystals we have, so he'll end up bringing the AniCrystal to us. We just have to be ready for it."

"You said that one of the princes of Atlantis is sympathetic to our mission?" Charles asked. He folded his arms and shifted his weight.

"M'balo, yes," Jen said. "He gave me this dagger." She unsheathed it from her belt and handed it to her father.

Charles inspected the gorgeously crafted dagger's hilt and blade. "Atlantis is where we need to go next." He handed her back the dagger. "And impress upon them that we need their cooperation before it's too late."

"For us and their civilization, too," Jen added. "I'm willing to bet that Malcolm wouldn't bat an eye over leveling Atlantis if it means getting the final MystiCrystal."

Both senior sorcerers nodded their agreement, and Jen told them of an idea that had just come to her before they broke off to return to the main group. She went over to Rez and took his hand, squeezing it.

"Tell them what you told me," she said in a low tone.

Rez took a deep breath and began. "I reckon Malcolm went into m'noggin when he froze me . . ." He looked uneasily at Jen, but she rubbed the side of his hand with her thumb and he continued. ". . . an' found out where the AniCrystal's located."

Mira's touch had seemed to work; Gavin's face looked a little softer around the edges, and Jen could tell that his fury was more in check. He took the news better than she had initially thought, which was good. For this to not implode, everyone needed to keep a level head.

Jen added, "He's already on his way to finding Fuzanglong, and"—she looked at Victor—"we have to assume he also plucked the memory of finding the TeleCrystal in Atlantis and failing to acquire it, so I, along with Vic and Charles, think we need to return to Atlantis before Malcolm can attack their kingdom."

She looked down at Hephalon, who hadn't changed positions since he'd become unconscious. Victor had slipped down to kneel next to him without Jen noticing. She was even more motivated to put an end to this so that no one else she cared about got hurt.

"The queen already kicked us out, basically banishing us," Gavin retorted. "What makes this time any different?"

Jen looked at her dagger's hilt, its marvelous pastel colors shimmering softly in the night as if it had its own reservoir of power.

"I have an idea . . ."

CHAPTER TWENTY-NINE

It was as if Malcolm had been there when the young telemancer, Rez, cracked the code to the AniCrystal's location. He'd never known how visceral telemancy was when you used it to read someone's mind. All the sights, smells, and emotions in that boy's mind had flooded into his consciousness simultaneously. Malcolm couldn't care less about the smell of Hephalon's boar's legs or the sight of Jen's "brother," Tyler, falling asleep at the table. What mattered most was the knowledge of where to obtain the AniCrystal—that and the fact that now he would beat Jen and everyone else to it, especially since Draconex no longer slowed him down.

Malcolm was also pleased to pick up a slightly older memory, one that made his jaw nearly drop: Jen . . . discovering *Atlantis*. It now made so much sense why the world couldn't explain where Atlantis, a society filled with technology so advanced for its age, had gone.

So it is *the Richat Structure . . . just made to look like a natural wonder by the power of the TeleCrystal.*

Malcolm ran the cold tips of his fingers down his cheek, feeling the slight raise of the scar that Skarmor had given him the night of the ambush on Watercress Castle. What were the odds that he would get a scar in the same place as Draconex? At least now he would never have to see his master's scar again.

Malcolm felt no remorse in murdering his master. Such was the cycle, after all. Draconex had disposed of his predecessor to claim the Dark Watcher throne, and now it was Malcolm's turn, as if in fulfillment of some prophecy.

And now, in one fell swoop, he knew where the last two MystiCrystals were. And he did it all without being the Light Bringer and deciphering Merlin's stupid lost journal.

A mischievous smirk curled his lip as he convinced himself that it was *he* who was destined to find the AniCrystal, collect the remaining four MystiCrystals, and finally free Lord Ferox from the Halostone. His destiny was made even clearer to him when Malcolm realized how to find the dragon of hidden treasures, Fuzanglong—and how fitting it was that Volcanor, whom he now controlled, had the innate sense for tracking down volcanoes, like a determined bloodhound on the hunt for a fox. His devilish wyvern dragon was born in the depths of the fiercest, most volatile supervolcano in the Vallei Mortic realm, so commanding it to find a volcano for him now was like going home.

Volcanor elicited a throaty rumble which preceded a hot snort that sent thick clouds of smoke out of its nostrils and straight into Malcolm's eyes. He blinked away the smoke, his eyes now itchy, but he could still see the massive caldera of what used to be a giant stratovolcano right on the border of China and North Korea. The caldera held a crater lake that stretched over nine square kilometers. Thankfully, the change in the seasons had already melted the snowy peaks.

With the aid of telemancy, Malcolm could infer that Volcanor was aiming for the deepest part of the lake, naturally situated in the middle of the crater. Pairing his strongest Mancy plane, terramancy, with the intoxicating powers of the ShadowCrystal, Malcolm rotated his hands in tight circles as Volcanor rocketed straight toward the center of the lake.

A whirlpool formed, a pinprick in the distance, but it quickly expanded into a swirling vortex that opened up a pathway hundreds of meters below to the crater bed. The reddened cracks of the dragon's skin became brighter as Volcanor pulled in its wings to cover Malcolm in a winged shield, fitting nicely in the vortex that the Dark Watcher had conjured. It carried with it an imposing roar as they were both swallowed up by the lake. Volcanor's skin-crawling roar was instantly muted and absorbed by the roiling waters, but not a drop of water landed on it as it burrowed deep into the crater in mere seconds.

Malcolm thought that the impact would have instigated an earthquake, but Volcanor became one with the volcano, barely slowing down as it penetrated the dense crater and entered into the stratovolcano's mantle plume. Blasting through a subducted part of the Pacific tectonic plate with ease, the wyvern dragon continued screaming deeper into the mantle, reopening millennia-old lava pathways that coursed kilometers below the Earth's crust.

Malcolm was in a cacophonous cocoon; harsh rumblings and grindings of material that was not meant to be moved rolled across Volcanor's surprisingly impenetrable skin as they traveled deeper and deeper. He felt Volcanor maneuver into a forty-five-degree angle, taking a new vector toward what Malcolm hoped was the lair of Fuzanglong, the dragon of hidden treasures. Mere seconds after the directional change, the rumbling and grinding subsided and dragon wings parted to allow foul-smelling, metallic air to assault Malcolm's lungs.

After spluttering and coughing for the first few seconds, he reformed his respiratory system by channeling his novice grip on astromancy to handle this level of atmospheric pressure and the harmful chemicals which laced the air like a thick, wet blanket. His eyes burned initially as well, but that was also quickly fixed once he could breathe.

Volcanor planted his gargantuan feet on the lower mantle floor, shaking its entire body to dispel any chunks of rock still stuck between the cracks of its thick hide. Malcolm was so in awe of what he was seeing that he was almost thrown off Volcanor's back along with the debris. With a firm grip on a crusty protrusion on his dragon's spine, the sorcerer looked straight ahead to see the sleeping form of another dragon that easily dwarfed Volcanor tenfold. Once the wyvern settled down and cleared off pieces of the Earth's mantle, Malcolm slid off and took a few steps forward, marveling at what was in front of him.

In the far distance was a lava waterfall, viscously cascading down into a cavern that was visually blocked by Fuzanglong's mountain-like body. Volcanor's raucous entry into its secret lair hadn't stirred the other dragon in the slightest. The fierce majesty of the slumbering dragon mesmerized Malcolm as he looked upon one of the oldest dragons to ever roam the Earth, revealed in the folklore of nearly every culture in human history.

Aside from the massive size difference, there were many features that Fuzanglong didn't share with Volcanor. Malcolm could not see any wings on the larger dragon as he traced its serpentine body with his eyes. Its scales displayed intricate patterns, bringing to the surface several stunning colors between yellow and dark maroon. The only reason he could pick out all the colors this deep down inside the Earth was the backlit lavafall and the shimmering radiance that reflected off the limitless treasure troves around it.

There it is! There is your bauble . . .

Malcolm's eyes were drawn to the opalescent crystal cradled in one of Fuzanglong's large, scaly claws. It seemed to radiate power. Smoother than he was expecting, the gorgeous crystal glowed yellow-gold with ribbons of more orange hues than red. Every so often, Fuzanglong's whisker-like tendrils on his snout slid over the AniCrystal's smooth surface as if it were protecting an offspring.

Malcolm salivated with anticipation. None had been this close to the AniCrystal since Lord Ferox held claim over it during the Great Battle.

Take what is yours . . .

You were destined to make it yours!

Malcolm looked behind him and saw Volcanor giving off submissive body language, showing almost instinctual deference to the immortal dragon in their midst. That surprised Malcolm—he had never seen Volcanor bow down to any creature, man or otherwise. He stopped to think about his next move, fighting the urge to just run up and swipe the AniCrystal before Fuzanglong stirred awake.

You must entice Fuzanglong, for he shall give up his prize to no one.

Malcolm rolled his eyes. Even though he relished having the power and assistance of the ShadowCrystal, there were times like this when he didn't appreciate its penchant for vague advice and cryptic riddles. Standing up straighter, Malcolm fell into a surface-level meditation. He clenched his fists so that his muscles pressed up against the ShadowCrystal in his gauntlet, helping him tap into telemancy. Malcolm lightly touched its mind, trying his best not to awaken the sleeping dragon. He was shocked at just how much knowledge it seemed to hold; he fought the urge to dig deeper—there would come a time when he would learn the secrets of the eleven known realms, but now was not the time. What he needed was to be able to get Fuzanglong on his side.

Malcolm's eyes didn't break away from the dragon. He watched its body roll as if sloughing off water as it woke. Finally, its eyes fluttered open, large orbs that reminded Malcolm of the most strikingly crystal-blue waters of the Mediterranean Sea. A harsh contrast to its fiery scales. Its pupils contracted to slits as it went rigid, clearly not expecting anyone else to be in its lair. Its deep, grisly, masculine voice boomed throughout the cavern, but its mouth did not move.

Who dares enter my domain?

Malcolm immediately sensed defensiveness and the budding of hostility in Fuzanglong's demeanor, so much so that he commanded Volcanor to bow in the hopes that seeing the respect of a distant draconic relative would lower his guard. At first, Volcanor shrank back, bringing a hellish wing up to protect its face from any sudden retribution, but Malcolm prodded further, edging the weak-minded wyvern dragon to finally submit. His winged servant slowly plodded forward, eventually stopping and dipping its head in a deep bow, its wings tucked into its body and hind legs in a kneeling posture. Malcolm lifted his chin, admiring the control he had over Volcanor, once the largest and fiercest dragon in all the realms. Now, it looked like a chew toy compared to Fuzanglong.

The devilish whispers of the ShadowCrystal rose in Malcolm's mind and he quickly silenced them as he brought a hand to cover his gauntlet. He would handle this uninterrupted.

Volcanor was helping his cause, though. Fuzanglong's whiskers twitched and his pupils dilated into a more friendly set of ovals.

Do you know who I am? I am Fuzanglong, the dragon of hidden treasures, knowledge, and prosperity.

Malcolm went onto one knee. *I am aware, Great One. I come with a gift,* he responded through their mind-meld as the dragon, intrigued, looked back at him after quickly making sure that nothing was missing from its boundless treasure trove.

Bring it forth. Fuzanglong tucked the AniCrystal under its belly.

Malcolm caught himself before he showed any disappointment, walking up to present one of his ring totems.

Hmmm, mumbled the age-old dragon, letting one of its thick whiskers slide onto the ring and bring it closer to an eye. *Fascinating. Clearly hand-crafted by a master blacksmith. He chose the material wisely. Not of this Earth.*

The cherry-red ruby inlaid in Malcolm's ring glistened as Fuzanglong inspected it further. Clearly pleased with his new trinket, he propped it atop a large mound of chests that overflowed with gold pieces and jewelry. The Earth trembled as the dragon moved its head back to look down upon Malcolm.

Now what is it you want?

Malcolm didn't catch an inflection in the dragon's tone, almost making it seem like the dragon had been visited before by wanderers wanting his help.

"I merely come to gaze upon your vast collection, Fuzanglong. You are a legend of the surface world revered by many peoples."

Fuzanglong slightly tilted its head, now inspecting Malcolm

like he had done with the ring. *The human condition is to want. You all always ask for something. Usually it is for a piece of my fortune so you can live a life of means above, or wisdom and power to rule amongst your own inferior species.* The immortal dragon scoffed. *You humans cannot see the bigger picture . . . except for one.*

"One?" Malcolm couldn't help but be intrigued.

One human long ago who had a heart of purity. I cannot say the same of yours. Fuzanglong's tone turned dark as it dropped its face in a look of judgment.

Malcolm quelled the nasty retort the ShadowCrystal wanted him to spew forth. He needed to redirect . . . change the subject so Fuzanglong's guard would lower once again.

"I could not help but notice the mesmerizing crystal you hold in your claws."

Giant eyebrows furrowed in slight confusion as he pulled the AniCrystal out from under his body, revealing it entirely as his claws opened.

Why mention it?

There was the inflection of a question. Malcolm knew he was starting to pique Fuzanglong's interest. He waited a few minutes before answering, letting the cascading lava *bubble* and *pop* its way into the bottomless crevasse, eroding the rocky walls that were unlucky enough to be in its way.

"There are four more just like it, each with different colors just as brilliant as yours."

Malcolm waited.

Fuzanglong's tail thumped the mantle floor, shaking the piles of treasure and sending a few coins into a golden avalanche that harmlessly stopped when it trickled to his gargantuan body. *Impossible. If there were more, I would have found them.* His pupils slitted even deeper.

"I didn't mean to insult you, Fuzanglong," Malcolm quickly said, feeling the intense jealousy and lust from the dragon. "I know where the rest are . . . and I can take you to them."

Volcanor had not moved since it bowed. Malcolm swallowed as seconds turned into minutes. His mind was holding down the lid to the ShadowCrystal, but the infectious voices were getting stronger and he didn't know how much longer he could keep them silent. He gulped and bit his cheek.

And they will all be mine? was Fuzanglong's reply.

"Yes, Great One. But I must warn you of the evil that guards them."

Tell me.

Malcolm let one edge of his mouth slightly curl in satisfaction. Hook, line, and sinker.

CHAPTER THIRTY

Jen found herself back on the outer ring of the Richat Structure, this time with Victor and Charles at either side of her. After Jen had filled everyone in on her idea, Rez had decided to stay behind to tend to Hephalon and Silvress, as had Jocelyn, who had volunteered to also keep watch over the Smiths. Gavin and Mira, of course, had been adamant that they be a part of the group that would return to Atlantis, even though they would be in the same lane as Victor, unable to understand Atlantean like Jen or Charles, the only omnimancers of the group. Now they had one person guarding every direction if the Atlanteans decided to surprise them again. Skarmor, Pernissa, and Kuirhan waited securely in the center of their protective circle.

Jen had no intention of waking up locked in an Atlantean prison again—and anyway, she knew if they attacked they wouldn't be taking any prisoners, based on the queen's thinly veiled threat moments before Jen and her friends had been forcefully escorted from the last kingdom of Atlantis several days ago. She nervously repositioned her shoulder bag with one hand and rubbed her thumb over the smooth hilt of Prince M'balo's ceremonial dagger, almost as if awakening a genie so she could wish for an abundance of strength and luck when it was time to confront Queen P'tara.

I believe in you, she remembered M'balo saying as he had handed her the dagger. *You have a kind heart.*

The arid breeze was making Jen's face drier by the second and she could feel the unrelenting sun's rays cooking her exposed scalp where her dark hair parted. Setting her teeth, she pulled out the three MystiCrystals, now glowing, from her shoulder bag and held them in front of her. Sure enough, the ChronoCrystal went translucent in her grip, slowly followed by the TerraCrystal and finally the AstroCrystal. An exhilarating combination of energy flowed through her body as she held the three softly humming crystals.

She waited, hoping this time the Atlantean guards would choose a different way to welcome them into their kingdom. She looked left at Victor, then right at Charles, before saying to Mira and Gavin behind her, "You guys see anything?"

"Nope. Just a lot of dry, cracked dirt," was Gavin's cheeky reply.

Jen playfully rolled her eyes, sighing, then returned her focus on their surroundings. There were no signs that Atlantis even knew they were there; that alone made her more alert, because if she had learned anything from her first time here, Atlanteans were masters at concealment. She counted out ten heartbeats, waiting for something, but nothing happened. She dared a glance at Victor and shrugged, not sure of how else to get the attention of the Atlanteans. It wasn't like there was a doorbell.

After a few more minutes, Jen decided to place the MystiCrystals on the ground next to the small part of the outer ring she was standing near. Just as she stood back up, a mirage rippled a few meters in front of her and out stepped M'balo with two guards flanking him.

"Omnimancer Jennifer," he said. His tone was light, but with a hint of reticence. "I'm sorry for your wait. I had to convince my mother to let me greet you."

Great, Jen thought. Just by that, she knew it would be a battle talking to the queen.

Putting on a smile, she said in Atlantean, "M'balo, good to see you. We need your help more than ever. You remember my friends, Gavin and Mira"—she threw a thumb behind her, even though she knew that they couldn't understand Atlantean, then motioned to her sides—"and this is my uncle, Victor, and my father, Charles."

M'balo bowed, his guards as unmoving as statues. "It is a pleasure to meet Jennifer's relations." He stood straight again. "Please, follow me." He waved them on, and once Jen picked up the MystiCrystals and put them back into her shoulder bag, she and the others walked through the invisible barrier.

Jen involuntarily sucked in as cool air surrounded her. She smelled a hint of some type of flower that was extremely pleasant, and her skin thanked her the instant she stepped into the climate-controlled city and out of the harsh desert conditions.

Her eyes were drawn immediately to the Akt'aron at the center of the kingdom—the resting place of the TeleCrystal, a shining beacon even in the brightest of days. Jen remembered the queen telling her about how it was solely responsible for keeping Atlantis concealed from the outside world.

The guards, with their wary and alert demeanors, split up, one hovering behind M'balo and the other taking up the rear behind Jen and her group. She shrugged at Mira and Gavin, then caught Victor and Charles silently admiring the unique, gleaming architecture. As Jen followed M'balo across ornate bridges that brought them to the inner rings, pedestrian traffic was fairly manageable and organized, especially since vehicle traffic was relegated to the sky. About one hundred meters above their heads, lines of hover-cars and cycles silently *whooshed* past as city life continued its regular ebb and flow.

Jen wished she could take a step back and marvel at the wonders of this hidden city, but her thoughts were too encompassed with seeing Queen P'tara and how much she was dreading it. She cycled through several different scenarios of how it could go, all ending with them being kicked out again as the best-case scenario. While her heart was on the verge of breaking out of her chest, she prayed that they could come to a mutual understanding. Everything seemed to hang on this meeting going well.

Some Atlanteans acknowledged her and her group as they passed, but most averted their eyes or spoke in hushed tones, especially avoiding her group's griffins and equivol. Clearly the queen's influence regarding outsiders was felt throughout the city. Jen did appreciate that they were allowed to walk on their own this time; that floating slab she had been carried on during her first visit had not been comfortable in the slightest.

They made it to the ring where the royal palace stood, its grand steps constructed from a curious mix of marbled sandstone and finely polished opalescent crystal. M'balo explained that Skarmor, Pernissa, and Kuirhan were not allowed in the palace and would instead be escorted by his guards to the palace gardens. After calming their animals and relaying that information to Victor, Gavin, and Mira—Charles, understanding Atlantean as well due to his omnimancy powers, helped explain —Jen watched as the equivol and two griffins were led around the side of the palace, out of view.

Two new guards took the place of the old ones and, at the behest of M'balo, they crisply saluted, turned ninety degrees, and leaned their chrome spears on their shoulders to allow Jen and her group through. They took the same path to the queen's regal chambers as when Jen was escorted out a few days before. Every step closer brought her more anxiety and dread, but she did her best to keep it under control. She knew she wasn't the only one scared witless about what might happen, so she promised herself to put on a brave front.

Born or thrust. Her consciousness echoed her dad's saying, the one Richard Smith would remind her of whenever she was feeling overwhelmed while growing up. Jen knew she wasn't a natural-born leader, but certain instances—like this one—called for her to rise to the occasion. She reset her teeth and pushed all that negative energy out of her body just as the massive chamber doors opened for them. *Thank you, Dad.*

Instead of being perched atop her raised throne dais, the queen was at ground level next to her other son, Sh'tam, squabbling with her head military commander—Kl'to, Jen remembered.

M'balo seemed to be expecting this behavior, as he turned to her and said, "Please wait."

Jen halted and updated everyone as M'balo entered into the heated conversation. Based on their body language, Jen inferred that Kl'to and M'balo were on one side of the argument while the queen and Sh'tam were on the other.

Queen P'tara raised her arms, her bangles and bracelets jangling down her stick-thin forearms, and elevated her voice, stopping any further dialogue. Apparently the queen had had enough. She looked menacingly at Jen and pushed M'balo aside, striding straight at Jen. Her hands were clenched tightly around her scepter and her lips were as thin as humanly possible.

"What did I tell you if you ever returned, girl?!" the queen screamed rhetorically, then her eyes widened. "And you stole our sacred *pugio!*"

"Mother!" M'balo yelled. He started after her, but his twin brother, Sh'tam, restrained him.

Jen nervously looked over her person to figure out what the Queen was referring to, her eyes eventually landing on M'balo's dagger. She was about to say something when her heart rate skyrocketed as she saw the queen take two running steps and lance her scepter through the air as if it were a javelin. Surprised that a woman who seemed so frail could send a projectile through the air that fast, Jen felt her nexus take over, guiding her hand to the dagger at her side.

SHIIIIING!

With lightning speed, Jen brought it across her body just in time to deflect the scepter before it could impale her. It ricocheted harmlessly straight up into the air. By the time the scepter came back down, Charles easily snatched it.

That action elicited a reaction from the entire throne room. Several hidden guards melted out of the walls, others repelled down from the raised dais, quickly moving to block off the only entrance to the throne room. Several dozen guards encircled Jen and her group before she could even take a breath.

They were closing in on them when Charles spun the scepter around and planted it on the ground, cracking the marbled sandstone beneath. His eyes turned into bright yellow orbs.

There was a collective gasp as the ground started to shake and the sky, through the glass dome, turned a familiar violet hue, followed by the entire room.

The queen halted in pure terror. *"Ennosidas,"* she whispered.

The earthquake quickly subsided; it seemed as though Charles only wanted to show them a small display of his power, and it clearly worked.

Jen was in a fighting stance, left foot forward, bearing the dagger in a reverse grip. No one moved; the whole room wanted to see what the queen would do next. It was Charles who spoke first, once his eyes stopped glowing.

"Queen Pt'ara, I wish that we were meeting under different circumstances, but we have no time to spare." His tone was much gentler than the power he had just displayed. He lifted the royal scepter, holding it horizontal as he took two steps forward. Jen could hear the soft clinking and sliding of the guards' chrome armor as they tensed in response to Charles's movement, but they paused when her father did the same. He then knelt and extended the scepter back to its rightful owner. "I am Charles Lancaster, father of Jennifer Lancaster and fellow omnimancer."

The queen still had an awestruck, terrified look on her face. Her hands shook as she smoothed out her regal gown and stepped forward, quickly snatching her scepter back and slamming its point in the ground. She seemed to be nonplussed when her attempt didn't break the ground underneath, and so with a scowl she twirled it under her right armpit, holding it at a downward angle with her right hand.

"I see the girl couldn't get her way so she brought back her daddy."

Queen Pt'ara's demeaning tone only augmented Jen's anxiety,

causing her hands to slightly shake. She flexed her grip on the dagger and took a calming breath.

"You think calling upon powers akin to Poseidon will cause us to bow down to you and relinquish our sacred Akt'aron?" the queen spat, referencing Charles's display from moments before.

Charles slowly stood back up. Jen started to move closer to him, but he flicked his hand out to his side, stopping her from getting any closer. It seemed he wanted to handle this alone.

Charles answered the queen's question with a question of his own: "Do you want to be the last ruler of Atlantis?"

Queen Pt'ara's posture went rigid. "Of course not! I wouldn't let that happen. I'd take down anyone who threatened this great city." She pointed the top of her scepter first at Charles, then at every other member of his group behind him, the wrinkles around her eyes deepening as she tightened her focus back on the omnimancer.

"Then you must put your prejudices aside and listen to us," Charles said.

"Are you threatening me, omnimancer?" the queen said, lacing her tone with frigid malice.

"It is not I who seeks to destroy Atlantis. My friends and I want to be your allies, and that is why we are here to warn you."

"You are bold, omnimancer . . . *too* bold."

"It's Charles, Queen Pt'ara. If we are to be friends, we must speak amicably to each other."

Clearly not used to being spoken to in this way, the queen scoffed and marched to Charles, stopping inches from his face. Her ornate footwear added several inches to her natural height, making her as tall as him.

The pervading silence rang in Jen's ears. Her muscles were getting sore as she maintained her fighting stance, but she dared not move and risk startling some easily excitable guard. She looked at M'balo, no longer being held by his brother. His body was rigid as though undergoing an internal fight to stay silent or speak up. His eyes darted between Jen and his mother before closing. He dropped his chin to his chest, seemingly defeated. Jen's heart dropped. She stole a glance at Victor at her right. He wore the same crestfallen look.

No, this is not how it will go down, Jen vowed. She had to do something. She—

"Mother, *stop.*" M'balo had slipped from his brother's second attempt at grabbing him and quickly ran to the queen's side. "Can't you see that they desperately need our help?"

Queen Pt'ara broke her long stare at Charles and whipped around to face her son. "I have had it with your unfounded sympathies toward these outsiders! They cannot be trusted, especially after they stole our ceremonial dagger." She pointed a sickly thin finger at the dagger Jen still held in a defensive stance.

M'balo took his mother's wrists and leaned into his next words: "I *gave* it to Jennifer, Mother. The day you banished them from our city."

The queen gasped, taken aback. "How dare you take something so sacred outside of our walls! I—"

M'balo cut her off. "And nothing bad happened to us, or to our *pugio.* Whoever keeps the dagger safe is worthy of our trust. If you do not believe me, remember the old texts. Mother, please."

Jen let her arms fall to her side—*finally*—and watched as the queen looked back at her, still allowing her son to hold on to her wrists.

"The old texts . . . are beyond refute . . ." A rare softness played across her face, and Jen could glimpse the woman she once might have been. But it was for only a second as the jaded bitterness returned with a vengeance. ". . . but are subject to interpretation." She broke free from her son's grasp and pointed at Jen and her group. "You still require the Akt'aron, which will make us visible and vulnerable to the unclean world from where you hail, essentially sentencing us to our ultimate demise."

"But that's just it," Jen finally spoke. "You don't have to sacrifice your existence. You will be able to remain hidden and safe even after you allow us to take the Akt'aron."

The queen furrowed her brow at Jen, her head slightly cocked to one side in confusion . . . or was it curiosity? She waved off her legion of warriors and they stood at ease. "What are you proposing?"

Jen walked over to stand next to Charles; he didn't stop her this time. "My father and I will do what our ancestors had done to our very own sacred place that we call Camelore. We will raise your kingdom into the sky."

* * *

Jen knew that the odds were against them, but these were desperate times. Camelore had been raised by the combined powers of the First Five, the original omnimancer clans, over fifteen hundred years ago. Now, the only omnimancer outside of Jen—if you could call her one since she hadn't yet completed her training in all five Mancy planes—was Charles, and he was still recovering from years of atrophying in the Dark Watchers stronghold, Feralot. But all that wouldn't matter if she couldn't come to an agreement with the queen of Atlantis to obtain the TeleCrystal. Jen knew that Malcolm would not bat an eye at leveling Atlantis in order to get it for himself. There was just no other way, and somehow Jen had to make Queen Pt'ara see that inevitability. And she thought she had figured it out, since her idea of raising Atlantis would not only keep the city hidden, but it would also not require the queen to keep the TeleCrystal.

Jen was wrong.

The queen barked with laughter. "You want to raise *my* Atlantis into the sky?" She quickly dismissed what she thought was a hilarious idea with the brush of her hand before taking on a belligerent tone. "You are the first person, Jennifer, to waste my time twice and still live."

She turned around and started to walk back toward her two sons when Jen yelled, "Queen Pt'ara, is this the proof you need?!"

Jen produced from deep within her shoulder bag the three MystiCrystals: the ChronoCrystal, TerraCrystal, and AstroCrystal. Now that they were free, they began levitating a few inches above her palms, the tips of their bodies pointing toward the Akt'aron and the TeleCrystal inside.

The queen slowly turned around, jaw clenched and wrinkles starker than ever before, but still she said nothing as the Mysti-Crystals floated higher, rotating around each other. Jen wished she had jumped and caught them, because now they were too high up and were only increasing their speed. Much like how Victor had entered her college apartment the night of her twenty-first birthday, the crystals flew through the glass dome of the throne room, making their way to the TeleCrystal. A faint light emanated from the top of the Akt'aron and the electromagnetic energy changed in an instant—not by much, but Jen could tell; she felt her terramancy silently awaken inside her nexus. The forcefield-like barrier with which the TeleCrystal protected Atlantis changed from a violet tone to a more normal, clear one.

Jen looked back at the queen and took a step forward, which caused the Atlantean guards to draw their weapons. Charles grabbed her wrist with the right mix of firmness and gentleness. She looked back and saw him slowly shake his head. Jen bounced her gaze from him to Victor, then to her friends, Mira and Gavin. They were all tense as if they could also understand Atlantean, acutely aware of countless weapons trained in their direction.

Gritting her teeth, Jen relaxed and looked back at Queen Pt'ara, who said, "Another cheap parlor trick you wizards enjoy so much." The queen turned back around, giving her the cold shoulder.

"We're *sorcerers* . . . there's a difference," Jen bit out quietly.

The queen didn't hear her; otherwise, she would not have let that kind of insolence go unpunished. She stopped by M'balo and Sh'tam and stroked M'balo's face, tracing her long, witchy fingers across his chin. "The most appalling thing you've done, Jennifer, is corrupting my sweet boy with your lies and propaganda." Sh'tam put on a wicked, smug grin at his twin brother being called out by their mother. "I should have you beheaded. I—"

M'balo grabbed her forearm, muting a few bangles as they got caught between his fingers. His eyes conveyed his hurt, so much hurt after searching for validation and respect for so long. "Mother, I can make up my own mind. How can you still see me as an infant?" Shaking his head, he let go of his mother's arm and walked over to stand beside Jen. He pointed at the center of the city to where the MystiCrytals flew and said, "What more proof do you need?"

Jen's headache-inducing frustration was quelled by M'balo's presence and his timely courage; she couldn't imagine how difficult it must be to stand up to this person who had raised him, shown him the way, and into whom he had put so much trust and respect. But sometimes you have to stand up for what you know is right, and Jen knew that M'balo wasn't as myopic and opinionated as his mother and, seemingly, his twin brother; M'balo was a visionary, and he understood the risks that were necessary so progress could be made.

Kl'to, the stoic military commander that he was, had been silent this entire time. He nodded once at M'balo and looked back at his queen, seeming to respect M'balo's stance but still honoring his devotion to the reigning queen.

Queen Pt'ara herself was silent as well. It was like M'balo had ripped out her vocal cords. Her lips quivered, but nothing came out. No retort, no backhanded response or dismissive comment, just silence. A lone tear trickled down her gold-flecked cheek.

Jen wished she felt bad for the queen, but her behavior and hospitality were sorely lacking in every regard, and Jen hadn't seen any redeeming qualities to make her feel that pang of sorrow. So she set her teeth and held M'balo's hand. He flinched ever so slightly at his first contact with her, but quickly recovered and kept his fingers interlocked with hers, squeezing her hand as he gave her a closed-mouth smile. His eyes told of the years of hurt, yes, but there was a resilience that had been born from that. Jen smiled back, tucking a loose strand of hair behind her ear. She looked back at the queen with a defiance she would have been missing if it weren't for M'balo.

Queen Pt'ara took a deep breath in preparation for what Jen could only guess would be the verbal lashing of a century, but just before she could assault the room with her shrill voice, a jolt traveled through the city, one so ferocious and sudden that everyone fought to keep upright. The throne room's glass dome cracked, creating small fissures that started to propagate and weaken its integrity. Luck seemed to be the only thing keeping the entire ceiling from raining down on them . . . as long as—

Another jolt—this time of much greater magnitude—was the dome's swan song. Shards of every size splintered from the once-ornate skylight ceiling, falling with a deadly grace toward everyone in the throne room. Countless pieces shimmered in the reflective light like diamonds as they cascaded downward in a waterfall of momentary death.

Jen and M'balo were the only people still upright, probably due to them holding onto each other, but losing their balance was the least of Jen's worries. Two jaw-droppingly large shards were falling directly at Jen and her group, another at Queen Pt'ara and Sh'tam, who were huddled together.

Jen didn't think; instead, she let her nexus take over and, in an instant, letting go of M'balo's hand, she conjured a torrent of air that blew him and her entire group outside of the throne room and into the hall, safe from their impending doom. In less than a blink of an eye, Jen effortlessly switched directions and flowed into animancy, launching herself toward the two remaining royals in the room with the speed of a greyhound. She wrapped them up in her arms and swept them away just as a huge part of the glass ceiling crashed in their wake. They all slid into the foremost dais wall as pebbles of glass bounced around them.

In the longest second of her life, the immediate threat was over. Out of breath, Jen propped herself up along the wall as Kl'to rushed over, sliding his shield, which was similar to an ancient Roman legionary scutum, onto his armored backplate.

"*Mah Roi'ta*, are you all right?" he said, kneeling down next to his queen and checking for any serious injuries.

The queen was still holding on to her son but looked straight at Jen. In a trancelike tone, she finally said, "Yes . . . I am fine." Not breaking eye contact with Jen, she picked herself and Sh'tam up just as M'balo rushed over, wrapping both her and his twin brother in a hug.

A small group of guards rushed up to Kl'to, asking for orders, as there came muffled screams and shouts from Atlantean citizens outside. A throbbing hum had grown in frequency, pervading Jen's hearing. To her, it sounded like the revving of a truck caught in a muddy ditch, stressed and overheating. Jen could see that Kl'to heard it, too, and he didn't look pleased.

"Get to ground level as fast as you can and raise the klaxons," he ordered his guards. "Man your defensive stations along the outer wall and wait for my signal." As they shuffled off, Kl'to lowered his chin and pressed the center of his chest. His chrome armor's colored outlines of light pulsated as he repeated the order to, Jen surmised, his other warriors who were spread across the city.

"The Akt'aron," M'balo said, diverting Jen's focus from Kl'to. He had finished checking on his family and was staring up toward the now-open dome.

"Why is it making that noise?" Jen asked. She took a step closer and accidentally brushed his bare shoulder with hers.

M'balo did not break his gaze from the sky, staring in both terror and confusion. He answered, "I-I'm not sure . . . I've never seen it act like this. But it is straining. It is protecting us from something that wants to get in, and badly."

Jen's instincts were telling her that this was somehow Malcolm's doing, but she had no answer as to how he had found this city, one that was supposed to be invisible to the rest of the world, and was able to shake all of Atlantis as if it were a snow globe. She looked down and saw Kl'to several meters away, tending to a wounded guard near a pillar next to the far wall. Jen's heart dropped, hoping that the guard's injuries weren't grave. She should have helped him as well, but her self-pity was forgotten as she was suddenly tugged backward.

Spinning around, she was met with the ashen face of the queen. Jen could tell that she was fighting to stay conscious, the sudden chain of events clearly taking a toll on her system.

"Mother," M'balo began, but was stopped by the wave of his mother's free hand.

The queen asked quite pointedly, "Why did you save me and my son?"

The question came out gruff and loud, startling Jen at first, but she composed herself as best as possible and shrugged, replying, "You were going to die. I couldn't let that happen."

Queen Pt'ara swallowed and let go of Jen's arm. The bangles on her arms were clinking and clacking in her agitation. "Even when I was so . . . so . . ." She put a hand over her mouth as she trailed off, almost like her body was stopping her from actually admitting any kind of fault.

Jen cocked her head and glanced at M'balo, biting the inside of her cheek to stop herself from smiling. If this was the closest she would get to an apology, she would happily take it. Jen could see the realization forming in the queen's eyes. Jen wondered if she had finally convinced her that she and her friends were here to help.

"We must get to the Akt'aron. We will be the safest there," the queen said, loud enough for both her sons to hear.

"Queen Pt'ara, this is the evil I have been warning you about," Jen said. "Atlantis is lost if you don't trust me. I can take the evil away."

The queen was about to bark an order to Kl'to but held her tongue and looked back at Jen. She stroked her scepter, biting her lip. Jen could tell she knew that time was running out and she had to make a decision one way or another.

"You saved my life without hesitation. Do you promise to do the same for my people?" The queen's eyes regained their hardness, but there was also a flicker of a plea, of the needing of a miracle.

"Yes. On my life," Jen replied.

The queen nodded. "Do what you must, and take this." She handed Jen her scepter. "No one will stop you with this in your hand."

With a whirlwind of thoughts in her head, Jen reflexively took what was given to her and nodded in return. "Keep safe," she said as she clipped toward the hallway. A few strides in she noticed that M'balo was following. "What are you doing?"

"I'm going with you," M'balo said.

"You should stay with your family."

"They are more than capable of running and hiding. It is what they do best. Me, I've never been good at that." He gave her a smile that exhilarated her.

"Okay," Jen said, adrenaline coursing through her veins like a torrential rapid. "Can you get me to my griffin?" she asked while handing him his dagger back.

"Yes, certainly. And thank you." M'balo slid it into his sash.

They had made it to the doorway just as the last of the palace guards were clearing out. Jen could see the heads of Victor and Gavin bobbing over the sea of helmets, clearly having no luck at getting back inside the throne room. They looked relieved when Jen came through the doorway to meet them.

"Jenny, thank God you're all right," Victor said as he quickly wrapped her in a hug, stopping her momentum.

"Nice save, thank you," Gavin chimed in, resting a hand on her shoulder. He winked at her while Mira nodded in agreement.

"That was some quick thinking, Jen," Charles said, hugging her. "Thank you."

Jen didn't want to be impolite, but time was not on their side. "Of course, there was no way I was going to let you all get squished. Come on, let's walk and talk." She pointed the queen's scepter down the hallway, which led to more stairs and eventually out into the palace square. "Do you hear that noise?" she asked everyone. "M'balo told me it's coming from the Akt'aron—the TeleCrystal. It's trying to keep the protective barrier up from something trying to get inside. And that something has to be—"

Mira quickened her pace to match strides with Jen. "Malcolm," she said solemnly, her eyes already steeled for the inevitable confrontation.

Jen nodded in agreement as she approached the stairs and fluidly flew down them. "I've gathered that something like this has never happened before, which is one of the reasons why the queen has agreed to our plan."

Victor was shocked. "She's actually allowing us to raise Atlantis and take the TeleCrystal?"

"Yep. I'll explain why later, but right now M'balo is taking us to Skarmor and the rest so we can reach the MystiCrystals quickly."

They finally exited the palace, Jen's eyes adjusting to the bright afternoon sun. The sky was a peaceful blue, something completely different from the streets of Atlantis. She skidded to a halt as another rumble seemed to split the ground asunder. People ran in all directions. Several guards were trying their best to organize the hysteria and direct their citizens to shelter. Off to her right, just outside of the city's outermost ring, was a plume of ember-flecked smoke billowing skyward.

"Jen." Charles put a hand on her shoulder. "We should raise Atlantis first. If we take the TeleCrystal from its perch, I fear the protective barrier will vanish and leave us completely vulnerable to Malcolm's wrath." He pointed at the dense plumes of smoke erupting all around Atlantis's perimeter.

"You're right," Jen agreed, tearing her eyes from the inferno outside to look at her father. She kicked herself for not realizing that potential consequence.

M'balo beckoned to the left. "Come, your animals are this way!"

"We're following M'balo!" Jen told everyone as she gripped the scepter tighter, sprinting to catch up to the Atlantean prince.

Thankfully the palace garden was not too far away, though they had to zig-zag through some hedges and massive topiaries just to get to the clearing that held Skarmor, Pernissa, and Kuirhan.

"Skar!" Jen shouted, running up to him. He was clearly agitated from the surrounding chaos, and she did her best to calm him while Victor and Mira did the same to Kuirhan and Pernissa respectively.

Just as she hopped on his back, the sky went dark.

An icy chill traveled down her spine as she looked up to see the sun being blocked by a dragon so large she thought the sky had split in two. Its serpentine body coiled and twisted like a banner kite caught in the wind as it flew over the entire city in what seemed like a second.

Gavin cursed. "What the hell is that?!"

Jen looked at Victor and Charles for reassurance, though she had a gut feeling about what Malcolm had brought with him.

"Fuzanglong . . ."

CHAPTER THIRTY-ONE

"I cannot believe my eyes!" Grand Mystra Cindergray exclaimed at the sight of Jocelyn Lancaster.

He thought Draconex had taken care of her for good . . .

He got off of his pegasus, Soter, once it settled on the soft grass of Camelore. The chronomancer had used his powers to rewind time, healing its injuries and reviving Soter.

"Grand Mystra," Jocelyn said as she hugged him. "How did you know I was here?"

He put on a caring smile. "Victor told me, and I had to come as soon as possible," he said, putting a large hand on the back of her head as she rested it on his chest. He surveyed the hut compound, slowly tracing his eyesight along the destruction that lay before him. A couple of huts had been cursorily rebuilt with torn sheets to act as makeshift doors.

Jocelyn pulled away and he continued, "Imagine my surprise when I learned that you were still alive." He looked deep into her eyes. "How are you doing, my dear?"

The woman sighed. "We really haven't had a chance to breathe since I made my escape," Jocelyn said. She wrapped her arms around herself.

"I can only imagine what you've been through, Jocelyn." He kept a hand on her shoulder.

Jocelyn bit her bottom lip and squinted off into the distance. She cleared her throat. "To be honest, I'm still having a hard time breathing, what with Charles and Jennifer still out there."

Cindergray didn't show his surprise. He rubbed his thumb on her shoulder and said in a concerned tone, "Oh, they're not here? What about Victor?"

"He joined them. They're probably already at Atlantis now." Jocelyn motioned behind her at the closest hut that was still standing. "I volunteered to stay behind with Hephalon and his son."

Cindergray's heart rate nearly doubled after hearing that Jennifer and her relatives had found the lost city of Atlantis, but his outward appearance showed no signs of his shock. "So Atlantis holds one of the MystiCrystals . . ." he said, more to himself than to Jocelyn.

"Yes, the TeleCrystal. Apparently the last surviving kingdom of Atlantis is actually the Richat Structure in Mauritania."

Cindergray hummed in acknowledgment as he stroked his mustache with his other hand.

Jocelyn added, "Amazingly, my Jenny was able to acquire both the AstroCrystal and TerraCrystal in the meantime." A proud smile was etched on her statuesque face.

Cindergray fought to keep his hand on Jocelyn's shoulder and not clasp her throat and squeeze. *He* should be the one lauded, since it was he who, in the shadows, had pulled the necessary strings so this momentous occasion could even occur. The fire in his eyes began to simmer as he remembered that finding the Halostone was what truly mattered, not who would be remembered as its discoverer. After all these years—*hundreds* of years—all five MystiCrystals were about to come together.

And he needed to be there when they did. He'd sacrificed too much.

"Grand Mystra?" Jocelyn's quizzical look brought him out of his thoughts.

His gaze didn't falter, he didn't even blink. "Yes, that is quite fantastic." He put on a smile again, retracting his hand, which was starting to tremble from the exhaustion of keeping his rage and anticipation under control. Cindergray was still astounded that Jen had been able to collect three, soon to be four, MystiCrystals. But how? Someone had to have deciphered Merlin's journal, which meant that someone was the Light Bringer.

A cold shiver ran down his spine as that revelation dawned on him.

"Grand Mystra, would you like to sit down with Rez and I? We were just about to put up some tea while we tend to Hephalon. I'm sure he'd appreciate your presence." She smiled.

Cindergray took a step back and slightly bowed. "No, I must lend my abilities to helping Jennifer complete her quest. Can you give Mystra Hephalon my regards, Diae—*dearest* Jocelyn?"

A few thumping heartbeats passed before Jocelyn said, "Of course." She returned his bow, albeit stiffly, but still had that gentle smile on her face.

Cindergray turned around and mounted Soter with the ease of a much younger man. The beautiful pegasus shook its mane and stretched its wings as it got up off the ground.

"You'll be safe here," he said as Soter took flight. He waved at Jocelyn as she shrunk in sight. She didn't return the wave; Jocelyn just stood there for several seconds before rigidly walking back to the hut where, he assumed, Hephalon and Resolved were staying.

Cindergray berated himself, realizing that he had probably tipped Jocelyn off on his true involvement in the war by nearly saying the name Draconex had bequeathed her before catching himself.

But it didn't matter. The MystiCrystals were about to be joined, and the only thing that mattered was getting his mother back.

CHAPTER THIRTY-TWO

Skarmor carried Jen to the base of the Akt'aron, the only structure in the entire city that was taller than the royal palace, located in Atlantis's central disc—a quick jump from the palace gardens in the first ring. The Atlanteans' holy temple loomed in front of her, its foundation set in sandy-beige marble with blue streaks inlaid in it like rivers cutting through a desert. As her gaze traveled up the temple, it transitioned smoothly into a beautiful crystal façade, one that shimmered in the daylight as it corkscrewed toward the sky, reminding Jen of a large spiral lollipop.

She dismounted her griffin as several temple guards ran up, their weapons at the ready. When they saw Jen holding the queen's scepter and that she was with one of the princes, they saluted and ran off to their battle posts after M'balo gave them their orders.

Jen caught herself smiling, amidst all this danger and chaos, at the prince before her. For the life of her, she couldn't understand why he was so trusting of her, and more importantly, why she was drawn to his presence. It was like M'balo could read her heart and showed the qualities Jen desired over anything else.

A small earthquake quieted Jen's inner monologue and made her aware that M'balo was staring at her expectantly. She blushed and said, "Good work." She gave him an awkward thumbs-up and he returned the gesture back, slower than usual, which made her think he'd never given a thumbs-up before. She chuckled and felt her cheeks begin to warm. To allay this newfound embarrassment, she looked up and saw that all air traffic had been grounded . . . and for good reason.

Jen could make out her three MystiCrystals orbiting the Tele-Crystal atop the Akt'aron. Fuzanglong made another strafing run, zipping across the sky as its staticky neon-green orbs of energy deflected off the telemancy shield, creating massive craters in the surrounding desert, but they were felt just as forcefully on the inside.

Interesting, Jen thought. *Fuzanglong doesn't breathe fire.*

Feeling sick to her stomach, she ran to Charles, who was still on Kuirhan. "It can't be safe to raise Atlantis any longer, not with Fuzanglong controlling the skies, right?"

Charles stayed on Kuirhan's back, looking up at the Mysti-Crystals. "We're still able to lift Atlantis in the air before we remove the TeleCrystal and the other crystals, so it can keep its shield up, but as long as Fuzanglong can track us, we'll be more vulnerable in the air than here on the ground. The sky is his domain. Either way, Atlantis can't last much longer." He looked the Akt'aron up and down, no doubt internally thinking through this problem.

Jen scanned the area too. Her eyes widened when she noticed the closest bridge behind them, the one they would have taken had they not ridden their winged creatures.

"I have an idea!"

She didn't wait for Charles to slide off Kuirhan to run onto the bridge. Gorgeous columns topped with opalescent orbs lined both sides of the bridge, as well as the other four that were spaced out around the central disc, giving passage back to the first ring. Jen picked the closest column and jumped. She activated terramancy to propel her high into the air with a few air blasts. When she was at the apex of her jump, her hand took on the composition of resilient diamonds, and she executed a quick inward knife-hand strike to break off the head-sized orb from its base atop the column. With the orb safely grasped in both hands, she softly dropped back onto the bridge. By then, Charles was waiting for her, holding Kuirhan's reins.

"This should do," Jen said with a smirk, turning the orb in her hands like a basketball. Surprisingly, it wasn't terribly heavy.

Charles had a confused look on his face, mouth slightly open and eyes bouncing from Jen to where the orb had once rested. She could see the rest of their group catching up. "What does this"—Charles finally said, pointing to the orb—"have to do with keeping Atlantis safe?"

Jen smiled as she continued to roll the orb between her hands. "We're going to employ a bit of deception." She waited for everyone else to arrive before continuing. "Do you all remember what Rez said about Fuzanglong, back on Camelore when we cracked Merlin's AniCrystal riddle?" She held the orb out in front of her, displaying it to everyone.

Another blast rocked the city's foundation as the bridge they were on began to crack. The water below churned and sprayed like the moon was pulling it in every direction.

"Jenny, can we speed this up?" Victor asked, nervously tapping his buckle totem.

"Right, sorry," Jen said, tucking the orb under an arm. "Rez said that Fuzanglong and the other dragons that settled in Asia desired power—power that came in the form of flaming pearls. So, I figured we light this orb up and send it as far away from here as possible so we can raise Atlantis and leave with all four of the MystiCrystals before Fuzanglong realizes it's not a pearl of wisdom at all."

Jen looked at everyone present as she waited to hear from someone.

"That's the best shot we have," Gavin chimed in. "I say we take it."

Jen nodded. "I'll light it and use terramancy to rocket it away from here. Just tell me which direction and—"

"Jen, you've seen how fast that thing is." Gavin pointed up into the sky. "It'll track down the orb in seconds. Then, when it finds out that it's been duped, it'll come straight back here with a deeper vengeance. No," he declared, "I'll take it and give Fuzanglong the chase of his life."

Gavin versus the biggest dragon Jen had ever seen? His determination caught her off guard and she had to process what that meant.

Mira, on the other hand, wasn't shy in voicing her feelings. "Gav, please." She grabbed his arms and shook her head furiously. "I can't lose you!"

Gavin took her trembling hands, kissed them, then wrapped her in a hug. "Don't you worry about me, babe. I can take care of myself."

"You know that's impossible—I always worry about you." Mira's voice was muffled in his chest.

He pulled away and wiped streaks of tears from Mira's cheeks. "There's just no other way for our plan to work."

Gavin looked over at Jen and this time she didn't stop herself from crying either. She knew that Gavin was right: Fuzanglong needed to be occupied long enough for her and her father to raise Atlantis in the sky and leave with the MystiCrystals, taking them away so the city was no longer in jeopardy.

She walked up and hugged him as well. He wrapped one strong arm around her tightly and gave her a single squeeze before letting her step back.

"I'll link us through telemancy so we know you're okay when we start this whole shebang."

Gavin nodded and flashed his trademark smirk. "We got this."

"I'll show you the fastest way out of the city," M'balo said from behind Jen.

"Thank you," she said.

Victor brushed past her with the orb. He had an air of solemnity as he walked up to the astromancer. Just then, Jen remembered how close Victor and Gavin were. Victor had been the one to save Gavin from Draconex in the Pit all those years ago and take him under his wing as he grew into not only a strong astromancer, but also an important member of the League of Light. Out of everyone here, Victor knew him the best, and as Jen watched him hand Gavin the orb, it was like Victor was also giving him his blessing to wear the rank of mystra.

Victor said something to Gavin, too quiet for Jen to hear, then hugged him and stepped away just as Gavin swung his legs back onto Pernissa. He cast a spell, putting a thin outer shell of alkali metal around the orb, which allowed him to levitate it. Victor conjured a small flame and whipped it at the orb, where it immediately spread to cover the entire surface area. Under the semi-translucent yellow-orange flames, Jen had to admit, the orb did pass for a very large pearl. She hoped Fuzanglong would take the bait.

M'balo quickly turned to Jen and said, "Even though it was brief, it was an honor standing by your side and helping you, Omnimancer Jennifer." He bowed the same way he had when he gave her his dagger—it felt so long yet was just a few days ago.

Jen chuckled. "You can call me Jen." She returned his bow. "And this won't be the last time we see each other, I think." She smiled at him as he started toward Gavin, flashing one of his own before he took a seat behind Gavin on the female griffin.

Skarmor chirped softly, making Jen feel his worry and concern, as Pernissa faced the same dangerous mission as Gavin and M'balo. Jen stroked his neck—the only actual thing she could do to help him feel better—as she watched Pernissa take flight. Jen led Skarmor over to Mira as Pernissa flapped her mighty wings, soaring in the opposite direction of the palace and leaving Jen to hope and pray that nothing horrible would happen to her friends. She gave Mira a side hug and rested her head in the crook of her neck. Jen could feel minuscule spasms as Mira continued to cry, though not as hard as before.

Jen knew that the city's klaxon bells had been steadily ringing since she had left the palace, but for some reason her senses were only now becoming acutely aware of them, almost as if they were reminding her of the urgency of her plan.

She picked her head up and stepped back so that she could see the last three remaining sorcerers of her group. "Time to get Atlantis airborne."

* * *

It took Jen a fair bit of focus and a lot of determination to replicate the feeling she got when Rez had opened up a channel to all of their minds. Out of all the Mancy planes, she wasn't too surprised that telemancy came the easiest to her, since Jocelyn, her mother, was a natural-born telemancer. Something she was extremely thankful for, because having the ability to communicate when every move needed to happen at precise moments was paramount.

To Jen's surprise, the Akt'aron was hollow on the inside, a vertical tunnel. As she made her way toward its center, Jen felt like she was entering the eye of a cyclone, the glow of the Tele-Crystal far above her acting as its eye. The structure's perfect blending of marble and crystal was a feat rivaling some of the greatest sculptors of the Renaissance era. She could see why this temple was the main focal point of Atlantis and not the royal palace. Objectively, its beauty was unmatched.

Jen wasn't paying attention to where she was stepping and before she knew it, she was on the ground, rubbing an elbow that took the brunt of her fall. "Ouch," she moaned, realizing that the toe of her boot had caught a small but firm root that was protruding from a crack in the marbled floor. Quizzically, she got up and then knelt to get a better look at the root. She could actually see it snaking, *moving*, through the opening and emerging more and more out of the crack.

"Uh, Charles, is this you?" she called over her shoulder, and pointed at what had tripped her.

Charles ran up to her, looking at the growing root. Victor and Mira were close to follow, the latter holding onto Skarmor's and Kuirhan's reins. The root started to thicken, causing more cracks to fork along the marbled floor.

"I haven't started anything yet," Charles said.

"Stand back," Jen said, getting up quickly and taking a few steps away.

Everyone else did the same as the root became more trunklike, growing vertically. A soft glow flowed through the trunk's striated bark as its top reached Jen's eye level, flowering with leaves. The tree continued to twist in its reach for the sky, causing her to notice a clump of leaves that were yellow—

. . . like the color of a ripe pear.

Her breath caught in her chest. Jen knew exactly what was happening.

"My God," she whispered, letting her fingertips brush the tree as it continued growing bigger and bigger. "It's Dimitri." She looked over at Mira and repeated her revelation louder. Her friend's eyes widened when she too saw Dimitri's birthmark. Jen faced her father and uncle. "This is an extension of Dimitri, the leshy who Merlin sent to protect me."

"The one that allowed you to escape Shangri-La, right?" Victor said, watching the tree fill the inside of the Akt'aron.

Jen nodded, bursting with tears. "I can't believe it."

She stepped closer and put both hands on the tree, sensing an abundance of comfort and peace. As she reached out with terramancy, she also sent feelings of gratitude and longing back to her leshy protector, and she knew right away that they were received. Dimitri returned a deep and endless feeling of loyalty and hope just before he separated himself from the tree in front of her.

She knew that meant that Atlantis was free to be raised at any point now. Even though Dimitri was no longer connected to the tree, it flowed with enough of his power to sustain itself, continuing its growth upward.

Just like the Arbor Sacré on Camelore, except this one would save Atlantis.

The Arbor Atlanti.

"Well, this cuts our work in half." Charles sounded relieved. He steadied himself on the tree when another seismic rumble passed through the city.

We made it to the western edge of the city! Gavin's voice came through their mind-meld crystal clear. *M'balo left to hold the line with his warriors over here, so now it's just me and Perny.*

Gavin, we're going to need you to fly as fast as you can when I say so, okay? Charles sent.

Jen looked at her father. He was back to being focused.

Copy that, Gavin responded.

To his daughter Charles said, "Okay, Jen, we have to tap into everything we have for this to work. I'll find you once we connect our nexi."

She nodded at him solemnly.

He squeezed her shoulder reassuringly. "Stand across from me and activate your totem. Hold your ground no matter what."

Jen side-stepped until her father was blocked by the tree and looked down at her bracelet. Before she closed her eyes and let the nexus take her, Jen realized that she didn't know what Charles's totem was.

Is he that strong of an omnimancer that he doesn't even need a totem to funnel his power? she thought.

You're sweet, but I just have years of practice, Charles said.

Jen blushed, realizing that they were all still joined by the mind-meld. Cheeks showing a touch of rouge, she leaned to the side so she could see her father again. His head was lowered, but his eyes were looking at her like he was expecting it. He winked and, smiling, Jen went back to standing firmly on both feet, feeling a little less nervous. She gave a parting glance to both Victor and Mira. Having people like them by her side galvanized her resolve and augmented her desire to see this through. She was ready.

Go, Gavin! Charles said.

Jen took a deep breath and closed her eyes. She felt her totem bracelet lift off and begin to rotate around her wrist as the Ring of Lancaster left her chest. They both coursed with the power of her now-awakened nexus. The best way Jen could describe what she felt was if she had opened up all the doors to her house on a warm, summer day and let the melodious chirping of birds, the comforting blanket of heat, and the invigorating wash of sunshine roll in all at once. With her spirit, she moved between all the Mancy planes and tapped into them in the span of one second.

Through telemancy, she felt her father's presence pull her to his side. In the limitless sea of their combined nexi, Charles guided Jen toward something that looked even blacker than the expanse they were in and told her to follow along. Strings of light came from every angle and entered Charles's presence. Like the smooth grace of a martial artist, he controlled it and redirected it out of his fingers, which were pointing directly at the blackest mass Jen's mind's eye had ever witnessed.

Hoping she wouldn't mess up, Jen opened herself fully to her nexus, and all of the doorways to each Mancy plane converged into one. She walked through, drawing as much power from each plane as she could and stockpiling it into the center of her being. Just when she thought she would burst, a blinding, shining light that streamed with vivid colors joined the light given off by Charles.

Jen wasn't used to being a conduit for this much power all at once, and before she knew it she was sucked straight into the light, like she had fallen into a raging river and the current was too strong to fight.

CHAPTER THIRTY-THREE

For how truly large Fuzanglong was, Malcolm was astonished at how quickly he was able to move. Moments after Malcolm had divulged the most likely location of the other MystiCrystals, Fuzanglong had set down the AniCrystal, not wanting to separate it from his massive collection of other priceless treasures, and burrowed a new tunnel through the mantle. Malcolm didn't hesitate to take this opportunity and quickly grabbed the AniCrystal, tucking it behind his cape before hopping on Volcanor and commanding it to follow in Fuzanglong's wake.

The much larger dragon plowed through the mantle with such force and speed that when he blasted out of the Earth's crust, a new volcano had formed. Malcolm felt the intense heat of lava as Volcanor barely escaped the eruption in time, now effortlessly matching the gigantic dragon's speed by flying in his draft.

Malcolm's whole body tingled with anticipation. He was at the cusp of having all the MystiCrystals, at which point the Halostone's location would finally be revealed—to him and him alone. After all this time.

He looked at his hands and noticed Draconex's totem ring, the one he had taken after ruthlessly ending his master's life. Back in Fuzanglong's cave, he had decided to keep that ring and offer his own totem to Fuzanglong instead, and Malcolm had no regrets.

He twisted the ring on his finger, smiling. He wanted to make sure that he would never forget who he vanquished to become the new and improved Dark Watcher commander.

As he was deep in thought, his eyes floated over to the ShadowCrystal gauntlet and his forearm below it. More vibrant purple veins licked out from where the crystal was touching his skin, multiplying seemingly by the hour. He looked over at his other arm and saw the same, the veins thinning as they traveled up his palm and reached the tips of his fingers. An involuntary twitch of his head brought the voices back.

See what you did with our power?

We deserve the same praise you give yourself.

We are *you.*

A tugging reminder of a partnership Malcolm had agreed to, but deep down he couldn't help but be reminded of the toxic relationship he had once had with Draconex.

And look how that turned out.

But Malcolm was strong. Stronger than Draconex. Definitely stronger than the ShadowCrystal. He could keep it at bay. The voices knew who was in charge. Malcolm ground his teeth together as he grasped for more control over his psyche, taming the voices and letting them know that they were not forgotten. What scared him was that he could feel their hold fortify, like vines wrapping around his lungs. Sparing a glance back over at his gauntlet, he decided he would let the ShadowCrystal in as long as it meant that he could fulfill his goal of releasing Lord Ferox. Then would he not only be a faithful student to the most powerful sorcerer there ever was, but also finally recognized as someone who mattered.

Malcolm picked up his head and looked forward, suppressing his feelings and focusing on the ensuing confrontation. He couldn't understand how Fuzanglong could fly without wings the size of Manhattan Island, but he didn't question it. Volcanor seemed in awe of the other dragon as well, like a little brother looking up to his eldest sibling. Another thing Malcolm had never thought he'd witness. There was always a bigger dragon.

Quick brushstrokes of clouds whisked by as the landscape below changed from verdant, snow-capped mountain ranges to rippling, azure waters to finally arid, forsaken sand dunes. Malcolm pulled out the AniCrystal from the backplate of his armor and held it in awe. It started to glow as if a fire had awakened inside of its casing. They must be getting close. Malcolm scoured the meandering sand dunes and cracked earth for the Richat Structure, the Eye of the Sahara. How could Atlantis fit in that place, he wondered. Was the kingdom underneath those large concentric circles of earth or merely shielded atop, made invisible by the TeleCrystal?

Then, almost as if to answer Malcolm's question, Fuzanglong released a stunningly green ball of energy that seemed to disintegrate the very air in its path, finally connecting several hundred meters below with something unseen. It ricocheted off into the desert, but not before sending a wave of discharge over a translucent dome that stretched perfectly over the Eye of the Sahara.

They were here. Malcolm laughed in glee as he commanded Volcanor to break away from Fuzanglong, letting him rest while he watched the larger dragon attack the shielded city with a vengeance. Another energy ball bounced off the barrier, creating a steaming crater around its perimeter. Malcolm could also see cracks start to form around its perimeter along the dry ground. He licked his lips; he could only imagine how the Atlanteans were reacting to this surprise attack.

There was no way that Jen and the rest weren't in the city. They would not allow themselves to be bested by Malcolm, a sorcerer of black sheep proportions. No one had ever given him the attention he deserved. It was time to take what was due to him. They should have recognized his importance long ago, and now he would make them beg for their lives and his forgiveness.

Fuzanglong circled over Atlantis like a starving vulture waiting for its prey to take its last breath. But it was Malcolm who was intent on being the one to stop it from breathing. Until motion out of Malcolm's peripherals caught his eye—and, evidently, Fuzanglong's as well.

Scowling, Malcolm brought Volcanor closer to Atlantis and channeled the eyesight of a bald eagle. His instincts made him think that it was Jen coming out to fight, but as his vision sharpened, he saw that it wasn't his former girlfriend, but the astromancer, Gavin. And floating behind him as he arched his griffin away from the beleaguered hidden city of Atlantis was a flaming orb of some kind.

It was clearly not a MystiCrystal, but it attracted Fuzanglong's attention nonetheless. The dragon almost immediately gave up on his relentless barrage on the city and homed in on the puny human on the griffin.

That is but a distraction!

Your dragon is like a moth to a flame.

Something is about to happen . . .

"No!" Malcolm screamed. He tucked the AniCrystal away and kicked Volcanor's sides, commanding his wyvern to follow Fuzanglong. The immortal dragon was now completely disinterested in Atlantis and flying away to catch whatever flaming ball of crap Gavin was taunting his vehicle of destruction with.

CHAPTER THIRTY-FOUR

Jen felt as if every molecule were about to be torn from her very being. Moments before, she was safely next to Charles and linked to his nexus, streaming all the Mancy planes into a dark void which she assumed was the spiritual representation of the entire city of Atlantis. An instant later, she was sucked into that void and spat back out into the physical realm. Back to standing in front of the Arbor Atlanti and fully conscious.

She felt like she was yelling, but she couldn't hear a sound over the vibrating efflux of energy both she and Charles were pumping into the Arbor Atlanti. She dared not look around lest she lose her focus, but she could feel Victor's and Mira's eyes on her as she gritted her teeth, blinking away tears.

As the magical tree continued to reach toward the sky, it seemed to flicker. Jen caught a few glimpses of Charles as the tree winked in and out, his eyes brighter than two high-powered flashlights. Jen bet her eyes were similar.

An unexpected weight crashed into her, making her legs buckle and her arms fight to remain outstretched. It felt like she was literally holding up Atlantis itself. Without thinking too much about how big the city was, Jen could only hope that she and Charles had been successful in separating Atlantis from the earth and were now lifting it into the sky.

Her joints screamed as the weight began to take its toll on her body, but the power of the Mancy planes gave Jen much-needed support. She felt her feet sink into the marble floor as if it were quicksand. The air seemed thinner as Jen strained every inch of her body, trying her best to keep her breathing rate static so as not to disrupt the flow of energy for which she was the conduit.

Just a little bit longer, Jen, her father's voice echoed around her.

Jen clenched her teeth together so hard she heard ringing, but she didn't relent. If anything, she opened herself more to the combination of every Mancy plane. Throughout her training, each plane felt a little bit different, but with them all commingled together, the resulting sensation was just short of breath-taking. She looked at her fingers, all splayed outward, and saw that a pure white light extended from their tips and wrapped around the surging tree trunk.

The light entering the Akt'aron began flickering, so Jen shut her eyes to avoid being distracted. Unexpectedly, she was thrown back into her nexus, but she still felt in complete control in the physical realm. Flashes of past events whipped across her mind's eye—

Malcolm attacking her in her apartment . . .

Draconex and his dragon attempting to kidnap her . . .

The deadly ambush during the Sesquimillennial Jubilee . . .

Being tied up in an Atlantean prison . . .

Watching Dimitri sacrifice himself so that she could escape Shangri-La . . .

Saving Queen Pt'ara . . .

—and her eyes started hurting as they darted every which way from the influx of power, so much so that she felt nausea set in. Jen opened her eyes to get her bearings but was horrified to see the light on her fingertips wan and the power flowing inside her nexus start to dry up as if someone was turning off a faucet. The Arbor Atlanti had also stopped growing, but was still drinking in the combined powers of Jen and Charles like a thirsty desert animal.

Guys, I don't know how much longer we can take this! Gavin cursed. His voice was fraught—Jen had never heard him sound that way. She needed to be done with her part so she could help him.

And without warning, the energy Jen had been drawing out of her nexus winked out. She stumbled forward, her head spinning, knees buckling, and vision blurring. She didn't even remember hitting the ground as everything faded to black . . .

CHAPTER THIRTY-FIVE

Jen awoke to bouncing blurry spots and an ear-piercing ringing. She furiously tried to blink away the vertigo as her senses acclimated and she saw Victor, Charles, and Mira kneeling over her. Victor was repeating her name, and as the ringing faded his voice rose up from the depths of oblivion.

"Jenny! Jenny, stay with me!"

He was careful not to shake her too much, but Jen felt the grip of a worried loved one. What made her the happiest was that they were all still here and Atlantis didn't drop out of the sky. The Arbor Atlanti's glow on Victor's hair made it seem like he was wearing a rainbow halo—another good sign that the tree had taken root in its new home. Jen didn't dare shake her head from fear of inciting a headache. She instead propped herself up on her elbows, looking at all three of them.

"How long was I out?"

"Not terribly long," Charles said, standing up.

"The longest minute of my life," Victor mentioned, helping her up.

Mira gave her a hug, then said, "Gavin was telling us that Pernissa was getting tired." She touched her temple to indicate the mind-meld. "But when you lost consciousness, our connection with him dissolved." There was a trace of worry in her voice; Jen couldn't blame her one bit.

"Oh, sorry . . ." Jen closed her eyes and tried to reconnect them all, but she couldn't pinpoint anyone in her mind; she could barely feel her nexus. That's when her extremities started to feel numb. "Oh no."

"What is it, Jen?" Charles asked, putting a hand on the center of her back.

She didn't want to open her eyes—she'd cry if she did, she knew she would—so she kept them shut, responding with, "I can barely feel my nexus." She picked at her fingers nervously. "I don't know what's going on."

She felt Charles's hand move soothingly up and down her spine. "It's okay . . . channeling every Mancy plane through your nexus was a lot, especially for someone who only started training a few months ago. Think of your nexus like a reservoir—it's not limitless, and after being under that much duress, it needs time to replenish."

Jen couldn't stop herself from shaking. Her eyes were still sewn shut. "How long will it last?"

"I don't know, but I'm also pretty sapped. We'll figure it out together, but we need to get to Gavin before it's too late."

Jen sniffled, finally opening her eyes and purposefully taking a few long breaths, which seemed to quell the tears. Charles brought her over to lean on Skarmor, taking the shoulder bag off her and putting it on himself.

"I'll grab the MystiCrystals. Get situated on Skarmor and I'll ride down with you, okay?"

"Okay." Jen nodded and watched him climb up the tree with the agility of a gibbon monkey.

Skarmor cawed softly and rubbed his head on hers. Jen couldn't help but smile and be distracted for a few seconds from the terrifying reality that she could barely feel her mystical connection with no guarantee when it would return. She bit her lip, shocked at how naked she felt without the touch of her nexus

—even though, up until a few months ago, she'd had no idea it even existed.

"Hey . . ." Victor soothed the griffin as he petted Skarmor's head along the grain of his feathers. Jen snapped out of her daydream and looked at him. He did a few more passes as he eyed Jen, then turned to face her. "That was some amazing sorcery, Jenny. I'm proud of you," he said. His eyes portrayed a smile just as big as his mouth.

"I never want to do that again," Jen said, exhausted, and let a weary chuckle underlie what she was saying. "I just hope my nexus recharges quickly."

"It will."

A muted sound that reminded Jen of pressurized air leaving a compressor made her look up toward the top of the tree. Even though she couldn't see through the dense leaves that had grown around the massive trunk and branches of the Arbor Atlanti, she knew that her father had made contact with the MystiCrystals and would soon remove the TeleCrystal from its perch atop the Akt'aron, allowing the Arbor Atlanti to take over as new silent guardian of the city. The light from above dimmed for a moment but was compensated nicely by the magical tree. Its thick trunk fit perfectly within the temple's hollowed, spiral tower and its branches created a multilayered helix around the trunk as they twisted higher, pulsing with a dazzling array of colors. The interior of the Akt'aron reflected the tree's vibrant lightshow, reflecting every hue of color on the floor like a kaleidoscope. Jen watched the prismatic lights dance all around her, feeling a peaceful serenity that she hoped would be felt by the city's entire population now that Atlantis was out of harm's way.

Down came Charles, masterfully finding hidden footholds in the Arbor Atlanti's trunk as the shoulder bag dangled across his body. The sound of a sharp inhale took Jen's attention away from her father.

"What is it, Vic?"

Her uncle had two fingers massaging his temple. "It's your

mother . . . she's sending a message through telemancy. Someone showed up on Camelore."

Jen's heart skipped more than one beat. "Malcolm?" she whispered, glancing over at Mira, who was still tending to Kuirhan. Could he have decided to return once he noticed Atlantis had disappeared?

"No," Victor said. He put a hand on Skarmor to stabilize himself. "Grand Mystra Cindergray."

Jen perked up when she heard the name. "Oh, really?"

"Something's . . . not right . . ." His face had turned ashen, and when he opened his eyes, Jen saw a look of true shock. "Grand Mystra Cindergray is on his way to Atlantis."

"Well, that's good . . . right?" But Jen had a sneaking suspicion that there was much more to it than she initially thought.

Charles came up behind her and held the shoulder bag by the strap. "Package secured. Let's go." He looked at Jen. As she took the shoulder bag back and slung it over her body, she gave him a worried look. He cocked his head slightly and his eyes went to Victor, surveying his friend's face. "Vic?"

Victor's fingers were slightly trembling. He tucked them into his palms, then said, "The Grand Mystra was at Camelore. He talked with Jocelyn before heading down to Atlantis."

"But Atlantis isn't down there anymore, as of . . ."—Charles checked his watch—"five minutes ago."

Victor's hand slid off the griffin's mane. He suddenly bolted for Kuirhan, saying, "It doesn't make any sense."

Charles's confusion was etched all over his face. "Victor? *What* doesn't make sense?"

Victor deftly jumped onto his equivol. "The Grand Mystra told Jocelyn that *I* told him where Jocelyn was." He took hold of the reins and stabilized himself as Kuirhan stood. "But I never updated him. And she thinks she heard him start to call her Diaema before he caught his mistake."

Charles murmured, "How would he . . . ?" Then his eyes went wide and he hopped on Skarmor. "Jen, get on."

Jen was behind him in an instant. Mira, just as silent, was with Victor atop the equivol.

Jen had a sinking feeling deep in the pit of her stomach as they galloped out of the Akt'aron's entranceway. Kuirhan took flight moments before Skarmor, and in a few seconds, both flying creatures carried their riders over the lip of the floating city of Atlantis. Ribbons of water cascaded over parts of the border, turning into fine mist before completely disappearing in the clear sky.

Jen peeled her eyes away from the floating kingdom, turning back around and holding on to Charles even tighter. She put her cheek on his shoulder and willed her nexus to wake up. Her gut was telling her that she was not going to like what they would find down in the Sahara Desert.

* * *

Skarmor rocketed toward the Richat Structure, with Kuirhan on his right. They stirred up wispy vortices as they shot through several cumulus clouds at breakneck speed. Jen's heart was rattling inside her ribcage, causing her arteries to feel like they were on the verge of bursting. She was scared of what might have happened to Gavin, exacerbated by the fact that she couldn't reconnect their mind-meld to ask him. And to make matters worse, she was trying to wrap her head around the sudden appearance of Grand Mystra Cindergray and how he fit into all of this.

How did he know her mother had been called Diaema? Had he known where she was all this time? Or did this go even deeper? Was he a double agent for the Dark Watchers?

Okay, now you're spiraling, she told herself.

It couldn't be that bad . . . could it? If that were true, it would be earth-shattering. Trying to clear her mind and focus on connecting to her nexus, she rested her forehead on her father's back. He was stiff as a board and silent, leaning forward as if that would help Skarmor fly faster. Now more than ever, Jen wasn't confident in their chances of succeeding, but she had no intention of giving up now.

The Atlantic waters looked so calm at this altitude, with the sun reflecting off the waves like microscopic diamonds. It was a harsh contrast to the scenery on the mainland, being not only a desert climate, but also a landscape torn asunder by a vicious, immortal dragon. The toll the area had taken today was steep. Deep craters littered the desert like a minefield, some still smoking from the powerful energy blasts from Fuzanglong. The Richat Structure was no more—only a large concave basin remained where Atlantis had once rested. Jen wondered when the world would be alerted to this, if they hadn't been already.

Jen craned her neck as she fought to focus on the center of the basin and her breath caught in her chest when she saw faint movement. The basin was so deep that it was engulfed in shadows of the setting sun, so Jen channeled the sharp eyesight of a bald eagle with the help of animancy to detect a flapping cape.

"There, look!" Jen shouted over the wind.

She pointed at what was left of the Richat Structure and Charles's eyes drew a line from her finger to the basin. The figures in the center were too small to account for Fuzanglong, but Jen knew that was where Malcolm was holding Gavin and Pernissa. With no sight of Fuzanglong, Jen's anxiety doubled.

Charles leaned forward and said something to Skarmor, and the griffin beat his wings furiously for a few seconds to catch up to Kuirhan. Jen kept a snug hold on Charles's midsection as he shouted to the riders on the equivol. He then leaned back and said to her, "Jen, this looks like a hostage situation. Stay close to me."

She hugged Charles tighter and said, "Okay."

Her gut felt as though it were being wrung out by vice grips. The reality of the situation hit her hard. The thought of Gavin and Pernissa, injured and imprisoned, made her nervous, but actually seeing it now solidified its bitter reality.

Skarmor and Kuirhan slowed their descent, aiming for the western lip of the basin. Once they touched down, no one moved. Jen looked down into the massive crater and saw the glowing red eyes of Volcanor. They looked to be staring straight into her soul, and she fought the urge to avert her gaze. It was unnerving that she couldn't see the rest of the dragon in the deep shadows. She could feel the moisture being sucked out of her skin. She began blinking continuously to keep her eyes from drying out.

"What are we going to do?" she whispered.

Her father didn't budge. "Make sure Gavin and Pernissa are alive. We worry about that first." Charles crossed his right leg over Skarmor's body and slid to the ground.

Jen's nexus was like a limb that had gone numb due to lack of circulation; she knew it was there, but it needed more coaxing to awaken. With hope, she tried testing her strength with any of the Mancy planes, but none of her totem charms moved. Feeling her breathing becoming more shallow, Jen slowly inhaled through her nose and held it for a few seconds before releasing the breath from her mouth. She could hear Kuirhan softly snort as Victor and Mira dismounted him. Jen still stayed on Skarmor. He didn't cock his head or show his impatience; he let her continue to sit as she calmed down and registered her senses. Even if she didn't have the full backing of her nexus, Jen would still fight her hardest to ensure her friends' safe return.

When she was ready, Jen leaned forward and rested her head and arms on Skarmor's back, smelling his sun-warmed fur and feathers. "Thank you, Skar," she said as she finally dropped to the ground and readjusted her shoulder bag.

Looking out over the edge of the large basin, Jen had a better view of who was all waiting for them. She turned to her left and walked up to Mira. She could tell her best friend was trying her hardest to stay strong, but her eyes told Jen another thing entirely.

Jen grabbed her hand and squeezed it three times before she whispered, "It'll be okay."

Mira didn't seem so sure, but she nodded anyway. Silent, she looked out over the abyss in the direction of where Gavin should be.

Victor stood next to Jen and said to the entire group, "We stick together, like Charles said. And above all, we need to stay calm."

He looked at Jen and Mira. "I don't like that we can't see Fuzang-long anywhere, so Mira, I'm going to need your help in being a lookout while Jen and Charles negotiate."

Jen could tell that Victor was giving Mira this task to keep her focus and thoughts occupied on anything other than Gavin and his safety. Plus, with Mira's animancy, she could pick up movement, sound, and smell well before anyone else could.

"Do you trust me?" Jen said to Mira.

"With all my heart," came Mira's reply.

Jen nodded and turned to look at Victor. Charles was now standing on Victor's other side.

"Let's go," Victor said.

He walked back to Kuirhan, followed by Mira after she hugged Jen. Charles was back atop Skarmor. When Jen made her way back, he held out his hand to her.

Jen smiled tightly and took it.

* * *

Malcolm let a hiss escape his lips as he saw Jen and the rest land at the western edge of the basin. Deep in the basin amidst the fresh shadows of the setting sun, Volcanor rumbled. It dug its taloned wings into the ground, newly exposed but still arid. Not breaking his gaze from the group, Malcolm soothed its mind, commanding it to wait patiently. He wanted Jen to come to him. He gripped the suddenly glowing AniCrystal in his right hand and knew that she had the remaining four MystiCrystals.

Gavin must have also seen his friends land. Malcolm heard a strained rustle behind him, and with an annoyed indifference, he glared at his prisoner from over his armored shoulder plate. Gavin fought his restraints, but they weren't going to relent, no matter how hard his muscles strained on the antimatter spell Malcolm had placed on him.

After letting Fuzanglong tire out the astromancer and his griffin, Malcolm had been able to capture Gavin without much effort. In a desperate ploy that had only prolonged the inevitable, Gavin

285

had disposed of his distraction, that large, flaming orb, launching it far enough away to divert Fuzanglong's relentless pursuit, which opened up a window for Malcolm to attack.

By the time Fuzanglong had returned from discovering the worthless bait, Malcolm had already bound Gavin and Pernissa. With the help of the AniCrystal's power, Malcolm was able to sway Fuzanglong from ending Gavin's and Pernissa's lives to searching for Atlantis's new location. The immortal dragon had spiraled high into the sky, giving Malcolm the time he needed to draw Jen and her group to him and prey on the feelings he knew she had for Gavin. Feelings that she had once had for Malcolm . . .

With their scouting done, he saw them return to their creatures and fly toward him. He clicked his teeth together in anticipation while staying alert for Fuzanglong. Malcolm didn't know how much time he had left until that dragon either found Atlantis and realized the crystals weren't there or gave up the search and returned, but for the first time in a while, he and the Shadow-Crystal were aligned.

This will all be over soon . . .

CHAPTER THIRTY-SIX

For the first several hundred meters or so, Jen felt like they weren't gaining any ground, even though Skarmor was clipping along at a decent pace. Not as fast as he was going when he had left Atlantis, though, and it didn't help that every five seconds or so her paranoia would cause her to scan the skies for Fuzanglong.

Where is he?

To keep herself from falling into a panic attack, Jen focused on relentlessly prodding her nexus, and with more than a touch of relief she could feel it faintly responding, sending pinpricks of acknowledgment back to her like that one limb that was finally regaining circulation.

She didn't realize she had closed her eyes—and wondered for how long—just as the slight vibration of Skarmor's hind legs hitting compact dirt jostled her out of her meditation.

And there he was.

Malcolm stood next to Volcanor, the wyvern dragon with those eyes as red as the pits of hell. Jen could hardly recognize him anymore. She could remember the time when he was once her boyfriend, back when she was so blissfully ignorant. Now, Malcolm looked like a shell of himself: face hardened with a nasty scar, eyes as black as coal, hair unkempt, and armor as jagged and deadly as a sword—and inspired by Draconex's look, no doubt.

The basin acted like a wind tunnel, augmenting the already sandpaper-esque, hot breeze to a new level of discomfort. Malcolm looked unaffected, standing in front of a hunched-over, kneeling form.

Gavin.

Jen suppressed the urge to run over and make sure he was all right. Next to the astromancer was Pernissa. She was hog-tied and lying on the ground, as if all her energy had been drained.

Jen could relate. She prayed that she could fully access her nexus before any fighting should occur.

Skarmor whined, breaking Jen's heart.

"Don't worry, Skar. We'll get her back." She rubbed his lion hide.

She waited until her father dismounted Skarmor to follow his lead. Victor and Mira did the same, surveying their surroundings. Jen stood next to Charles as Volcanor dropped its head low, eliciting a low rumble that preceded wisps of opaque smoke from its nostrils.

"You know what I want!" Malcolm yelled. There was a gravelly churn to his voice that Jen had never heard before. His eyes bulged, black as bottomless pits.

"Malcolm, the Halostone—"

"Deserves to be found!" Malcolm blurted, cutting Charles off. His head twitched a few times as his arms shot out stick-straight. "The eleven realms have gone too long being disjointed, and they've only gotten more unruly since Ferox's disappearance. He was a *visionary*! He was at the cusp of bringing complete *order* and true peace to the realms!"

"Malcolm—" Jen said, but she was drowned out by his tirade.

"Jen, *don't* get me started!" He pointed an accusatory finger at her. "You ended up on the wrong side of this war."

"Well, maybe you should have handled yourself better on my birthday. Believe it or not, trapping and hurting someone doesn't exactly make them want to join you."

His lower lip quivered as a tear streaked down his face, getting caught in the bottom part of his scar. "We could have ushered in a glorious new era together, Jen. You, an omnimancer, and me, the commander of the Dark Watchers . . ."

"I'll never join you. You tricked me, kidnapped my parents, and now have my friends." Jen fought to keep her voice level, but she could hear a faint tremble encroaching.

Malcolm clenched his jaw and pushed his cape to one side. He reached behind him and, just as Charles slid into a fighting stance, pulled out a glowing amber-yellow crystal.

Jen stiffened. The AniCrystal. He actually had it.

"I know you have the rest. I can feel the AniCrystal pulling toward you."

"Malcolm, we can end this now," Jen pleaded. "You don't have to do this."

"Oh, but I do." Malcolm shot a malicious stare at Victor. "I have been invisible, deemed insignificant, for far too long. My potential has been squashed by my so-called *mentors* who were supposed to *encourage* my growth, not *stunt* it!" He was still staring at Victor. "It's time I proved how wrong you were."

Jen looked at Victor. He was standing strong, not giving any intention of responding. How can you try and reason with someone who was so far gone?

His silence only angered Malcolm. He contorted as spasms wracked his body. He opened his mouth and let out a throat-bursting scream. His neck bulged with purple veins, and more sprouted all across his face.

Volcanor chimed in as well, issuing a horrific roar that shook Jen to her core.

Malcolm spun around and wrapped an arm around Gavin's throat, putting him in a choke hold. He raised the hand that still held the AniCrystal. "Give me the other crystals or I'll club your boyfriend's brains out." His totem ring glowed a deathly red.

Jen unconsciously put both her hands on her shoulder bag. Ignoring her father's warnings, she said, "Fine, here!"

She whipped off the shoulder strap and held the shoulder bag out in front of her. Even Victor and Mira stopped and rushed over to her. Before they could hold her back, Jen had already taken out the lost journal and tossed the shoulder bag toward Malcolm.

It landed by his feet. With his mouth parted in an evil sneer, Malcolm let Gavin go, pushing his head into the ground. He indifferently waved his hand and Gavin was sent flying into Jen, his magical restraints completely gone.

Gavin!

Jen saw stars when her head walloped the ground as she tried her best to catch the six-foot-two, two-hundred-pound man. Those stars, though, didn't go away, but morphed; they turned into streams of light and traveled down her spine, exciting her nerves, and . . . and . . .

Her nexus was restored!

"Jen, what have you done . . ." Gavin whispered.

Even though his voice was soft, his tone was full of nothing but disapproval and disappointment. Jen was too distracted by her totem bracelet levitating off her wrist to let his words sink in.

She extricated herself from Gavin and looked back at Malcolm. "And Pernissa." It wasn't a question, but a demand.

Malcolm had already picked up the shoulder bag, but before he reached in, he looked back at Jen. She stood to meet him at eye level.

"Unfortunately, she stays with me. Unless you take her place. After all, I still need your blood to complete the spell."

"Jenny . . ." Victor said, shaking his head.

Jen bit her lip, then looked at Skarmor. He took a step forward and cocked his head at her.

"*Now*, Jen, or you can claim her corpse!" Malcolm seemed more agitated.

Volcanor beat its venous wings and stomped toward Pernissa.

Jen froze. Her eyes flicked from Volcanor to Malcolm, who was staring into the sky. She looked and saw, to her horror, Fuzanglong, high up in the dusky sky, rocketing toward them with the speed of a jet fighter.

You broke your promise, human! a deep voice boomed. It was so clear Jen thought the dragon was next to her ear. *No one takes*

Fuzanglong for a fool and remains breathing. He was at least a few miles up in the sky, but that distance would vanish in just a few seconds.

Malcolm unsheathed a dagger and was about to plunge it into Pernissa's neck when Jen dropped the lost journal and channeled the speed of a cheetah. The millisecond before she got to Malcolm, she compounded her speed with the battering force of a black rhino. She connected with his chest plate right as he was bringing the blade down, and they tumbled away from Pernissa.

Behind her in the distance, Jen could hear Skarmor's cry as he swooped in to protect Pernissa from Volcanor; Mira and Victor screamed her name, but she didn't let up and continued fighting Malcolm. The collision caused the four MystiCrystals to roll out of her shoulder bag, and a well-placed kick from Malcolm sent Jen flying backward.

Stopping her roll, she flicked her hair away from her eyes to see Malcolm scramble to grab the AniCrystal, which had also been thrown from his grasp. As he crawled to get it, the fiery crystal wobbled and flew over his shoulder into the hands of a much older man standing next to a newly arrived pegasus.

"Grand Mystra?" Jen said, shocked.

He wore an expression she'd never seen before as he took his other hand, which was holding his totem pocket-watch, and froze Fuzanglong in midair.

Charles was the first to Jen's side, helping her up while Mira and Gavin cut Pernissa free and Skarmor distracted Volcanor.

Victor shot into Jen's field of vision but was also stopped in midstride with a chronomancy spell as Cindergray brought his pocket watch in Victor's direction.

"I'm sorry it had to happen this way, old friend," Cindergray said as he slowly walked to where the other MystiCrystals lay.

Jen told her body to charge the Grand Mystra, but realized that she was frozen in place like everyone else.

The true power of Grand Mystra Cindergray was in full force, and it severely frightened Jen. She tried speaking, but her vocal cords were just as frozen as every other inch of her body. A painful silence swept over the entire area as Cindergray laid out all the MystiCrystals, each one touching the next. They were all emitting steady light, and once he connected the AniCrystal to the chain, a shockwave rippled forth, churning the ground as if it were a stormy ocean, and a large white tube of light shot skyward—

And Jen was released from Cindergray's spell, as the old man was the first to be hit with the power surge.

Malcolm was pushed farther away from the beam of light while Jen tried to regain her footing; it felt as if she were learning to walk all over again. The Grand Mystra's full mustache hid a lustful grin as he stumbled backward, his hands outstretched in beckoning wonder, discarding his time spells.

Jen didn't know if this beam would incinerate anyone who came within its touch or act as a portal to an unknown realm, but she had no choice but to stop Cindergray from whatever he was going to do next. As Fuzanglong careened into the desert several hundred meters away, the ground underneath Jen was swimming and carried her almost in a semicircle; before she could blink, Jen found herself almost straight behind the Grand Mystra.

Someone shouted her name, but there was too much cacophony for her to tell if it was Charles or Victor. Praying she wouldn't get distracted, Jen channeled all her focus into terramancy. She felt as if her nerve endings had extended through her feet and into the ground. Connecting her senses with the very molecules beneath her, Jen was one with the undulating ground.

As if paving a path ahead, she held the ground before her in place, then took a step.

Then another.

And another, until she was running like she was on a solid surface, sending spells into the ground in front of her just as she released her hold on the areas where her feet had just been.

Jen could see Cindergray regain his balance and stagger toward the beam as if heavily impaired. Her nexus seemed to be telling her that the beam was more than likely a portal than a death trap, and so Jen planned to tackle him before he could reach it. Who knew how long it would remain open.

She was steps away when she felt as if she were trying to run on smooth ice. Jen lost her balance and flailed into Cindergray, knocking them both into the sheer, white tube of light.

CHAPTER THIRTY-SEVEN

"JEN!"

Victor yelled his niece's name, helplessly watching as she bowled into Grand Mystra Cindergray, sending them both into the light beam produced by the MystiCrystals. He was caught up in a tidal wave of moving ground, unable to make any progress toward the beam, and straining to keep his grip on Gavin, who was still supine. Victor felt as if he were in a horrible dream, trying desperately to run but not gaining any ground.

In awe, he watched as Malcolm leapt into the beam seconds later. Victor needed to follow Jen to make sure she was okay. He looked around and saw his group scattered all around, Charles several meters to his left, and Mira a few meters behind, to his right; Skarmor and Pernissa were in the air, grappling with Volcanor.

Cindergray's pegasus, Soter, was the last of the animals to take to the air. Clearly spooked, it flew away like its life depended on it, just as Fuzanglong released a deafening roar that stopped the ground from moving. The massive dragon clawed at the desert floor, kicking up chunks of dried crust as it picked up speed. It planted its four feet firmly on the ground and launched straight into the right side of the vertical beam just as Jen, Cindergray, and Malcolm shot out the left side.

Victor's heart nearly exploded as he helped Gavin to his feet and ran toward Jen. He could see Cindergray and Malcolm attempt to get up, but they both collapsed back on the ground.

"Go to Jen. I'll keep my eye on the other two with Mira," Gavin said as his girlfriend arrived on his other side.

Victor nodded and looked back at Jen. She was lying a few meters from the men, showing no signs of trying to get up. He skinned his knee as he slid next to her and turned her over.

"J-Jenny?" he said, then froze when he saw what Jen was lying on.

Her eyes fluttered open and she pushed him away, yelling, "I didn't mean to!"

The look in her eyes broke Victor's heart. She looked terrified, scared of him.

His eyes were drawn back to the object on the ground. It was the size of his hand, polished smooth and oval in shape. Alternating bands of brilliant purple blended perfectly together while a natural ring of pure gold cut through the purple as if intentionally poured there.

He had no doubt what it was.

He picked it up and looked at Jen, who seemed ready to counter with her own set of spells should Victor attack her. Gavin and Mira were silent behind him and were met with Charles. He had to figure out what happened to her on the other side of the portal, but he couldn't get over what he held in his hands.

"Jenny, you found . . ." His voice cracked. "How did you find the Halostone?"

* * *

Before Jen could comprehend what had happened, she tumbled out of the white beam. She rolled over carefully manicured blades of grass and went into a crouch, ready for when the Grand Mystra came out of the beam . . . but nothing happened.

She looked down at the greenest grass she had ever seen and caught a strange sense of *déjà vu*. She looked warily around and realized she was inexplicably back in the Elder Synod's courtyard, the place where she had passed the Chimera Course several months before. It was empty and Watercress Castle was still standing.

"Impossible . . ." Jen breathed.

She looked over at the Chimera Course, with its perfectly trimmed hedges that led up to the altar's pedestal. Resting atop the pedestal wasn't the metal orb—she had used that very mineral to make her totem bracelet—but instead a large, oval stone with the most brilliant bands of purple and a natural ring of gold.

Jen immediately thought—*knew*—it was the Halostone. If it truly was, why was it out in the open like that?

She started toward the outer edge of the left row of hedges when a column of flames scorched the grass in front of her. Jen whipped her head to the right just in time to duck and roll out of the way of another blast of fire. She felt the uncomfortable heat even after the flames abated to reveal Mystra Stonebridge, the Elder terramancer.

Jen was too stunned to speak. She thought he had died in the Sesquimillennial Jubilee massacre.

"Stay *inside* the course," he commanded.

He lowered his hands as Mystra Skycap soared over his head, coming straight at Jen like a lioness pouncing on her prey.

Jen let out an involuntary shriek as she dodged the Elder animancer and sprinted a few meters before diving into the Chimera Course's pool. But she didn't have time to stay hidden under the water. If that was the Halostone at the end of the course, she needed to get there before Cindergray did—wherever he was. With resolve, she pushed off the side of the pool and swam like a sailfish to the other end. Pulling herself out of the water, she remembered who had tried to stop her next: Mystra Étoilier.

As she dried off, Jen waited for that big slab of carbon to block her way, but it didn't come. She looked to her left to see Étoilier standing behind the row of hedges, looking straight ahead like he didn't even notice her.

Jen's instincts told her to look to the right and she saw, up at the top of the courtyard's highest wall, the imposing form of Grand Mystra Cindergray. Arms crossed, he didn't move. Instead, he silently watched her with his blue, glistening eyes—exactly where the Dark Watcher assassin had attempted to murder Jen.

Jen was trying to catch her breath when movement at the edge of her peripherals made her look back toward the altar—

And who else stepped in her way other than Victor.

"Vic!" Jen yelled in relief.

She ran toward him, but something in his eyes made her steps falter.

"You caused this, Jen," Victor said, lifting his arms, palms up. "You gave up the MystiCrystals, and now we are doomed."

He clamped his hands shut, and tree roots wrapped around her feet, binding her to the ground.

"No, *no*, I didn't mean to!" Jen started hyperventilating. "Malcolm was going to kill Gavin. I-I couldn't let that happen!"

"And let the entire fate of the eleven realms die instead?!" Veins popped from Victor's neck as he brought a torrent of water crashing into Jen's back, knocking her down.

Jen tried screaming "No!" but the water gushed over and around her head, sucking all air from her lungs.

This can't be reality. Nothing here makes sense.

Jen tried to calm herself and fought to bring her hands to her feet. She channeled terramancy and loosened the roots chaining her feet to the ground and let the water carry her forward. Fully expecting to slam into her uncle, Jen braced herself, but instead of his body, she felt his hand shoot out and grab her by the throat.

The water left as quickly as it had come, and Jen was left sopping wet and fighting for air as Victor let her dangle two feet off the ground. Her eyes felt like they were bulging out of their sockets as she looked to her right to see the glistening Halostone just within reach. It didn't have a drop of water on its smooth surface.

"You failed us, Jen," Victor spat. "You are too weak to do what needs to be done." He tightened his grip around her throat.

"No—" Jen gurgled, grabbing onto his strong arm. She flailed her legs in a futile attempt to make contact with any part of his body.

Jen needed oxygen badly, and her nexus understood that. It was as though she were on autopilot as the door to telemancy opened and she saw her white-knuckled hands disappear.

Victor blinked and let go, stepping away to look for his now-missing niece as Jen collapsed to the ground and sucked in air. Her legs and arms felt afire as she tried to stand. She had no choice but to push through the pain.

Her hand reappeared just as she reached for the Halostone.

* * *

Cindergray landed hard on his side and barrel-rolled on scorched earth until he was stopped by a large boulder. When the wince left his face, he looked upon what was beyond the scope of his belief.

There was his aunt, Gwendolyn Lancaster, curled up in the center of a fresh graveyard of sorcerers. His eye caught the full moon up above, and he admired how purple it was. Wincing again, he propped himself up just as Gwendolyn stirred. She let out a weak moan as she held both the Halostone and the Ring of Lancaster out in front of her. Her light sobs pulled at Cindergray's aching heart.

Cindergray could tell she was running out of time. He remembered when he was eight years old, Stor Winspoc, the head guardian of the Camelore Twenty-Four at the time, telling him of how his aunt had passed away. How they had arrived at the site of the Great Battle just in time for Gwendolyn to bestow upon them the Halostone and her family ring before she had passed from her injuries.

As Cindergray looked at his aunt now, he struggled between rushing over to help her and remaining where he was. He didn't know if this was truly the past or some hallucination he was experiencing.

With trembling hands, Gwendolyn laid both of the items on

the ground and touched the totem ring she wore to the Halostone. Mist lifted from the stone and settled to its right, coalescing into an exact duplicate of the Halostone. Gwendolyn then extended her arm toward the moon and a red light shot forth from her ring. Cindergray assumed that was the beacon spell meant for the Camelorean guardians, but a few minutes later a long silhouette formed in the middle of the moon. He tensed and positioned himself behind the boulder as the pinprick quickly became the slender form of Fuzanglong.

The massive dragon landed at Gwendolyn's feet.

Gwendolyn.

The dragon knew his aunt's name?

"Fuzanglong . . . I need you to take this stone to your realm, Empyyr."

Cindergray almost crumpled to the ground.

Empyyr? There is a twelfth realm?

Blinking away his surprise, he could tell that his aunt's life force was waning. Gwendolyn didn't have enough strength to pick up the Halostone, instead rolling it to the dragon.

Your injuries . . . Fuzanglong started. *Let me heal you.*

"No. The true location of the Halostone must die with me." Gwendolyn gurgled out a wet cough. "If Philip can become Lord Ferox, imagine the army he could raise if he was ever let out."

Cindergray's world shattered. He was only an infant when Lord Ferox began his rampage on the First Five clans, massacring one after another in order to gain possession of the MystiCrystals they had been protecting, setting in motion the legendary Great Battle. No one had told him that his father *was* Lord Ferox. He was told by Mystra Winspoc, the leader of the Camelore Twenty-Four who took him under his tutelage, that Ferox was the one who had killed Philip, his father, to get to Genevieve, since she was the Lancaster clan's keeper of their MystiCrystal, the Chrono-Crystal: the final MystiCrystal Ferox needed in his conquest.

Gwendolyn's next words brought Cindergray's focus back. "This stone . . . holds Lord Ferox, an evil . . . so great it would doom all of our realms if . . . it was released," she labored.

You have been a true friend to me, Gwendolyn. I will do what you ask.

Fuzanglong picked up the Halostone with its whisker-like tendrils and a beam of white light descended from the sky, covering the dragon's head. The serpentine body entered the radiant beam until it was gone and the light faded away, leaving Gwendolyn with the Ring of Lancaster and the exact copy of the Halostone.

Seconds later, a group of sorcerers arrived and huddled around the injured Lancaster. Cindergray spotted Stor Winspoc, the first to kneel next to Gwendolyn. Cindergray couldn't make out exactly what the head Camelorean guardian said to her, but he witnessed a different guardian recite the Sorcerer's Oath. His aunt's body disappeared and was replaced by several balls of white light. They defied gravity and twirled up into the night sky.

Her soul had been returned.

He saw the replica of the Halostone get tucked away into the folds of Winspoc's cloak, along with his family's ring, as the group of sorcerers walked around and gave the same courtesy to the other fallen sorcerers.

A woman's voice crept up from behind Cindergray: "Now you know what really happened, my boy."

He spun around to see Genevieve, his mother. A shimmering aura surrounded her as she floated a meter away.

"Mother," he breathed. A tear ran down his cheek and got caught in his beard.

She held out what looked to be the Halostone.

"I've never stopped searching for you," he said between sobs. "I was the only one who believed you weren't dead."

"You are right . . . the spell I used brought me into the Halostone as well. I am sorry I wasn't there for you as you grew up."

Cindergray squeezed his eyes shut as more tears threatened to flow. He grinded his teeth so a whimper wouldn't escape.

"But I caution you with what you will find," Genevieve warned, "should you release its contents."

"There's been nothing more important than finding you," Cindergray said.

"Even if that means releasing Ferox as well?" Genevieve cocked her head slightly and retracted the Halostone.

"I am prepared to do anything to get you back. I've waited in agony for too long." Cindergray's voice was stern.

Then he reached out for what he hoped was the real Halostone.

* * *

Malcolm spit out coarse sand after faceplanting into the ground. He cursed and tousled his hair to let any remaining pieces of sand fall out as jeers and yells took over his hearing. Under flickering fluorescent lights, smudged Plexiglass walls separated him from scores of bystanders. The men and women closest to the walls were pounding relentlessly on them as this memory came back to Malcolm.

He was in the Pit.

Opposite him in the ring was the small boy he had beaten all those years before. As he walked closer to Malcolm he seemed to age with every step, and after five steps he was a young man in his midtwenties, and he looked alarmingly like . . .

"Gavin," Malcolm whispered. He swallowed the silty residue of the sand that was still sticking to his tongue and stood up.

A black mass caught his eye off to the left and he saw the corpse of his late master, Lord Draconex. Malcolm involuntarily recoiled, surprised at the sight. There Draconex was, crouched in the exact same spot Malcolm had left him in the cave, spear sticking out of his throat and all.

"You like picking on people smaller than you, huh?" Gavin said icily. He popped his totem orb from his pendant necklace and enlarged it.

How had Malcolm not realized it before? It all made sense now. The boy Victor ended up saving from the Pit—the boy his master had chosen over Malcolm—was now fighting by his side.

Malcolm's rage fomented as he glared at Gavin. He spun and kicked up a dense wall of sand that he then shot toward the astromancer. Almost as if expecting it, Gavin rolled the orb in his hands, and the sandstorm halted in midair and the specks of sand turned into fine white crystals.

Nonchalantly, Gavin walked through them unharmed.

"Or you fight dirty to eke out a victory."

Gavin sneered and his eyes turned frigid-blue as he jutted his free hand out and down, slamming Malcolm to the ground with the invisible hand of gravity. His joints screamed as his lungs overworked just to suck in the bare minimum of oxygen he needed to remain conscious.

Gavin knelt by Malcolm and showed him his orb, which transformed into a stone that looked eerily similar to the Halostone he had spent countless hours researching. He lightly tossed the Halostone in his hand, saying, "If only you knew what cost you'd end up paying for the Halostone . . ."

Malcolm channeled terramancy and felt the hard, dense quartz spear that was pinning Draconex to the wall. With a flick of his fingers—the only part of his body he could move except for his eyes—the spear dislodged from both the wall and Draconex's throat and sliced through the air, straight toward Gavin's head.

Gavin's instincts saved him but at the cost of releasing his gravity spell on Malcolm. As Gavin twirled around to catch the spear, Malcolm did a kip-up and found himself inches away from Gavin's face.

Gavin snickered and plunged the spear into Malcolm's chest just below where his armor ended.

"You're not ready for the sacrifice you must make . . ."

Malcolm's diaphragm spasmed as the crowd's roar caused his hearing to pop. Gavin didn't pull the Halostone away, and so, banking on the feeling that this wasn't reality but the stone maybe was, Malcolm reached for the Halostone.

CHAPTER THIRTY-EIGHT

Back in the basin that was left by Atlantis, Jen's mind started to connect the dots. The surreal experience she'd just had back in the Chimera Course was a result of going through the portal to some other . . . dimension? New realm? Her eyes flicked from Victor to the base of the white beam to see that the MystiCrystals had formed into a ring and were spinning like a fan.

Holding her throat where, moments before, she thought Victor had been strangling her, she looked back at a concerned Victor, who was holding the Halostone, waiting for an answer she didn't quite have.

"I-I . . . I'm not sure," Jen forced out.

She tried to stand, but her legs were too shaky. She felt steady hands catch her. She looked up into Charles's eyes. Feeling a tug on her neck, Jen looked down to see the Ring of Lancaster, now glowing, being drawn to the Halostone.

Victor sharply inhaled through clenched teeth and dropped the stone, which had also started to glow. "It's burning up," he said as he rubbed his hands. "Jenny, Charles . . . don't touch it."

Jen knew that if any of her blood got on the Halostone, a chain reaction would cause it to release what was inside. Behind her, Gavin and Mira were holding each other, watching.

Victor wrapped a portion of his cloak around a hand and

reached for it again when it flew away from him and into Cindergray's hand. Smoke erupted from his palm—clearly the stone was searing his skin, but the Grand Mystra didn't show any pain.

Victor quickly put himself between Jen and Cindergray. "I don't know why you want Ferox released, Grand Mystra," Victor said, "but I'm not giving you that chance." He dropped into an L-stance and brought his arms out in front of him, displaying his totem rings on his fingers. "I won't let you get to Jen or Charles."

The Grand Mystra chuckled. "What an altruistic sentiment, Victor, but I do not need them. You see, *I* am a Lancaster too."

Jen's first instinct was to look at Charles, who looked just as stunned as her. She turned back to catch Cindergray biting his other hand hard enough to draw blood. He raised his maimed hand over the Halostone and squeezed, his blood dripping onto the relic. The droplets sizzled like water on a hot frying pan and the polished surface of the stone began to crack.

"I am Philip Lancaster II, son of Philip and Genevieve!" Cindergray bellowed, his eyes manic as they watched the Halostone continue to splinter like the shell of a fragile egg under pressure.

CRACK—CRACK—CRACKK!

Blinding light emanated from the jagged cracks and a power surge plowed forth, one so great that it sent Jen and everyone else tumbling backward while breaking the connection between the MystiCrystals, deactivating the portal. Jen put her chin to her chest to protect her head as she rolled for several seconds.

When she stopped she could no longer see the Halostone but instead two cloaked figures—a man and a woman—with their arms locked as they stared at each other. The woman had long, curly dark hair and wore a velvet cloak the color of port wine; and the man, much taller, was draped in a sickly dark-green robe with a long hood obscuring most of his face.

Jen turned nearly catatonic when she noticed the Ring of Lancaster was no longer around her neck. She looked up and thought she saw it glistening on the right hand of the woman as she shoved the man away and, almost immediately after, conjured a spell that engulfed the shrouded man. It coursed through his body—white outlines of his skeleton briefly crackled in and out like he was in an X-ray—seconds before his silhouette faded away.

When the bright spell had ended, the man was no more; the only thing in his place was his heavy robe, tattered and charred.

The woman stumbled forward and crumpled to the ground.

"No!" Malcolm screamed off in the distance, reminding everyone that he was still alive.

Victor sent a slew of spells toward his old tenderfoot, but they harmlessly ricocheted off his shielding spell. Volcanor swooped down from the darkening sky and completed the arc as Malcolm deftly jumped on its back. The wyvern dragon rocketed off into the dusk, carrying him away, his entire plan having been dashed.

Cindergray was already next to the fallen woman, hugging her to his chest. He stayed there for a bit until a forceful spell from Charles wrapped up the old sorcerer and knocked him away from the woman. Jen felt uneasy at the sight of Cindergray writhing on the ground, shouting and crying hysterically as he tried to break free of Charles's spell.

Victor was right behind Charles as they sprinted to the woman. Jen wanted to join them, but, awestruck, she couldn't move. Gavin and Mira went up to Jen, and it was Mira who asked:

"Is that who I think it is?"

Jen took a few stuttering steps closer to the felled woman then stopped, trying to process the last few seconds.

"I think so," was all she could manage.

So many things had happened in such a short amount of time. She had to think aloud.

"Did she just . . . *kill* . . . Lord Ferox?"

Jen turned around and pointed at the heap of robes.

Gavin and Mira both shrugged, but the looks on their faces answered Jen's question enough. Skarmor and Pernissa touched down next to her while Kuirhan did the same by Victor. Holding on to Skarmor's wing, Jen was led to where the woman lay. The closer Jen got to her, the more she saw a family resemblance.

She had to be Genevieve Lancaster.

Cindergray was incoherently muttering as sobs racked his senile body. Every so often Jen could hear the word "Mother" escape his lips.

Jen was now practically hovering over the woman when her eyes fluttered open.

"Gwendolyn?" she murmured. Her eyes adjusted, and she brought her hands up in a protective manner.

"We're here to help," Victor said, trying his best to hold her without causing any more concern. One of his hands supported the woman's head. "Can you tell me your name?"

His question hung in the air for a few seconds before her breathing slowed. She answered, "Genevieve Lancaster. Who are you?"

By now, everyone was huddled around Genevieve. Jen wondered who would be brave enough to try and explain everything. She felt a hand hold hers and give a squeeze, and looked to see Charles. The look he gave her made her realize that in a span of minutes, two more Lancasters had been found, making a total of five: Jen, Charles, Jocelyn, Cindergray—Philip—and now Genevieve.

Just as Victor was about to respond, Genevieve convulsed, causing her body to go rigid. A whimper escaped her tight lips, and then she went limp.

"Mother!" Cindergray shouted from several meters away. Charles flicked his wrist and a light pink spell hit the Grand Mystra in the face, knocking him out.

Victor picked Genevieve up and said in a declamatory tone, "Okay, we gotta get her to Camelore for medical attention."

"What about the Grand Mystra?" Jen asked as Victor walked toward Kuirhan.

"We take him with us too," Charles said, glowering. His eyes told it all: he was hurt at how Cindergray had not only manipulated everyone, but was also complicit in both her parents' disappearances. "Cindergray—or whoever he is—has a lot to answer for."

Jen squeezed her father's hand both out of sympathy and to remind him to stay strong. No one could have possibly foretold that this would have been the outcome of destroying the Halostone, but Lord Ferox was gone for good. The only evil that they still had to worry about was Malcolm.

Charles looked at her, his eyes softening. *Thank you,* he sent through her nexus.

Jen watched him walk over to collect the strewn MystiCrystals after picking up her shoulder bag. She noticed that the crystals were dormant as Charles secured them in the bag, leading her to believe that, since the Halostone was destroyed, their collective power had been severed.

Her father, deep in thought, fixed the broken strap before slinging the shoulder bag across his body and going over to where Cindergray lay in the fetal position. Like he was picking up a sack of flour, he hoisted the unconscious sorcerer over a shoulder and made his way to Skarmor.

Jen didn't say anything to him as he passed, respecting his focus and thoughts. Her gaze instead trailed to where the portal had opened. What remained was an indentation of a circle with a diameter no greater than two meters. Jen wondered what kind of realm it was, and if she would ever be able to return to it.

Her mind wandered as the desert breeze blew through her sweat-soaked curls. It felt a lot less harsh than before—maybe because it was just after sunset or maybe because the thousand-year war had just ended with Lord Ferox's sudden demise.

Jen breathed in and tilted her head toward the clear night sky. Almost directly above her was the Orion constellation. Her eyes were drawn to the twinkling stars that made up the Belt, which calmed her more.

"Rez will not believe this," Gavin commented, sending a light, exhausted chuckle through Jen.

Her eyes remained fixed on Orion's Belt for a few seconds

longer before she turned around and, without hesitating, wrapped him and Mira in a big hug. Together, they all cried.

"Come on, let's go home," Jen said, just now realizing how tired she was.

As they made their way to the griffins, Gavin, who had picked up the lost journal, said while mindlessly strumming the pages' edges like they were guitar strings, "What ever happened to Fuzanglong?"

Jen exhaled. "Beats me. I'm glad he's nowhere in sight."

That seemed to be a sufficient answer for Gavin. He just shrugged and kept walking.

Charles was already on Skarmor, Cindergray's body draped in front of him. He tried making room for Jen, but she waved him off.

"It's okay, I'll ride with Mira and Gavin."

"Sounds good. I'll see you up on Camelore, Jen," her father said before he commanded Skarmor to take flight.

Victor was the next to leave. He let Genevieve rest on his back, her hands securely strapped around his midsection. "Race you there!" Victor shouted as his equivol kicked off the ground, fading into the dark sky right behind Charles and Skarmor.

Jen smirked, always enjoying her uncle's playful banter.

"Hey, where did that portal take you?" Mira asked once they were all on Pernissa.

"Oh my god, you won't *believe* it," Jen started.

She then began to explain the dreamlike experience in an undiscovered realm as they followed the two elder sorcerers toward Camelore, leaving the basin fully deserted. A shift in the arid wind caught the tattered robe that once belonged to Lord Ferox, sending it luffing and twirling on an indefinite journey through the sands of the Sahara Desert.

On a calm night, miles above the Earth, so high up that not even clouds could reach, five of the last remaining League of Light sorcerers flew to Camelore. With them was the surviving contents of the Halostone: Genevieve Lancaster.

Atop his stalwart equivol, Kuirhan, Victor Huxley led the way for Skarmor and his riders, Charles Lancaster and the unconscious Grand Mystra Cindergray. Pernissa took up the rear, carrying Jennifer Lancaster, Mirabelle Amian, and Gavin Kingsland.

The temperature had been steadily dropping as they gained altitude, and beneath the light of a full moon, Genevieve's eyes fluttered open. The eyes had flecks of purple and auburn-gold amidst a sea of hazel; eyes that had seen the world fifteen hundred years younger; eyes that now turned a sickly dark green as they drank in the remote lunar landscape thousands of miles away.

A sinister grin curled her lips as Camelore grew in sight.

ABOUT THE AUTHOR

Gregory Heal is an independent author who is always trying to find creative outlets to express himself.

Having grown up in Southeastern Wisconsin, he enjoys downhill skiing, boating, and sailing. He also loves to paint and practice percussion when he is not working as a mortgage broker.

Manufactured by Amazon.ca
Acheson, AB